Dracula vs. Hitler

PATRICK SHEANE DUNCAN

INKSHARES

Published by Inkshares, Inc., San Francisco, California
www.inkshares.com

Edited and designed by Girl Friday Productions
www.girlfridayproductions.com
Cover design by Dan Stiles

ISBN: 9781942645085
e-ISBN: 9781942645092
Library of Congress Control Number: 2016938143

First edition

Printed in the United States of America

Dedicated to the two Laurels, Cleon and Boullosa—kind beings who have had a great influence on me.

EDITOR'S NOTE

Accidental discoveries. You're looking for one thing and discover something else of even more value. I'm rummaging in the junk drawer, searching amid the usual dresser jetsam for that thingamabob that goes to the whatchamacallit, and then come across my old Hopalong Cassidy penknife. And it is the perfect tool for opening those damned CD security tapes.

Or, doing research on Medal of Honor recipients for a documentary and stumbling across the story of Mary Walker, the only woman to receive that award, which leads to ruminations about women in combat and subsequently to a very successful screenplay and movie.

Luck, I guess, curiosity and the ability to tell the difference between gold and iron pyrite, literarily speaking.

If you've ever had to search for any government document, you cannot help but be reminded of the last shot of the first Indiana Jones movie as the boxed Ark is hauled into what appears to be an endless warehouse filled with stacked crates extending into infinity. I've been inside those warehouses. They exist, scattered around the fringes of Washington, D.C., and other parts of the U.S. This is one place where reality and movie fantasy merge. In fact, the reality makes the movie image seem feeble.

There are warehouses that are miles in length. Endless corridors and shelves filled with government detritus. Mostly paper. Documents from the inception of our government and before. Logs and letters and inventories and forms. Paperwork from every branch of government: Presidential papers, the document-spewing House and Senate, agencies that spit out paper like babies fill diapers. The military wallows in documentation, in triplicate, the Navy floats on it, the Army hurls it at the Pentagon, and the Air Force drops it by the ton. And the IRS? Enough said.

And they keep it all. Every single page. In warehouses like those sur-rounding D.C., stored underground in old salt and gypsum mines scattered across the country. Miles of files. Mountains of memos. So much paper. Untold reams of reports. Centuries of forms, letters, and ephemeral data.

And, as you would expect, things get lost.

I, myself, was certainly lost. In a labyrinth of metallic shelves three sto-reys high, each shelf stuffed with boxes. They smelled of mildew, and my allergies were acting up. I was researching an HBO project about female spies in Europe during World War II. I was on the hunt for a batch of old wartime records from the OSS—precursor to the CIA—concerning the use of women in "ungentlemanly warfare," concentrating on the adventures of those female agents who spied for us in Nazi-occupied France: Yvonne Rudellat, a receptionist turned spy, Chilean actress Giliana Balmaceda, and Virginia Hall, an American journalist with a wooden leg she called Cuthbert.

As usual the document I wanted, needed, was missing. Well, more accurately, it was not where it was supposed to be. But according to the government troll who sat in the tiny office a few miles behind me, it was indeed "*in here somewheres.*"

I searched the boxes stacked around the designated area, on shelves above and below and adjacent. Still nothing. Then I saw something stuck behind a sagging brown file box.

Out of nothing but curiosity, I slid the interior box into the open. My hand left a mark on the dusty lid. The top was bound with yellowed string that, as it unwound, came apart in my hand.

Inside the box a single sheet of paper with the bright red declaration "TOP SECRET" lay upon a briefcase. As I set the sheet aside, its edges crumbled at my touch, raining yellow confetti onto the concrete floor. I examined the briefcase. Brown leather; faded gilt lettering stamped on the flap bore the legend *J.M.H.* The brass clasp and trimmings were tarnished with green verdigris. When I flicked open the clasp and lifted the flap the desiccated leather cracked like cheap plastic. I couldn't help but glance around to see if there were any witnesses to my destruction of what could be some historic heirloom. There was no one around. So I continued my examination.

Why did I continue? I am a writer by trade. Curiosity is in the job description.

Inside the ancient briefcase, still smelling of old pipe smoke, were a variety of documents:

A leather-bound diary, the cover rubbed to rawhide in places, the same initials, *J.M.H.*, embossed on the lower right corner, any hint of gold long worn away. The tattered remnant of a marking ribbon hung like a rat tail from the binding. I thumbed through the wrinkled and stained pages; the odor of mould was enough to make me sneeze. The writing was some sort of shorthand in a variety of pen inks—black, blue, a faded purple, and even red—plus pencil notations.

Putting this volume aside I pulled out a crumbling envelope, emblazoned with Russian characters that were later translated as "MOST TOP SECRET." Inside was another diary, in thick binding, written by hand in German, using a variety of inks, but obviously in the same hand. The edges of the pages were blackened as if they had been in a fire. Some fell loose as I opened it.

After this I found a reddish-brown accordion file that contained a thicker document, this one stapled, the metal fasteners staining the paper with rust. It was three or four inches thick and typed on thin paper, all carbon copies, some of the letters so vague as to make the text near indecipherable. Rubbing my fingers on the back of the paper, I could feel the indentations the typewriter keys had made on the almost transparent vellum. An original document. The first page had a title: "*The Dragon Prince and I*, a Modern Novel by Lenore Van Muller."

Next was a manila folder, once held together by a rubber band that was now rotted and snapped but still stuck to the cardboard. Inside was a stack of old copy paper, the thermal facsimile type from the pre-Xerox era. The print was a brownish blur on stiff, fragile, and very thin paper. They were copies of German documents, many topped with the Nazi symbol, that eagle holding a swastika. My eyes kept fixing on two words I did recognize: The first was "Hitler." This name was mentioned repeatedly alongside one just as infamous if not even more so—"Dracula."

The combination of those two names was enough to send my curiosity into overdrive.

The very last item at the bottom of the case was a file folder of dark brown pasteboard, cracked in two at the fold. Between the halves were thirteen loose sheets of manuscript, handwritten in a small, tight hand. The paper was crumbling at the edges. The ink had faded so much that later it would take some scientific wizardry to bring out the text, infrared and a few other colors of spectrographic scans. At first examination, considering the other documents, I took the language in this manuscript to be German also, but it proved to be Dutch. I did recognize the one name at the top of the first and the bottom of the last page—Abraham Van Helsing.

My HBO project was now completely forgotten. I quickly but carefully returned the items to the briefcase, put them back into the box, and I have to confess I slid the "TOP SECRET" cover sheet under the shelf. Checking out the box was easy—too easy, if you ask me—as it was listed in the vast computer catalogue by only another number, no details other than the notation "Misc." As you might expect, a good part of these vast government holdings had yet to be catalogued.

It took months to have the diary transcribed. The shorthand was not Gregg, but a version of the Pitman system. Through the Internet I found a retired legal secretary from Wales who was familiar with the style. Her legal background and innate suspicious nature proved to be an initial stumbling block, as it took a month just to get her to sign a nondisclosure agreement.

Finding a translator for the German documents was easier (as was that nondisclosure negotiation).

The thermal paper was more problematic, as it was in a very delicate state, some of the pages disintegrating at the slightest touch. I had an archivist mount each page between plastic sleeves—an expensive undertaking.

The Dutch translation was easy; a former teacher of mine in Michigan was sworn to silence and did the work. I will always remember his phone call asking me if this was some kind of prank I was playing on him. Thanks, Milt.

As for authentication, I sent paper samples and certain mundane passages to various experts and laboratories. Due to the extraordinary contents of these documents, it was imperative that the authenticity of the various papers be proved.

The papers were put through more than one testing facility and all passed. Chemical analysis and fiber identification were conclusive as to the period. Forensic document experts agreed with the source of each manuscript as indicated in the text. Dates and references within the texts have been checked and rechecked. Most turned out to be concurrent with the events of that time. The few conflicts are easily attributed to the imperfection of memory.

Sadly, all attempts to locate and interview any of the participants mentioned in these documents has been futile. They are either long dead or untraceable, at least by the Internet missing-person-location services and the various private detectives that were hired. How these documents found their way to Maryland I have no clue. Why they were never published or released before is obvious: What they reveal would cause more controversy than any government would want. By releasing them now, I hope that other individuals or agencies with more resources than my own will pursue this investigation.

After careful and repeated readings, I have edited the documents to provide one linear narrative, quoting from the particular document that provided the clearest or most complete version of the events. As with any eyewitness testimony, there are inherent contradictions in the documents, and in those cases I took the majority opinion or left the contradictions in place.

I am convinced that there is little doubt, though scant physical evidence, that the events described actually took place, however unbelievable and incomprehensible this may appear on a first reading.

I'm sure that there will be a whole slew of people who will think this all fell out of a horse's ass. That's okay. Let the reader decide on the verity of the original authors and the story they tell.

Patrick Sheane Duncan—2016

FROM THE DESK OF
ABRAHAM VAN HELSING

(Translated from the Dutch)

11 NOVEMBER 1896

If this document is being read, then it is upon my death, and I depend on the reader to take the proper actions to resolve the plight I have created. To make the reader aware of the dangers, I am writing the following account of the circumstances that led to the quandary you will find yourself confronting. I cannot stress enough how great the jeopardy one will face in correcting what might have been a great blunder on my part. I apologise. But failure would imperil not only the brave soul who deigns to embark upon this task but likely hazard the entire world. Please do not take this as an exaggeration. The entire world.

After our astounding final encounter with the Vampire, I was not content that we had ended the affair satisfactorily. I believe we had been so relieved and intoxicated by our monumental achievement and the release of Madam Mina from the vile Creature's entrancement that I am afraid we had neglected to make certain that the Beast was indeed destroyed. I dwelled upon this while the other participants were making arrangements for the transportation of poor, deceased Quincey Morris back to his family, and themselves back to England. As for myself, I decided to remain in this mysterious country for a few months of research and inquiry.

After checking on Madam Mina and assuring myself as to her continued recuperation, I stole away from the commotion and ventured into the village, where I rented a horse-drawn carriage, an enclosed transport wagon used by the local milliner to haul perishables. At a tavern servicing the peasantry, I was able to engage four burly fellows to assist me. A familiar type of rough rustic, willing to do most anything for lucre. Still they drove a dear bargain for a day and night's work.

Despite their rough countenances, they did show some misgivings when they witnessed my purchase of a casket at the local undertaker's. I suppose any sort of container would have sufficed, but after much searching I determined that the ideal vessel for transporting a body is indeed one from the mortuary. A simple pine box was my preference but there were none at hand, or so said the daunting proprietor. He offered one to be built, but I was not willing to wait the two, possibly three, days. I knew this to be a sales tactic, but I was in no mood to wait or haggle, and I purchased a black lacquered affair (for far more than it was worth, I am sure). The dastardly man prattled on about the craftsmanship of the casket, the lush satin interior, hand-rubbed brass handles, and so on until I felt as if I were being fitted for a new suit.

Finally we were on our way, I guiding from the open driver's perch with two of my hirelings, the other pair inside the wagon with the casket as there was no other place for them to ride. They were not happy with the arrangement and had insisted on drawing straws for the berths. Only I knew that they would be even less content when they discovered exactly what was going into the coffin.

Finding the spot where we had finally confronted and defeated the Vampire was quite easy. The place had been burned into my mind like a silver photoengraving. We travelled on the rough road, for a road of an ancient and imperfect kind it was.

The box containing our Un-Dead foe had been pushed into the river, and I had only to follow the course of the current for a few hundred metres. I finally spied the box caught up in a tangle of flood debris piled near the bank. The container was in the grasp of tree limbs, their claw-like branches gripping it firmly.

One of my henchmen waded out into the rapid eddies with a rope tied to his waist for security. His fellows held the other end as he struggled against the fierce current, but he was able to tie another rope to the box.

It took all five of us to pull the box from the water and up the muddy bank. When these stalwart men saw what was inside they withdrew with the timidity of a maiden spying a snake in the rose garden. Even the horses began to scream and tore at their tethers till I calmed the beasts. When they did feel my hands on them, they whinnied low as in joy, and licked my hands and were quiet for a time.

I left the soothed beasts and examined the condition of the corpse. There was no evidence of the decay often found with water immersion, but this was not surprising, the weather being quite cold and the subsequent icy waters most likely acting as a cold storage preservative. What was surprising, most remarkable in fact, was that I found the Vampire's throat halfway healed. Despite the deep slash delivered by Harker's kukri blade, the wound had closed and new tissue was forming. I should have taken this as a warning.

The other wound was made by the late Quincey Morris's Bowie knife. Being nearly the length of a Roman short sword, the blade had been thrust into the Vampire's chest with such force that it had pinned the creature to the bottom of the box, very much like a mounted insect. We discovered this while transferring the body into the casket. It was my decision to leave the Bowie knife in situ, assuming that this was the reason for the Creature's demise. Assumed in error, to my later regret.

As we loaded the coffin into the wagon, a chill wind began to blow and a scattering of snow pelted us. The horses trotted away as I gave the site one last mournful look, in remembrance of our companion, the brave Quincey Morris. The somber clouds overhead matched my dark mood.

A thaw and the rain from the night before had turned the roads into muddy bogs, then the cold temperature had frozen this mud into a turgid crenellation most difficult to traverse. Our wheels bounced and jolted, and the wagon was tossed about like a ship on a rough sea. It became slow going, to say the least, a bitter wind in our faces. The two men riding up front with me were probably wishing they had done better on the straw draw.

The farther we travelled the more ragged and difficult the road presented itself, and our progress slowed more than I desired. My consternation increased as night loomed before us, the dim light behind the low ceiling of bruised clouds diminishing by the moment. I knew that the night was the Vampire's dominion, and even though he seemed to be without power at this moment, a deep, antediluvian dread haunted me.

Our passage led us through desolate rural areas, tiny houses with small tilled plots now scoured of any fall crop, the orchards naked of leaves. These small farms were often walled with stone harvested from the fields, and these walls hemmed in our route.

The road became rougher, our jostling more violent, to the point where we were almost thrown from our seats more than once. I heard an occasional curse from within the wagon as those men were tossed about. Despite the threat of night falling upon us, I had to order my driver to slow his horses before we lost a wheel or broke an axle.

Suddenly, as if a gas jet had been turned off, night was upon us.

I do not know if one of the men inside the wagon—out of innate curiosity, or thinking to steal the Bowie knife—opened the Vampire's casket and removed it, or if the constant bounding and bucking of the carriage simply loosened then displanted the blade. Either way, our first indication that something had gone awry was a sharp scream from inside the wagon, followed by a great commotion from therein, a knocking and pounding to rival the wagon's outside agitation.

Another horrible scream, this one clearer and louder, as the rear door of the wagon flew open and a man was propelled out that door. It was one of my hirelings. He tumbled onto the road behind us, his body rolling in that familiar limp and loose tumble as only the dead perform. There was more thrashing and yelling from the open door, then another scream from the depths of hell, this one abruptly truncated mid-note, quickly followed by the appearance of the second man's body, obviously thrown from the carriage's open back doors. There was something peculiar about the fall of this body, but I had no time to ponder. My other two hirelings looked at me in consternation.

Then a hand appeared over the wagon roof just above the open rear door. We all craned our heads to watch as a face rose into view, like a pale moon over a dark horizon.

The Vampire. His red eyes burned like hot coals; a matching scarlet smeared his mouth. His smile was depraved, the gruesome fangs shining brightly.

The two men on either side of me, so full of bravado and manful bluster when I engaged them, blanched and leapt from the wagon at this sight of the Un-Dead. I do not blame them. My first instinct was the same.

But I felt the debt owed to Morris and the lady Mina, how brave they had been in crisis, and so I reached down to retrieve the reins so that I could regain control of the horses before they ran us off a cliff or into one of those stone walls.

The Vampire rose and stepped upon the carriage roof. He clutched something in his left hand. I could not make out the object, as the darkness and a sudden ceiling of overhanging trees had plunged my view into a complete penumbra. He threw this object at me. It struck me in the chest and by reflex I let loose of the reins to catch it, clutching it to my breast. When I once again had enough light I saw that I was cradling the dismembered head of my hireling. I have to admit that, even with all of my experience at the dissection table and my familiarity with the human anatomy, I was momentarily paralyzed with shock.

I quickly tossed the repulsive visage into the night and, rousing myself from my stupor, regained my senses in time to see the Vampire stride across the wagon's turbulently rocking roof as easily as if he were on a stroll down a park path. I turned just in time to see his foot rise to kick me in the chest and send me flying off the wagon. I bounced off one horse and fell between the pair, catching myself on the braces. Not a conscious act at all, I assure you, but some kind of desperate survival instinct.

The horses, sensing some atavistic threat above them, no doubt, became wild with fear. I was barely holding on to the leather straps, flying hooves inches from my face, my hands. I knew I was but a hairbreadth from being trampled to death or crippled by an ironclad hoof. My back hung low enough to scrape and bump against the rock-hard pinnacles of mud protruding from the road. Each stab and abradement was a vicious blow that almost knocked me loose.

The Vampire leaned down from the driver's seat and planted a foot on my chest. He said something to me but I heard it not, as the clatter of the horses' hooves drowned out all sound. With a sardonic sneer he applied pressure with his boot until I had no choice but to release my grip. I fell onto the harsh road, the horses' hooves pounding so close that I felt the wind of their passing upon my face.

I bounced a few times, my forehead striking the undercarriage with a brutal blow. The spinning wheels barely missed my limbs. I do not know how, but once more some primal survival instinct caused my hands to desperately reach out, and I found purchase on the rear axle.

I instantly suffered a beating as I was dragged behind the wagon at full gallop. If only to escape further battering, I painfully hoisted myself up and into the wagon interior. The inside walls were painted with blood. I could see that the casket had been flung open. Slinging one of the ropes over my shoulder, I proceeded to climb to the wagon roof as had the Vampire before me. I confess that my short trek across the jittering roof was not as surefooted as that of my foe.

But I had the advantage: He was unaware of my approach as he urged the horses on at a breakneck speed. When I was a pace behind him I threw a loop of the rope around his neck and hauled him out of the driver's seat. With all the strength within me I twisted tight the rope.

He fought the improvised noose, clawing at the rope that bit into his neck. The struggle was so vigorous that it caused us both to roll around on our precarious perch. I held on, knowing my life was forfeit if I failed. I knew I could not strangle the Vampire, as he did not breathe. My hope was to haul it off the carriage and, if the Almighty was smiling upon my efforts, thrust it under the wheels. I think that the Creature's previous battle, days before, had weakened it, if not the wounds and submersion in freezing water, because otherwise I would have had no success against his prodigious strength.

Meanwhile the horses had gone wild, mad with fear. Unfettered by the reins, they raced in a fright-fuelled frenzy, straying from the road. The carriage scraped rough-hewn walls, sparks spitting where its steel wheels struck stone. The Vampire was getting the better of me, and I tried to concentrate on the task at hand, but my pummeling beneath the carriage had taken a toll on me. I never saw the great oak ahead of us.

I did feel the collision as the carriage struck. The impact was tremendous, a great smashing that sent the Vampire and me sailing through the air. I struck the ground so hard that I was rendered insensible for a brief moment. Regrettably, the Vampire recovered immediately and was instantly at my throat, one hand on the crown of my head, pushing it aside to bare my neck. I came to my senses, finding his face inches above me, mouth open and fangs on full display. I kicked out with my legs, knocking his out from under him, causing him to sprawl and simultaneously freeing me from his deadly embrace.

I rose to my feet and so did the Creature. We rushed at each other and collided like two battling elk. We grappled, and even in his current weakness the Vampire was able to overcome me. I struck him a few blows that had no effect upon him. He struck at me, and those clouts did indeed have a disabling result upon my own vigor. I could not continue for long in this sort of combat.

A strike at my head caused a bit of vertigo, and I began to search desperately for some source of salvation, any sort of deliverance. I spied behind the Vampire the wagon, listing to one side where a wheel had broken. The rim and steel-clad wheel was gone, the hub sprouting only a few naked and shattered spokes, which splayed out like the fingers of an opened hand.

"Now I will be rid of you once and forever," said Dracula as he approached me with dire intent.

Once again he grasped the top of my head with one hand and pressed the other upon my shoulder to bare my throat.

I ducked my head, freeing myself, and pressed my shoulder into his mid-section. Digging my feet in, I charged ahead, propelling the Vampire backward. I gave all my remaining strength to this drive until we came to a sudden stop.

I backed away and saw that the Vampire had become impaled by one of the wheel spokes. His eyes glared at me in fiery rage and emitted a horrid screeching, and then that malefic light faded and his writhing body went slack, as if he had died. I was not fooled—after all, he was the exemplar of the Un-Dead.

I watched the Vampire until I could catch my breath again. He did not move.

When I had recovered sufficiently I went in search of my hirelings. The two survivors had reunited and were sitting under a great pine, smoking and huddled against the cold. I spied the flare of their cigarettes before seeing them. We backtracked in a search for the bodies of their compatriots. Both of those men were quite dead, the neck broken on one, who had also been drained of his blood, the other dead from multiple injuries, his entire rib cage stove in like a busted crate. It took us another hour to locate and reunite the poor fellow with his head.

We marked the road where they lay with hastily created crosses, something to poke out of the gathering snow so that we could collect them on our return. The wind came now in fierce bursts, and the snow was driven with fury as it swept upon us in circling eddies.

The two men still living seemed not overly affected by the death of their companions—a statement on the hard life in these lands, I suppose.

They were more skittish when we came upon the Vampire. Even in his deathly repose Dracula had a viperous air. We set about removing the broken wheel, carefully making sure that the impaling spoke remained in his body. I was confident that this was the cause of his demise and immobility—such as it might be—temporary or otherwise.

Mounting the spare wheel was a dirty, strenuous affair. That done, we went in search of the horses. They had broken free but not wandered far, and they did not resist being hitched back into harness. Dracula was restored to his coffin, and this time the lid was secured by multiple turns of our rope.

And we returned to our journey. The snow was now falling heavily and angrily swirled about, for a high wind was beginning to blow. I advised the driver to go slow for fear of the jostling that might have freed the Vampire before. We actually had no choice in the matter, as one of our other wheels and perhaps an axle were impaired from the collision.

Finally we passed through the tiny village that was my destination.

The hamlet had been abandoned after a series of floods, the houses buried up to their hollow-eyed windows with sand and rock, bush and saplings thrusting out of roof and open room. A solemn and sad sight, what was once so full of life and hope now a monument to the fragility of man and his feeble efforts to create some permanence.

A distance farther from this sad, empty town was a hill where a church once lorded over the land, safe from the raging waters below but not protected from the parishioners. There was something wild and uncanny about the place. It is told that the priest, after a succession of plagues ravaged his flock, had lost his faith in God and in a scheme to prove His existence attempted to raise the Devil: the priest's perverted logic that if Satan existed so too must his God. To summon the Dark Prince the priest performed sacrifices in some black rite—human sacrifices, infants, stolen from the surrounding villages. He became a wolf preying on his own flock.

Suspicions led to action by the townspeople, and the skeletons of his victims were discovered in an old hideaway dug under the rectory. The villagers set fire to the church with the blasphemous priest trapped within.

The burned-out husk of the house of God was now overgrown with weeds and inhabited by bats that flew up in a ghostly flutter as we approached. The church itself was of no interest or purpose to my aims. It was the adjacent cemetery I needed. In my research to find the home of my enemy, the Creature in the casket, I had come across this profane site and a certain tomb related to the Dracula family.

We found it without difficulty. Huge it was and nobly proportioned, the structure surpassing all other vaults in size and bearing. A large mausoleum of black stone dominated the graves, which clustered around it like chicks to their hen.

The casket was manhandled, with some bother and hardship from the wagon into the tomb, there being just the three of us: I was injured from my battle, one of the other men had a useless arm, and we were hampered by the loss of the two others who had helped load the coffin. But we managed and then secured the door from the outside. My hope is that this desolate and cursed place will serve as security until I can return and seal it even further. I might find a way to also bind the coffin in a more impenetrable manner.

Why do I go to these lengths instead of destroying the King-Vampire? I am not sure. I tell myself that it is pure scientific curiosity, the why and how of such a being, that we could learn things that might be of immense value to humankind. I do hope this justification is not some vainglorious enterprise. It could be the doom of me—and the world.

We return home, to gather our dead and proceed with our lives. My own future is a mystery to me, as it should be, I suppose.

So, it is now upon the shoulders of you, dear reader, to decide what is to be done with this creature. The future, if my own era is any exemplar, I am sure will be witness to scientific miracles. It will no doubt be a better world, and I hope that in those better times people will be able to solve the rebus I have left you.

Good luck, and God help you.

Abraham Van Helsing
11 November 1896

DATED: 15.4.41
TO: SS-OBERGRUPPENFUHRER REINHARD HEYDRICH, REICH
MAIN SECURITY OFFICE
CC: REICHSFUHRER-SS HEINRICH HIMMLER
CC: ALLGEMEINE-SS WALTER SCHELLENBERG, CHIEF AMT VI,
SD—AUSLAND
FROM: DESK OF MANFRED FREIHERR VON KILLINGER, GERMAN
CONSUL, BUCHAREST, RUMANIA
(BY DIPLOMATIC POUCH)

MOST SECRET

On the dawn of the bold Operation Barbarossa, against
our great enemy the Soviet Union, and the long-awaited
eradication of the Communist poison, our Rumanian allies
are not as prepared as we would prefer. Conducator
Antonescu is eager to attack his historical enemy,
but the Rumanian armoury is still non-standardised,
obsolete, and foreign-sourced. They are making great
strides--as usual, with our aid. The influx of German
instructors and advisors has made a major impact in
modernising their program, but they have still a long
way to go and, alas, will not be fully prepared for the
coming offensive.

They are hampered by over twenty years of French-
inspired defensive operational philosophy. Even so,
we have witnessed a considerable gap between French
theory and Rumanian practice.

Still there is the fact that peasant soldiers such
as these are generally able to subsist on lower-scale

rations and worse conditions than typical German infantry. They can be hardy and uncomplaining in harsh circumstances.

A saving grace: There is sufficient manpower to throw against the Russian line. Enough to do some damage, divert Soviet resources, consume the enemy materiel, and decimate enemy forces, rather than sacrificing good German resources and soldiers.

They also have a cavalry of decent quality, but I do not see much use of such in the era of the blitzkrieg.

The Rumanian populace was initially rebellious at the Soviet annexation of Basarabia and Northern Bucovina and the awarding of Southern Dobrogea to Bulgaria and Northern Transylvania to Hungary. These were offered as an appeasement against the threat of our military might. Antonescu seems to have accepted the state of things and now has become an ally, after we supported his government against the attempted coup by Sima and the Iron Guard. I do recommend that we keep Sima and his cohorts alive and under our thumb in German territory as an inducement to keep Antonescu cooperative.

Meanwhile, the Rumanians have been purging all non-Rumanian ethnics from their current borders. The loss of which makes their army more homogeneous and, therefore, more reliable. How reliable that may be is yet to be determined. The battlefield will tell the tale.

On a note of caution, we must be circumspect with Antonescu, who is acutely aware that his Ploesti oil fields are vital to our war efforts. He has positioned a large cordon of his troops around the petroleum facilities.

We can be sure that, besides forming a protective ring around Ploesti, the Rumanians are prepared to sabotage the oil fields (as the British did in the Great War) if ever the tide turns against the Reich. I am clear on your directive that we must do everything possible to maintain this vital resource, and we will act accordingly. With this in mind, the assignment of our elite Brandenburg Battalion to abet the 18th Security Detachment in Ploesti will serve our purposes very well.

Recent oil shipments to Germany have been disappointing, I know, below the level you desire, but a shortage of tanker cars has made rail transport difficult. As soon as the Danube thaws completely, we can resume full capacity with barge shipments.

There is one fly in our ointment. Recently the area around Brasov has been the focus of targeted resistance. If this rebellion continues and bleeds past the Carpathian Mountains, Ploesti may be in jeopardy. I am forwarding to Captain Lobenhoffer and his detachment instructions to work with the local militia and suppress and destroy this spark before it starts a fire of resistance and terrorism that could spread across the country.

Any further suggestions would be appreciated.

Heil Hitler.

Dnr.--Manfred von Killinger

TO: MANFRED VON KILLINGER, GERMAN CONSUL, BUCHAREST,
RUMANIA
FROM: CAPTAIN GEORGE LOBENHOFFER, MILITARY ATTACHE,
BRASOV

MOST SECRET

SUBJECT: INCIDENT REPORT

<u>4.4.41</u>--Rumanian Military dispatch rider travelling
via motorcycle on the road N of Arnesti encountered
piano wire stretched across road. Decapitated.
Documents regarding Rumanian troop movement missing.
Also sidearm and uniform.
   No arrests made.
   Assailant(s) unknown.

<u>6.4.41</u>--Three SS Auxiliary Police, formerly local
Volksdeutsche, eating lunch at an outside cafe in Rasnov
killed. Shot at their table by assassin bicycling past.
   Cafe owner and staff detained and interrogated. One
detainee died under questioning.
   Assailant(s) unknown.

<u>7.4.41</u>--Troop transport vehicle in queue at roadblock
outside Sacele destroyed by grenade inserted into gas
tank. Twelve occupants, Rumanian conscripts wounded,
three killed, including one officer.
   Various witnesses describe perpetrator as woman,
man, child.

No arrests.
Assailant(s) unknown.

<u>11.4.41</u>--Outside Codlea. Convoy ambushed. Was able
to speak to the lone survivor in the hospital. Statement
follows:

"My name is Radu Lepadatu. I am Private in First
Mountain Division. Was on patrol through farm country
evicting Jews, gypsies, troublemakers. Last stop this
day is farm of Leibu, Jew. Raised corn, hay, peppers.
We confiscate what we find. Not looting. Re-allocation.
Leibu family have no need where they are going. Put
Leibu, wife, two children on truck with others. Maybe
twenty prisoners. Take chickens. Take cow. Find good
boots for me. Many socks, hand-knitted. Gets cold in
mountains. Everyone angry at Private Lazar Tuca. He
is dead now. Lazar shoots cow before we put in truck.
Takes six men to load dead cow onto truck. Dead weight.
Alive cow walks onto truck. Tuca stupid. Sergeant calls
him village idiot. Farmer's daughter weeps at death of
cow.

"Convoy drives back to Base. Five trucks. Fords.
Good trucks. Made in Rumania. [Note: This is true. Very
capable trucks. But only assembled in Rumania from
imported parts. Parts import has ceased. Reliability
of these vehicles will most likely deteriorate as
conflict endures. CPT. L.]

"First truck contains soldiers. Twelve men. Second
truck and third filled with captured materiel and
provisions and cow. And chickens with legs tied. Truck
three full of prisoners. I in last truck, fifth, with
six other soldiers. Tuca next to me. He smells like
dung. Tuca, like village idiot, lifted rear end of cow.

"We drive through forest. Narrow road. Rough road.
We bounce like ball bearings in fruit jar. Butt sore.
I stand. Use knees like car springs.

"Dense forest. Huge old trees. So big man cannot put arms around trunks. Branches meet overhead across road. Road like tunnel with green ceiling.

"I see man on side of road. Steps from behind tree. Ax held over head. I think lumberman. He brings down ax. Chops rope. I follow rope with eyes.

"Rope frees log suspended up in air. Big log. Thick as a fat man. Three, four feet thick. Twenty feet long. End chopped to point. Log swings from two ropes. Goes faster, what you say? Momentum, yes. Hits my truck hard. Big crash. Knocks truck over.

"We spill out like beans from bag. Men scream. Some trapped under truck. Yell in pain. I lose rifle.

"Stand up. Lead truck knocked over same way.

"Other trucks have to stop. Trapped on road.

"Then we are attacked. From woods. Both sides. Gunfire. No place to hide. I find my rifle. Never get to shoot. Knocked down. Hit in leg. Doesn't hurt. I look at hole. I am shot, I think. Can't find rifle again.

"Battle over in seconds. My ears ring. From gunfire.

"Now leg hurts. Hurts bad. Big pain. Want to scream. But see Tuca next to me. Jaw gone. Just upper teeth seen. Can see all of them. Rotten teeth. Blood fills hole. He looks at me. I watch Tuca's eyes go dead.

"People come out of trees. Carry guns. Civilians. Maybe thirty. All carry guns. I play dead. Old man yells orders, "Collect all weapons. Ammunition. No prisoners."

"They start shooting soldiers. Even dead men shot. Woman walks over, shoots dead Tuca. I squint, see her. Beautiful woman. Like goddess. Red hair. She stands over me. She kicks wounded leg. I grunt. Open my eyes. She looks down at me. Holds pistol. Points at my face. Barrel is so big. I could crawl inside like sewer pipe. She shoots me. In head.

"I wake up in hospital. I have hard skull. Father always tease me. Skull like rock. Maybe he right."

(Note: PVT. Lepadatu is a very lucky man. The bullet did not penetrate his "rock-like" skull, just plowed between the bone and skin to exit out the back. The leg wound is worse, having shattered the bone. He is due for amputation.

(But his testimony reveals an uncomfortable fact. An organised resistance group has established itself in the area around Brasov. Highly organised, if the Private is to be believed. And I do believe him. He is too much a primitive to be disingenuous. I and my unit are putting the spur to the local militia to quell this problem before it gets out of hand. CPT. L.)

DATED: 20.4.41
TO: OBERGRUPPENFUHRER REINHARD HEYDRICH
CC: REICHSFUHRER-SS HEINRICH HIMMLER
FROM: MANFRED FREIHERR VON KILLINGER, GERMAN CONSUL,
BUCHAREST, RUMANIA
(BY DIPLOMATIC POUCH)

MOST SECRET

I am forwarding the following report from SS Captain
Lobenhoffer concerning the resistance effort in and
around Brasov. It seems that the Captain and the local
militia are having little effect on this burgeoning
underground terrorist campaign against our operations
in the region.

Maybe it is time to increase our presence in this
area. I have spoken with Antonescu about this, not
wanting to frighten the Rumanians with any thought
that we are encroaching upon their domestic affairs.
He stated that he was open to any assistance against
these rebel forces. They obviously pose as great a
threat to his rule as to our own goals.

I will allow the Captain's report to speak for
itself. I do not need to remind you that Brasov is less
than a hundred kilometres from the vitally important
Ploesti oil fields.

Heil Hitler.

Dnr: Manfred von Killinger

* * *

DATED: 19.4.41

TO: MANFRED FREIHERR VON KILLINGER, GERMAN CONSUL,
BUCHAREST, RUMANIA
FROM: CAPTAIN GEORGE LOBENHOFFER, MILITARY ATTACHED

MOST SECRET

SUBJECT: FIELD REPORT

This last week in Brasov and the surrounding areas there
we have witnessed a plethora of sabotage incidents and
outrageous attacks on military personnel and materiel:
the demolition of a Brigade fuel dump, electrical and
communication lines routinely cut all over the district,
the torching of barracks and vehicles, military
personnel lured into alleys or ambushed and robbed of
their weapons, papers, and oft-times uniforms. There
have been numerous break-ins and pilfering of armouries
with a loss of over a hundred weapons (a more accurate
account is difficult, as the Rumanian inventory system
is a travesty), including pistols, rifles, light and
heavy machine guns, even a wheeled howitzer plus a
Company level mortar. Ammunition was also taken.

Things have gotten out of hand. The Rumanian
authorities have not made one legitimate arrest.
Token apprehensions have occurred, followed by crude
interrogations. Suspects have confessed under duress,
but those confessions are suspect as none of them are
corroborated. The confession, however forced, seems
enough for these barbarians. These arrests are shams
and have done nothing to abrogate the terrorism; in
fact, they may be adding fuel to the fire. The local
militia appear to be totally helpless in the face
of these insurrections and do nothing but turn the
population against our cause and to the side of the
resistance.

A good part of the problem lies in the attitude of my Rumanian colleagues. They totally ignore every bit of advice I provide to them. You would think that a soldier of my pedigree, stature, and training would be a valuable resource to be mined for my wisdom and expertise. But I have found that these are an arrogant and stubborn people, and my counsel falls upon determinedly deaf ears. Do they not know that my family has been soldiering since Frederick the Great?

On 18 April I accompanied Legion Captain Cuanda on a mission to round up some Jews in Brasov proper, where we were to shut down a local newspaper with leftist leanings, the Brasov Autonom (Independent). This journal has a history of Communist and anti-government/Antonescu propaganda. Also, its editor and publisher, Israil Zingher, is a Jew.

The newspaper offices occupied the ground floor of a four-storey building near the centre of town. The Rumanian soldiers destroyed the printing presses with more zeal than was required--tossing the various parts through the front windows and into the street, along with furniture, boxes of type, rolls and bundles of paper, and even Zingher himself. Any protests from this Jew were silenced by the boots of the soldiers.

A door-to-door search was made of the top three floors, part of which was the residence of the Zingher family. Other apartments also were cleared--not a delicate operation, I'm afraid, as the living quarters were demolished by the overzealous and thuggish soldiers. More furniture was thrown out the upper windows and smashed onto the cobblestones below.

The residents, too, were not spared from this brutish behaviour. One protesting man was shot on the spot. A few women were also assaulted in the manner soldiers have used throughout eternity. It is my opinion that this kind of mistreatment by our allies can only reflect negatively on us Germans and be ultimately detrimental to the Fuhrer's goals. We are better than this.

Across the plaza, Captain Cuanda stationed a single old Renault FT-17 tank next to a tall building, more as an intimidation factor than anything. The tank commander, a Legion Lieutenant, Codrin Dalakis, stood in the open turret observing.

Unseen by him, a second-storey window above and behind the tank opened. Out of the window slipped a long stick with a loop of wire at the end--much like the snare wielded by dogcatchers in my hometown of Dusseldorf.

The snare was snapped over the tank commander's head, the wire drawn tight. Then the strangling, struggling Lieutenant was hauled out of the turret by his neck and lifted up and into the building via the window.

At that point a resistance fighter dashed out of the selfsame building, scrambled up the side of the tank, and stepped into the hatch, closing it behind him. The three gunshots, muffled by a few inches of tempered steel, were not heard above the commotion at the apartments. These actions were deduced after the fact.

The tank hatch was opened, the bodies of the crew hauled out and replaced by three subversives.

None of this was observed by myself or Captain Cuanda and the rest of the detachment as we supervised the assemblage of the apartment occupants. These people were lined up for an examination of their identity documents. Those with suspect papers were loaded into trucks brought for this purpose. Much weeping and begging was displayed. To no avail, of course.

A woman in the line piqued my own interest. The Captain had inspected her papers and passed her over with a second glance, an entirely justifiable second glance as her beauty was worthy of that and more, luxurious black hair not sculptured as the current fashion requires, falling in natural waves about her shoulders, framing an alabaster face with sunburned cheeks, intelligent green eyes, and a fine if overripe mouth. But what caused her to stand out from the crowd was her disposition. While the other detainees demonstrated fear and apprehension, this woman showed no fright but instead a certain self-possession, a rather superior bearing that, I have to admit, went against the grain.

I, too, inspected her papers, identifying her as one Lenore von Muller.

"You do not reside here?" I asked, as the document stated a residence on the other side of the city.

I spoke in German, waiting for the Captain to translate, but she answered me in my own language.

"I was visiting," she told me with a hint of defiance.

"Perhaps warning them," I proposed.

She did not reply. In fact, her visage took on an angry glare.

I decided that this Fraulein von Muller should be subjected to a more thorough interrogation back at my personal office, and I took her arm to escort her to my vehicle. At this point, Captain Cuanda grinned at the woman as he reevaluated her figure, which I must say was equal to her face. He addressed her.

"Maybe I can find a use for you in my quarters," he offered in his crude German, groping her about the bosom and lower. I am ashamed to say that I did nothing to stop this loathsome act. "Many uses indeed," he said.

"We've heard what goes on in your quarters," she said and then proceeded to spit on his boots. A most vulgar act for such a refined beauty, I thought.

The Captain lifted a hand to strike the woman and I restrained his arm. I am not one for brutalising women and children, like some of his barbarian brothers-in-arms.

This was when I heard the tank rev its powerful engines and the telltale clanking of steel tread across the cobblestones.

I was, I have to admit, surprised. It stopped within a few metres of where I stood and the turret gun rotated with a loud whine of hydraulics until the muzzle of its cannon was aimed at my head. I could see the lands and grooves curling down the barrel. Then I heard the unmistakable clink and clank of a round being loaded into the breech of that howitzer. A more ominous sound I have never heard.

I stared at the black maw, contemplating my own death, wondering why a Rumanian crew would be helping these traitors. Then the turret hatch clanged open and a man, a scarf obscuring his face, popped up and addressed me.

"Let her go," he ordered in Hungarian. I did not move, not understanding the local language. The woman repeated the order in German, and I realised that I still had one hand clutching her arm. I hesitated, moved toward my personal vehicle. With a whirr of engine and clatter of the ratchet, the big tank gun tracked my every step. I stopped. The gun also ceased moving. I released the woman.

She relieved me of my sidearm, pulled the cocking lever of the Luger to chamber a round. She handled the pistol with familiarity and very professionally.

The cannon rotated to aim at the Rumanian soldiers gathered around the truck filling with prisoners. Three similarly scarf-masked men disarmed the soldiers. Where they came from I do not know.

The man at the turret issued another order, "Tell your men to release those people." This was addressed to me. I decided that this was not the time to argue that these were not my men, and I relayed the demand to Captain Cuanda.

He issued the order to release the prisoners. The Jews on the truck also seemed too shocked at the turn of events to act, and the black-haired woman rushed to the truck waving my pistol, shouting at them, "Hurry! Run! Go!"

They quickly scurried to vacate the truck and departed with the waiting masked men, disappearing down an alley.

At this point the black-haired woman walked past me to face Captain Cuanda. She addressed him, "By the way, I have no use for you, whatsoever." Whereupon she raised my Luger and struck him on the temple. He fell to the ground.

Before I could react, the tank cannon fired. The round hit a truck, which exploded. The Rumanian soldiers sought cover. I prostrated myself upon the cobblestones.

The woman boarded the tank and it began to back out of the square.

Captain Cuanda gathered himself, crawled to a soldier wounded by the exploding truck, and stripped a grenade from the man's body. Rising to one knee, Cuanda prepared to throw the grenade at the departing tank, or the woman. We will never know.

He was instantly cut down by a burst from the tank's Hotchkiss 8mm machine gun. He fell upon his own grenade, and the resulting explosion lifted his body into the air. What landed only millimetres away from my face was but mangled meat.

I immediately took charge, but without weapons we could not pursue. We gathered our wounded and dead and returned to the security of our Base. Rearmed and with reinforcements, we returned to the "scene of the crime," and I led a search for the assassins. Not a trace of them or the prisoners was found. I assume the citizens gathered in the initial raid are now being secreted out of Rumania. The tank was discovered abandoned in a potato field at the edge of town. The interior had been set afire, igniting its load of 37mm cannon shells, thereby destroying the vehicle entirely. The dead body of Legion Lieutenant Dalakis was found in a local quarry, stripped of his uniform.

As this incident demonstrates, the resistance is obviously becoming bolder. Larger terrorist operations are expected. I want it to be clear that none of this is my fault. I assure you that these activities are a direct result of the local military commanders ignoring my professional guidance, which is of the highest standards set by the Reich. I recommend that I be given command of an SS unit to put down this rebellion before it spreads across the country, particularly south toward Ploesti. A Battalion would be welcome (and of course the promotion inherent in the command), but I would accept a Company. If we have learned anything from Poland and other occupied territories, it is that small acts of insurgency must be extinguished before they become open revolution--the type that inspires an already recalcitrant populace.

I await your orders.

Heil Hitler.

CPT. G. Lobenhoffer

(Note: The Luger that was taken from me was an old Lange Pistole 08, presented to me by my father, a General in the Artillery, when he was given his new Walther P38. I am anxious for its return as it has great sentimental value, and I would appreciate an alert be posted across Rumania.)

EXCERPTED FROM THE UNPUBLISHED NOVEL
THE DRAGON PRINCE AND I
by Lenore Van Muller

[Editor's note: Lucille Van Helsing is obviously the true author, as evidenced by her use of the name "Lenore Van Muller," a version of the alias during the *Brasov Autonom* raid.]

A war is a war is a war is a war.

The band on the *Titanic* played until the ship sank into the cold, merciless sea. Music to lull doomed souls. And the passengers danced. To their deaths.

The world is at war. Rumania is in the iron grip of Hitler's toady, Antonescu. This country, my country, the whole of Europe, is at war.

And the fine folk of Brasov dance. They put on a festival. St. George's Day, a trifling celebration. The first day of spring. Villagers will rise before dawn and bathe in the cold river in the primitive belief that doing so makes them healthy and strong. This in the age when planes drop hell from the sky.

While the world shudders, the young maidens of Brasov plant basil, storing the seeds in their mouths to ensure the health of their crop. Madness. Their country has become an offering on Hitler's altar of war, and they spit seeds like country bumpkins.

The previous evening when the clock struck midnight the locals extinguished the lights in their houses, turned the kitchen utensils topsy-turvy in the drawers, and hung bundles of garlic over doors and cow sheds for protection against the malefic creatures that haunt their medieval imaginations. While the real danger was the conscription of their menfolk to feed the German war machine.

Some farmers took their cows to pasture so that they could carefully watch over the beasts and protect them against witches intent on stealing the milk. Others hit each other with nettles to ensure their health for the coming year. Sometimes Lucille thought she did not live in the twentieth century but the sixteenth. There was evil out there. Not in the form of witches and goblins and Blajini. The true evil seeped from Berlin like dark floodwater.

These were the thoughts of Lucille Van Helsing as she bicycled her way down the country path into town. The last vestige of a fog lay low about the fields like frosty breath from the squatting remains of haystacks.

Lucille knew from her own St. George's Day memories that in the village square confectioners were now setting up tables laden with sweets. Gypsies were erecting stands for fortune-tellers and other diverse entertainments. There would be a puppet show for the children, acrobats tumbling across the cobblestones, a stilt walker making everyone crane their necks as the village wits asked about the weather "up there."

A fire-breather would belch flame to the alarm and subsequent delight of all. A wire would be strung from the Town Hall bell tower to the building across the plaza so that a tiny man in tights could precariously stride from one end to the other as the crowd below oohed and aahed.

And if one of the gypsies lifted a wallet or snatched a watch off an unsuspecting wrist, caused a necklace to disappear as if by evaporation, the pilfering did not seem to dissipate anyone's enjoyment any more than the war that loomed over Europe.

Even the Rumanian soldiers would be in high spirits, laughing and drinking, partaking of the foods in the various stalls. A few would even pay.

On the doomed ship the music played and the passengers danced as the icy seas crept to their knees.

Lucille's father had driven into town earlier, called to a meeting of the town leaders by the local Nazi Liaison Officer, Captain Lobenhoffer. Usually Lucille attended town meetings with her father, but today's presence of the German prohibited her. Lobenhoffer would have recognised her from the incident at the *Brasov Autonom* where she had absconded with his Luger. During the encounter she had worn a black wig, but she wasn't sure that was enough disguise to fool even the dense Nazi.

She was aware of the irony as she carried the German's weapon nestled inside her knapsack like a loaf of fresh-baked bread for Grandmama.

Lucille did not mind having to bike into town. It was a trip she had made so many times as a child. On this very bicycle. She turned onto the main road. Memories ambushed her from every house and farm field she passed. She soaked in the sights and sounds of spring, the budding flowers in the fruit trees, apple, plum, pear, and cherry, mixed with the acrid bite of manure spread about the freshly turned fields. The brilliant green grass spread beneath the trees was decorated with fallen petals as if carefully laid there by an artistic carpet designer. She almost lost herself in the bucolic, verdant scenery.

The ship's band played on. But Lucille was one who did not dance to their funereal song.

Most of the houses along the road were deserted, the occupants already in town for the festival, the roads likewise as empty. In the blue sky a flock of starlings swarmed in an undulating cloud, a collective mindless flight much akin, she thought, to this collective, mindless war.

Lucille tried to lose herself in the halcyon springtide. And it seemed to work. Her angry thoughts were slowly being ameliorated by the pastoral view. Until she heard a great rumble and engine growl behind her. Glancing back, she was able to see a convoy coming down the road.

She pulled her bicycle over to the narrow shoulder before she was forced off the road. Teetering at the edge of a drainage ditch, she was buffeted by the gusts thrown at her by the passing vehicles.

They were German.

Every human knows the value of appearances, women more than men; a red dress makes one kind of statement, a black sheath another. The proper coif, the persuasive artistry of make-up, and the right shoes, always the right shoes.

So Lucille could appreciate the adroit hand that was behind the creation of the German uniform, especially that of the dreaded Waffen SS. Comparing the grey, stylish, imposing Nazi SS uniform to the baggy brown serge of the Rumanian Army livery was the difference between a falcon and a yard chicken. Even the German transportation exuded ruthless power.

Lucille watched them pass, the lead vehicle a half-truck/half-track combination, rubber tyres up front and steel treads in the rear. The only passenger was an SS Major standing upright, one hand braced casually on the machine gun stand mounted in the centre of the vehicle. Lucille's eyes were drawn to the officer's dress hat and the dreaded death's-head insignia. Under the shade of the cap bill were the cold, blue eyes of a man as hard as the steel upon which he rode. Over his shoulders, a long, black leather coat hung to the ankles of his black boots. He stood erect, as if he were a statue carved to honor the German Teutonic ideal.

He passed Lucille without a glance in her direction. This was in itself unusual, as Lucille Van Helsing was used to being appreciated. Her radiant red hair, striking features, and lithe but curvaceous body usually caused at least one look, more often a second and third. She took no great pride in this. It had been a fact of her life since her teens. She just took it for granted. And yes, she had used it more than a few times, but regarded it as no more than a bit of luck in the hereditary lottery.

The half-track rattled past her, the slapping of the steel treads a loud obscenity in the rural idyll that surrounded Lucille. Four trucks followed, filled with German soldiers, also standing. What lower-ranking man would dare sit if their commandant stood? Their uniforms were smart, clean as the rifles and machine guns strapped across their chests. Every truckload that passed sent a chill through Lucille. These were not peasant soldiers. These were hardened troops, every man having the countenance of a combat veteran. Lucille knew the difference. She recognised the look, had seen it in her own mirror. These were killers.

The game had changed.

As soon as the last truck had passed, Lucille remounted her bicycle and pedalled as hard as she could into the dusty wake of the convoy.

She had to warn her father and the others.

As she neared the outskirts of town, she began to see familiar landmarks with new eyes. With German eyes. The fire-blackened hulk of a tank, pushed to the side of the road. The graffiti scrawled in whitewash on the turret: "Antonescu Die!" A series of Rumanian Army helmets set atop fence posts— all riddled with bullet holes. The Resistance had displayed these trophies in the same manner that medieval legions set out the decapitated heads of their enemies. Lucille now had second thoughts about the taunts and worried that they would suffer for it.

She redoubled her pedalling. The air was rent with the pealing of bells from the Brasov churches, whether tolling in celebration or warning, Lucille could not tell. She did notice that one of the bells gave off a discordant note as if cracked. She had never noticed this before. Was this a recent event, or were her nerves magnifying her senses?

The convoy roared through the narrow streets of Brasov. With a silent, raised hand from the Major, the half-track stopped a dozen blocks from the square. The following trucks lined up behind it. Lucille saw them park and she made a brisk turn down a side alley. In her handlebar mirror she could see the Nazi officer consult a map and spit out orders to his underlings.

Racing through the narrow side streets and alleys of Brasov, her mind flew from one frightening scenario to another.

Her father was in danger. The committee meeting was a trap. The Resistance had been betrayed. Who? Why? What could she do? She had to do something. Anything to save her father. Anything!

She entered the Old Town section, speeding through the narrow paths between the ancient Saxon buildings, having to tuck in her arms to escape brushing the thirteenth-century walls. She curled around the old Greek Orthodox Church, brilliant white in the noonday sun. Past the graveyard of Rumanian and German dead from the First World War, the German crosses still visible on the weatherworn cement markers, poking their grim heads over the tops of the uncut grass.

The band played an old familiar song.

At the Schei Gate she almost collided with a gaggle of schoolchildren. They were dressed in traditional costume for the St. George's Day pageant. She sped past the Johannes Honterus School and approached the Black Church, so named from when it was burned down by the Austrians during one of Brasov's many invasions. Her bicycle rattled over the cobblestones so violently that she was afraid it would shake itself apart.

Dumping her bicycle against the church wall, she snatched her knapsack from the basket and entered the small door at the "wedding" portal. The church interior was dark and smelled of sandalwood incense. Lucille hurried down the aisle, past the wooden pews alongside the nave reserved for the old Guilds, their emblems emblazoned across the fronts.

Checking to make sure the church was empty and she wasn't being observed, Lucille hurried toward the bell tower stairway. She paused but a second and dashed up the spiral stairs. The climb seemed to go on forever, and her breathing became loud, deep, rasping gulps of air. She felt a stabbing pain in her side. When she had reached the belfry landing, she took a moment to catch her breath before peering out one of the tower's narrow slits.

Lucille remembered how she and her girlfriends used to sneak into the church and climb these endless steps to hide in this belfry and smoke illicit cigarettes while they giggled over the racy bits of *Lady Chatterley's Lover*, the only sections they actually read. Had she ever been that innocent? It was also here that she secretly read that Forbidden Book, by herself, of course.

From her sixty-five-metre-high vantage point she could view the entire Brasov Town Square below her. The festival looked like an Arabian bazaar, most of the town having turned out for the celebration. The food stalls and gypsy entertainment were at full frolic. Children's laughter and adult shouts of joy rose up to Lucille's ears. The pleasant aroma of *gomboc* and *budinca* mingled with the noise.

Reaching into her knapsack, she withdrew the Luger. Pulling back the toggle, she chambered a round, flipped on the safety, and stuck the pistol into the pocket of her sweater—rather, a sweater of her father's that she had claimed as her own. The weight of the handgun pulled down the ancient knit until it hung a foot below the other pocket. That wouldn't do.

Pulling the pistol out, she instead stuck it in the back waistband of her pants, the motion <u>reminding</u> her of a Bogart/Cagney gangster movie for a brief moment. She felt foolish.

But then, recalling the impending danger, she fumbled in her knapsack for her binoculars. She often bicycled around future ambush sites, playing the role of bird-watcher, peering through her glass at various birds, even cataloguing her sightings in a tiny notebook. She had, of course, studied a guide on Rumanian birds in case a suspicious soldier stopped and queried her. She could recite enough particulars to fool any amateur and probably a few professionals, being fully knowledgeable about the short-toed and golden eagle, the black woodpecker, assorted dippers, and the scarce ring ouzel. It was a way to monitor troop movements without arousing too much suspicion.

Lucille was usually able to bat her lashes and twist a flirtatious finger through her copper hair and talk her way out of any encounter, more of them lately, but the notebook, the binoculars, and her avian spiel were always ready to prove her case. The pistol, if they failed.

So far the use of the Luger had not been required.

She focused her glasses on the building at the centre of the plaza—the three-hundred-year-old Town Hall. Two storeys tall, with a clock tower adding a third. In the old days the Council House was where the one hundred privileged citizens, representatives of the various Guilds, used to rule Brasov. With the power of the Guilds now only history, today the upper floor contained the Mayor's offices, his own inner sanctum facing the Square, fronted by a large portico. This porch, roofed, but with large, open, arched windows, was where the town leaders were now meeting, the men drinking and dining alfresco, able to gaze down at the festivities in the plaza below.

She could see the men gathered in the portico. They were obviously waiting for something or someone. They ambled about the great office, glasses of sherry in hand, smoking the sulphurous cigars handed out by the Mayor, who kept the good tobacco for himself in a humidor hidden in his side bar.

Lucille knew them all. General Suciu, the Rumanian commander of the Mountain Division, which held dominion over Brasov and the surrounding area of Transylvania. He was a lackadaisical officer, wearing his wrinkled, ill-fitting uniform as if it were a pair of overalls. Never comfortable with his military position, he spent more time with his lumber business, fleecing the government, selling overpriced green wood. Business was good. War, as always, was good for business.

The General had recently expanded his interests into a manufacturing plant in Targoviste, relining gun barrels to enable various field cannon to fire the same 75mm round the Germans used. Not coincidentally, his own units were ordering these artillery refits in large numbers. Lucille had personally put his factory on the Resistance's list for sabotage.

He was a soft-looking man, always seeming distracted from the conversation at hand, his Division known for their lack of aggression and general slovenliness. Every Resistance mission was grateful for this listless attitude. There were rumours that Suciu regularly stole his men's rations for resale and that one could purchase an officer's rank or a promotion within his organization with coin or, in one instance, a land deed. He was doing well in the war and so was his tailor, who kept busy letting out the waistband of the General's uniform trousers.

Right now the fat-faced General was leaning out the window, his dishwater-grey eyes enjoying a bird's-eye view of the women's cleavage below. Since it was proper during festivals to wear the traditional open-necked peasant blouse, his eyes were flitting about in his head like a canary trying to escape its cage, and his little pink tongue constantly slimed his lips.

Father Petrescu, the Catholic priest, was glancing at the General with resigned contempt. Though most of Brasov was Lutheran, Petrescu was the agreed-upon religious leader in the area, a position earned by his Krakow University education and his equanimity in any dispute. His face was always red, made more so by the stark contrast with his white collar and black cassock, his skin burned by the sun in the summer and chafed by the wind in the winter, as he bicycled from one end of the parish to the other trading selected morsels of gossip for food and drink. For the isolated farmers, wives and children of the valley, he performed the roles of newspaper, radio, and, every once in a while, priest.

His whippet-thin physique induced every woman on his route to try to fatten up the cleric with a hearty meal, often providing provisions for the road, which he parcelled out to the least prosperous of his flock. It was a tribute to the man's conviviality and charity that a good many of his invitations often came from non-Catholic homes.

Constable Chiorean leaned over the priest to refill his glass. The regional police officer was a great bear of a man, his imposing height and barrel chest enough to intimidate any criminal or rabble-rouser. Yet he combined this with a benign calm in any situation. No matter how excitable anyone else became, the good Constable's quiet demeanor, accompanied by his giant hand laid upon an angry shoulder, was enough to defuse any volatile situation. He was also the hairiest human Lucille had ever encountered. His mustache sprouted from nose to sideburn, his hands were carpeted with hair long enough to braid, tendrils of hair curled out from his collar and tufted out of his ears, and his eyebrows grew like one long hedge over his brown eyes.

The Constable and the priest were in deep conversation with Mayor Muresanu, a tiny man who compensated for his bald pate with an explosion of beard. His face was dominated by a nose the size of a pear that was tapestried with a filigree of red and blue veins. He assumed the mantle of office as if it were a birthright and strutted around Brasov like the majordomo of an exclusive French restaurant, his self-importance bloated miles beyond his station.

Lucille's father, Professor Abraham Van Helsing, was accepting a light for his cigar from Captain Lobenhoffer. She would chide him later for this; he had promised to give up nicotine, which he himself declared a poison. He was in his eighties now and, by his own diagnosis, his lungs were not what they were. Lucille was going to give him hell—if he lived to hear it.

The Nazi, Lobenhoffer, was a tall, sallow man with glasses who always appeared to have a bad taste in his mouth. His thin, blond mustache seemed to be constructed of only twelve hairs and hovered over a wet, thin mouth that twitched when he was frightened. Lucille knew this firsthand.

The Captain and her father were in deep conversation, most likely about Lobenhoffer's distinguished heritage going back to Gebhard von Blucher, the famous Teutonic General. Her father had told Lucille that Lobenhoffer could recite his lineage like a child declaring the alphabet and did it with the same singsong rhythm. The trouble was that the German could never remember whom he had told, therefore Van Helsing and everybody Lobenhoffer encountered in Brasov had heard the list of ancestors so many times they could repeat it back to him.

Her father, who still maintained a remarkable memory, was probably biting his tongue to keep from finishing the recitation for Lobenhoffer.

From Lucille's view, the group in the Mayor's office seemed a congenial lot. They were completely unaware that the dreaded German SS were about to interrupt the conviviality.

Lucille tried to think of a way to warn her father, pull him out of danger. She could not do it herself; Lobenhoffer might recognise her. Was there a phone downstairs in the church Chapter-house? Could she enlist one of the gypsies to carry a message? She surveyed the crowd below and spotted Janos. Janos!

Lucille and Janos had been lovers since the partisans had ambushed the convoy in the forest, their union the result of a celebratory bacchanal. He had also played a major part in the *Brasov Autonom* rescue, commandeering the tank, but he had covered his face with a scarf so Lobenhoffer would not recognise him. Janos could go warn her father and the others. Was it worth the risk?

Focusing her binoculars on the plaza below, she found Janos gorging himself on *pup de crump* at Afina Vula's table. The woman was throwing her great bosom into his face at every opportunity, feeding him with her own hand like one would offer an apple to a horse. Somehow grated potato crumbs kept falling into that great chasm of cleavage, forcing her to forage for them. It appeared that Janos was suffering from momentary vertigo as he watched her fat fingers dive into that fleshy abyss.

Lucille decided to go down and pull him away, if not to warn her father then to save him from himself, a task she had performed before. She began to slip her binoculars back into the case when she heard that terrible clatter and roar as the SS convoy rolled into the Square from all directions, the trucks blocking any escape routes out of the plaza.

The half-track with the upright officer plowed directly through the carnival, crushing stands and stalls under its wheels and tracks without regard to any pedestrians who might be in the way. The startled populace frantically fled out of the mechanical beast's path. Janos snatched a frozen, transfixed child into his arms, seconds before the little one was run over.

Those not in harm's way just stood and stared as the Nazi troops leapt off the trucks and aimed their weapons at the crowd. There was an efficiency and sureness about their movements that indicated they had done this before, and more than once. The commanding officer dismounted his vehicle with an imperious nonchalance. He turned to his adjutant and spoke an order. Not loudly—Lucille couldn't make out the words. He was the kind of leader who believed that men who spoke too loud did so out of weakness.

Lucille could not hear what was said, but she need not have worried, as the adjutant repeated the command in a shout to his men.

"Arrest the gypsies!"

And the soldiers rushed to obey. The gypsies tried to flee, but there was no sanctuary to be found. Every street was blocked. A gypsy man clutched his wife and tried to enter the front door of the bakery, most likely to escape through the back door. A gunshot barked and the man fell. The shot echoed across the square and was replaced with the wail of the fallen man's wife.

Everyone in the Square froze where they stood. SS soldiers dragged the wounded gypsy and his weeping woman to one of the trucks and tossed them into the bed. The rest of his people were now easily rounded up and loaded into the trucks.

The commanding officer strode into the Town Hall without a glance at the turmoil he had just created.

Lucille held her breath. She was too late to give any warning. Her father was sitting by the window, staring down at the tragedy happening below him. Lucille tightened her view until his face filled the glass. She stared into his heartbroken eyes and muttered one plaintive cry.

"Father."

* * *

Professor Van Helsing listened to Captain Lobenhoffer scamper through the branches of his family tree like a squirrel after acorns and let his mind wander to more weighty concerns—such as how and why some cultures came to consider themselves better than others.

He had witnessed it all over the world. The British lording it over the East Indians, the Turk's disdain for the Armenian, the Germans looking down their noses at, well, everyone, the rich thinking the poor were a lesser species, his own Dutch and their low opinion of the African, the Oriental.

In Van Helsing's wide experience, every race displayed the same panorama of human attributes, from the most low to the highest, intelligent and idiotic, good and evil in equal proportions. And then there was that most dominant, most dangerous characteristic, the feckless passivity that allowed evil to prosper. What seemed to unite the arrogant was simply power over their assumed underlings. It was rare to find one of these vainglorious egotists admitting that they held such a lofty status by mere accident of birth—like this Teutonic blowhard Lobenhoffer.

And what was it in the German character that induced them to initiate so many wars in the last hundred years? If Lobenhoffer were any example, it was that very presupposition of superiority. The only catalyst needed for this poisonous brew was a charismatic politician who knew how to capitalise on that presumption.

Lobenhoffer had reached the Hapsburg twig of his great Austrian oak when the recitation was interrupted by a substantial din coming from the Square outside the open windows. The cacophony of steel striking stone leapt into the Mayor's office, and everyone rushed to view the source.

Van Helsing saw the Germans roll into the plaza below. He recognised the emblem of the SS and knew at once that the game had just escalated. He watched the SS troops collect the gypsies with efficient brutality. He saw the calm shooting of the man attempting to escape—Traian, a stalwart member of the Rumanian Resistance.

The Professor scanned the Square, seeking another freedom fighter, Janos. The young man had gone back to manning the table peddling his mother's *wiener schnitzel*. Janos was excitable, a reactionary, not necessarily a leader but a fierce soldier. Van Helsing had put him down at the festival when the meeting in the Mayor's office had been announced. Janos and three other men were to provide some security. Van Helsing would have preferred his daughter to lead this contingent, but she had made her face familiar to the German Captain and some of his men, so she was left to pacing the floor at home.

Janos looked up and their eyes met across the Square. Van Helsing gave a small shake of his head. Janos nodded, for the moment controlling his baser urges. He desired nothing more than to kill Germans; his sister had been raped by a gang of Nazis in Bucharest. Her subsequent suicide only added fuel to the fire that burned in the lad.

Van Helsing turned his attention to the SS Major, who had stepped down from the lead vehicle and was making his way to the Town Hall. The Professor and the other men in the Mayor's office were silent, listening to the crisp footsteps on the stairs that led up to the Mayor's office. Van Helsing turned accusingly to Lobenhoffer.

"I am sorry I could not tell you," Lobenhoffer apologised without sincerity. "Military secrets."

Lobenhoffer had called a meeting of the Brasov community leaders for what he described as a very important announcement and then, when everyone was assembled, had waffled and treaded conversational water. Meanwhile, cigars had been distributed, Van Helsing accepting even though he knew that Lucille would smell it on him later and lecture him. Sherry was consumed. Conversation stretched until it gave way like taffy pulled into too fine a string.

And now the waiting was over. *A lot more than the wait might be finished*, Van Helsing thought with some trepidation.

The new SS officer strode into the Mayor's office, stopped short within the doorway, and took inventory of the occupants, his blue eyes without expression, flitting from one man to the next, like a sharpshooter seeking targets.

Captain Lobenhoffer, straightening his tunic, stepped forward and snapped to attention, aiming his palm at the Major. They exchanged *Heil Hitler*s; the Major's salute much more offhand.

"Major Reikel, so very glad to meet you. I have heard of your exploits in Poland."

The one called Reikel only nodded. Lobenhoffer went on.

"I have gathered together the local leaders as you requested. This is Mayor Muresanu, Father Petrescu, and Constable Chiorean."

Reikel nodded to each man in turn. The Mayor offered his hand, but it was ignored by the Major, and Muresanu let his hand slowly drop to his side as if the appendage itself were sighing in regret.

Lobenhoffer clapped Van Helsing on the shoulder with a hearty bonhomie.

"And this is the renowned Doctor Van Helsing. He was building a university here before the war."

Reikel gave the Professor a more thorough inspection.

"You are Dutch?" It was more a statement than query.

"Yes," Van Helsing replied. "I married a local woman and settled here."

"A medical doctor?" Reikel asked. "Your specialty?"

"I have some medical training, but mainly as an academic interest. I hold doctorates in philosophy, anthropology, languages, and assorted other fields. Still, I help out the locals with a general practice clinic."

"An educated man." Reikel turned back to Lobenhoffer. "Captain, you are dismissed and ordered to report to General Schubert and the Eleventh Army."

"The Eleventh . . . ?" Lobenhoffer could not contain his shock. "Basarabia. . . . Facing the Soviet line . . . ?"

"Yes," Reikel said with that nod. "Immediately."

Lobenhoffer stood rooted in place, calculating his future. The numbers were not turning out in his favor.

"No need to tarry," Reikel prodded the reluctant hero.

"But may you not need me to . . . brief you on the area, the, uh, local conditions, status of our anti-resistance operations, my understanding of the . . ." Lobenhoffer swam against the current, searching for a life preserver. Reikel pushed the man under.

"I have been briefed. I read your reports. Go."

The last word was the softest and at the same time the most forceful order Van Helsing had ever witnessed.

Lobenhoffer snapped his heels together with an audible clack, saluted, and left like a man walking to the guillotine, which was close to the truth. The rumours were that the Russians were amassing an army of millions on the Soviet line in preparation for the inevitable German invasion. The non-aggression pact was nothing but a delaying tactic for both sides as they gathered their men and materiel for what was inevitably going to be a bloody slaughter.

Van Helsing heard the Captain's steps fade down the stairway and then the cough of his staff car, the banging of the engine as the man rode away to his grim fate.

Reikel turned to the others.

"As I said, I have been briefed on the nefarious activities of the terrorists operating in this area." He eyed each man as he spoke. "None of you would know anything about these resistance activities, of course."

"We know nothing," Mayor Muresanu announced. "We have done every-thing in our powers to stop them. But . . ."

The Mayor's shrug was most European. It spoke volumes.

"Everything," General Suciu confirmed.

"Why would you do anything else?" Reikel's lips formed what Van Helsing interpreted as a smile. Reikel put both hands behind his back, cocked his head.

"Let me explain my theory of war," Reikel began. Van Helsing recognised the posture of a man about to give a lecture he has given before. "It is not the theory that they teach in our military academies. *Honor on the battlefield.* This code of the *gentleman soldier.* I attended Heidelberg, heard this romantic philosophy of war, and assumed it into my very being, like every young cadet. Then I put these teachings to the test. In Warsaw. And they failed. Yes, they failed completely."

Reikel strode to the open arch, gave a perfunctory gesture to the men below. He continued to speak to the men in the room with his back to them, words so soft that those gathered had to strain to hear them, the priest stepping forward and cupping an ear with one hand.

"Poland changed my mind about these theories. I realised that they were a nineteenth-century concept, destined to die on this modern battlefield. How I came to this reversal is of no significance to you. It is the idea that is important."

There was a commotion down in the Square. Cries of protest, sounds of struggle, and wails of fear. Van Helsing had to restrain himself from rushing forward to see what was the cause. He could see the others of the council were also fighting the urge.

Reikel turned back to face them.

"Total war. You do not win by pretending that war is anything but slaughter. He who slaughters the most—wins. No caveats. No quarter given. None expected. Do you understand?"

The Mayor nodded, but Van Helsing could tell he was not really comprehending. General Suciu and Chiorean followed suit. Van Helsing saw no reason to answer and edged toward the open arch. Reikel countered the move, stepping in the Professor's path, that thin smile returning.

"For example, this resistance," he continued in his lecture mode. "It is ultimately futile and will cost your people more than can be gained. The question is how to communicate this message. Quickly. Efficiently."

He waved a hand toward the archway, as if he were a waiter offering a table, inviting the five men to step forward to view the plaza below. Now they could see the SS soldiers herding the people in the Square and lining them against the walls of the surrounding buildings.

"What is the meaning—?" Mayor Muresanu began, but was halted by Reikel raising a silencing hand. Then the Nazi turned to Chiorean.

"Constable, give me a number from one to ten."

Van Helsing felt the room grow cold, a heaviness forming in his chest. Chiorean was caught by surprise.

"I, uh, I cannot think of one." He was by nature a plodder, not a fast thinker by any means. Sudden fear had paralyzed him.

Reikel shrugged as if the answer were of no importance and turned to Father Petrescu. "Then you, priest. Those in your field are fond of numbers, the Holy Trinity, Ten Commandments, seven deadly sins . . . A number, please."

The priest's thinking was a bit faster than the constable's. "I know you and your kind disdain any religion but your god Hitler. But I will not stand for any mockery of mine."

Father Petrescu stood straight, chest puffed as if bravely facing a firing squad. *Priests,* Van Helsing thought, *always trying to become saints, preferably the dead sort.*

Despite his own misgivings, Van Helsing found himself stepping in front of the Nazi Major, meeting the German face to face.

"I do not know your game, Major," Van Helsing said, "but we will not play."

"Maybe you have no choice." The Major's eyes glinted with a sudden enthusiasm. He had finally found a worthy opponent.

"We always have choices, Major," Van Helsing said to the German in the man's own language.

"You speak German? Of course you do. You are Dutch. We are of the same native blood, are we not?"

"We have no more in common, Major, than the worm and the apple it infests."

The Nazi's eyes went dead. "You, my Dutch friend, you will state a number."

"And if I refuse?"

"Have you heard of the East Indian bed of nails? I have a variation of this trick I would be happy to show you."

Van Helsing's dread came creeping into his consciousness with bared claws.

* * *

What to do? What to do? Lucille was desperate, her mind a whirligig of myriad responses. She could rush down into the Square to her father's rescue. But there were all those armed men between here and there. And she with only her pistol. There had to be something she could do. Anything.

She dug into her trouser pocket and withdrew a handful of coins, quickly sorting through them. How many were in the Mayor's office? Five. She picked out five coins, a one-, five-, ten-, twenty-, and fifty-lei denomination.

Returning the rest of the change to her pocket, she set the five coins on the cement floor at her feet. Knowing she did not have the power or the expertise to protect everyone in the office, she designated the fifty as her father.

Dragging a knuckle across an exposed nail she waited for blood to well in the cut. First she kissed the fifty lei, then pressed her blood upon its surface and laid it on the floor. Mumbling a protection spell in crude Portuguese, she drew a circle of blood around the coin. It took a few tries, as the cut wasn't deep. Doubts intruded upon her thoughts as she chanted, hoping that she remembered the spell correctly.

On a visit to Brazil, Lucille had learned the Macumba magic from a Santeria High Priestess. It was probably the only white magic the ancient woman knew except for some love spells that could go hideously awry if the purchaser somehow offended the prickly witch. Lucille had seen the horrifying results.

She arranged the other four coins into a square around the fifty, bent over, and spit on each of them. Finished with the spell, her mind became frantic with the thought that she might have made a mistake in the ceremony that would result in serious if not deadly consequences.

Lucille hurried to her view port, staring at the Town Hall, wishing she had a spell to see through walls.

* * *

"Is this how your new style of war works, Major?" Van Helsing met the German's cold stare with his own. He was not afraid of the Nazi. Van Helsing had faced more formidable adversaries. "Through threat and bluster?"

"There is no threat or bluster, Professor. Quite the opposite. I am a man of action and results. As you shall see. Right now . . ."

Frown lines formed on the Major's forehead, and his gaze left the Professor and stared beyond the old man as if he were not there any longer. There was a blank, fugue-like moment, and the German officer suddenly turned to the Mayor. It was as if the confrontation between Reikel and Van Helsing had never happened. Van Helsing was confused over the Major's sudden change of focus. The Nazi was acting as if Van Helsing were no longer in the room.

"Mayor?" Reikel's voice was insidiously calm. "If you will oblige me, a number."

"Could you tell me what you are getting at?" the Mayor asked. He was beginning to grasp that the Nazi was heading toward something dire. "What are your intentions, sir?"

Reikel ambled over to the Mayor's desk, casually picked up a framed photo, and seemingly admired the picture. "Your family?"

"Yes." Muresanu's face became as white as his beard.

"Major." General Suciu stepped forward. "I do not like what is going on here. This is my area of responsibility. I am in command. State your purpose."

Van Helsing had never seen the man so imperious and was surprised at his temerity. It was the first time Suciu had ever impressed him.

"My purpose, dear General, is to rid you of the vermin that have spread from *your* area of responsibility, that have polluted *your* country, endangered *your* people and *our* mutual goals. For some reason you have failed to eradicate this pestilence yourself. I could step aside and allow you to pursue whatever plan you may have, if that is what you desire. And I assume that you will also accept the full responsibility for the success or failure of your actions."

Once again that little smile, a barely discernible upturn of the very edges of his mouth.

"And of course," he continued, stepping forward so that his face was inches from the General's. Suciu flinched. "Then you would also accept the consequences of any failure on your part. By the way, your lack of success so far has been pointed out to your commanding officer."

The General backed away a step. "I have neither the inclination nor the manpower to pursue these rebels. They are all yours."

Reikel nodded, went back to the Mayor as if he had never been interrupted. He contemplated the photo. "Your daughter, she is beautiful. How old?"

"Seven," Muresanu said with a trembling voice.

Reikel turned back to the open archway and spoke to the SS Lieutenant below.

"Seven, Lieutenant Guth. The number is seven. Adults only."

Leaning over the balustrade, Van Helsing watched Guth, a thinner, younger version of the Major, his blond hair sheared close to the sides of his head, blue eyes without emotion. Guth walked over to the line of Brasov citizens who stood against the walls of the storefronts that lined the plaza. He drew his pistol from his holster and began counting the people, skipping the youngest.

"Eins, zwei, drei . . ."

"No." Van Helsing heard his voice utter that single word.

At the count of *"sieben,"* Guth shot the man standing in front of him, Mihail Palade, a taciturn truck driver and sometime taxi service. Van Helsing winced as if he had been shot himself.

There was an audible gasp from the people lining the Square as Palade's body slumped to the cobblestones.

Guth proceeded counting without pause. He reached *"sieben"* again and fired another shot. Another innocent, Nadia Tiriac, a woman who took in cleaning and sewing, very popular for her communion dresses. She collapsed like a string-cut puppet, a bullet in her head.

The people lining the Square roused from their shocked silence. A few began to protest. These were instantly and brutally clubbed by SS rifle butts. Other protestors were held back by the threat from the other end of the rifles pointed at them.

Guth kept on. Bodo Frontzek, an ironmonger and plow repairman, father of eight girls.

Counting and shooting. Again and again and again. The people of Brasov began turning their heads away at every seventh count.

Van Helsing knew every one of the victims. Knew their children, their parents, their wives and husbands. He felt every bullet.

One man, Mik Banfy, shouted, "Take me!" as the woman next to him, the widow Abady, faced the seven count. His appeal made no difference.

Women wept and wailed. Grown men cried. Walderman Zirndorf raised up his hands, either to beg or futilely ward off the bullet that tore through his palm, then his face.

Janos Maer, former carpenter, now fierce partisan and lover of Van Helsing's daughter, stood farther down the line. He could take no more and pulled his ancient Wembley pistol from under his shirt.

"No! No more!" he shouted. "Let's take them! We outnumber them!"

And he fired at the German Lieutenant. The bullet chipped the stucco in front of Israil Zingher's candy store. Guth did not even duck.

Janos was instantly the target of a dozen rifles and machine guns. His body danced for a brief second under the fusillade's impact, then fell. The plaza was quiet, the report of the guns still echoing off the surrounding hills. The Germans eyed the residents with an intense vigilance, anticipating another outburst. It did not come.

"He does not figure in the count," Reikel said in that quiet voice with the same insouciance as he did everything.

Van Helsing could only grit his teeth. He had heard a cry when Janos pulled the gun, a female voice that sounded much like his daughter, Lucille. He searched the faces in the plaza, but could not see her anywhere. He reversed the process and examined the line again, but still no Lucille. Had his mind played a trick on him, presenting his worst fear in this dreadful moment?

One man looked down the line and visibly counted the people from one victim to himself. The result was obviously a multiple of seven and he began to keen like an injured cat until the bullet from the German Lieutenant's gun mercifully silenced him.

Guth kept counting and shooting, the shock weakening at every killing until toward the end his victims just stood and waited with a fatal torpor, standing in place as Guth reloaded, shot, and reloaded again. A large Corporal followed, handing him full magazines.

Van Helsing could barely restrain his outrage and grief, grinding his teeth until the muscles in his jaw ached.

"Barbarous," Van Helsing spat, glaring at Reikel. The Nazi Major met his gaze without emotion.

"Exactly," Reikel replied. "Total war. Nothing less. Once people witness the consequences of any hostile action, they will cease their futile resistance. Or their wiser neighbours will persuade them. Oh, I forgot." He leaned out the archway. "Lieutenant Guth, prepare a bed for the Mayor."

Then he turned to the office entrance where Van Helsing could see two SS waiting patiently. Had they been there all along? He could not remember them arriving. Reikel nodded to them and the two soldiers quickly approached the perplexed Muresanu and, before the little man could react, grabbed him by his feet and shoulders and tossed him over the portico wall.

Van Helsing and the others rushed to look down and saw six German soldiers standing at rigid attention below, bayonets mounted on the barrels of their rifles, weapons held at the vertical.

The Mayor fell upon the upright knives and was impaled. He screamed in agony, writhed like a snake struck by a hoe.

Reikel, too, leaned out and impassively regarded the poor wretch.

"Finish him," Reikel ordered softly and quickly withdrew his head.

The six soldiers fired their rifles, perforating the man stuck to their weapons. There was a report, a fountain of blood and meat spewed into the air.

"You bastard!" growled Constable Chiorean and lunged at the Nazi Major. Van Helsing put his body between the policeman and Reikel. The impact was formidable, staggering Van Helsing. The two SS soldiers used their rifle butts to knock Chiorean to the floor, and the air went out of the man.

Reikel surveyed the angry faces of the four remaining men.

"It is always best to make an example of one of the elite, to show that no one is immune from reprisal." That fiendish little smile played across his mouth. "Absolutely no one."

Reikel took the seat behind the Mayor's desk, made himself comfortable, tossed the photo of the Mayor's family into the trash basket. He looked at the four men as if he were surprised that they were still there.

"You are dismissed."

* * *

"Revenge has no place in war." This was a pronouncement from Lucille's father after a partisan raid when many of her Resistance comrades were killed. Lucille's anger and sense of loss had overcome her, and she had been about to shoot a captured soldier. Her finger tightened on the trigger of the Schmeisser she had pointed at a poor Rumanian soldier's weeping face. But her father gently pushed the gun barrel aside and whispered those words into her ear.

She had relented and later contemplated that wisdom. The curious morality of war was thus: War was about killing the man who was trying to kill you, killing the man who was thinking about killing you, killing the man who had the potential to kill you. He had killed your friend—was that not reason enough to exact some kind of justice? She still disagreed with her father's pronouncement. These were her thoughts as she dashed down the belfry stairs, taking them two, three at a time, in one headlong rush.

Lucille Van Helsing opened the church door and slowly walked across the Square, one hand deep inside her sweater, fingers tight around her Luger, ready to kill the SS Major if her father was to follow the Mayor out the window. Revenge might not be justifiable in war, but on a personal level revenge would be all that she would have remaining to her.

Lucille's confidence in her protective spell had completely evaporated. In the belfry, peering through her binoculars at the Town Hall, she had heard a clink and looked down at the coins arranged at her feet. One of them had just flipped over, as if by an invisible finger. And at that very instant the Mayor had been tossed out the window to his gruesome death. She feared the worst. Had she botched the spell? Seeing the barbarous murder of the Mayor made her shudder in horror, and knowing that her father could be next, she flew down the belfry steps.

In the plaza the dead were being collected by their families under the watchful eyes and guns of the SS troops. Lucille saw an old woman, Ecaterina Tula, cover the dead face of Janos Maer with her tatty shawl while his mother moaned in misery.

Lucille did not pause to mourn. There would be a time for that later. She had learned this during preceding months, in raid after raid, losing one compatriot after another, some of them friends, close friends. The ordeal had taught her another lesson: Don't become emotionally involved with anyone who fought alongside her. Until Janos. He had been a slip, one that she knew she would pay for in tears. She swore, not for the first time, never to let anyone get close to her again.

The only exception, of course, was her father. Father and daughter were exceptionally close due to the death of her mother when Lucille was ten. The mother was much beloved, and after the loss Lucille clung to her father and he to her.

The Professor had always treated his perspicacious daughter as an equal. Lucille, thrust into a sudden maturity, tried to take her mother's place in the household, cooking, supervising the help, assisting in the clinic. Her intelligence and lively mind made her a formidable companion. As a teenager, her mind became more than a match for his own far-ranging intellect.

He tutored her himself, outside the local school curriculum, and furthered her education at Swiss private schools. He brought her with him for his own lengthy studies in Munich, Prague, and Zaragoza. Her enrollments at a succession of private schools were brief due to what she called "an independent spirit" and the schools labelled in other terms.

She always rejoined her father, telling him that she learned more in a week with him than in an entire semester with immature, rich brats and boring, doltish instructors. He wondered if she was just trying to flatter him, if there was a spoonful of honey in that tea, but she meant every word.

To tell the truth, she was a daddy's girl, as lonely without him as he was without her. This was why Lucille was determined to personally assassinate every German in Brasov, Rumania, the entirety of Europe, if the Major had so much as harmed a hair on her father's head.

But just as she was fuelling the furnace of revenge, within a few steps of the Town Hall entrance, her father walked out of the doorway with General Suciu, Father Petrescu, and the Constable. Each man at the moment appeared intent on being somewhere else. Professor Van Helsing was last, his face twisted with his inner thoughts.

He saw his daughter. "Lucille, what are you doing here?" He glanced back at the two SS soldiers who braced both sides of the door. Neither paid particular attention to the Van Helsings. And Lobenhoffer's men had obviously left with their Captain.

He put an arm around her, whether for support or comfort she could not tell, as he led her toward the small group of mourners gathered about the bodies scattered around the plaza perimeter. Lucille also felt weak, the familiar aftermath of a spell casting and the usual residual headache that threatened to split open her skull.

"Did any of them survive?" he asked, mournfully perusing the aftermath.

"They are all dead. The Germans are, if nothing else, efficient." Lucille pulled him away. "Please, Father, leave this place now."

"What are you doing here? You could have been shot," he chided in alarm. "Like those unfortunate ones."

"I was in the bell tower," she told him. "I saw . . . everything." Her voice was filled with bile. "When they killed the Mayor . . . I came down. I couldn't . . . there was nothing I could do . . . nothing."

"I know," he whispered. "I know."

"I just stood there while they executed innocent people." She shook her head at her own failings. "I am a coward. I am ashamed."

"We live to fight another day." Her father offered what little comfort he could. "We could have fought. And all died. Then who would resist the barbarians?"

"Janos fought them."

"And Janos fights no more. What good is he to the Resistance now? We don't need martyrs. We suffer under a surplus of martyrs."

He sagged against her shoulder. She led him around the corner of the church. Her father paused to glance back at the Square. She turned, too, in time to see a giant swastika flag unfurled from the Town Hall portico.

"There are not that many of them," she said. "We can eliminate them. Every single one of the bastards."

"They have plenty more in Berlin," her father said.

They collected her bicycle and walked in silence toward the outskirts of town and around the green dome of Tampa Mountain. Their house sat in the southwest shadows. They trod the entire way to their tiny villa without a word spoken. Lucille did not mention her spell cast. Her father was a man of science, a non-believer in the arcane arts. This despite his own experience with that great, emblematic creature of the occult. He was unaware of his daughter's dabbling in the mystic arts, and she wanted to keep it that way, avoiding any useless confrontation. Her only regret was that she had not the strength to save everyone in the Mayor's office, protecting only her father. She took the death of the poor Mayor on her own shoulders.

Sucking on her torn knuckle, Lucille observed her home as if she had never lived in it. A hundred-year-old cottage, its outside walls plush with climbing roses just beginning to bud. Her mother had planted them, and her father had faithfully tended the vines. The buds were but hints of colour, red, pink, yellow, and white, so full of promise that Lucille felt the irony deep in the pit of her stomach. Janos . . .

She fought the pull of her memories of the young man as a drowning victim fights for air, clawing toward a surface that kept receding as she sank into the depths of despair. The buoy that saved her was the thought of revenge. She clung to that desire to keep herself sane.

They were approaching their own door when her father finally spoke. "We need to reevaluate our tactics. Circumstances have been altered."

"I'll call a meeting," she told him as he opened the door, glad to have some thought other than that of Janos to occupy her mind.

"Be most careful," he advised, hanging his hat in the hall. "I have a feeling that this . . . Major is not so tepid an adversary as Lobenhoffer."

A noise drew their attention to the front window. Coming down the road was another German convoy, trucks filled with stoic SS soldiers. The column of dust raised by the vehicles took forever to settle in the windless air.

"Reinforcements already. We have to be careful," her father repeated. "Very, very careful."

The knock at the back door startled both of them. She put her hand on her pistol and went to answer. Easing the door open, finger on the trigger, she saw a nervous figure standing in the shadow of the eaves. It was Closca, one of the partisans.

"We have caught us a spy," he said.

Lucille's first and only thought: *Revenge.*

FROM THE WAR JOURNAL OF
J. HARKER

(transcribed from shorthand)

APRIL 24, 1941

Some bloody spy I turned out to be. Not behind enemy lines three days and I was on my way to a prisoner-of-war camp to sit out the rest of the war. Silly sod. King and country would be so proud—not to mention my mum.

Of course, I could just get shot. The thought did cross my mind. More than once. Maybe every ten seconds or so. I had no idea who had nabbed me. The hood over my head was completely opaque and cinched at my neck. The raw burlap rubbed the skin around my throat, causing an irritating burn. The least of my worries, I kept reminding myself, but the chafing was extreme. Plus, I was re-breathing my own hot breath over and over, creating a suffocating claustrophobia. I tried not to hyperventilate, as I knew I would pass out from oxygen deprivation. My hands were bound behind my back, otherwise I would have been clawing at the damned sack like the trapped animal that I was.

I called out to my Sergeant a few times and received no answer, not that he could have responded or would have in his current state. I assumed that he was similarly trussed. Rough hands manhandled me out of the paddock where we had spent the night. The thugs who awakened us so rudely trundled me into the back of a lorry of some sort. I found myself lying upon a steel bed reeking of manure and hay. There was also a sharp odour of diesel fuel, and I heard the rhythmic rattling of a four-cylinder engine. I bounced about the hard floor like a marble in a cigar box, rapping my skull more than once. Nothing like tenderizing the meat before tossing it into the cooking pot.

There were a few stops, more than a few turns. I tried to keep track of the twists and turns, but soon lost any sense of distance or direction. I could hear other engines, some passing. I could hear voices, but just a murmur, no words that I could make out.

After a while—time was immeasurable—the lorry stopped, and I was dragged across the floor and hoisted by my shoulders and feet like a sack of grain. I felt a brief flash of warmth as the sun seeped through the bag over my head, then darkness again as I was carried down a flight of stairs, my abductors grunting with the effort. I was put on my feet and eased into a sitting position on a hard chair. Retreating feet climbed the stairs, I heard a door close, with the creaking of hinges moaning for a bit of oil, and then I was left alone for what seemed like hours.

The possible loss of my life or years of imprisonment were nullified by an even more pressing concern. During this whole ordeal my bladder was near bursting. I am a man of habits, one of those being the emptying of such organ first thing every morning upon waking. Subsequently, the trip in the lorry was a circle of hell for me; every bump and jolt had been like somebody beating my bladder with a truncheon. Sitting in that chair, the wood jabbing into my bones, the urge became all-encompassing, and finally, to my dismay and profound embarrassment and, I have to admit, some relief, nature took its course. I almost wept in shame.

So, when I finally heard footsteps descend the stairs and that cursed hood was at last removed, I felt no solace. I was more worried about my abashed condition than any consequences from being caught a spy. I crossed my legs, attempting to hide my offence. My hands were unbound and I felt the sting of blood returning to those extremities. That pain was increased by the wounds in my palms and I could barely contain an anguished cry. I was determined not to allow my captors the benefit of my suffering.

It took a minute for my eyes to adjust and when they did I saw that I was ringed by three men, one holding my own pistol, not exactly pointed at me but his eyes were vigilant. He wore a beret and sported a Stalinist mustache that drooped at the ends. Another man, tall with a military bearing, grey hair in a brush cut, was untying my Sergeant, who sat in a chair a few yards in front of me. The third man, a dark-complexioned fellow with eyes crinkled as if smiling at a joke only he was privy to, emptied my kit onto the floor and began rifling through my possessions. I watched this with some trepidation.

He found my pipe, which was more than an ordinary Meerschaum, then examined my assortment of ink pens. I held my breath until he discarded them. But then he opened the box that contained what appeared to be a lump of coal. He tossed it from hand to hand, studied it, perplexed, then was about to pound it on the stone floor. My sphincter tightened, the action having nothing to do with my usual morning alimentary ablutions.

"Don't!" I finally shouted in Rumanian. "Stop before you blow us all to kingdom come!"

He froze. So did the other two. They stared at me, then past my shoulder. I turned to see my Sergeant sitting behind me, similarly bound to a chair. He grinned like a tot on Christmas morning. "BOOM!" he shouted, startling all of us. I was relieved to see that he appeared to be in good condition, at least not impaired any more than before.

"And how does a lump of coal present such a danger?" a voice at the top of the stairs asked.

I stared up at the black silhouette as the figure descended. As he came into the light, I could see that he was a distinguished-looking gentleman, at least in his seventies, a large head, clean-shaven, a broad forehead with bushy eyebrows, and a wide set of intelligent blue eyes.

And then down the stairs, like an angel descending from heaven, came a young red-haired female who might have been the most beautiful example of her gender I have ever encountered. Her brilliantly red hair was long, falling over her shoulders in great rubiginous waves; startlingly green eyes peered through a profusion of bangs much like a wary jungle cat watches through tall grass. Her skin was pale to the point of luminescence. She seemed slight of figure, but this was hard to discern under the bulky sweater and baggy men's trousers held up by what appeared to be a knotted man's tie in lieu of a belt. Her sensual aura hung about her like the nimbus behind a sunlit cloud, and my curiosity about the form beneath that sweater overrode the circumstances of my capture.

Or the fact that she was pointing the barrel of a German Luger at my chest. It came to mind what my father said when the government announced the drafting of women into the armed forces.

"You can't give a gun to a female," he declared. "Women become flustered under any stress. They're much too fragile creatures, too emotional." At the time I concurred, despite the hearty tongue-lashing from my mother. I never conceived that I would be put into a position to test his theory.

"Who are you?" she demanded. I had never seen a human so ready to kill. The look in her eyes was frightening in its intensity. She *wanted* to kill me, she was *eager*.

"The other side of the coin is who are you?" I countered as I glanced at the lapel of my jacket where I had pinned a cyanide capsule. It had been given to me by an American OSS agent in London, to take in the event of enemy capture. The dilemma for me: Was I brave enough to take that grim route instead of revealing my secrets under torture? To my dismay, or delight, the bloody little death pill was gone, probably lost in our disastrous river crossing.

"What do we look like?" the woman asked. "If we were the Rumanian Army, you would be in shackles and on your way to Bucharest. If we were German, you'd be minus a few fingernails and blithering about what colour bloomers Churchill wears on Sunday."

What she said made sense.

"Code name?" the old gentleman asked in English that was tainted with a dash of an accent, not German, but in that linguistic family.

"Purfleet," I replied. I had picked it myself.

"Commanded by?" he prodded.

"Major Samuel F. Billington."

The old man nodded. Now it was my turn.

"Code name?" I asked.

"Ledhrblaka," he said. It was the right response; this was my Brasov contact using an Old Norse word for "leathery wings." It fit the man; his skin was as creased as old saddle leather.

"You can call me Professor. We apologise for your rude welcome, but there have been reports of Germans and Rumanian spies impersonating English commandos in order to infiltrate the Resistance."

"No worries," I said. "Tithes of war and all that."

"We waited for you at the designated drop zone," the old man said. "What happened?"

"My pilot mistakenly dropped us up near Red Lake," I told him. "We had to make our way here by hook or crook."

The woman fixed me with her emerald eyes. "What are you doing here?"

"And you are?" I asked, not so much for intelligence work, but to put us on a less formal basis.

"Maybe your worst enemy." She stepped over so that she stood directly in front of me. I suddenly became aware of the ignominy of my condition and the accompanying odour emanating from my lap.

"I am not as trusting as my father," she continued, her dour demeanor assuring me of her conviction. "Again, why are you here?"

This was my moment. The trading of our clandestine pro formas over and done, I was finally allowed to deliver the speech I had rehearsed since the day I met Guy Gibbons at the St. James Club and he asked if I would be interested in joining the SOE.

I stood up for my recital. My wet pants stuck to my thighs in a most uncomfortable manner. I tried to put aside my odious state and concentrate on my words.

"I am here to provide an operational link between your local Resistance and Britain."

"Why do we need you?" The young woman again.

"Please don't interrupt." I was afraid if she did so I would lose track of my recitation and have to start over again. "We know that the Germans only succumbed in the First World War because of a collapsing morale and an economic disintegration caused by the British naval blockade, in addition to conventional warfare. We have seen that organised Resistance movements in enemy-occupied territory, comparable to the organizations such as Sinn Fein in Ireland and the Chinese guerillas operating against the Japanese, can have a profound impact on that morale."

"So far you're just carting coal to Newcastle." She was becoming less attractive by the moment.

"Um, British blockade . . . organised resistance . . . Ireland . . . Oh yes, we at the SOE plan to supply and to mobilise secret armies across Europe. For one, to tie down Axis forces when invasion eventually takes place."

"And until that wishful 'when'?" She was quite a corker.

"To kindle and fan the flames of revolt in the enslaved lands of Europe, using different methods, including industrial and military sabotage, labour agitations and strikes, continuous propaganda, assaults against traitors and German leaders, boycotts and riots, plus missions of strategic significance." I was proud I had gotten the whole spiel spot-on.

"A very pretty little lecture." She smiled sardonically.

Despite being a bit browned off, I had to admit I felt a stupefying shock to my libido when she deemed me worthy of that smile.

"You deserve a pat on the head, I suppose," she continued, the sarcasm a tad heavier. "But one last time, what do we need of you?"

"I can coordinate airdrops of weapons and munitions, anything else that you may need," I replied. "For example, that bit of coal. It is really a small explosive that you can toss into the coal car of a locomotive. Thereby, say, turning an enemy train's journey into a bit of a shambles. Or one could stash it in the stove or furnace of a military barracks and render their sleep permanent."

The three men examined the lump of coal with a bit more respect.

"And how do you go about getting us these airdrops?" she asked.

"By radio."

"And your radio is . . . ?"

"Um, a bit buggered at the moment," I confessed sheepishly. "On the trek here. Lost it on a river crossing."

She shook her head at me.

"There were wolves," I added.

"Hopeless" was all she said, and my heart plummeted into a deep dark chasm.

"Young man," her father addressed me in a kinder tone. "Have we met before?'

He searched my face with those penetrating eyes and I in turn examined his features.

"No," I admitted. "I don't recall encountering you before this moment."

"Nevertheless," he continued, "the acts of resistance you describe do not come without consequences. Our German occupiers guarantee reprisals."

"We have been victims of those consequences," his daughter added, and a pall seemed to invade the room. "This very day."

They began to relate to me the events at the St. George's festival in Brasov, the arrival of a certain Major Reikel, and his immediate predations on the populace.

While they did this, I watched the man called Ledhrblaka remove the bandage from my Sergeant's head and examine the wound underneath with a professional manner that made me think he might be a doctor.

"This is a most severe wound," he said. "I'm surprised that you are conscious and ambulatory. What happened here?" he asked the Scot, who just stared blankly into the distance.

Indeed the injury appeared worse than the first time I saw it, the skin an angry red and pulled away to reveal the shiny skull beneath.

"On our parachute drop the Sergeant struck his head on some rocks. Miles from the designated drop zone, the result of what I would call, to say the least, a distracted pilot. Since he regained consciousness he has demonstrated some mental defectiveness, a bit of a muddlehead, I'm afraid to say."

I gave them a brief recounting. (I did not dwell upon the perilous risk of my own life rescuing the Sergeant from a precipice, though I mentioned the injury to my hands.) I added a short recitation of our trek from the mountains around Red Lake to Brasov, our encounter with a kindly old crone who tended to our wounds, the assistance of her relative as he drove us by lorry to a rendezvous with another Samaritan, who took us on a perilous trek through the mountains by horse, and the loss of our radio during a hazardous river crossing. I omitted the chase by a wolf pack so as not to sound melodramatic.

The old man ran his fingers over the Sergeant's skull with tender precision. The Sergeant just sat there as if he were being measured for a derby hat.

"What is his name?" the woman asked. "Or code name, if you insist on your clandestine tomfoolery."

"Uh." I was suddenly shamefaced to confess that I did not know the Sergeant's name. At my first meeting with him at the Egyptian airfield, the din of the airplane propellers had rendered our introductions incomprehensible, and I had heard not a word he uttered. At the time I shrugged this off, assuming I would have plenty of time later to elicit his particulars. That moment, because of his later head injury, never came. Since then he had answered no questions and I had only addressed him by the rank displayed on his uniform before he changed into his civilian spy attire.

The others looked at me, waiting for an answer.

"Uh, he goes by the code name Renfield," I told them with as much confidence as I could muster. I thought I heard the woman gasp and the old man gave me a peculiar frown. I do not know where the name came from.

Yes, I do—my preoccupation with that damned novel and its hold upon me now that I was in the land of its origins.

"Cats on the rooftops, cats on the tiles,
Cats with syphilis, cats with piles,
Cats with their assholes wreathed in smiles
As they revel in the joys of fornication."

The Sergeant—I suppose I must refer to him as Renfield from here on— sang as in a school recital. Everyone stopped and stared at the chanticleer and I felt a touch of embarrassment. Some first impression we were giving, me in my soiled pants and a vulgarian Frank Sinatra.

"He does this," I told them. "Ever since the knock on his brainbox. Or it may have been a habit from before I met the chap."

Renfield continued his warble:

"The hippopotamus, so it seems,
Very seldom has wet dreams.
But when he does, he comes in streams
And he revels in the joy of fornication."

"Are you a doctor?" I asked the Professor, trying to distract them from this quirk.

"Among other things," he said and turned to me. "You said you injured your hands. Let's see."

Carefully removing my gloves, I held out my damaged hands for his inspection. I couldn't help but wince as he removed the crone's poultice.

"That is quite the abrasion," the old man stated, gently probing my torn palms. "He needs a clean dressing." The old man said this to the ginger girl. She nodded and climbed the stairs.

"I was hauling the Sergeant off a cliff by his parachute lines and the nylon slipped through my hands," I told him. "I couldn't let loose or he would have plummeted to his death, I'm sure."

The redhead returned, handed her father some bandages, and began to clean the Sergeant's wound, dabbing it with cotton swabs soaked in what smelled like Mercurochrome.

"Sounds like you had quite the hike," the redhead commented, and I felt myself blush.

"What is this ointment?" The old man dipped a finger in the paste covering my palms and sniffed it.

I explained that the old woman in the mountains kindly applied the poultice. He smiled in admiration and told me that my hands were well on the way to healing, and to my surprise and delight they were just so. Under his questioning I described the old crone's potion, and he mentioned his own studies of native folk remedies before his research was interrupted by the war.

Finished with my hands, he went back to Renfield. With the assistance of the woman he sewed the wound shut and wrapped the Sergeant's skull with a very professional bandage. A great improvement over my amateur efforts.

"Your fellow traveller has suffered severe trauma to the cranium. There is nothing we can do here, nor do I think any nearby hospital or doctor is capable of handling a case such as this. Much less the danger of him serenading a Rumanian hospital staff with a ribald aria, in English, thusly revealing his origins. He would be arrested immediately," he said. "My advice is to leave him be and hope for the best. He may improve on his own."

As if on cue Renfield continued his tune:

"The ostrich has a funny dick,
And it isn't very often that he dips his wick,
So when he does, he dips it quick
As he revels in the joys of fornication."

By now the novelty had worn off, and no one stared at the Sergeant anymore. It made no matter to him. I think he sang only to entertain himself. The Professor turned his attentions to the wound on my knee, sustained in my tumble in the river. He showed no disgust as he raised my urine-stained pant leg, and I was grateful for his professional objectivity. He told me that he would need to clean the wound and maybe some stitches were required. And he promised me a bath and change of clothes.

Renfield's head was as wrapped as King Tut's and he beamed at everyone with an imbecilic grin.

"You revel in the morning with an upright stand
(It's urinary pressure on the prostate gland),
And you haven't got a woman so you jerk it off by hand
As you revel in the joys of fornication."

To my astonishment the Professor and the redhead broke out in loud guffaws at the last stanza and the others joined in the laughter. So did I.

The old man led us up the stairs, and on the way I probed with questions about the recent SS incursion. They expanded on the events at Brasov Square, the massacre of the civilians, and the impalement of the Mayor. I was struck into shocked silence as the others related their account of this barbaric slaughter. Everyone fell into a somber silence.

Oft-times, this is all we can give the dead, a respectful quiet. This was not so for the daughter. Her face clouded and she spoke quietly. "I will kill them all. Every one of the bastards. I will kill them all."

It was then that I knew I was in love.

DATED: 25.4.41
TO: SS-OBERGRUPPENFUHRER REINHARD HEYDRICH
FROM: SS MAJOR WALTRAUD REIKEL
(VIA DIPLOMATIC POUCH)

MOST SECRET

Have established authority with local populace in Brasov. Rumanian military have given us carte blanche. Proceeding to root out resistance hierarchy. Detaining suspected members and through various interrogative techniques will ultimately provide linkage to leadership.

Simultaneously, public demonstrations of our principled stand concerning any insurrectionist acts have been put into effect.

Heil Hitler.

FROM THE WAR JOURNAL OF
J. HARKER

(transcribed from shorthand)

APRIL 27, 1941

This SS bastard, one Major Reikel, has further demonstrated his brutality in regard to his hunt for anyone involved with the Resistance.

The first morning after the St. George's Day massacre, nine homes were raided by the SS and a total of fifteen men, old and young, were taken to the Town Hall and imprisoned in the basement. Screams could be heard throughout that night by the women gathered outside, mothers, wives, and daughters of the arrested men. The cries of pain from inside mingled with the wailing of these poor women outside, a mournful madrigal that haunted anyone within hearing.

One of these men, snatched from his home before his mother's terrified eyes, a fellow named Vuia, was actually a member of the local partisan cell. The Germans found a number of Rumanian Army uniforms buried under his chicken coop floor, plus a cache of weapons in an abandoned well on his property.

We were taught in our SOE training that everyone breaks under torture. Everyone. So it becomes a matter of how long you can hold out. But at the same time, it is incumbent for every man to remain silent as long as he is able, to give his compatriots the time to flee.

Vuia talked within a day. The Resistance had prepared for this in their organization, creating independent cells of two and three among the lower echelons. Vuia gave up names. One Zsigmond was dragged out of his own butcher shop, still wearing his bloody apron. He had been ordered to flee, but he bought into the myth that a strong man like his dear friend Vuia could stand up to anything the Nazis could dish out. That and his business and large family connections rooted him in the town, and he resisted all pleadings to run.

The Schmeisser and grenades Zsigmond hid in the carcass of a hog were confiscated as further proof, if any was needed, of his guilt.

The third leg of their cell followed orders and fled to another partisan group up north, avoiding capture. He left only hours before the Nazis appeared at his upholstery shed.

Reikel must have thought that he had wrung as much intelligence as he could from the two unfortunate men. Two days after their capture both Zsigmond and Vuia were paraded through town, then lashed upright to a machine-gun stanchion mounted in the bed of a three-quarter-ton lorry. Word quickly spread, and even I was allowed out of hiding to witness the spectacle that followed:

The Professor, his daughter, and I walked a short distance from their home, a half mile or so, where a scattering of locals had gathered at the intersection of two roads. Above us a murder of crows lined up on the telephone wires as if to view the scene for themselves. I tried not to take this omen too seriously. My error. At the approach of the Nazi lorry and accompanying vehicles, the birds took flight, swirling over our heads like some E. A. Poe harbinger of death.

Both men's faces were bloody, swollen, bruised, and cut, Vuia's face so plethoric that his eyes were but two slits. Their hands were mangled, malformed, fingers bent in ways not natural at all. There were large bloodstains in the crotch of their trousers, the cause not evident, but forcing your imagination to horrid conclusions.

Zsigmond tried to hold his head tall, defiant, but his strength or his pain betrayed him and he kept sliding down the pole that supported him. The two guards would haul him back to vertical by his hair. Vuia kept his head down, eyes to the floor, if he could see anything through the swelling. Whether his posture was from defeat, shame, or exhaustion one could not tell.

Some of the citizens lining the road stared, some averted their eyes, a few turned their backs. There was no indication whether the latter behaviour was out of repugnance or to protest the demeaning of these two brave men, poor, doomed souls that they were.

The procession, two German military cars front and aft of the lorry, stopped at the crossroad intersecting the main northern thoroughfare entering Brasov. Stakes were driven into the ground and both men were tied hands and feet to them, spread-eagled so that their bodies spanned the narrow road.

By this time, traffic had backed up six or seven vehicles deep. No one dared to complain. The cordon of armed Nazis was enough to discourage any protests. So we waited, mostly silent, only a low murmur of hushed voices, as if the audience were inside a church rather than out in an overcast spring day.

The arrival of Major Reikel, about whom I had heard so much, bestirred the crowd. The gathering was growing by the moment. Passengers from halted vehicles disembarked to see what was causing the delay, and folk from the neighbouring area arrived to see what the commotion was about. The Major rode up in a noisy half-track.

I was standing in a pasture along with thirty or forty observers, feeling like a hedgehog in a cat's litter. I was not yet comfortable in my clandestine cover of worn baggy pants and a leather coat that hung on me like a tent without poles. But the Major, standing high on his perch, paid me no special attention.

Reikel—I was informed that this was the very beast from the Town Square massacre—stepped out of his half-track with an imperious air and strode over to the two partisans staked out across the road. He didn't say a word, but examined them for a brief moment, a nearly imperceptible smile upon his cold face, then just walked back to his vehicle and mounted it. Standing erect, he nodded to his Lieutenant.

This Lieutenant, Guth by name, shouted out to the assembled crowd, "Let this be a warning. Any terrorist activity will be punished. Not only against the perpetrators. The citizenry who allow these insurrectionists to hide among you will be punished at the same quota established by your former Mayor. Seven to one." Then he walked to the first vehicle in the queue. It was a big two-ton flatbed hauler driven by a heavily bearded man.

"Proceed," the Lieutenant ordered the driver.

The man looked down from his cab at the two men prostrate in his path. There was no way to drive around them, with a steep drainage ditch on one side of the road and a high kerb bordering the other. The driver shook his head.

The Nazi stepped up onto the running board, drew his pistol, and put the barrel to the recalcitrant driver's temple. The man put the lorry in gear. The vehicle began to roll forward slowly.

Vuia and Zsigmond turned their heads to watch the approaching wheels, big, black, knobby tyres.

"Fast!" Zsigmund cried out.

The driver closed his eyes and stomped on the pedal. The engine roared and the great mechanical beast jumped forward.

The massive wheels rolled over the men.

The driver, tears in his shut eyes, flinched at every bump.

A scream was heard from one of the victims, which one it was hard to discern. There was also an outcry among the spectators.

After the German leapt from the running board, the driver sped on, eager, I suppose, to put the whole nightmare behind him.

The next car was forced to do the same, then the next, and so on. Over and over, the gruesome exercise in terror continued, until the two men were but bloody smears on the road. One driver, a young man with a profound harelip, screamed to himself as he drove the short distance.

Reikel watched us with a look of business-like satisfaction, and then rode away, his point made. The crowd of witnesses dissipated like morning fog under the glare of the sun.

As I followed the Van Helsings back toward my warren in the basement, the old man, my contact, and his irritating but beguiling daughter paused to converse with a pair of men lurking in the shadows of a great elm.

I stopped with them, wanting to ask the Professor about his efforts contacting London, requesting an airdrop to provide me with a new radio. But the atmosphere was glum, properly so, and I decided not to broach the subject. We all looked at each other.

"A warning, they say," one of the men said. "More like a display of savagery."

"It is a preview of the world to come," the Professor said.

"You have to agree, Van Helsing," the other man said. "It is time for the turtle to pull in its head."

Van Helsing! I was dumbfounded. The utterance was like ice water thrown into my face. I heard no more of the conversation as that name echoed around my brain like a shout inside a tunnel. Van Helsing!

On the trek back to the cottage I was in a dream state. *Van Helsing.* I watched the old man before me. It was as if a personage of myth and legend had materialised right before my eyes, as if Ulysses or King Arthur had suddenly appeared and asked me to high tea. Van Helsing: the Dutch physician, philosopher, man of letters, lawyer, folklorist, teacher. My grandfather's colleague. The hero of The Book.

When we reached their house I was told to return to the basement, and I did so reluctantly. Would one want to leave the presence of the Scarlet Pimpernel? But I went.

I descended the stairs in a fugue state and found Renfield, for that was what everyone called him now, being kept company by our three abductors. The room had a dirt floor, smelled of earth and onions from the racks where an assortment of vegetables was stored. Shelves were filled with jars of home-canned goods, more shelves with tools, cans full of nails and odd bits, bicycle parts. A coal chute was the only other exit, no windows, the walls constructed of smooth river rock. The dank centre of the room was furnished with a few unmatched chairs, a small table sporting a wine bottle encrusted with a kaleidoscope of wax drippings, and two folding cots that had been brought in for the Sergeant and me. A dismal affair, all in all, but not uncomfortable considering that a few days before I had been contemplating a prisoner-of-war camp or worse.

"Show us your toys," said the one who called himself Horea. No one had so far revealed their real name, just code names to maintain our covert mode.

Earlier I had engaged in a bit of a chin-wag with Horea and the two chaps, Closca and Crisan, my kidnappers. They all seemed as attached to each other as if they were triplets. Horea was the short man who sported a quite impressive Stalinist mustache, one wing of which was in a constant droop, making his face seem lopsided. He wore a beret, not, I suspected, as a sartorial choice but to conceal an excess of scalp in the northern realm. He was a staunch Communist, having been educated so in the Soviet Republic.

Closca was his opposite, a tall, older man with crisp, grey, short-cropped hair, like the bristles on a brush, standing straight up, wild eyebrows curling toward his widow's peak, and a steel-like posture as befitted an ex–Iron Guard, the legendary Rumanian Legion of the Archangel Michael, religious fanatics who openly courted martyrdom. They had assassinated four

Prime Ministers before Antonescu had them disbanded and many of them imprisoned.

The third man, Crisan, had that dark gypsy complexion, constant black stubble, and eyes ever squinting as if peering through a smoky room. He had a ready laugh, and he laughed often, the gold in his teeth flashing like Ali Baba's treasure in a dark cave.

These men had nothing in common. In fact, in different circumstances they might have warred with each other, but a hatred of the Nazis and/or Antonescu was enough to unite them for now. What would occur between them after the war was grim to imagine, but for now they were allies.

Under the baleful glare of an overhead bulb, I opened my kit and proceeded to give them a little show of the trinkets provided by my dear friends in the SOE research and science departments, plus a few items an American OSS mate had given me to "field-test" for his own spy bureau.

There was my pipe that could provide a decent smoke until the proper occasion presented itself and then, with a twist of the stem, fire a bullet.

I demonstrated the invisible ink, which no secret agent is complete without. A miniature camera the size of a wristwatch and disguised as such. The Welrod pistol with silencer. Black Joe, the explosive in the guise of a lump of coal. They were particularly tickled at a similar device in the shape of a horse turd.

The trio became fascinated by the cigarettes treated with tetrahydro-cannabinol acetate, an extract of Indian hemp that supposedly acted as a truth drug. The theory was to provide the ciggies to the enemy in a social circumstance and then be able to pump them for information.

Crisan wanted to test one on Horea to see if he actually was receiving the favors of a certain Floarea, but I had to refuse as my supply was limited.

Lastly I gave a small chalk talk, sketching on the earthen floor with a bit of wood, on the uses of the pen fuse, a pocket-sized time-delay incendiary. SOE called it the time pencil, and each could be set to go off for units of ten minutes to thirty days. You only had to press a ridge on the device to release acid that ate through a wire. When the wire snapped, the explosive inside detonated, igniting the attached explosive.

We had a lively discussion over the practicality and possible uses of these various diabolical instruments, they smoking fags and I trying to keep my pipe going for more than thirty seconds. I still had a small tin of Arcadia tobacco. We consumed a bottle of middling Tokay that Closca materialised from his leather coat like a magician drawing a bunny from his hat.

Their enthusiasm for my little presentation was fulsome, and they wanted demonstrations of everything. Since it all was in short supply and with no radio to call for more, I steered them away from the more dangerous creations and let them experiment with the invisible ink, adding that milk and urine could provide a suitable substitute. This prompted a testing of all three liquids. Subsequently there was a tincture of asparagus in the air, and I took the opportunity to update this journal.

Renfield meanwhile busied himself with his own kit containing a few boxes of gelignite, blasting caps, fuses, detonators, and spools of wire. I kept an eye on his handling of the explosives, enough to obliterate the house we occupied, but he was as conscientious as if he were in full use of his faculties. He checked every cap with the delicate care of a watch repairman, returning each metal tube to its berth in the specially constructed shock-absorbing box. The gelignite, itself a powerful explosive, was inert until primed, and he was careful to keep it separate from the ignition devices.

The project seemed to calm him and, rather than singing one of his obnoxious ditties, he happily hummed to himself like a busy bee. I think I discerned the melody of "Boo, Boo Baby, I'm a Spy." As impaired as he was, did he still retain a sense of humour?

While he was so occupied, my mind went back to my astounding discovery—Van Helsing.

As a child, I was acutely aware of the dark secret that shadowed my family, the Thing of Which We Must Never Speak. My father and mother were both adamant that The Book and anything to do with it were forbidden subjects in our house. Of course this taboo was itself enough to prick my adolescent rebelliousness. Hence, I strove to unlock that mystery at every opportunity. My grandfather, the font of this secret, discovered my interest, a scrapbook that I hid under my bed during one of my frequent visits to his home. I had diligently filled it with film reviews, magazine articles, and assorted material, everything I found concerning The Book and The Movie. If my mother's and father's attitudes toward the subject were any guide I was expecting a severe castigation from him.

But in a tribute to my grandfather's intellect and perspicacity, in lieu of punishment and further admonitions, the old man brought me into his confidence, a secret society of two, never telling my parents of our shared communion with his past.

There were no documents, no evidence of the truth of the matter, just The Book, the scar on my grandmother Mina's forehead, and the contents of my scrapbook, the trivial musings on a bit of popular fiction. I hung on his every word as he related the events, tragic and otherwise, that had transpired so many years ago. I knew the story by heart, and it was as much a part of me as if I had personally participated. His version often varied from The Book, such as my grandmother's scar, which in the printed story miraculously disappeared but in actuality was seen every day, hidden behind a fringe of hair she wore over it.

All in all the two accounts stayed true, at least in the larger narrative if not in the particulars. Yet, because of the variations, I suppose there was always a part of me that thought it all might actually be a fabrication, a divertissement for my beloved grandfather as he bonded with me, maybe a chance similarity of names that he took advantage of and I, a gullible child, embraced. This niggling doubt had always chewed at a corner of my mind like a rat at a block of cheese.

But now I had evidence! Van Helsing! Another name linked to the story. In the country of its origin! My curiosity was a fire within me.

I heard the basement door open and the daughter's voice announce supper. We went upstairs, where a pleasant and hearty repast was laid upon the dining room table. The daughter, Lucille—at last she had revealed her name—had prepared an Italian meal of noodles and a pesto sauce, trout from the local streams, crusty bread from oat flour, and olive oil for dipping. The wine, a Grasa de Cotnari, 1928, more than earned its title of Rumania's Bloom.

The home was a small Saxon cottage, three bedrooms upstairs with modern bathrooms. The downstairs also had a recent renovation to contain the Professor's vast library and a separate medical receiving and examination suite. The furniture was a variety of styles and eras, and every room was crammed with objects collected, I assumed, from Van Helsing's wanderings about the globe. Curiosities abounded: stuffed creatures, shrunken heads, bits of stone with hieroglyphics, ancient jars. He also seemed to have a predilection for modern devices, from stereopticons to electric massage instruments. Besides a most impressive library, there were books and periodicals stacked on every available surface in every room, even the kitchen and the loos. Recording devices seemed to be a particular obsession of the old man; wire and wax recorders of various types and manufacturers were piled willy-nilly in one corner of the downstairs parlour.

As we dined, a great blaze flamed and flared in the fireplace, sending a hollow roar up the chimney. The warmth sunk through my flesh and gave me such lethargy that I had to move myself away.

During the meal the Professor, who ate sparingly, passed around a leaflet that the Germans had posted all over Brasov. In Rumanian, it declared that the area was henceforth under martial law, announced a curfew that went into effect immediately, and warned that any transgression or "acts against civility or the peaceful enforcement of military rule will be met with instant and considerable justice."

"Justice," the daughter spat.

"They think this will stop us?" Horea declared defiantly.

"Many more reprisals like the slaughter in the Square will turn the people against us," Closca warned.

Crisan nodded. "We cannot risk the lives of innocents."

"What are you planning to do?" I asked Van Helsing. I had been watching the man, hoping to find a way to ask him the myriad questions filling my head.

"The council will be meeting to consider our next step," he replied.

"I think you knew my grandfather, Jonathan Harker, from Essex," I ventured, finally opening the door that had been closed to me for so long a time.

"My word!" he exclaimed and dropped his fork. He then proceeded to examine my features like a lost man peruses a map. "Of course! You have the eyes, the nose, and chin. How is your grandfather, you say? The years . . . How is the lad, uh, fellow? He was a solicitor, if I remember correctly."

"Well, he left the law to become a vicar after your . . . adventures. Church of England, of course. He is very well. Spry for his age, last I saw him."

"And your grandmother? Wilhelmina, right?"

"Yes, though nobody ever called her that—she went by Mina. We lost her in '36. Influenza." I remembered my grandmother's kind face, how every time she brushed aside the bangs that hung to her eyebrows I would catch a glimpse of the scar on her forehead, the mark of the Host, and her macabre history, with my grandfather and this man.

"I am sorry. Ah, that wonderful Mina, pearl among women. A vivacious and beautiful girl. So intelligent. And very brave during what you call our 'adventure.'"

"I am proud to have her maiden name as my middle, Jonathan Murray Harker, sir."

And I offered my hand. He took it in his own, the skin as dry as autumn leaves, the fingers long and delicate. His grip was firm for a man of his years. How old was he? His whole aspect was of vitality and a rapacious intelligence.

"To think, after all of these years, the chance of our meeting, here . . ." He shook his head in wonderment.

"Not much chance to it, sir. I requested this posting, fought for it, actually. When I was but a boy, I would sit at my grandfather's knee and he would recount the events that befell you and him, along with Mina and that fellow Morris, Dr. Seward, poor Lucy . . ."

I suddenly realised how his daughter, Lucille, had come to her appellation. No one called me on the slip of my tongue. I glanced at Lucy. "Lucille" was too formal an appellation for such an Amazon. I was a bit abashed, but she only smiled at me. I think I detected some new respect or interest in my personage, and I could not help but feel more confident under her gaze.

"Lucy Westenra . . ." the Professor mused. "Poor, poor Lucy." He slipped into the embrace of Mnemosyne for a moment.

"I was named after her," Lucy said, most likely to cover for her father's momentary lapse.

"Named after the one I lost through my own failures as much as the depredations of an evil force," Van Helsing said with a slump of his shoulders and a sadness which demonstrated that the passing of the years had not assuaged his feelings toward the matter.

"I haven't found out if it is a blessing or a curse," Lucy said. "Yet."

"You have fashioned your own path, my dear." Her father laid his hand on hers, and she glanced at him tenderly. "A crooked path at times, one that has wandered the ends of the earth and strewn broken hearts at your feet for paving stones, but you are your own woman, of this there is no doubt."

I turned to her and summoned what courage I could muster, perhaps from the beneficence of the wine.

"So you have travelled a bit?" I asked her.

"My father, to his credit, encouraged me to become a cosmopolitan being and, thusly, I travelled. I schooled in Switzerland, Spain, even England."

"No school could tolerate her behaviour for more than a semester." Her father shook his head.

"My behaviour"—her eyes fixed on mine as she spoke, and I could not help but be transfixed by those verdant eyes—"was the consequence of a medieval scholastic philosophy and an equally antiquated view of what a female should or could accomplish. Narrow-minded academic twits. Especially in England."

"After school, you came back here?" I offered, attempting to calm her ire.

"Not for a while. I travelled. Spent some time in Berlin, Paris. Ah, Paris . . . Paris was . . . disappointing. Then I went to North America. New York was fun. I spent a short time as a chorus girl in an abysmal musical, even though I have the terpsichorean abilities of a plow horse. Then I crossed the continent by rail—hoboing, they call it—reading Edgar Lee Masters, Odets, Steinbeck, and Frost. For a bit I worked on a fishing boat in Sausalito, California. I'll never eat another sardine. Drove through the Central and South Americas with a Portuguese opera singer and her gigolo in a touring car with bad springs and a radiator with more holes than a colander. Took a tramp steamer to Indochina, flew across China with an aviatrix under the influence of opium and Sappho—she, not I. Trekked Greece, Italy, and found myself back in Berlin, living in a rat-infested garret with six penniless artistes until the fascists made life unbearable."

"My God, woman, you have lived ten lives!" I exclaimed.

"She never lights on one flower for long, much like the hummingbird." The Professor looked me in the eye. A warning perhaps.

"My wings are a blur, but my beak is sharp." Lucy laughed, a silvery, musical sound, like the tingling sweetness of water glasses when played by a clever hand. The sound stopped my heart. I felt a wicked, burning desire for her to kiss me with those tumid lips.

Van Helsing regarded me with some sympathy. No doubt he had witnessed a plethora of young men falling under the enchanting spell of his daughter.

"She came home only to warn me about the gathering storm in Germany. About which she was entirely prescient," her father added. "'In the nightmare of the dark / All the dogs of Europe bark.'"

"Yeats." I recognised the quote. "The 'beast that prowls at every door and barks at every headline.' MacNeice."

"Oh, you're one of those," Lucy said. "You parry quotation with quotation. Poetry is not for dueling, sir."

Once more I was abashed and could not meet her eyes. After supper was done the three rebels departed, Horea being teased about the aforementioned Floarea and the other two creating rather juvenile, vulgar rhymes about their relationship.

When I found myself alone with the Van Helsings, I could not allow myself to tarry in Lucy's presence, afraid of any faux pas I would most certainly make in my current state of infatuation. I sought refuge upon my narrow cot in the badger burrow of the Van Helsing basement.

Renfield was already asleep, and I had no one to share the recent cracking revelation with, even though he was probably in no state to appreciate it since he had more than a few pages glued together. The Sergeant slept a lot; whether this was his customary habit before his accident I did not know, but I assumed the rest would be good for his recovery. The bare bulb cast the corners of the room in deep shadow, but I dared not turn it off. When I had done so previously, Renfield put up such a fuss that I had to turn it back on. It seemed he was deathly afraid of the dark. Again, whether this phobia was from before his accident or after I did not know.

I lay on the taut canvas of the cot, staring at the ancient wooden beams over my head, spinning scenarios of Lucy and me conniving against the enemy. I am afraid that too many of these fantasies resembled Hollywood tales, with me in trench coat and snapped brim hat a la Bogart or Brian Aherne, kissing Lucy on some foggy, foreign street, danger around every dark corner.

This sweet reverie was interrupted by the creaking of the door at the top of the stairs. I could see only bare feet, but I knew them to be Lucy's. She descended the steps and revealed herself like a curtain slowly rising. First I saw the hem of a green silk kimono, then more, the material embroidered with white storks, wings extended in full flight. The hints of her body, the curve of her hip and the rise of her bosom, were highlighted with shiny reflections. Her face was in shadow but the glow of the lightbulb set her russet tangle into frozen flames. Blast, I was barmy about the girl.

"English?" she whispered. "Are you awake?" She did not wait for an answer, but took my rising as confirmation.

"Come," she intoned softly.

I hastily re-belted my trousers, which I had loosened for comfort as I prepared for sleep, and followed her up the stairs.

Without another word she preceded me through the kitchen, the living room, to the stairs leading to the rooms above. She waited for me at the third step, and when she saw that I was indeed behind her, she continued the climb. I was in her thrall, mesmerised by the sway of her hips under that silk, hearing the soft rustle of the cloth, whispered inducements as I imagined every caress of the material against her skin.

She paused again at the door to what I assumed was her bedroom. Or was it her father's? I panicked, thinking I had presumed too much, that this was an invitation to an innocent meeting.

"Come to me, Jonathan. Come, and we can rest together," she said. There was something diabolically sweet in her tone.

But then I could see a struggle on her face. She resolved her quandary and opened the door. Taking my hand, she led me inside and closed the door behind us. The click of the lock as she turned the key was like an electric shock down my spine.

My eyes followed her hands as she released the belt at her waist and a mere shrug of her shoulders caused the robe to fall from her body like a green waterfall. She stood before me in naked glory.

I heard a moan and surmised that this noise had been emitted by my own throat. Her hands then went about relieving me of my clothing. I stood there immobile, unable to assist her in any manner, paralyzed by my own concupiscence. I felt a stupefying vertigo, as if all the blood had left my brain and gone elsewhere. When she had stripped me of my trousers and underthings, I was confronted, as was she, with evidence to support this circulatory hypothesis.

When her bare hands made contact with my turgid plight I almost fainted and was saved only by her pushing me onto her bed.

I am too much of a gentleman to detail what followed, but I can confess this much: What transpired put any youthful erotic imaginings to shame. Repeatedly. Again and again. Until we both fell into a deep, exhausted slumber.

* * *

Another entry. I am back in my own bed, for propriety's sake, and I have to admit still in some sort of swoon. She is one of God's women, fashioned by His own hand to show us men and other women that there is a heaven where we can enter and that its portal can be here on earth. So true, so sweet, so noble . . . on second thought, more bittersweet.

***

APRIL 28

This entire day I have been in a complete fog. Last night's beatitude seems like a delirium. Breakfast and a midday meal were announced, but only the Professor was present. Whether the fair Lucy was avoiding me or, as was explained by her father, truly arranging a meeting of the partisan cell leadership I did not know. I ate little, positively moonstruck, dwelling on sweet, dare I say, tumescent memories of the night before. Renfield's appetite was formidable, in no way diminished by his incapacitation, and he could spend hours sitting by himself with only his thoughts to occupy him. What these thoughts might have been, I had no clue.

My own thoughts drifted to fantasies of Lucy and me. I envisioned dramas of my perilous efforts, commanding brave partisan raids and returning to her welcoming arms, she bandaging my various minor wounds and rewarding my exploits with tender lovemaking.

These daydreams are obviously drawn from the font of my juvenile interests in Kipling and Tennyson. As a boy, the stories of the British Raj in India fascinated me. *The Lives of a Bengal Lancer* was read, re-read, and acted out with my mates in backyards; we killed each other with our stick swords and pantomime guns over and over and over. I sat through *The Iron Mask* multiple times at the local cinema and recited the plot to my school chums, re-creating every bit of Douglas Fairbanks derring-do.

My father, who had served in the trenches during the Great War, showed concern and disapproval about my enthusiasm for the romance of war. But romantic, knightly notions of *affaire d'honneur* are not discouraged so easily.

And one important part of these stories is the rewards of glory—the love of a beautiful woman. That my prize has come so early, before I have proven my worth on the field of battle, I have no regret. In fact, my desire to prove myself has increased manifold.

It was almost poetic, my current state. I have a formidable enemy, his evil aptly demonstrated in the Brasov massacre and at the crossroads, and I have a beautiful female paramour to recognise any heroics I might demonstrate.

Now all I need is a mission to prove myself.

Wandering downstairs I found the Professor reading, deep into some obscure text, bent over a book on his desk, unaware of anything but the page inches from his nose.

I scavenged some cheese and bread from the pantry, a bit of sausage, and a local cider. After feeding Renfield and myself, I couldn't wait any longer and interrupted the Professor, asking the whereabouts of dear Lucy. He assured me that she was soon due, but I could see the worry in his face. I shared his anxiety, coupled with an almost overwhelming desire for her embrace, if not more.

As if by my bidding she suddenly came through the door, out of breath, discarding her binoculars and undoing the garters that bound her pants for bicycling.

"The meeting has been called, in less than an hour," she said. "I notified everyone personally. There are checkpoints all about town. That is why I am delayed."

"You couldn't use the phone?" I asked, somewhat peevishly, resenting my exclusion from her escapades.

"We cannot chance that the Nazis are eavesdropping on the lines," she told me.

I cursed myself for not thinking of that devious stratagem. Who was the spy here?

The Professor grabbed his coat. "Have you eaten?" he asked his daughter. She nodded.

"I assume that you can drive." He directed this to me. I said I could. I had noticed that the kind doctor spoke none of the fractured English as was characterised in The Book. Might he have learned better in the ensuing years? Or had the Irishman gilded the lily in that respect?

The automobile was a magnificent 1930 Bentley Speed Six Sportsman Coupe fastback in immaculate condition. It started on the first try, and the engine purred as smoothly as an old maid's tabby. The Professor explained that he had used his standing as a medical man to receive an allotment of fuel outside the normal Rumanian war-time rationing, much like the police, fire, and, of course, military vehicles.

Lucy sat beside me and gave me directions as I focused on staying on the correct side of the road. She gave no hint at what we had shared on our night of bliss—a pose for her father, I assumed. We were stopped twice at SS roadblocks, once on the outskirts of the town and once more in Brasov proper. Each time papers were demanded, my SOE-forged documents passing muster easily, and we were lectured about the curfew. The Professor cut these reprimands short with a letter of dispensation from the Rumanian military declaring that he was a medical doctor. He sported the universal black bag to reinforce his legitimacy and introduced Lucy as his nurse.

"On an emergency call," he would explain. "Sick child."

As I gripped the steering wheel I realised that my hands no longer pained me, a mere stiffness from the healing scabs and scar tissue. The old crone must have been, as I suspected, a witch. Still, I wore gloves as a bit of protection and to hide the still-healing wounds. The gash on my knee was mending nicely and pained me not at all.

Somewhere in the midst of the Brasov warrens I was told to park. I had no idea where we were, having little knowledge of the town outside of a dated Lydecker I had purchased in a London bookstore. I had kept it in my coat pocket, but that cursed river crossing had plucked it from my person as easily as the Artful Dodger. I tried to keep track of our movements, but the walk through the maze of narrow streets only confused me more with no landmarks but the high walls closing upon me.

"My grandfather did not tell me that you were a medical doctor," I said, as we walked the dark narrow streets. "I received the impression that your degree was in philosophy."

"That and sociology, psychology, history, and botany. At that time I only had a modicum of medical training. I wished for more," he said without a tinge of arrogance. "When I settled here, there was a paucity of medical men, and so I furthered my medical education a bit more to fill the void. And lately some astronomy, a little physics."

"The hummingbird doesn't fall far from the tree," Lucy chimed in and they shared a laugh.

"Halt!" Out of the shadows stepped two German soldiers. We stopped. One, a Corporal, aimed his Schmeisser at us. The other, his Sergeant, eyed us with suspicion.

"What are you doing out after curfew?" the Sergeant demanded.

"I am a doctor." Van Helsing straightened his posture and took on an imperious air. "I have an emergency. A child with appendicitis." He handed the Nazi Sergeant his dispensation papers and hefted his black bag to waist level as if it were proof of his profession.

The Sergeant inspected the paper while his Corporal did the same for Lucy. I swallowed my anger at the blatant sexual overtones of his examination. He even stroked his mustache like a silent movie villain, the rotter.

"And the girl?" the Corporal asked.

"I was a girl when you were counting the hairs on your balls," Lucy sneered at the man. I saw her hand slip into her coat where she carried that ridiculous Luger with a barrel as long as a carbine.

Van Helsing glared at his daughter.

"My nurse," Van Helsing explained. "And my impertinent daughter."

"A nurse." The Jerry grinned. "Maybe she could look at something for me. Sometimes it swells to alarming proportions."

I held myself in check. Lucy had not the self-control.

"I'm quite familiar with those symptoms," she said. "I recommend you handle it the way you usually do. If you need, I can write you a prescription for a lamb."

The Nazi raised a hand to strike her. Lucy's hand slipped into the depths of her coat, hugging herself as if against the cold, but I knew she was holding her Luger at the ready.

I stepped toward the Corporal. The Sergeant put himself between us.

"And you are?"

"Their driver."

"Why don't you stay with the car?" he asked. I was not ready for this question and my brain did a tap dance to find an answer. Van Helsing saved me.

"I do not like to walk alone at night," the Professor announced. "I have treated a few of your soldiers, and the partisans resent my ministrations. I am afraid for myself and my daughter."

"And you think this will protect you?" The Corporal eyed me with derision. I bristled at the slight but was able to contain myself with a super-human control I did not know I possessed.

"What is in the bag?" asked the other.

"The ghastly paraphernalia of my beneficial trade," Van Helsing said. The Corporal just frowned in puzzlement.

The Sergeant returned Van Helsing's papers and waved us on our way.

When we were far enough away to be out of hearing Van Helsing turned to Lucy. "Antagonising them does nothing for our cause," he reprimanded her. "All it does is make you feel superior for the moment. We must appear harmless."

"They see only my tits," she scoffed. "To them I am already harmless."

I was shocked at her vulgarity. How could all of these contradictory characteristics exist in the same creature? The enchanting playfulness and then confrontational antagonism. She brings to mind the object of Byron's verse:

"She walks in beauty, like the night
Of cloudless climes and starry skies;
And all that's best of dark and bright
Meet in her aspect and her eyes."

Such a sweet visage with the tongue of a fishwife.

After wending our way further through the moonlit labyrinth of alleys and narrow streets, we finally reached our destination. It was a small shop; a conservative gilt sign in the window discreetly declared "Mihaly's Fine Men's Fashion—Bespoke Suits."

Van Helsing checked the street in both directions, searching for any observers. There were none, and he opened the door and hastily ushered us inside.

The store was composed of dark wood shelves where bolts of cloth poked out, and display cases containing shirts and ties. The ties were the only splash of colour in the store, and the cloth nestled in the cubbyholes was in the grey, brown, and black spectrum, giving the whole store a masculine but gloomy atmosphere. Mannikins were dressed in what looked to be very well-tailored suit jackets, if not au courant.

A bell above the door pealed out our entrance and a small man answered. I was introduced to him, a dapper gentleman advertising his wares in a beautiful herringbone pant and vest. This was Mihaly, the proprietor and best tailor in Brasov. His pencil-thin mustache was as rectilinear as if made with a straight edge, his skin the white of a frog's belly, his brilliantined hair black and shiny like wet paint.

Professor Van Helsing introduced me only as the Englishman, and Mihaly accepted this. Peering from behind his father's hips was Mihaly's son, eight or so, a miniature version of the father, sans mustache.

The Professor bent down to address the boy.

"How is your appendicitis, Toma?" he asked.

"Terrible." The child melodramatically clutched his stomach. "Do you have some medicine for me?"

"I do," Van Helsing said and produced a licorice stick from his coat pocket. "But you are not to take it until after your supper."

The proprietor led us to a viewing cubicle, a tiny room the size of a telephone kiosk, mirrored on three sides floor to ceiling so that a customer could properly admire his new attire. Stepping onto a small wooden platform, Mihaly reached up and pulled on the light fixture inside the tiny closet, one of those old brass hanging lamps that had been converted from gas to electric. At this, one of the mirrored walls swung inward, revealing a set of stairs leading down into a basement.

I followed the Professor and Lucy down the concrete steps. A lone, bare lightbulb hung from a wire in the centre of the subterranean room, the limited light casting dark shadows into a great number of nooks and crannies. Bolts of cloth, jars of buttons, spools of thread mounted on pegged boards, and a great miscellany of goods crowded onto shelves that went from floor to ceiling and wall to wall. In one of the dark recesses I saw a stack of weapons, five Mannlicher rifles, and a bucket of ammunition for the same. Next to a mannikin pinned with a paper pattern leaned what appeared to be the tube and base plate for a 60mm mortar, and next to a stack of ancient yellowing celluloid collars sat a pile of French-style grenades.

Everything we would need to begin a well-dressed revolution.

Under the glaring light squatted a long table upon which lay a long, wide length of grey pinstriped cloth, a tissue pattern pinned to it. Above it floated a great pall of cigarette smoke produced by the three smoking around the table. One of those was introduced as Anka, a short, stout woman with a black-and-grey rat's nest of hair, and black eyes that stabbed at you with malice and skepticism. Her face was lined with deep crevices where her cynicism toward this bitter life had been as permanently engraved as a woodcut. Her downturned nose and theatrically placed warts only reinforced the resemblance to an Arthur Rackham illustration of an evil witch. Sitting with her were two <u>battle-weary-looking</u> men introduced as Pavel and Farkas, as suitable noms de guerre as any.

Pavel was a tall, scholarly-looking chap with a great halo of curly hair and black-rimmed spectacles. Farkas was pale, blond, slight, an almost effeminate fellow. Both looked haggard, the same look I had seen on the soldiers returning from Dunkirk.

Van Helsing introduced me by my own pseudonym and vouched for me. We sat with the others, circling the table.

"Don't touch the cloth. Very expensive," warned the man called Farkas, pointing at the table, and for caution's sake I edged my chair away.

"Where is Vasile?" Van Helsing asked.

"Arrested," Anka pronounced. "Taken to the castle."

"Castle?" I queried. The woman squinted at me as if she suspected me of arresting this Vasile.

"In Bran," Farkas explained. "An old fortress from centuries ago." Bran was a tiny village less than twenty miles southwest of Brasov.

"*His* fortress," Pavel intoned.

"Who?" I asked.

"He whose name we do not speak," Anka replied.

My mind sprinted after the thought. Could they be speaking of the one who haunted my Transylvanian ruminations? I knew that Dracula's castle was located in Bran.

"The Germans have abandoned the Town Hall, except as an office to coordinate their patrols and roadblocks."

"Why Bran?" I asked. "Why not use the Citadel?" The Citadel, built in the middle ages, was a massive fortress on the north side of town, overlooking the entire city.

"Too large to hold with the men they have. Bran is smaller, more easily defended," Anka said. "Though they have also added another company of SS to their number."

"The Huns now have at least three companies of SS and a garrison of Rumanian traitors," Pavel said. "They have moved all prisoners from the Town Hall to the castle."

"Vasile will talk. He knows who we are," Lucy said.

"Not Vasile," Farkas defended his comrade.

"Everyone talks," Lucy replied. "Eventually."

"He will not talk," Anka said flatly.

"We cannot be sure of this," Lucy cautioned.

"He hung himself in his cell before they could torture him," Anka said. It was very quiet for a moment. Farkas produced a bottle of wine from within his greatcoat and poured the contents into six jars and passed them among us. He raised his.

"To Vasile," he toasted, and we drank. It was sharp, bitter claret— appropriately so, I suppose.

"And Iaon?" Van Helsing inquired. "I hope his excuse for being late is not so tragic."

"He has fled to the mountains," Pavel told us. "They burned his house. Killed his dog."

"He loved that dog," Farkas said with some sadness. "A gentle beast but gassy."

"I brought bread," Pavel announced. "It is still hot."

He passed around a warm loaf of rye. The smell was amazing, and I tore off a chunk. I had just eaten, but I could not resist. It was delicious. Lucy turned to me just at the moment when my mouth was full, of course. I smiled at her, my cheeks puffed like a squirrel storing nuts. This woman had a way of finding me at my most awkward state every time.

"So we are reduced to what you see," she said, gesturing around the table.

"What have you learned concerning this Major Reikel?" Van Helsing asked.

"This Major Reikel," Anka began. "I asked one of the soldiers whose laundry I wash about this man. Reikel made a name for himself in the Poland invasion. He was a Captain commanding the *Einsatzgruppen*, the paramilitary death squads, during Operation Tannenberg. Twenty thousand Poles were executed. The Captain was promoted to Major for his efficient rendering of this mass extermination."

"Reikel did this?" Farkas asked.

"The same," Anka answered.

"So, I assume that if we continue to resist he will do the same here in Brasov," Pavel stated.

"It seems prudent for us to cease our operations," Van Helsing said. "At least for the moment. Until we can evaluate our opposition."

"No!" Lucy cried out. "No! We quit?! Never!"

"Not quit," Anka responded. "A pause."

"It's quitting," Lucy argued. "What did all of our friends die for? What did Janos die for? All those people we lost fighting . . . No."

"We fight, we get innocent people killed," Pavel said.

"There are no innocent people," Farkas replied. "We are all soldiers. We are all at war."

"Platitudes are very nice when your family is not at risk, nor your children," Anka replied, her eyebrows drawn.

"So, we just sit on our hinders, waiting for the Germans to go away? Until the war is over? After the Nazis have taken all of Europe, England, the world?" Lucy had worked herself into a proper snit.

"My dear Lucille." Van Helsing laid his hand on her shoulder to calm her. It seemed to be the unction to quell her fire. "We know what is at risk. Our task is to find a way to hamper the enemy without destroying our own viability. If we incur too many civilian deaths due to reprisals, we may find our own people turning against us."

"We don't need them," Pavel stated, chin thrust out stubbornly.

"Yes, we do." Anka glared at him. "You do not know how many people know about us, our activities."

"We have security in our cells," Pavel protested.

"Our security is a joke," Farkas replied. "This is a small town. Everybody knows everybody's business. A young lass is found pregnant, they know who the father is, when the deed was done, behind whose barn, and whether they did it standing up or from behind."

"And what colour her knickers were," Pavel said with a nod, conceding the point.

"Is this true?" I asked in momentary panic.

Lucy just shrugged. "Our command cell is well secreted. But . . ."

"I have the cheese, cascaval," Crisan said and produced a large cloth-wrapped wedge. Peeling away the cloth, he withdrew a rather large knife from his boot top and carved off a chunk for himself, then passed the blade and cheese around the assemblage. It was a tasty yellow cheese, not too sharp, somewhat like a Swiss Emmental, and it went very well with the bread and wine. Our conversation ceased for the moment, as any talk does when food intrudes, no matter how serious the conversation.

"So we agree," Van Helsing said. "We will suspend all."

"No!" Lucy declared. "We do not agree!"

"Never," Pavel added.

I felt the same outrage as Lucy and Pavel. For different reasons, I suppose. Here I was on the precipice of my first induction into the war, ready and more than willing to begin my cherished mission, and the very people I was supposed to organise and lead into battle were calling it quits. A great melancholy settled upon me, my whole purpose draining away.

"Tell them, Farkas, what the bastards have been doing," Lucy urged.

"They have been arresting people off the street and from their homes," Farkas answered. "*Arrested* is the wrong word. Kidnapping. There are no charges. People are just . . . taken. Gypsies, Jews, and others. Sometimes relatives are told that these detainees are suspected of 'malicious activities,' but often there are no reasons given at all."

"Haven't the local authorities been able to do anything?" I asked.

"Constable Chiorean has abandoned Brasov," Van Helsing stated without emotion. "He has decided to spend some time with his sister in Belgrade."

"I would have thought better of him," Lucille said, disappointed.

While they gossiped, my attention was on that delectable cheese and knife as they circled, eagerly awaiting my next turn with mouthwatering anticipation. I had already re-filled my glass with the heady wine and filched another chunk of that glorious bread.

"No one knew he had a sister, much less one in Belgrade," said Farkas. "Father Petrescu has appealed to the Pope. The Vatican replied that this is a political situation, not ecumenical, and they stay out of the politics."

"*Pula calului in virful dealului,*" Pavel spat.

"Also, our appeals to the Antonescu government have fallen upon deaf ears," Van Helsing added. "We are to face this brutality by ourselves."

"And that brutality has escalated," Lucy said. "There have been rapes, seemingly at whim; every woman who encounters a German is at risk. Families keep their daughters and wives imprisoned in their homes, not allowing them on the streets, day or night. Not even for church. And when the Nazis invade a house the women must be hidden, under beds, in cupboards and chests, even in barrels. Still, some are . . . found."

It was evident that Lucy had been doing more than arranging a leadership meeting while she had been out today.

"There is also much theft," Pavel told us. "They steal property, not just money, but jewels, silverware, take paintings right off the wall. Anything."

"You fret about . . . things," Anka chastised him. "While they rape and torture and kill our people?"

She turned her fevered eyes to me. "They suspected Emil Rusu to be one of us and killed his family before his eyes, trying to force him to confess. His eight-year-old son, his ten-year-old-daughter, his wife, throats cut in front of their helpless father. He cried for them to kill him instead. That he knew nothing. Nothing. And it was true, he knew nothing. So they shot him in turn."

"And we know this for a fact?" I asked, as I knew that rumours often were prone to exaggeration.

"His seven-year-old daughter was in the room, cowering atop a tall wardrobe where her father had hidden the poor child." Anka glared at me and I felt properly reprimanded.

"The sad fact is that these depredations in the village pale to what is happening within the castle," Farkas gravely intoned. "Anka has placed some of her people within those walls."

"Less said the better," Anka warned.

"Of course." Farkas nodded. "But we have been tracking those who have been apprehended."

"Abducted," Pavel corrected.

"So far, four hundred twenty-two have been taken into the castle," Farkas continued, ignoring the harsh tone of his compatriot. "Seventy-three have been released."

"Every one of them has been tortured," Anka said. "In horrible ways. Skin flayed from the bottoms of their feet. Then forced to walk. Excruciating." She shuddered.

"Genitals have been . . . mangled," Pavel said. "This was done to men. They made a machine to do this."

"We have been able to discern, via Anka's inside informants, that there are, as of today, two hundred sixty-eight prisoners held within the castle," Farkas said.

"That leaves eighty-one unaccounted for," I interjected, math always a strong point for me.

"Where are they?" Lucy asked.

"A pit outside the castle has been discovered," Pavel sighed heavily. "An old cistern gone dry. We do not know exactly how many bodies it contains. At least forty. To accomplish a full count would mean emptying it—which, of course, we cannot do without some jeopardy."

"Some of these bodies were recognised." Anka stopped suddenly and turned to Lucy. "Someone should tell Horea that his Floarea is among the dead."

Lucy nodded, accepting the burden. A pall hung over the room, thick as the nimbus of cigarette smoke.

"These bodies . . ." Anka continued. "Those that could be seen have been mutilated."

"Torture of the most fiendish variety," Pavel said.

"The screams are heard throughout the castle," Anka said heavily, and I realised that she was the inside informant and she was the one who had witnessed this depravity. The cheese, much diminished, had finally come around and I eagerly cut myself a modest piece, then felt a pang of guilt and conscience. Here I was thinking of my stomach while we discussed the tragic fate of our peers. Sometimes I can be a right prat.

"Monstrous," Lucy declared.

"Exactly. This Reikel is a monster," Anka said, and the others nodded in grim affirmation.

"They are all monsters, the Huns," Pavel muttered.

"How do we fight a monster?" Lucy whispered, a curse in her voice. She stared into her wine, seeking an answer in the bloodred depths.

Van Helsing, who had been uncharacteristically silent during this recitation of evil, taking it in as if he were attending a lecture at school, took a deep breath, as if preparing for a plunge into dark waters.

"I once fought a monster," Van Helsing said quietly. "He was also . . . formidable. And more than a match for these beasts."

I was stunned. I almost choked on a mouthful of bread and cheese. Was he speaking about the same monster that came to my mind?

We all turned to the old man. There was a sharp intake of breath from Lucy. "Father . . . no."

EXCERPTED FROM THE UNPUBLISHED NOVEL
THE DRAGON PRINCE AND I
by Lenore Van Muller

Her father had never spoken of what had brought him to Transylvania so many years ago, but Lucille had heard the stories, lurid tales too outlandish to be believed. She heard them as a child, murmured about at school, overheard in stores and shops whenever people saw her, whispered recountings of the tale. Lucille's mere presence seemed to prompt the repeating of the legend.

In response, she had prodded her father, even tried to provoke him into telling her something—anything—about that part of his life. But his silence concerning the subject was absolute, and she soon learned to never bring up the matter.

The mystery grew from a seed into a great, dark tree that cast its shadow over their otherwise happy lives. When her mother was still alive, Lucy had pressed her, too, but she would never part with any information, acceding to her husband's silence.

That left Lucille to compile what she could from the snippets of village rumour, secondhand accounts, and, of course, that novel. Her father had received numerous copies, sent to him by the author and aficionados of the book, some requesting his autograph or an interview, and he burnt every one in the fireplace. She found a copy in the school library and stole it from the shelves. She read the forbidden tome in secret, hiding it at home, and reading bits in the bathroom and by lamplight under her blanket as if it were pornography.

She wanted to ask her father so many questions. How much of the book, the myth, the gossip, was true? Was the creature real or an exaggerated version of some madman killer?

These questions returned to her as they left the tailor shop. But she said nothing on the drive home. Harker, possibly sensing her mood, was also silent. The questions swirled around her brain, as if she were standing outside a carousel with taunting wooden horses passing by, mocking her over and over. By the time they reached the house, she had decided, she was going to finally confront him. Now was her chance to have some answers.

One clue was evident. Her father had just admitted that much. The monster was real. And that fact tinged her decision to question him with a dark sense of apprehension.

"Father, do you intend to enlist the . . . vampire in our cause?"

"I do."

"So it exists," Harker said.

"It does," her father replied.

"It was not destroyed," Harker persisted. "As was described in the book."

"The book, pfui!" Van Helsing spat.

"I'm going with you," Lucille immediately announced.

"I forbid it," her father answered.

"I think I am far beyond the age where you can forbid me."

He went from room to room gathering diverse items off tables and from assorted drawers and tossing the objects into his black bag. Lucille followed, arguing with her father every step. Harker trailed close behind, deep within his own thoughts.

They travelled from parlour to library, into the medical examining room, to the attached shed where her father had a wood and metal workbench on which he tinkered with his inventions, back upstairs to his private quarters.

All the while the two Van Helsings tossed the same argument back and forth in some verbal tennis match.

"Why can't I come with you?" she finally demanded.

"Because it is too dangerous," her father said as he put his shaving mirror into his medical bag.

"More dangerous than a German bullet?" she asked.

"Decidedly," he replied and went about collecting any other mirror that he could find. She and Harker followed him from room to room like two puppies after their mother.

"Even more reason for me to accompany you," she said.

"I'm sorry, Lucille, but no."

One hand mirror was too large to fit into his valise, and he laid it upon the floor. To her astonishment he stomped on the glass and broke it into pieces. It had belonged to her mother and was sacrosanct. At least until now. He bent to the floor and carefully picked up the shards and put them into his bag, muttering to himself, "So sorry, Lyuba, but you would understand, I'm sure." Harker went to his knees and helped collect the broken glass.

"You cannot stop me." She stood in front of her father, blocking the doorway. "I am an adult now."

He stood and they faced each other, both ramrod straight, both equally stubborn by blood, neither ready to give ground.

Her father laid a hand on her shoulder and appealed to her with his greatest weapon.

"My dear Lucille, I am the only one who knows this creature and its insidious ways, hence, I am the only one to do this. But in attempting such I must be in complete command of my faculties. Having you present will only create a distraction, one that could get me, us, killed. Or a fate worse than death. I need to focus, as if this were surgery, an operation where life hangs in the balance. As it does. So I ask you, for me, for the success of this travail, for your country, stand aside and let me do this. Alone."

She took a moment to consider his argument. And as he expected, as he knew she would, Lucille consented with a slight, reluctant nod of her head.

"But take someone with you. Farkas," she suggested.

"Farkas is too superstitious. He would be more of a hindrance than help."

"Pavel, then," she offered.

Harker, standing behind her father, urgently raised his hand like a schoolboy with a ready answer and an eagerness to please the teacher.

It was her father's turn to nod. "Pavel, then. I will ask him, but these local people have strong feelings—"

"And me!" Harker finally exclaimed like a balloon filled to the bursting point.

They both looked at him. He nervously stroked his thin line of mustache.

"Me," he repeated. "Please. Take me with you."

FROM THE WAR JOURNAL OF
J. HARKER

(transcribed from shorthand)

I suddenly found myself overcome with nerves. This was it. I was finally going to see for myself what had changed my grandfather's life so profoundly that he left the law and became a man of God. That had such an impact on my grandmother that if the devil's name was spoken in polite conversation her hand reflexively went to the scar on her forehead. I was now embarking on my own encounter with the wellspring of all of those macabre tales.

We picked up Pavel, who was waiting at a crossroads south of Brasov, and I followed Van Helsing's directions to the village of Sacele. We were stopped by one German and two recently established Rumanian Army roadblocks. The Professor's medical papers and the lie that Pavel's wife was in the midst of a difficult birth were enough to allow us safe passage. There was no doubt that Pavel's fidgety and pale appearance gave credence to the lie.

I drove along the twists and turns of the narrow roads, past a tiny, pastoral village. The countryside was lovely and most interesting; if only we were there under different conditions. How delightful it would have been to see it all, to stop and meet people and learn something of their lives, to fill our minds and memories with all the colour and picturesque scenery of this whole wild, beautiful country and the quaint people. But alas . . .

One turn and the pavement gave way to gravel, and another turn led to two muddy ruts that were deep enough to control the Bentley so well that I could let loose of the steering wheel, and we rode along as if on a train following tracks.

All three of us were silent the entire ride, each deep inside our own thoughts. I noted that Pavel, sitting in the passenger seat next to me, stank of garlic, and I was able to discern a garland of it strung around the man's neck. I was reminded of the Mohammedan tale that when Satan stepped from the Garden of Eden, after the Fall of Man, garlic sprang from where he placed his left foot and onion from where his right touched.

I also noticed that Pavel now wore a rosary made of some dark wood with a large silver crucifix that hung almost to his belt. I had not seen him wear this religious symbol at the meeting before, and I had been told by dear Lucy that he was a steadfast Communist, rejecting religion as "the opiate of the people." But I guess everyone falls back on what comfort they can when they are frightened.

The road became overgrown with weeds and brush. Just when I thought we could push no further through this dense foliage, Van Helsing told me I could stop and then ordered us out of the car. Van Helsing opened the Bentley's boot and gave Pavel the tyre jack carried therein. He then led us away from the car and around a lilac hedge the size of a London bus.

Our path entered a twisted mass of trees, the corridor blocked with recent growths. Pavel walked ahead, slashing at the foliage with the long knife he wore sheathed at his belt. I wished I had brought my grandfather's kukri. The blade, if nothing else, could serve as a comfort in this twilight grove of grotesque and vine-encumbered trees, the branches distorted, shrivelled, and decaying. The very look of this dark realm was enough to stir a morbid fancy. My own doubts and fears crowded upon me, and I was struck by the grim adventure I had embarked upon.

"'Beware the Jabberwock, my son!'" I quoted. "'The jaws that bite, the claws that catch! / Beware the Jubjub bird, and shun / The frumious Bandersnatch!'" My attempt at some humorous relief fell on deaf ears, the other two men as grim as last week's mutton.

The shade grew denser as we meandered through this twisted, macabre wooded labyrinth, and the air filled me with a brooding fear. What eldritch dream world was this, which I had entered?

We finally stepped out of these wind-whispered woods, and I found myself facing the ruins of a church. Crumbling walls displayed elaborate carvings worn to illegibility by eons of rain and wind. The grey stone was black with mould and a green verdigris of lichen. Fallen blocks lay helter-skelter among the weeds and briars. I examined the remains of a doorway arch and the peaked forms of absent windows; shattered white marble tiles were scattered along the interior, which was spotted with tufts of wild grass. Some of the base stones conveyed the semblance of a wall that hinted at an early Roman influence or even construction. What remained of the steeple was a stone cross propped up against a sagging, weary wall.

A gravestone lay in pieces on our pathway, the shattered remains like a puzzle hastily reconstructed. I could barely make out the name, the carving made smooth by the decades: Varney.

At the back end of the ruins was a cemetery. A rusted iron fence was failing, and the headstones had been untended for so long that an oak had sprouted from a ground-level tomb, splitting the marble and heaving it aside, along with a few other grave markers.

While I took in this sad ruin, Van Helsing jolted me out of my melancholy.

"We must hurry while we have the light." Van Helsing urged us forward through the graveyard, his black bag tinkling like a wind chime in minor chord. Past the fence was another, smaller cemetery. Many of these graves had no stones at all, just iron stakes holding tiny vertical glass panes that had once displayed a piece of paper, long disintegrated, the iron itself corroded with knobby barnacles of rust.

"Unconsecrated ground," Van Helsing explained. "For murderers, apostates, and the unknown dead."

There were a few headstones and a large mausoleum with maybe a hundred cubicles inside. There was nothing to mark the names of those interred. I commented on this.

"Influenza epidemic," Van Helsing explained, as I examined the tomb's mouldy interior. "So many died that there were not enough survivors to identify them all."

At the very back of this poor, ignominious graveyard was a larger tomb, twice the size of the mausoleum, carved of black granite flecked with glints of silver and veins of red running through it like tributaries of blood. Ancient carvings along the sides and front had been abraded by the elements, but I could make out a pair of dragons flanking the entrance, their tails curled around a Gothic letter D. Someone had chiselled a crude cross into each of these reliefs.

The entire circumference of this imposing edifice had been wrapped in strands of wire, spaced a foot or so apart, and between the stone and wire a variety of crosses had been inserted. There were crucifixes by the hundreds of every size and type imaginable. Plain wooden crosses, some evidently carved by hand, crosses of brass, copper, steel, iron, some of intricate design, some with Christ, a variety of effigies, from crude to life-like, in his agony or in peace, accepting his pain or crying out, eyes cast down in suffering or uplifted, asking the eternal question.

"All these crosses," Van Helsing muttered to himself. "Where did they come from? Who could have done this? I thought my secret was well kept."

The three of us stood there at the tomb's entrance, I in thrall, Van Helsing most likely in reminiscence, Pavel crossing himself and whispering a prayer. The wind rustled the leaves of the trees, and their branches rattled against each other like the clattering of bones.

Finally, Van Helsing opened his medical bag and pulled from it a pair of wire snips. He cut one wire and a cascade of crosses tumbled to the ground. Pavel scurried to gather them off the dirt. Another wire was cut, the pile of crosses increased.

After severing the last wire, Van Helsing stepped back and gestured to Pavel, who inserted the wedge end of the tyre jack between the tomb door and jamb. He applied some pressure, but the huge stone door moved only a mere inch. There was a loud grating as the rusty iron hinges protested years of disuse. Pavel's face grew red, and the tendons in his neck went rigid as he dug in his feet and leaned into the pry bar.

With a great grinding that was as loud as Pavel's grunts, the door finally gave way and opened enough for me to get a grip upon the inner edge and help slide the huge chunk of stone open. I was prepared for some unpleasantness, and indeed a faint, malodorous air seemed to exhale through the gap.

One of the iron hinges, rusted completely, fell off and clattered to the stone floor. Inside, a small window set high in the wall across from the door spilled light upon a black marble sarcophagus that was set in the centre of the tomb. Two steel bands were strapped about the sarcophagus and bound with a pair of rust-encrusted locks. The whole interior was lit by an eerie orange light, and I could see the sun setting behind the tomb in a crimson death. *Most appropriate,* I thought.

Van Helsing stepped inside, and I followed him. Pavel hesitated, began praying under his breath again. Abject fear was evident on his face and he seemed unable to cross the threshold with us.

"Pavel." Van Helsing's voice was soft, soothing. "You've faced Nazi machine guns, been bayoneted and shot. Surely you can do this."

"I . . . cannot." The poor man shook his head. "My mother told me . . . stories."

"Then wait here," the Professor told him and took the tyre jack from the man's limp hands. Pavel stepped farther away from the tomb.

There was an odour of mould, damp, and something more—corruption. I tried to breathe through my mouth as the Professor looked around at the black brick walls. The aged mortar was crumbling, a few bricks fallen to the floor. The tomb was grim and gruesome; spiders had assumed dominance over the discoloured stone and dust-encrusted mortar.

The Professor stepped up to the small window and knocked out the glass with the tyre jack. The sudden wanton destruction surprised me. I had never seen the Professor in any mode other than the intellectual. Brushing the broken shards outside, he then plunged his hand into his magic bag and produced a compass and what appeared to be a farmer's almanac. Consulting this periodical, he took an azimuth reading through the window.

Then we went to work. The sun was gone and we worked by torchlight, Van Helsing stationing Pavel at the window to shine his own battery-powered lantern through the smashed window to imitate the dawn. The Professor kept having to adjust Pavel's angle as the man's arms tired. I was kept busy driving wooden wedges into the wall mortar at Van Helsing's direction.

As I did so, I could not help but glance frequently at the sarcophagus that dominated the small room. It was so close. The object of terror and bloodshed that might lie within was almost beyond comprehension. Almost. As it was, the proximity was frightening enough, and I found it difficult to concentrate on the simple work of hammering wood into the ancient cement.

Even more disconcerting was the constant sound of breaking glass as Van Helsing smashed his collection of mirrors, one by one, into smaller fragments. The sound of glass scratching stone has always been one of those sounds that curdles my blood and makes my skin crawl. To hear it all night was making me slightly mad. The daemonic and ghoulish atmosphere did not help my mood any. More than once I had to restrain myself from shouting at the Professor to "stop, for God's sake, stop." But finally he was done breaking the mirrors and became busy setting the glass upon my wedges.

It took hours and, in the midst of the black night, Van Helsing proposed a break to sup on the bread, cheese, and wine Pavel had brought with him. The usually ravenous Pavel declined, and so did I.

"Let's just be done with this," I said, and the Professor acceded.

Our labours were interrupted once more. I suddenly felt a gust of wind buffet my face, and I turned to witness the strangest spectacle. A burst of flower petals, deep violet, wafted in the air above the sarcophagus, like a flock of tiny bluebirds flitting about the room before my amazed eyes.

Van Helsing caught one of the petals in his open palm and examined it in the dim light. "Monkshood," he remarked, looking around for the source of this strange phenomenon.

"Must have blown through the window," I offered, but I could tell the solution wasn't sufficient for him. Silently he went back to the task at hand. I took the cue and resumed my own work.

We finished about an hour before dawn, the Professor constantly adjusting his construction, the kind where one move upsets another, which in turn causes another change, one after another, a cascade of tiny remedies. We did this until mentally exhausted, and when I protested that, certainly, enough was enough, Pavel agreed with me.

Van Helsing gave this reply: "Our lives are in the balance, gentlemen. We do this properly or we die. And possibly many others. And death is the best of our options. We do this right or we suffer in dire fashion. Believe me."

I believed him. My grandfather had planted the seed of horror, and now Van Helsing was nourishing the carnivorous plant that was devouring my courage.

Finally he gave the word, dismissed Pavel, and hung a cloth over the window while I set down my mallet. We went outside, and I could see the sun turning the eastern sky pale. I stared at the dawning as if it were the first I had ever seen.

My arms ached from the work, and I could see Pavel trying to massage out the kinks in his own arms, as he had been holding the lantern over his head for hours. Van Helsing glanced at his watch and looked up at us. He appeared tired. For the first time since I had met him he seemed old, the burden upon him sapping his normal vitality.

"Dawn is upon us," he said, hefting the tyre jack from where it leaned against the crypt. "Now we see if we are as smart as we think."

He stepped into the tomb and I followed. All of a sudden I wanted out of this lordly death house in this lonely churchyard, to be away to teeming London where the air is fresh and the sun rises over Hempstead Hill and where wildflowers grow of their own accord.

"Close the door," Van Helsing ordered Pavel, and my skin crawled as stone ground against stone, cloaking us in darkness with but a faint glow from the cloth-covered window. I was overcome with fear, the smell of the grave permeating the core of my being. Van Helsing turned on his electric torch, handed me the tyre jack, pointed to the locks securing the steel bands that encompassed the sarcophagus. The locks broke easily and the bands, three inches wide, fell to the marble floor with a clang that startled us both.

I reached down and put my hands to the lid, the same red-veined, black granite that clad the outside, but this was polished to a high gleam that could be seen under the layer of dust. Van Helsing added his strength, and we slowly slid the heavy slab away. It fell to the floor with a loud thunk that shattered some floor tiles.

"Is everyone all right in there?" Pavel called from outside. His voice sounded small, a thousand miles away.

"Yes, yes!" Van Helsing shouted.

I stared down at the casket, black lacquered wood, simple, elegant in its own manner.

"'Of witch, and daemon, and large coffin worm, / Were long be-nightmared,'" I quoted. This time I elicited a response.

"Keats," Van Helsing noted correctly as he took the pry bar and inserted it under the coffin lid. He levered the jack up and down a few times and, with a crack, the seal was breached. With another tug and push, the lid sprung up a few inches on its hinges. Tossing the pry bar aside with a loud clang of steel against marble, Van Helsing then used his hands to push the lid up into the vertical.

Dracula. The legend, the myth made corporeal, that very creature lay there in state. I knew him at once from the description in The Book: the waxen face, the high, aquiline nose on which the light fell in a thin white line, the slightly open mouth with sharp white teeth showing between blue lips. The mustache that trailed to his jawline and shoulder-length hair were a brilliant white. His hands, long-fingered, the nails a soft purple, still clutched at the rounded, wooden stake that pierced his chest. The top of the wood was splintered.

I held my breath. I was here, standing before the fabled monster, the locus of my grandfather's tales. I was finally confronting the being that had preoccupied a good part of my life.

"This is why I volunteered for the SOE," I whispered to the Professor. "This is why I cajoled and pleaded to be assigned to Rumania."

"And the reason I stayed," he replied.

Van Helsing was also contemplating the body, deep in his own thoughts, memories.

"I thought you destroyed it. Cut off his head and all that," I ventured.

"That book!" the old man spat, then settled into his professorial mode. "I could not. The scientist in me, I suppose. Such a unique specimen. I wanted to study the phenomenon of the creature. That was why I began to delve deeper into my medical studies. Then . . . life took precedence, a marriage, a child, my practice, the offer to build a university, and now the war. I never got around to it. Maybe I was . . . avoiding the whole endeavour. But I knew he was here . . . waiting."

We both examined the form in the casket. Despite the history, it was a noble visage, broad of forehead, a Romanesque nose, and a surprisingly sensual mouth.

"Strange," the Professor went on. "It is as if time had not passed since I and the others stood here so many years ago. The body appears exactly the same, not a bit of decomposition that I can see. No change of any kind is evident, no lengthening of the nails or hair as the dead oft-times exhibit. The flesh has not sunken or contracted; there seems to be no desiccation of any form. Though the hair has turned white. Curious."

He was bent over the coffin, his eyes inches from the corpse, scrutinising every inch of exposed flesh, assuming the mantle of scientist.

"Remarkable," he whispered.

I, too, perused the cadaver, with a less scientific bent and a bit more trepidation. Were we really contemplating the revivification of this monster? Was this action at all proper? Was this act not impious sacrilege? Would Van Helsing and I leave this tomb alive? Would we suffer the fate worse than death that Van Helsing had referred to more than once?

Van Helsing steeled himself and wrapped both hands around the stake that penetrated the creature's chest.

The sharpened wood came out easily enough. There was no blood or gore, just a blackish residue adhering to the stake.

We both took a reflexive step back as if we had just opened a box of venomous snakes. But Dracula did not move. The body was as still as before.

"I thought as much," Van Helsing said as he tossed away the stake. It landed on the tiles with a clatter. The Professor went to his medical bag, withdrew a syringe, and slid up the sleeve of his shirt and coat to expose the ropey vein at the crook of his elbow.

"No! Use mine," I said, astounding myself.

I slipped up my own sleeve and offered him my arm. I do not know why I did this. I tell myself that it was because the old man looked so tired and I thought that a loss of blood might further weaken him. If there were any deeper reason, I do not want to contemplate such.

Van Helsing stared at me for what seemed to be an eternity, studying my face, searching for that same rationale. He finally turned his attention to my arm, regarding the filigree of bluish veins that weaved under my skin. Selecting the most prominent blood vessel, he pierced it with the point of the needle. I prided myself that I did not flinch, but this was more, I think, the skill of Van Helsing's phlebotomic finesse than my bravery.

Dark, scarlet blood filled the glass tube. When it was full, Van Helsing slid the needle out of my skin. Again he bent over the coffin, poised the syringe over Dracula's chest, and pushed the plunger. A stream of bright red arced into the puncture wound. Then he moved the needle up to the dead face and squirted the remaining fluid upon the vampire's mouth. The blood seeped between blue lips and disappeared.

I gasped and Van Helsing turned from his kit to look. In alarm, I could only point with a shaking hand at the chest wound. The dead flesh was healing before my astounded eyes, scar tissue forming over the gaping hole and then, just as swiftly, that shiny skin transforming to a firmer state.

Dracula's body arched. Then contracted. The eyes snapped open. The mouth flew agape. The fangs were displayed.

Van Helsing leapt away, retreating until his back hit the rear wall. My reaction was a mite slower. I stood there for a second, mesmerised by those eyes. They were of a yellow-green cast, like those of a black cat once owned by one of my aunts. Trying to gather my senses, I took a step to the rear and my foot stumbled over the discarded stake, causing me to fall on my pipe and drum.

Dracula leapt from the casket with feline grace, stood glowering at Van Helsing and then at me. But his strength seemed to abandon him, all of it spent on the quick exit from the coffin, I suppose, and his legs gave way. He was obviously weak, his muscles not performing properly.

Using the sarcophagus for purchase, he pulled himself back upright and turned his head slowly, taking in his environs. Those vulpine eyes passed over me, I still on my arse, then fixed upon the Professor, huddled against the wall under the tiny window.

Dracula extended one long arm, and with his trembling white finger pointed at the old man he instantly recognised.

"Van Helsing!" The voice was a dry rasp, like old parchment being crumpled into a ball. "You!"

The creature summoned what strength he had and charged across the tomb toward Van Helsing, who whipped the improvised curtain off the window.

A long shaft of sunlight stabbed into the crypt. Striking a mirror set upon one of the wedges I had driven into the opposite wall, reflecting light onto another piece of looking glass that bounced the sunbeam to another side wall and onto another bit of mirror and another until the tomb was crisscrossed by streams of sunlight.

Dracula recoiled from one, then the other until he found himself backed into a dark corner. He hissed in rage and frustration, like a wolf fighting the trap that snared his leg, and, as any cornered beast, his eyes desperately sought an escape path, any way out.

He lurched toward the door, but found it blocked by three beams of light. He tried another path. Also blocked.

Van Helsing stepped forward just short of obstructing a beam himself so as not to destroy the sun-ray cage he had constructed.

"You are trapped," he told the creature.

I rose from the floor, finding a space that did not interrupt the reflected columns of light.

Dracula, furious, reached a hand toward Van Helsing. The sunlight struck his skin as if it were a blowtorch. The flesh was instantly burnt, blistered before my eyes, blackened. Smoke wafted from the infernal broiling, and I could detect a rotten sweetness in the air.

Dracula was forced to snatch his hand back into the shadow.

"What do you want?" Dracula snarled. The fangs were no longer in evidence. The canines were rather long, but not anything I hadn't seen in normal people. "Why have you roused me from . . . that?"

He gestured to the casket.

"I have a proposition for you." Van Helsing spoke calmly, as if he were a solicitor discussing contracts. "Your country has been invaded."

"Again? And the invader?"

"The German Army."

"The Hun . . ."

I noticed that Dracula was paying scant attention to the conversation, but instead was studying the arrangement of the broken mirror pieces perched upon the shims inserted into the brickwork. I had a feeling he was not admiring the workmanship.

"This is the Germans' second try at a world war. Global domination is their goal," Van Helsing continued, watching the vampire with the caution a rabbit gives a hawk. "They are back and they are vicious. More brutal than ever. Your country's leadership has surrendered territory, some of it your homeland, and now cooperate with the Germans. Your people are suffering."

"My people . . ." Dracula sneered. "They despise me. They regard me as a beast. Less than a beast. To be hounded and killed."

He studied the beams of light as if they were a knot to unravel.

"You were once a patriot," Van Helsing continued, never taking his eyes off the vampire. "A champion to your people, your country."

"True, this. I drove out the Turks, the boyars," Dracula said with a certain pride. I caught a glimpse of the nobleman who once resided in the creature.

And now I knew it was true. This was Vlad Tepes, who had ruled ancient Wallachia brutally, but fairly, in the 1400s. He had fought the Ottoman Empire and won, driven the Hungarians from his lands. His name translated as Vlad the Impaler, famous for mounting his enemies on stakes. The Ottoman Army, it was said, once fled in fright after seeing thousands of its fellows, all rotting corpses, displayed on the banks of the Danube like so many rats on skewers.

I was musing on my historical studies of this man when Dracula's hand shot out, like a snake strikes, and snatched the wooden stake from the floor and threw it at a mirror shard. The glass shattered and fell from its place on the wall and suddenly a whole section of Van Helsing's sunlight prison was gone.

The vampire leapt at Van Helsing, fangs bared. The Professor's hand went to a pocket, pulled forth his shaving mirror, and bounced light from the window directly into Dracula's face.

The creature gasped, his face raw and red where he was burnt. Half-blinded, he once again sought the sanctuary of shade.

"I could put you back into your tomb," Van Helsing threatened.

"Do so," Dracula softly replied, shielding his eyes. "There is no world out there for me."

"Your people revile you only because you preyed upon them." Van Helsing kept his shaving mirror at the ready, dancing the reflected beam above and around the vampire. "I am offering you an opportunity to redeem yourself. A chance to make up for all the misery and pain you have caused."

"Redemption is not for me." Dracula shook his head. "It would take a score of lifetimes to atone for my depredations."

"From all accounts, you have those lifetimes ahead of you," Van Helsing said, but Dracula, arms still over his eyes, just shook his head again.

"How about something else?" I asked.

Dracula took his arms from his face and turned toward me. I found my hands were trembling and hid them behind my back.

"Blood" was all I said.

"Blood." Dracula spoke the word as if it were holy.

"Nazi blood," I continued with more confidence. "The blood of the invaders. You can have your fill. And be a hero to your countrymen once more."

"The blood of my enemies." There was a crinkling of the eyes, the hint of a smile. "I have a powerful thirst."

"There is more than enough blood to satisfy even your overwhelming thirst." Van Helsing picked up the argument. "But you must promise to kill only our enemies."

"Why would you trust me?" Dracula asked.

"A fair question. One I have pondered myself," Van Helsing answered. "I have long studied your history, volume after ancient volume, and, despite your unholy appetite, you were once known to be an honest ruler, a man of his word. I now ask for it."

"My word then. To feed only upon my enemies."

"*Our* enemies," I corrected.

"The enemies of my people. Agreed. My oath. You have it," Dracula vowed.

"Agreed," Van Helsing said.

Dracula peered at his former foe, now ally. Van Helsing stepped into the path of the light beam, breaking asunder the reflected prison. Without the glare from the window Dracula could see the old man clearly now and was obviously stunned.

"You are old," Dracula said in astonishment.

"True, I am old," Van Helsing acknowledged. "And you are . . . but for the colour of your hair, unchanged."

Van Helsing walked around the crypt and knocked the bits of mirror to the floor, smashing them. I slipped a hand into my pocket and wrapped my fingers around my pistol, doubting it would prove to be any defence against this creature. The vampire noticed my movement and appeared to be amused at my nervousness.

"You, too, seem familiar," he addressed me.

"I am the grandson of Jonathan Harker."

"Harker . . ." Dracula thought for a moment. "The solicitor from England?"

"The same."

"Grandson." Dracula shook his head as he walked freely about the crypt, ducking under the window. He paused in front of Van Helsing, who did not even flinch.

I kept my hand in my pocket, seeking security in the steel of the Browning. I realised that Van Helsing had no such talisman and was helpless before the creature. This raised my estimation of the Professor and how brave a man he was indeed.

"You are most wrong about me, Professor," Dracula said, his voice becoming more human with use. "I am not totally unchanged. On the contrary. I have changed in many ways, I think."

He continued to walk, gaining surety in his gait as he did so, turning once again to the old man. "What do we do now?" he asked.

"We wait for nightfall, I suppose," Van Helsing replied. "For your convenience."

"I need to feed. I am weak and my thirst is strong. Very strong." His amber eyes flitted from me to Van Helsing and back. My free hand reflexively went to my neck and, although I tried to cover the gesture with some fiddling of my collar, the vampire caught the motion and gave me a wolfish grin.

"Control yourself," Van Helsing said. "You are not an animal."

"Not quite," Dracula said. "But neither am I human, am I?"

He smiled again. It was a wicked smile, the canines not fully extended, but still prominent enough to give him a predatory aspect.

"How long have I been . . . in state?" Dracula asked. "What day is it? Or should I say year?"

"Year," I told him. "Nineteen forty-one."

"Nigh fifty years . . ." Dracula absorbed the information. "And the world has changed much?"

"It has," Van Helsing replied.

"Aircraft. We have machines that fly," I supplied. "And drop bombs, men."

"We have methods of slaughter that would impress even you," Van Helsing added. "There was a world war. Now there is another. The first tallied deaths in the millions. I think we are destined to top that number this time."

"There is a man called Adolf Hitler . . ." I began.

The history lesson, with many digressions, lasted until sunset. Van Helsing and I tossed historical benchmarks back and forth like a vigorous badminton rally, trying to encapsulate a half century of human achievement. The vampire took particular interest when Van Helsing told him how Transylvania had been absorbed into the Rumanian Union after the Great War and the disintegration of the Austro-Hungarian Empire. The rumours that Hungary would soon be given the Szekely Land of Eastern Transylvania irked him even more.

"My country is but a lump of bread to be shared at the table of my enemies, a piece torn off here, another there?"

Pavel was called and passed a wine bag and victuals through the window. Van Helsing and I supped, and I even offered some to the vampire to see if he would accept. He declined.

"The nourishment I need flows through your veins," he said and leaned toward me, inhaling through his nose. "It was your blood that revived me, yes?"

I could only nod, chilled to the core of my being. Suddenly my hunger faded, and I went back to my history and the expansion of the American sphere of influence.

When the light from the small window finally failed, the Professor nodded to me and I put my shoulder to the crypt door and hollered for Pavel to assist me. We were able to leverage the door open and the three of us stepped out into the night air.

Oh! But the world seemed fresh and pure after the terror of that vault. How sweet it was to see the clouds race by and the passing gleams of the moonlight between the scudding clouds—like the gladness and sorrow of a man's life; how sweet it was to breathe the fresh air that had no taint of death and decay.

Pavel stumbled backwards at the sight of the vampire, muttering a prayer, *"In manus tuas Domine commendo spiritum meum,"* clutching his rosary with one hand while making the sign against the evil eye with the other.

Dracula was oblivious to the man. Instead he tried to adjust his tattered apparel, a black suit and white shirt that had not withstood the years as well as their wearer. The cape fell to the ground, and his shirt showed through gaps in his coat where the material or stitches had rotted. Dracula appeared disgusted, even a bit embarrassed, at the state of his attire.

He glanced at the night sky, at the moon beginning its climb.

"The skies have not altered," he said as Van Helsing led us out of the graveyard. "Are you going to shoot me or not?"

Van Helsing and I turned to see Pavel pointing a large revolver at the vampire's back.

"Pavel, please," Van Helsing pleaded, and Pavel pocketed the weapon. We trudged on, past the other cemetery, the ruins of the old church.

"I do not know this place," Dracula observed.

"Few do," Van Helsing replied. "I made use of a tomb built for one of your ancestors who died in Istanbul. His body was lost in the Black Sea, hence the sarcophagus was left empty. I thought it best not to draw attention to your resting place."

"Resting." Another enigmatic smile flickered across Dracula's face.

When we reached the automobile Dracula insisted on examining the Bentley. He was keenly interested in the vehicle's workings, especially the instrument panel and the function of every switch and toggle. He was stunned when I told him that there were millions of such machines all over the earth, most not so fine, of course. And he was even more surprised when I informed him that in some countries even the common man, the peasant, owned such a luxury.

Then he turned to me and reached out a hand. Surprised, I took it in my own, and he shook it.

"Thank you for rescuing me from that interminable state," he said with some formality and a slight bow. His clasp of my hand was with a strength which made me wince, not lessened by the fact that the flesh was as cold as ice.

"You are, uh, welcome," I replied trying to recover.

Pavel would not sit with the vampire. The Professor instructed him to instead drive. I assumed that this was to keep the obviously frightened man busy with something physical. Van Helsing sat up front with Pavel, to give instructions, thus leaving me to ride in the back seat next to my grandfather's greatest foe, what he had called "the epitome of evil."

I found myself struck dumb, awed at being in the presence of this creature of myth and imagination. My befuddlement was a bit mollified by the fact that Dracula stank of mould and decay. I did not know if this was inherent in the vampire's very essence or his clothes, which kept falling to pieces and littering the floorboards. But the odour was enough to prod me into opening my window. When I did so, Dracula turned to his own window lever, inspected the chrome knob, and wound down the glass.

Poking his head out and into the drafting wind stream like a spaniel on a Sunday outing, Dracula inquired, "At what speed are we proceeding?"

Van Helsing leaned over to glance at the speedometer. "Forty-seven kilometres per hour."

"Most impressive," Dracula said to himself as he popped his head back inside. A phrase came to me, "A stranger in a strange land"—a line from Exodus, I think.

This childish delight displayed by the heinous monster was enough of a tonic for me to ready one of the thousand questions flitting about my brain like sparrows trapped in a house. Trying to be nonchalant, I began inspecting the vampire, searching for the pointed ear tips described in The Book, and I was disappointed to see that his ears were as characterless as my own. Examining his hands, I could see that there was no hair on his palms, nor did the fingernails match the description I had memorised; they were not cut to sharp points. Sigh. And I leaned forward one time to catch a whiff of his breath, expecting the foul stench of the grave, as per The Book, but this, too, did disappoint. There was no demonstrative exhalation to be seen. None. I chastised the novelist for his fictional exaggerations and turned to what I knew to be fact, history.

"Uh, the impaling of your enemies," I asked. "Uh, exactly how was that accomplished?"

"Simple, actually." Dracula shrugged. "The stake was laid upon the ground, a post prevented the base from sliding, the pointed end of the stake aimed at the . . . how do you say . . . anus, the legs of the person each tied to a horse, a flick of the whip, the horse charges away, and . . . impaled. Then you lift and plant the stake into the ground for display to all."

My own sphincter involuntarily tightened at the thought.

"Did, uh, many survive the, uh, initial impalement?" I figured, in for a penny in for a pound.

"A surprising number did. Some would live for days."

"It must have been agony," I said.

"Of course. But that was the point, yes?"

The disgust must have been evident on my face.

"The times when I was *voivode*, as ruler, were, how you say, primitive. For a primitive people one must be crude, obvious. For theft in one village I would have the thief's feet skinned, then salted. Sometimes my more enthusiastic and creative followers would gather goats to lick the salt. Very painful. The thief's screams would be heard throughout the village. Even better, the story would travel to other villages, the punishment becoming worse with each telling. The people begin to understand. Stealing will not be tolerated. No exceptions to the law. I punish all men, women, I punish old, the young, the rich and poor, no exception for class, religion. And soon, thievery begins to decline. You see my point."

"I do."

"Then you see the importance of impaling my enemies."

"I guess."

"I learned this from the Turks. They held me prisoner for a time. A most dispiriting time. They whipped and beat me for days until I could stand no more. Later, after I was free and became ruler of my country, the Ottomans sent Turkish envoys to demand tribute of my people. I had their turbans nailed to their skulls."

"Message sent and received."

"You understand. My older brother . . . they blinded him, buried him alive at Targoviste. When I had the opportunity I impaled twenty thousand Turks outside Targoviste. As you say, 'Message sent, message received.' No?"

"No. Yes. I mean, I, uh, understand."

Van Helsing turned in his seat to face us. "Now you see why he is the perfect match to send against the Nazis. It is a kindred barbarism with which we will fight them."

"Barbaric acts that were for barbaric times," Dracula said.

"Welcome to *our* times," Van Helsing said and turned back to the front. He was quiet for the rest of the drive. As was I, thinking about what we were about to unleash upon the world.

We stopped at a village to allow Pavel to use a phone and call the council to a meeting at the tailor shop.

As we entered Brasov, the vampire sat up and peered out the windows, intent on the passing landscape, his head swiveling from side to side, examining the buildings. He stared at Tampa Mountain, and I remembered from my studies that he had impaled forty merchants on that peak. He showed particular interest as we passed Catherine's Gate, and he seemed excited when he spotted the Black Tower and then the White Tower.

Pavel parked the Bentley, and the four of us walked through Brasov proper, the vampire hunched over like an old man, his steps unsteady, even feeble at times. I offered a shoulder for him to lean on but he imperiously brushed me away. The streets were deserted, the curfew obviously being obeyed. As we walked the silent streets I began to hear the howling of dogs, at first one or two, and then they were joined by others until there was a canine chorus all about us. It seemed as if every cur in town had chosen this moment to cry at the night sky, and I could not help but wonder if the presence of the vampire was the cause of this unnerving choir.

Dracula gazed at the buildings as if he were a traveller who had been away for a long spell, which I guess was closer to the truth.

"Brasov has changed," he remarked. "Grown. A multitude of buildings. Which is only expected, yes? These lamps do not flicker."

He was staring at a streetlight and then the shaded lamp hanging over a storefront.

"They are electric," I explained and was well into a lecture on Edison, the lightbulb, and the results of the industrial revolution when I was suddenly interrupted.

"Halt!" Two SS soldiers stepped into the narrow alley to block our path. They were the same Germans who had intercepted me and the Van Helsings on my first trip to meet with the council.

Their weapons were pointed at us.

"Doctor," the Corporal addressed Van Helsing. "On your rounds again? Where is your pretty nurse? I have something only she can treat."

"My daughter, you mean?" Van Helsing asked, not hiding his indignation. "I would appreciate it, sir, if you would speak of her with respect. If you must speak of her at all."

"Watch your mouth or you'll be setting your own bones," the Sergeant snarled. "Who are these people? Papers."

Pavel handed his to the German. The soldier examined the document, then reached into a jacket pocket and produced a sheet of paper that he held up to read by the streetlight.

I paid little attention to the sentries and instead watched the vampire, who seemed to be fixated on the death's head symbol on the SS uniform. Thusly I was caught by surprise when the Corporal announced, "You are under arrest," and pointed his weapon at Pavel's face.

The Nazi Sergeant was regarding Dracula with some suspicion. He reached out and curiously fingered the vampire's shoddy attire, the remnants of the cape. A bit of cloth came away in the German's hand.

"And who might you be, beggar man? Identification," he demanded.

"I am called Wladislaus Drakwlya, Prince of Wallachi, Vlad the Third."

Both SS soldiers frowned. Dracula ignored them and turned to Van Helsing. "These, I assume, are our enemies."

"They are," Van Helsing confirmed.

"Then with your permission . . ." And with supernatural speed the vampire seized the Sergeant by the back of his head, yanked it to one side to bare the man's neck, and sank his suddenly elongated fangs into the soldier's throat.

And he fed.

The Corporal turned his gun away from Pavel and aimed the muzzle at Dracula. Before I or Van Helsing could react, the vampire moved. With his mouth still feeding on the Sergeant, Dracula's arm shot out and gripped the other German's helmet and crushed it, steel helmet and the skull inside cracking like an egg in a fist.

The Corporal's body went limp instantly but hung suspended by Dracula's extended arm, while the vampire's mouth remained sucking at the other soldier's neck. The demonstration of strength astounded me.

The soldier under Dracula's feeding tried to scream, but no words came. His face, turned red at first from the exertion of his struggle, paled and then went completely white with blue tinges. In mere seconds he was drained of blood.

Dracula's eyes became red around the amber, almost glowing, the veins in the whites of his eyes becoming engorged as he drank.

Finished with his feasting, Dracula snapped his victim's neck and dropped both bodies. So fast was this action that by the time Van Helsing, Pavel, and I had recovered from the spectacle, Dracula was already striding away. I paused in the narrow street and found myself fixated on the crushed helmet that lay upon the cobblestone. There were indentations in the grey steel, in the shape of a hand, the four fingers and thumb as clear as if pressed into mud, all in all a remarkable artefact.

The difference in the vampire was astonishing. He now walked tall, full of power.

"I feel much better now," he casually remarked, as if after an aperitif, which, I suppose, this was for him.

"What about the German?" I asked, hurrying to catch up. "Will he not become a vampire now?"

"Not if I kill them before the transformation," Dracula said. "It is a beautiful night, is it not? Late spring, if I am not misled."

I noticed that the man's mustache had gone from white to a dark grey, black hairs now intermingling with the white, and his hair had undergone the same change. There was also a flush to his cheeks, the waxen appearance now disappeared.

He paused to let Van Helsing and Pavel catch up; they had lingered behind to drag the bodies into a shadowed recess. I waited, still attempting to absorb what I had just witnessed. What manner of man was this, or what manner of creature was it in the semblance of a man?

I remembered a phrase oft repeated by my grandfather: "Hell has its price."

EXCERPTED FROM THE UNPUBLISHED NOVEL
THE DRAGON PRINCE AND I
by Lenore Van Muller

While her father was away confronting his ancient enemy, Lucille spent that entire night and the following day on edge, trying to read, needlessly cleaning. She had not the temperament to be a fastidious housekeeper, but her father, except for his stacks of reading material piled willy-nilly about the house, was an orderly man, so she only had to clean up after herself.

After the bout of tidiness, she went into the basement and tried to chat up the British Sergeant, but it was like attempting to converse with an organ grinder's monkey. He was in one of his fugue moments. Until she innocently asked about one of his devilish devices.

"This is a fuse?" she asked, prodding him into some kind of interaction. "It is longer than the usual blasting cap."

"Aye, that's 'cause 'tis a time fuse." Renfield's usual dim appearance took on a canny intelligence. "We call them 'time pencils,' or 'switch number ten.' Mind you, originally a German device, developed further by the Poles. Coded for the time delay: black, ten minutes; red, thirty; green, five and a half hours; yellow, twelve; and blue, twenty-four hours. Exact timing dependent on temperature."

He went on about the components of the fuses, "steel wire tension springs," "glass ampules of copper chloride," and how an "addition of glycerol, because of its higher viscosity and anti-freeze qualities" led to a considerable increase in delay time.

Then he went on to other devices. His lucid lecture was for the most part informative and interesting to Lucille, who was a woman who cherished learning anything new. But as Renfield's discourse wandered into the proper formulation of a foaming agent called Vulcastab, used to sabotage locomotive boilers, Lucille's mind began to wander back to her father and the perilous task he had set upon.

Her mind kept dwelling upon the more violent aspects of the vampire tales that she had heard as a child. Growing up, it seemed that every Rumanian adult and child could vividly recall some chilling story of the un-dead. The gory details that had once thrilled a little girl now became her most horrid nightmare.

She fretted and paced and tried to engage Renfield in a discussion of his past, his family, but his damaged brain was like an old radio; even when the tubes warmed up, he could dial in only the one frequency. After a while the channel faded and he was back to his mute self, interrupted by some occasional dirty doggerel. Lucille gave up and went back upstairs.

After a long bout of internal argument she finally succumbed to temptation. Going to her father's bedroom, she collected a small tangle of his white hair from his brush. She fingered the fine, silken hairs as she tied them into a bundle with one of his shoelaces. He would be upset later when he found one of his shoes disabled by her pilferage—if there was a later for him. Outside she plucked five blue monkshoods from the garden. Her mother had planted them, hopefully giving them more power.

In the kitchen she created a salt circle on the table. Stripping the leaves from the monkshood stem and decapitating the flowers, she cut the stems to length and built a five-pointed star within the salt circle. The flower petals were piled in the centre of this pentangle and the bundle of hair placed upon the blue bed.

Pricking her finger with the point of a paring knife she let a drop of blood fall into each of the five points of the star. The protection spell was one she had learned in Paris from a warlock under the tutelage of Maria de Naglowska, a renowned Luciferian. But before she uttered a word, she was reminded of the spell that she had cast for her father at the Black Church—and the omission of the rest of the men in the Mayor's office and the consequences of that omission.

Hurrying to the basement she searched the Englishman's cot for hairs left behind, and was dismayed to find only three meager tendrils. Not enough, she thought, to have any power over the individual. Then she remembered the wound on his knee and rushed back outside to the refuse barrel. The contents had not been burned yet and she rummaged through the debris until she found a discarded bandage that her father had removed. She was delighted to see that there remained a brown patch of blood on the gauze.

Taking this into the house she cut a small swath of the blooded cloth and laid it carefully alongside the tuft of her father's hair. She was stymied over what to do about protecting Pavel and finally scrapped the clot that had formed on her cut finger and used a bit more of her blood to write Pavel's real name on a scrap of paper. It would have to do. This joined the tokens of her father and the English boy.

She began the spell, muttering it in Latin and French for insurance, three times for each language, and at the end setting fire to the hair, blood, and paper. Suddenly the monkshood petals rose into the air of their own volition, swirled a moment, and dashed toward the ceiling in a violet cloud that disappeared before hitting the rafters. The spell done, she gathered up the remaining components, folded them into a sheet of clean paper, and carried it outside to bury under a yew tree.

Now all she could do was wait. Wait and fret.

She spent the rest of the night alternating between pacing and fitful sleep. She fed the Sergeant and tried to make some order of the stacks of periodicals and books strewn about the house. Dawn came, and her worry now put her in a state of numb desperation, sitting in her father's favorite chair. As she waited for the phone to ring, she took some comfort in her father's familiar smells still held in the chair's leather.

It wasn't until hours later that the phone did finally ring. She was suddenly hesitant to answer, afraid to face the possible loss of her dear father.

But when Pavel told her that everyone was well and that the vampire had been revived, she was speechless. She could hear the hesitation, even dread, in Pavel's voice, but she did not care. The only thing of importance was that her father had survived. Pavel passed on her father's request for an immediate meeting of the partisan leadership that evening. Happier now with something to busy herself, she made a few phone calls and went about the preparations for the trip into Brasov. She wanted to get there before dark fell and the curfew was in effect.

Travel at night would be difficult without her father's dispensation papers, and the problem was magnified by the presence of the daft Renfield. She did not want to leave him by himself. The German raids on homes had lately become more frequent and always unannounced. She would hate for them to come across the addled man while she was away. He would be caught for what he was, a spy, and the consequences for him, not to mention the Van Helsings, would be dire. There was no one to call to baby-sit him.

The three Marx Brothers, as she called them—Horea, Closca, and Crisan—were on a sabotage mission outside Ploesti, coordinating a plot to contaminate the axle boxes of tanker cars servicing the oil fields. Harker had introduced them to a method of mixing carborundum powder into the axle grease, forcing the bearings to seize up and, therefore, totally disabling the trains. No, she would have to take Renfield with her.

Taking him upstairs, Lucille stuffed one of his cheeks with a wad of cotton until it puffed out like he was bee stung. Then she wrapped one of her scarves under the jaw and tied it at the crown of his head. A floppy hat hid his skull bandage. The man looked ludicrous, but she knew from experience that silly and weak was better than appearing suspicious.

They walked toward Brasov, soon hitching a ride with a farmer hauling a load of goats to the butcher. Approaching a German roadblock, Lucille's hand slid into her coat pocket, the inside sliced away to allow access to the Luger stuffed through her waistband.

The roadblock was perfunctory, Lucille blathering about taking her "cousin" to the dentist for the emergency removal of an infected tooth. Of course Renfield chose that moment to render to the guards a bawdy serenade, but all that was heard out of his cotton-packed mouth was muffled noise, and the SS ignored him, taking his singing for pain-induced moans.

Brasov seemed different now. Maybe it was the swastikas festooned all about, businesses declaring their allegiances, if not in heart then for protection and lucre. She felt a foreigner in her hometown.

They were early, so she stopped at the Catholic church a few blocks from Mihaly's. There she and Renfield supped with Father Petrescu in his office. The old priest was a garrulous sort. Everyone knew that what he heard in the confession box often leaked into his conversation. The local Catholics frowned on his lack of circumspection. But some of the German soldiers were Catholic, despite the Nazi taboo against worship of anything but Herr Hitler, thusly the priest had become a receptacle for all sorts of intelligence. Lucille hoped to glean information about what was happening in the castle and among the SS occupiers.

From what Petrescu had heard, the Germans had increased the number of prisoners in the castle and there was no room left.

"The conditions are terrible," Petrescu lamented. "The poor people are packed together like potatoes in a bag. So crowded are they that some must sleep standing. Whole families of gypsies and Jews have been imprisoned. Children, women, living in their own filth. It is . . . a sin."

"But I heard from a farmer just tonight that they are still rounding up people every day," Lucille said. "Where are they going to put them all?"

Lucille let the talk wander into local gossip, the latest concerning who might be the father to poor Ecaterina's baby. Her husband had been conscripted into the Rumanian Army and stationed on the Yugoslavian border for over a year without leave. The betting was all over the place. Ecaterina had been in possession of a woman's body since the age of thirteen and had proudly displayed this gift from God to a wide variety of very interested fellows before and after her marriage.

Father Petrescu licked his lips and stroked his nose as he recounted Ecaterina's exploits, and Lucille pondered what Jung would make of the priest's physical tics.

At one point in the meal Renfield, who had been mute to this point despite the removal of the cotton wadding to facilitate his eating, burst into song.

"The object of my affection
makes my erection
turn from pink to rosy red.
Every time she touches the head
it points the way to bed."

The priest, who was fluent in English, was flabbergasted. Renfield abruptly ceased his singing as quickly as he had begun. Lucille went on eating as if nothing had occurred, and soon the priest was back to drink and the contemplation of Ecaterina's love life.

The clock on the wall declared with a mellow bonging that it was near time for her partisan meeting. Lucille excused herself and Renfield, cutting short any further scandalmongering. She knew that the priest was dismayed; the old Father could and would gossip until the candles guttered.

Besides, Lucille was in a hurry. During the whole scurrilous monologue her mind was elsewhere, fretting about her own father. Every time she caught a glance of the silver crucifix hanging from Petrescu's neck, her thoughts went to the vampire legends and the accompanying banes: garlic, wild rose, hawthorn, mustard seeds, crosses, and holy water. Her father had left with none of them.

She stuffed Renfield's cheek with the still-damp cotton wad. Soaked with saliva, it had shrunk, so she filled the lack with her handkerchief. He was as compliant as a child during this folderol, allowing her to re-tie the scarf. She made their good-byes, the priest adding his usual plaintive but vain request to see the Van Helsings at the next Sunday service.

Because of the curfew they encountered no one on the walk to Mihaly's and, with a few changes of direction, avoided the German patrols. The tailor escorted them through the hidden entrance and down into the basement, where Anka was already waiting.

Lucille removed the cotton and handkerchief from Renfield's mouth, unknotted the scarf. Renfield grinned at Anka like an idiot and began to sing.

"Let me ball you sweetheart,
I'm in bed with you.
Let me hear you whisper
That it's time to screw."

Anka was dumbfounded and turned to Lucille for an explanation.

"He has a brain injury." Lucille lifted Renfield's bandage to show the recent red scar where her father had stitched his scalp back into place.

Anka nodded. "My brother was kicked by a horse when he was eleven years old. Kicked in the forehead. Teach you to never linger behind a beast that kicks. Never tasted again. Nor smelled anything. Could not tell sweet from sour, spices had no effect. Couldn't figure numbers, either. But has eight children, ninth on the way."

"Obviously it did not hinder any performance below the neck," Lucille commented.

"To his wife's delight." Both women laughed.

Renfield discovered the cache of land mines in the corner and went after them with the delight of a child given an alarm clock to take apart.

Anka made tea on a hot plate set up for that purpose. The two women traded what intelligence on the Germans they had gathered since the last meeting. Lucille kept glancing at the stairs, waiting for her father to step into view at any moment. Anka noticed Lucille's preoccupation and the apprehension that accompanied that watchful look.

"I told him not to go," Anka said. "It is a wrong thing to do."

Finally Lucille heard heavy footsteps above their heads, the squeal of hinges as the concealed door was opened. Her attention was riveted on the old, worn, wooden stairs. But it was only Farkas descending. He greeted the women, and Anka briefed him on Renfield, who decided to serenade them.

"My bonnie lies over the ocean.
My bonnie lies over the sea.
My father lies over my mother,
And that's how I came to be."

Lucille was too concerned about her father to pay notice to Renfield's duncery. Recently she had become acutely aware of the old man's age and that she might not have many more years with him.

Not that he was fragile at all. He was as robust and intellectually vigorous as he had ever been. But she had, as her father's nurse, witnessed a sudden turn to illness by many of his elderly patients. One day they were out pounding dust from a rug on the line, the next morning in bed after a fall from which they never recovered. So, lately she kept an eye on him, alert to every cough, pain, or tic of his daily movements—at times, much to his annoyance.

And the dangerous work in which they engaged only made things worse for her. He insisted on leading some raids himself and participated much more than was appropriate for one of his age or standing. That the same could be said of Lucille was shrugged off her young shoulders. "Like father, like daughter" was never more true.

More footsteps were heard over their heads. Lucille's heart leapt at the sound. Farkas slid a hand down to the short-barrelled shotgun he carried by a strap slung under his long coat. The incessant SS raids had put everyone on edge. So far the leadership cell had not been penetrated, but Reikel and his interrogators were climbing the partisan vine, linking one cell to another, arresting them as they filled in the puzzle.

Lucille reached for her Luger. Once again the secret door at the top of the stairs opened. Lucille took a deep breath and then watched her father's worn shoes descend the steps. She rushed forward to embrace him. They being not a physically demonstrative family, her father was surprised at her touching display, but hugged her back with equal enthusiasm.

"You're safe," she whispered.

Lucille was so caught up in the reunion that she took little notice of Pavel or the Englishman's entrance.

But the next man to step into the basement drew her attention, as he did everyone else. They all were suddenly in thrall of his presence. Even Renfield discarded his lethal toys to stare.

The first thing she noticed was his posture. He was a tall man, three or four inches over six feet, and the top of his head was near brushing the ceiling beams. But he neither ducked nor bent as Harker, not nearly the same height, often did. He walked the room upright as if daring anything to have the temerity to knock him in the skull.

He surveyed the room, taking in everything and everyone with curious amber eyes. He seemed to have an avid interest in all that was around him, like a child in a museum. Finally his eyes fixed on Lucille and she felt a trembling begin in her chest that flowed out to her hands and knees. She backed into one of the support posts and pressed her shoulders into the wood, trying to steady herself. Four years ago Lucille had been in the States visiting the Grand Canyon with an actress friend, Daphne, who was sharing her bed with a young man who had a summer job at the Hoover Dam. The place had just opened, and they took the art deco elevator down into the concrete depths.

Lucille was already awestruck by the massive concrete edifice, but when they entered the cavernous room containing the megalithic turbines and transformers she felt the hairs on her arms rise, the down on the back of her neck tingle. The room thrummed with a life of its own, and she could feel the presence of the immense power lying in wait, the vast force being kept at bay, an energy that could light—or destroy—an entire city.

This was what she felt when Dracula entered that basement, including the risen hair, as did the others. Farkas stumbled back until a chair stopped his retreat. Anka crossed herself and made the sign of the *mano cornuto*, or horned one.

Renfield stood, the mines forgotten, his mouth agape, mesmerised, eyes fixated on the vampire. He muttered one word: "Master."

"You did it." Anka glared at Van Helsing. "You had to do it." She spat out the words.

Farkas dug into his shirt and pulled out a tiny gold cross that hung around his neck by a thin gold chain. He brandished the small crucifix at Dracula, who merely bestowed a benign smile upon the man. It only confirmed Lucille's concept of the absurdity of the human animal.

She had seen the same religious conversion repeatedly on the battlefield, as many of her partisan mates were Communists. Lying there, bleeding, some dying, they all seemed to fall into the same fearful state, believing that if Stalin could not save them then maybe the god they had rejected so fiercely would. Sad to say, both usually failed the doomed men.

"This is Farkas, Anka, and Sergeant Renfield, another Englishman," her father introduced everyone. "Count Dracula."

"Prince," Dracula corrected, and made a slight, formal bow. At this Renfield moved forward with an alacrity that Lucille had never seen, startling everyone, and threw himself at the vampire's feet.

"Master," Renfield whispered in what could only be said was reverence. Harker pried the man off the floor and sat him in a corner where the Sergeant eyed Dracula's every move.

"This is an abomination," Anka said with a harsh tone.

"Desperate diseases require desperate remedies," Van Helsing told her. "He has agreed to fight for us."

"No." Anka shook her head. "Never."

"None of my people will fight alongside this . . . repulsive demon," Farkas swore.

"Watch your tongue," Dracula warned and stepped toward Farkas, who leapt away. "You are a fortunate man. I swore to Doctor Van Helsing that I would not harm any of his allies. But that does not give you the freedom to treat me with disrespect."

"Everyone, please." Van Helsing raised his hands for some amity. "We all agree that we need to do something to abet our cause. Does anyone have an alternative?"

No one spoke. Lucille smiled and filled the silence. "Can we just put these old superstitions aside? We need all the help we can find."

She had been scrutinising the vampire, curious, comparing what she saw before her with the image from the sensational accounts she had heard as a child. She was confounded by the mustache. Bela Lugosi was clean-shaven. And this one did not skulk as the actor had, but held himself in a stately, regal manner.

He became aware of her inspection and she saw that he was suddenly self-conscious about the state of his garments. His knee poked through a rent in his trousers, the once-white shirt was discoloured by a meandering splotch of green-black mould, and his dinner jacket was barely hanging together by a few strained threads.

Lucille caught a glimpse of his discomfiture, a fleeting hint of his embarrassment that he quickly covered with an imperious nonchalance. She found the reflex humanised him, a peek at the mortal who once resided inside.

The duality made him unexpectedly attractive.

Dracula was in turn examining Lucille. In his eyes she was beautiful, none of the maidenly reticence that he remembered of most women.

Van Helsing saw the silent interaction between the two. "So sorry. My manners. This is my daughter, Lucille."

Dracula frowned at the Professor. "Your daughter?" He turned back to the young woman, perusing her features. "Ah, yes, I see the resemblance, the intelligence in the eyes."

She smiled at him, accepting the compliment.

"May we return to the discussion at hand?" Anka demanded. "Without the presence of . . . this." She turned a cold eye to Dracula. Lucille stepped forward, between the vampire and Anka, staring down the old woman.

"Do that," Lucille said. "Meanwhile I'll take the gentleman upstairs and put him in some decent clothes."

"That would be much appreciated." Dracula smiled at her in thanks. "If I walk around in these rags much longer I might find myself in a state of dishabille. It might shock your delicate sensibilities."

"I doubt there are any to shock, sir," Lucille replied.

Van Helsing was acutely aware that there was something happening between the two and was immediately afraid for his willful daughter. Harker was also aware of the subtle signals the pair was sending. But both men had more important matters on their hands and turned to deal with the recalcitrant partisans.

"Come with me." Lucille started toward the stairs. "I'm sure Mihaly has something that will fit."

Lucille walked up the stairs and Dracula followed her. Renfield rushed to join them and once again Harker had to restrain his demented Sergeant.

Dracula entered with her into the haberdashery. The proprietor and his son were absent and, from the clatter of cutlery and dishes she could hear from the floor above, Lucille presumed that the family was at their supper.

"I'm afraid that I have no means to pay at this moment," Dracula said.

"My father has an account," Lucille said. "Credit, actually—he removed a rather large gallstone from the owner two winters back."

Dracula tried to remove his jacket, but the cloth was in such a sad state that slipping out of the sleeves was near impossible and he was left with nothing to do but tear it off.

Lucy sorted through the trousers first, trying to appear casual.

"Count Dracula . . ." she mused. "I've heard stories about you."

"Not Count," Dracula corrected her. "Voivode, or Prince in English, of Wallachia, three times, if I may vaunt. Or my proper name, Wladislaus Drakwlya, named after my father and grandfather. My mother was Princess Cneajna of Moldavia. You may call me Vlad. Or as my intimates once did, Val."

She handed him a couple of pairs of trousers and began to sort through the shirts.

"Your father told you about me?" he asked.

"No." Lucille shook her head. "He never spoke of you. I had to find out things on my own."

He stripped off the rag that was a shirt and let it drop to the floor. Lucille noted some red stains on the tattered cloth. Could that be blood?

She held a new shirt to his naked chest, checking for size. His skin was blue-white. His physique was lean, but he was well-formed, muscled.

"This looks about right," she said. "Is it true that you are immortal? That you cannot die?"

"With some stipulations," Dracula replied. "I think your father proved that."

Their eyes met. Lucille had to pull herself away. There was something about his proximity that made her feel vulnerable, not in control. She prided herself on her control.

For something to occupy herself, she rummaged for socks. Checking his feet, she saw that his shoes were coming apart, the sole of one flapping like a dog's tongue.

When she turned back, he was wearing a pair of the trousers and slipping the shirt on.

"Check the shoes." Lucille pointed. "They're over there. Not much of a selection, but . . ."

She watched him walk over. The pants fit him pretty well, the shirt, too. She had dressed a few men in her time.

"You'll need a coat." Her hand played contemplatively among the racks. "Here's a nice camel hair."

Dracula eyed her choice, shook his head.

"I prefer something more . . . a cloak perhaps."

"Cloak?"

He found one at the end of the rack, black with a short opera cape.

"A cape?" She squinted at the garment. "More suitable for the opera, I think. A bit old-fashioned, is what I'm trying to say."

"I am old, thus my fashion would be much the same. Would it not?" Dracula donned the cape, regarded the result in the mirror, nodded with approval.

"This will do nicely," he said. "I will repay your father. I have hidden some treasures."

Lucille frowned at his reflection.

"You can . . . be seen in the mirror."

"Of course. Why should I not?"

"There are stories that you cannot be reflected in a mirror."

"Ah. Superstition." He emitted a slight laugh. "And how would that operate, scientifically?"

"I don't know. Tales, you know."

"Well, I cannot defy the laws of physics." He laughed again, then put himself directly in front of her. "But, this I can do."

He raised his hand and waved the open palm inches from her face, then put the full power of his own eyes upon hers.

"Look now," he whispered. The voice came to her as if from a great distance. "You cannot see me."

She turned to the mirror. And even though Dracula was standing beside her, she saw only her own reflection in the glass.

"What did you do to me?" Lucille cried with some alarm.

The vampire made another pass with his hand and he immediately reappeared in the mirror.

She turned to face him, her anger evident.

"You bastard. Don't you ever play with my mind. Don't ever."

"I am sorry. It was only meant as a demonstration . . . to answer your question . . . I am sorry."

Dracula was confused. Not at her response, but his own apology. Why did he feel the need to defend himself to this woman, this human? She had just made a vulgar imprecation that in a previous time would have resulted in a duel—if she had been a man. Which she was most decidedly not.

They stared at each other for a moment that seemed for Lucille to stretch time. She stepped closer to him. They were inches apart. She reached out a hand to his face, a desire to touch him, to make physical contact, a need that overwhelmed her.

Was this another of his mesmerising tricks? She didn't care. He just stood there, waiting, not resisting, and her fingers trembled before his cheek.

"We have come to an arrangement." It was her father.

She and Dracula both took a step back from each other, like children caught in some deviltry.

"The Englishman has presented a most perspicacious plan," Van Helsing said.

Young Harker stood behind him beaming at Lucille.

She ignored the boy and turned to her father, who obviously knew he had interrupted something between his daughter and the Prince and was happy for it.

"You can fight for us," he said. "For the moment. The others are, shall we say, reticent. But you will prove yourself, I know."

Farkas, Pavel, and Anka appeared behind him. Anka stepped forward, the short, stout woman pushing her way through the men like a tank breaching a wall.

"The first time you attack one of my people you will be destroyed," she addressed Dracula.

"You want him to help us, but you threaten him?" Lucille asked defiantly. But Dracula laid a hand on her shoulder. She felt the coolness of his flesh as one finger touched her neck.

"You do not have to defend me," he told her and faced the others. "I deserve whatever opinion they have of me. And more. I thank you all for the opportunity to serve my country and my people again."

He made that little bow and in doing so saw his bare feet poking out from under his trouser cuffs. He wiggled his toes, which Lucille found endearing.

"I need shoes," he said. "And then we go to war."

FROM THE WAR JOURNAL OF
J. HARKER

(transcribed from shorthand)

When Lucy left the meeting and took the vampire upstairs to outfit him in a new wardrobe, I was torn between accompanying them or staying to plead my case. I needed the partisans to act, to continue the fight. Duty won out.

I monitored the discussion among the partisans, looking for an opportunity to interject my carefully rehearsed speech. I had been putting my case in order ever since the last meeting, when the decision had been made to cease insurgent activities.

Anka and Farkas were still espousing vehement declarations that they would not fight alongside the vampire.

"You have not stated your position in regards to the Count, Pavel," Van Helsing addressed the man.

"In *Das Kapital*," Pavel began, "Karl Marx uses the vampire as a metaphor for capitalism. The exploitation of labour is akin to draining the blood of civilisation."

That gave us all pause, and in the midst of everyone's puzzlement I used the silence to speak.

"I think I have a solution to both of our problems," I said. "The danger of incurring reprisals for any partisan acts in and around Brasov—and your apparent antipathy to the Count. There is another possible course you could take." Every face turned toward me. I did not want to muck this up.

It was at times like this that I cursed my looks. It is an unfortunate statement of fact that I appear ten years younger than I am. Well, maybe five. It is not unusual for me to be asked at pubs for some kind of verification that I am of age, and any encounter with a woman, well . . . 'Struth! If I had a tuppence for every time some comely woman had asked me, "How old are you, dearie?" I would be as rich as Farouk.

"You could take your resistance efforts to another part of Rumania; leave the Brasov province undisturbed until the Germans leave."

Van Helsing looked at me with what I could only call respect. I continued, "Our goal, yours and mine, is to make life difficult for the enemy, correct? Does that have to be only in Brasov? We could target the oil fields in Ploesti or interrupt the chromium transports from Turkey, which are of immense importance to the Rumanian and German war machine. There is much mischief to be had in other areas of your country."

There was a moment of quiet as they all weighed my proposal. I held my breath, not only because of the pall of smoke that hung in the air like a diaphanous dirigible.

"That seems to be a perfect alternative." Van Helsing pursed his lips and nodded. "Kudos to our British ally."

Even Anka was responding with what I perceived as acute interest. She nodded, frowning in contemplation.

"And we could take the vampire with us," I pressed. "He can thusly prove his worthiness—or not. And you will not have to accommodate his presence, if that is an anathema to you."

To my surprise they responded affirmatively. I could barely pay attention to the discussion among them as a little man inside my head ran about in delirious circles shouting, "I did it! I did it!" I was putting a match to the fire Churchill wished to light in this part of Europe. Despite my bungled performance so far, I was beginning to render my mission and fulfill the promise that Gubbins had seen in that artless boy at the St. James Club. I could not wait to relay my triumph to HQ. Of course I had no transmitter, and that realisation brought me back to the conversation.

The debate continued as they parsed procedural, tactical, and logistical concerns. I withheld comment, deciding my part had been accomplished and not to push my luck. To be honest, I was fearful of getting rather outside my brackets.

During their discussion my mind once more returned to what might be happening on the floor above me, Lucy and the vampire. Doing what?

Finally a consensus was agreed upon. Anka would continue to monitor Reikel and the German occupiers (as they had come to be known). Farkas and Pavel would spread the word among the local partisan cells to stand down momentarily, but to keep their members in readiness.

Lucy and I were going to take the sabotage efforts south, her father to stay in Brasov and hold the local Resistance together as best he could. When I heard the pronouncement pairing me with the fair Lucille, my mind tumbled into a mental maelstrom, drowning in an undercurrent of Paphian delight.

I was in a turmoil, the thrill of finally embarking upon a war mission, to take the first step toward my destiny, to fulfill my commission, to engage the war personally. And to do so with Lucy, my beloved. I had dismissed the brief encounter she had with the vampire at Mihaly's. When I saw them together, to be honest I did envy the solicitude she displayed to him. But I pushed aside my jealousy—it is true that is what I felt—and calmed myself with the obvious fact that there was no possibility that an ancient creature such as he and a vibrant young woman such as dear Lucy could ever find any commonality together, much less share the bond that Lucy and I had found. She has made a commitment to me, carnal though it may be, that will only grow in affection. I look forward to our future as I have anticipated few things in my life. I am impatient, hungry for the adventure to begin.

I thought about going upstairs as soon as we returned to the Van Helsing residence, to knock upon her door and enter that den of delight once more. I imagined her sleepy smile, a welcoming kiss. and the warm invite of her bed, the cozy comfort under the covers, and the erotic entwining of naked flesh.

But I held that impulse in check. I did not want to be rude or thought impetuous, maybe even desperate. And there was the possibility of putting a match to the tinderbox that is Lucy's temper. She was an irascible sort, like most women, of unpredictable and tempestuous nature. A minefield of emotions that I, at the moment, dared not venture into for fear of losing an appendage. Any appendage, if you know what I mean.

EXCERPTED FROM THE UNPUBLISHED NOVEL
THE DRAGON PRINCE AND I by Lenore Van Muller

After the meeting at Mihaly's, the cell broke up and everyone went their separate ways, each exiting at carefully timed intervals.

Harker and Renfield accompanied Anka. She had asked the British agent to reconnoitre and acquaint himself with the Bran Castle, since it was now serving as SS headquarters. Plus she had some papers taken from a Rumanian Army dispatch rider for him to inspect and determine if they would be of any value to his superiors.

Harker decided to take Renfield with him, but the Sergeant, out of character, resisted. He had to be physically led away from Dracula, with whom he seemed to have an extreme fascination. Harker was also apparently disappointed at abandoning the vampire and Lucille, but acceded like the good soldier he was.

Lucille left with her father and Dracula. She felt a tumultuous excitement blossom within her as she watched the vampire stride ahead of her with a cat-like grace. She did not analyze this feeling, rather indulged in it, as she had not felt this way since her adolescent days of girlish crushes on movie stars. She remembered her collection of postcards, giddily swooning over Victor Vina and Jean Angelo.

"You spoke of changes," Dracula addressed Lucille's father. "But you did not apprise me of the shift from the patriarchal to a matriarchal rule."

"I do not perceive your meaning, sir," her father said.

"When did the female gender overthrow the rule of men?" Dracula asked.

"That, I assure you, has not occurred," Lucille interjected. "Not yet, at least."

"Then why is that shrew allowed to command?" Dracula looked to her and her father for an answer. "War is the provenance of men."

"A man's business?" Lucille eyed the vampire, her brow furrowing. "The Resistance is everybody's business."

"Anka is an able and passionate partisan. She is often loud, brash, and obstinate but more than capable," her father replied.

"More capable than you?" Dracula asked.

"She has the trust of the local people," Van Helsing said. "I have lived here for near half a century and they still refer to me as 'the Dutchman,' 'the foreigner.' Anka is one of their own. Her family has resided in this valley for untold generations. She is one of them. I am not."

"Still, war is not for the female. Their sensibilities are not suited to the harsh realities of combat."

"I would disagree," Lucille said. "In fact, I think you have a lot to learn about modern women."

"I fear that I have offended you," Dracula said to her. "I am eager to learn anything you can teach me. But the biological imperatives are not to be denied."

Lucille decided to allow the argument to die for now. She did not want to annoy the vampire. Why, she did not know.

As they trod the empty streets, Dracula paused at a spot where the pavement glistened, having recently been splashed with water.

Dracula exchanged a look with the Professor.

"I had Mihaly send some of our people to clean up," Van Helsing remarked. "And take away the bodies. They will disappear."

"This ground has been fought over for centuries," Dracula said. "By the Wallachians, the Saxon, the Turk. There is hardly a foot of soil in all this region that has not been enriched by the blood of men, patriot and invader." He shook his head and they continued on to their car, which was muddied from the previous day's excursion.

Lucille drove, her father on the seat next to her, as he described the brief confrontation with the two Nazis and their dispatchment. Dracula rode in the back with the privileged air of a potentate. She stole a glance into the rearview mirror and Dracula caught her peeking. He made an exaggerated version of the gesture he used to hypnotise her and smiled playfully.

Lucille could not help smiling. He was so different from the personage portrayed in The Book, the movies, the folktales. She wanted to know more about him.

"The women in your castle, were they your wives?" she asked.

"The women in my castle . . . ?" Dracula frowned. "You heard about these women where?"

"The book," Lucille told him.

"The book . . . what book is this?" he asked.

"There is a novel, well, I'm not sure if it is fiction or . . ." she stumbled.

Her father saved her. "There is a book that takes liberties with the story of our encounter in England, Harker's experiences in this country, and melds them with some fantastical rubbish," her father explained. "Written by a vaudevillian."

"It would be interesting to compare your version of the events with those in the book," Lucille offered. "And yours," she said to the vampire's reflection in the mirror.

"I cannot conceive of a more useless endeavour than comparing fiction with what may or may not have happened almost fifty years ago," Van Helsing said. "Let us speak of it no more."

The last was directed at Lucille. She nodded, but her father knew that the subject was not closed. His daughter was tenacious and not easily swayed from anything that piqued her interest. And Dracula, he had noticed, had ignited her curiosity. It worried him. No, it frightened him.

She examined the vampire's face. It was a strong one, no doubt, aquiline, a lofty forehead, eyebrows thick, his hair bushy, curls in profusion, a rather cruel-looking mouth, red lips, broad chin, and an extraordinary pallor. There was an intelligence in those amber eyes that reduced her general feeling of superiority over most men. The mustache seemed old-fashioned but enhanced his aura of masculinity. There was no evidence of the oily, smarmy air seen in the Lugosi performance.

His hands surprised her. Not the hands described in the novel, not coarse or broad, with squat fingers, but long, artistic fingers as those of a pianist she had once met. Nor were the fingernails long and cut to sharp points, hair supposedly growing in the palms.

And although she had read that his breath was rank with the emanation of carrion, she had caught no such odour when they had been so close at the tailor's.

In fact, as she now watched his chest, having some experience as her father's nurse, Lucille was astounded to observe that he seemed not to breathe at all. What did she expect? she scolded herself. He was, after all, dead, was he not?

Once they arrived at the house, the three of them settled themselves in her father's library. Dracula wandered the shelves, his long white fingers trailing across the spines of the books as if he were caressing the ribs of a beautiful woman. Lucille went to the kitchen and prepared a plate of meats and cheeses. She sliced some dark bread and brought a bottle of wine and three glasses.

She set the plate on the low table centred between three wingback chairs and a leather chaise lounge. Taking her seat on the chaise, she nibbled and watched Dracula take one of the chairs and page through an anatomy text. Her father sat and watched the vampire as he would a feral dog.

"Wine?" Lucille offered. "There is chicken, ham, some fine cheese from Luxemburg, a local white cheddar."

"I do not sup, thank you." Dracula waved the offer away.

She saw her father was staring at the floor, and he bent to pluck a monkshood petal from the carpet. Frowning at it, he turned his gaze to Lucille and seemed to be ready to ask a question. She purposely interrupted the incipient inquiry.

"Wine, Father?"

She poured a glass for him as he made himself a sandwich, his thought lost to the ethers. Lucille watched the two men, not sure what she was expecting. Maybe an explanation of what had occurred between the two of them, an evaluation of the legend versus the actual events, some revelation of the truth behind the myth.

Instead it became an elucidation of what had transpired since Dracula had been "away." "Sleeping" was her father's term.

The Professor began with the Boer War, the Spanish-American War, and the unraveling of the Ottoman Empire, which pleased the former Prince of Wallachia.

Lucille interrupted with a short discourse on the theory of social Darwinism and the spread of democracies.

"The masses ruling themselves." Dracula shook his head. "It will never last. The masses are ignorant."

"But we are educating the masses," Lucille objected.

"Education does not make a man intelligent," Dracula said. "Ignorance, willful ignorance, and mental laziness are hallmarks of the masses. They need leaders. They cry out for leaders and do nothing by consensus without them."

Van Helsing used this moment to describe the pervasiveness of mass production and its impact on Europe and the United States. He spoke of the changes the automobile had made on society, the promise of heavier-than-air flight.

Dracula seemed most surprised by the telegraph and telephone, especially the trans-Atlantic cable—that one could speak to another hundreds if not thousands of kilometres away instantaneously or near that.

Lucille broke in to extol the potential of the cinema and radio; this led to her enthusiastic gush about the phonograph and recorded music. She leapt up to demonstrate, but her father stopped her with a hand.

"It is a frivolity," Van Helsing said. "Some other time."

And in his most professorial tone, her father launched into an exposition of the Great War: the poison gas attacks, machine guns, artillery, tanks, submarine predation, and casualties into the millions, nearly seven hundred thousand dead at Verdun alone, the participation of the United States tipping the balance, resulting in an uneasy and ultimately unsuccessful peace.

Dracula listened with avid curiosity and enthrallment, asking piquant questions.

He followed the description of the Russian Revolution, but dismissed their socialistic aims with even more vehemence than his opinion of democracy. "The Russians worship their Czars as they do their icons," he said. "They seek a ruthless, strong leader the way bees need a queen."

"Another biological imperative at work?" Lucille smiled to take some of the bite out of the remark.

Her father rhapsodised about Einstein and tried to explain the accomplishments of this genius, but Dracula became mired in the philosophical implications. He finally called a halt to the discussion. "This is too arcane for my medieval mind. You must give me some books to supplement my shortcomings."

Van Helsing agreed and moved on to the worldwide Depression, how Germany rose out of the ashes of the First World War, Hitler and his expansionism, the other fascist movements, Spain, Italy, and the simultaneous spread of Japanese imperialism into China.

"War. War again and again. Humankind does not change," the vampire mused. "The efficiency of their war machines may, but the basic instinct to kill each other for causes great or small never ceases to amaze me."

"You killed more than a few yourself," Lucille ventured.

"As a monarch, yes. Because I realised something that your Kaiser, your Hitler, Mussolini, emperor, and premier know. Oftentimes the only way to deliver a message that everyone understands is to pile the bodies up so high that all can see." Dracula shrugged, such a human gesture that it unsettled Lucille.

She looked away from him and noticed that the dawn light was beginning to climb the opposite wall.

"Oh my God, it's morning," she cried.

"You must get some sleep, Lucille," her father said, hoping to put some distance between his daughter and the vampire.

Lucille turned in concern to Dracula. "Don't you have to climb into . . . a coffin or something?"

"No, no." Dracula smiled. "But a room where I can pull the drapes to block the light would be greatly appreciated."

"We can accommodate that," Van Helsing replied. "The guest room will suffice, will it not, dear?" Lucille nodded in assent.

"And maybe I could partake of your library?" Dracula asked. "To pass the time. Books have always been amiable companions. They have given me many hours of pleasure."

"Of course." Van Helsing smiled. He was proud of his collection, not unduly, and led Dracula to the shelves.

"Let's see . . . maybe we should start with *Mein Kampf*. That would inform you about our enemy."

"Freud!" Lucille exclaimed as she found the volume and passed it to the vampire. "In order to really know the self-hating martinet."

"And some Shaw, for entertainment," her father added and passed the book to Dracula.

"H. G. Wells, then," his daughter countered. "And Oscar Wilde! You will love Wilde." She excitedly searched for and found a collection of his plays in the stacks.

"Well, some Conrad, Chekhov, Tagore. Proust?" Van Helsing was snatching books from the shelves with the same enthusiasm as his daughter.

"Not yet," Lucille said. "But Joyce, certainly."

"Ah! Pirandello!"

"Ibanez!"

"Karel Capek!"

"F. Scott Fitzgerald!"

"Remarque!"

"Kafka!"

"Graves!" her father shot back. *"Fisher's History!"*

"Joyce!"

"You already pulled Joyce, dear," her father noted and they both faced each other, glanced at Dracula, who had a stack of books in his hands that reached his chin. They broke into laughter and the vampire joined them.

The sight of the legendary creature laughing like a schoolboy at a classroom joke caused Lucille to gape at him in astonishment.

"Well, I think we have suitably armed you with enough reading material for a few fortnights, much less the day," Van Helsing said. "Lucille, if you will show our guest his room. I must retire. As amusing and convivial the night has been, my old body does not have the stamina it once did." And he walked to the door. "I bid you good night, rather, good day." And he exited the library.

Lucille watched him leave, his shoulders bent, his fatigue evident. She regretted keeping him up so long. But she would not have traded this night for any other in her life.

"Come this way," she told Dracula and led him to the guest bedroom upstairs. He had to duck beneath a shaft of sunlight beaming through the stairwell window. Lucille entered the bedroom first and closed the curtains while he waited in the hall.

"You can come in now," she said, turning on the bedside lamp. "Maybe tonight we can talk. Just you and me. Not a history lesson but . . . more personal."

"I shall look forward to it," Dracula whispered. His accent gave his words a quality not unlike a cat's purr.

They stood there for a few seconds, inches apart. And Lucille confirmed her earlier assumption. He did not breathe. His chest neither rose nor fell, his nostrils did not flare, and she felt no breath from his mouth.

The realisation so disturbed her that she involuntarily stepped away, then fled the room, closing the door behind her.

She found her father waiting for her in the hall.

"I know you are not of an age to need or take advice from an old man . . ." he began.

"I have always respected your advice, Father," she told him in all sincerity. "Whether I take it or not is another matter entirely."

He smiled ruefully.

"Keep your distance from that one," he said. "He is most dangerous and, though he may appear civilised at the moment, you have no idea the barbarous acts that are within his capability."

"But you trust him."

"With reservations," he said. "With great reservations."

And he pulled her into his arms with one of his rare embraces. Two in the space of a day. Lucille held him for a bit longer than he was comfortable with, but he allowed it.

"Get some rest," he told her. "Tomorrow you take our new weapon to war."

(Translated from the Dutch)

What have I done? Have I, by this brash act, endangered my colleagues, our effort against our enemy? Have I put my own dear daughter in peril?

To unleash this monster upon the world is a formidable responsibility. Only I know how evil were his predations, how corrupt were his deeds upon the innocent and weak. Now he is free to prowl the earth again. Am I able to control him? Is anyone?

And if we are so fortunate as to succeed in vanquishing our adversaries—what then? What do we do with our "monster" after the war is over? Do we put him back in his box like the Christmas angel?

These questions haunt me like the ghosts of poor Lucy Westenra and Quincey Morris.

What have I done?

FROM THE WAR JOURNAL OF
J. HARKER

(transcribed from shorthand)

MAY 17, 1941

When the partisans asked me to reconnoitre the castle Bran and examine the captured documents, I have to admit I was a bit miffed at being separated from the vampire and dear Lucy. I had so many questions to put to him, and so many things I wanted to say to my love. But the presence of the vampire dominated my thoughts. I was kicking myself for not asking more questions of the creature when I had the opportunity. I craved knowledge. I needed to fill in the gaps between my grandfather's stories and that damned Book, which was so vague in so many areas and quite often contradictory to my grandfather's version of events.

Lucille, the other thorn in my brain, left with Dracula. And I was not unaware of the certain magnetism between them, at no time more evident than when we walked in on the pair as she clothed him. I was indubitably aware of my own feeling at the moment—jealousy. But of whom I was jealous I was not sure. I wanted time with each of them.

The reconnaissance of the castle came a cropper, as we could not get within a mile of the ancient palace. Nazi roadblocks and sentries blocked all roads to the fortress. From a distance it did appear to be formidable, perched high upon a promontory much as these medieval structures are, with steep walls and towering battlements. It is of yellow stone topped with red tile roofs, the walls rising from equally vertical cliffs, with but one curving approach, heavily guarded. Impenetrable in its day, but with today's aerial bombing, just another target. I made notations on a map provided by Anka, for any future attack.

After this we drove to what appeared to be an abandoned livestock barn and pens situated alongside the railroad tracks. Inside a smelly, shambling structure, I was presented with the dispatch rider's documents by a waiting Pavel. I noticed a bullet-riddled motorcycle sitting in a stall and a Rumanian uniform laid out to dry on a rusty cart. There were holes in the uniform jacket that I doubt were caused by moths. The remnants of the luckless dispatch rider, I supposed.

The documents concerned the Rumanian Army's recent shortening of the training periods for military recruits and a desperate need for soldiers who could read, write, and hopefully do the basic math needed to run the logistics of a military operation. Suggestions were made to start conscripting teachers in those very subjects and to establish schools for military typists. Also included were a list of promotions, enlisted and officer ranks, plus some vehicle and parts requests. I properly complimented Anka on the capture and told her to forward the whole package to London, as the experts there probably would be able to harvest all sorts of intelligence from these bits and pieces.

Pavel meanwhile took Renfield to a trapdoor covered in six inches of cow dung. The manure was shovelled aside and the trapdoor was lifted to reveal an arms cache. We inspected the weapons, a hodgepodge of German, Rumanian, and French small arms with accompanying ammunition, some of which matched the calibre of the arms, some not.

Renfield became enamored with three cases of German land mines, mostly anti-tank and anti-personnel. The Sergeant became a bit giddy at the sight and instantly took one apart in front of us. He was smoking a cadged cigarette, and the ash kept falling onto the exposed explosive charge. We all watched with dread, expecting the butt to fall from his lips and blow us all to kingdom come, but he was as sure-handed as a watchmaker, and our fears were for naught.

Finally we pulled Renfield away from his latest crush and were driven to the basement of a Brasov bakery, where a stack of flour sacks was provided for our repose. Unexpectedly, taking into account my preoccupation with Lucille and Dracula, I immediately fell asleep. But my dreams were a phantasmagoria of vampires, blood, graveyards, and falling under the rapacious fangs and claws of a pack of wolves, one of which transformed into the naked form of Lucy and proceeded to devour me.

I was jolted awake from this deranged nightmare by the rattling sound of a machine gun, but when my senses returned me to this world, I realised that the sound was the rattle of the giant floor mixer in the bakery above my head.

I glanced at the glowing dial of my watch. It was only a tick past three in the morning. The rattle and clang, with the muted voices of the bakers working above, kept me awake for only a brief minute, and I slipped back into a more peaceful slumber, the sweet smell of yeast and the comforting redolence of baking bread wrapping me in the arms of Morpheus as easily as if in the arms of my mother.

Two hours later I was awakened by a series of kicks upon my leg. It was Pavel and Farkas. They led us upstairs, where I was allowed a brief, unsatisfactory wash in a sink and the use of the facilities. Then, after I was provided with a hot cruller and a cup of thick coffee, we were taken back to the Van Helsings'.

EXCERPTED FROM THE UNPUBLISHED NOVEL
THE DRAGON PRINCE AND I
by Lenore Van Muller

After more than a few ignominious escapades, Lucille Van Helsing learned quickly that one cannot dwell on regrets. One must acknowledge the blunder, the momentary weakness, and plunge ahead with one's life.

The assignation with the English boy was one of those lapses. She could excuse it; tell herself that this was all related to her loss of Janos. That love affair had been spurred by the aphrodisiac of war. She and Janos had succumbed to the knowledge that death was only the next mission away. They tried to live for the moment and the future be damned. They wallowed in the passion fuelled by near escape and the urgency of no tomorrow.

But she was not even sure if the impulse to bed Harker was that deep. Perhaps all she desired that evening was not to sleep alone, to merely hold someone, anyone, to find a bit of comfort in the arms of another.

Or she was just randy. This had happened before. She was a woman who was aware of and at ease with her own lust.

She had also found, through her few but busy years, that it was beneficial not to think about these episodes too much. Not during times such as these.

Her problem with the infatuated English boy was now complicated even more by her sudden attraction to the Prince. Not necessarily romantic, but she could certainly feel the pull of a certain fascination.

Lucille found little sleep, knowing that the vampire occupied the room next to her. She wanted to go to him, pummel him with questions, scientific and otherwise. She was curious about how the vampire was able to exist, how he metabolised blood into sustenance, how his organs managed without oxygen.

And there were personal questions. She wondered what her father had been like fifty years ago. Before he met Lucille's mother. What had actually occurred in England. Why had he seduced—or, to be blunt, preyed upon—the two women. So many questions, one leading off to another, like the spreading limbs of a tree, branches and twigs of query.

Finally she dressed and left her room. In the hall she resisted the impulse to knock on the Prince's door. There would be time later, on the coming mission to the south. She was not a child who couldn't wait for Mos Nicolae.

Downstairs she could hear young Harker in the basement speaking to Renfield. She considered going down and dealing with the situation she had created, but she was not in the mood to unravel the emotional knot she had tied. Maybe she just did not have the courage to make another man unhappy just because she was too weak to control her own base needs.

She heard an engine outside and peered through the lace curtains to see her father arrive in the Bentley. Lucille was surprised; she had assumed he was asleep in his bedroom. But he had risen early and gone into Brasov to obtain papers for the vampire. No one could travel anymore about the countryside without the proper documents, and the partisans used a friendly printer in town to counterfeit any needed papers. The identification, ration and business card were made out for a Vlad Wallach, a mortician from Fantana Alba in Bukovina. Lucille smiled at her father's sense of humour.

"I'll give them to him," she said and took the papers upstairs. She knocked first.

"You may enter," the Prince announced in an imperious tone.

Stepping inside she found him smiling at a book. He held up the cover for her to see: *The Pocket Book of Ogden Nash*, an American poet and humourist.

"Most amusing, this fellow," he said, closing and setting the book aside.

"You'll lose your place," she noted.

"I memorise the page number where I stopped reading," he told her. "I've quite enjoyed many of the tomes you have recommended. A rich and enlightening repast. Thank you."

"You're quite welcome," she said. "Just let me know when you need more. We have acquired some documents for you. To allow you to travel."

She handed him the papers and he perused them with little interest, not commenting on the name, not even the profession.

"We'll leave at dark," she told him.

"I look forward to the journey," the Prince replied. "And to punishing our enemies."

"So do I," she replied, and said it again to herself. *So do I.*

She left him to his reading and went back downstairs to find Horea, Closca, and Crisan had arrived. Her father called down for Harker and Renfield to come up. Lucille rummaged in the kitchen for something to feed everyone, and her father helped. This prompted a mundane conversation about the latest German demands from the Rumanian farmers: potatoes, sugar beet, and wheat stores that the locals had been holding for themselves.

"If they keep this up there will be not enough to feed our own people," Crisan complained. "Our own production is already down, because so many young men have been taken off the farms and conscripted into the army."

"That is part of the German plan," Closca said. "Why they invaded, using us and the other countries they conquered as provender for their war machine."

As they ate Lucille was very conscious of young Harker's constant attention to her every word, her every move. At every chance he managed to brush up against her, touching her hand when she passed him the butter, laying a palm on her shoulder when he leaned over to pour her a glass of wine, searching, she knew, for a signal that what happened the other night was the beginning of something, not the end.

But Lucille, to his apparent dismay, acted as if the tryst had never occurred. She noticed her father was eyeing both of them, aware that there was some kind of perturbation in the ether around the two.

Later, when the sun began to disappear behind the mountains, they began loading their vehicles. All that Dracula carried, his only possessions in this new world, was a stack of books borrowed from Professor Van Helsing, the volumes bound by an old belt as a schoolboy would have done.

The Prince had to smile when he saw their transportation, which gave meaning to the profession noted on his newly minted documents. Horea had procured a hearse for the journey. That allowed her to use her nursing credentials and for them to pose as an improvised medical transport to a Bucharest hospital, their patient being the injured Renfield. Her father provided a vial of phenobarbital, with which she injected the demolitions expert so that he did not suddenly burst out into song at some inopportune moment and give away the game. The vampire would assume the role of hearse owner, allowing its use for this "emergency." Taking into consideration the vampire's sensitivity to daylight, the decision had been made to travel at night whenever possible. The romantically befuddled English Lieutenant drove. Horea, Closca, and Crisan followed at a discreet distance in a rusted old truck, carting a few boxes of pickles purportedly headed for the brinery near whatever village might be ahead.

Horea argued that it was the wrong time of year for pickles, and the shrivelled lot in the barrels would not pass inspection by any army roadblock, especially if the guard had any farm experience. This devolved into a useless argument among the Marx Brothers until Lucille finally put a stop to the debate with a few well-chosen words and the order to move out. Before they drove away she received a heartfelt farewell from her father with his request to be vigilant and careful.

Then forty kilometres down the road Harker had to stop the hearse when they saw the truck pulled over to the side of the road. Horea was quibbling with a farmer over a few barrels of last season's apples. A deal was struck, and the pickles were dumped and replaced with the withered apples. The alibi now was that the Marx Brothers were on their way to a cider mill. This seemed to be an amiable solution for all three.

Lucille was too aggravated to even join the discussion.

The explosives and weapons had been packed into a hidden compartment under the floorboards of the hearse. Harker kept his pistol under his seat, but Lucille would not part with her Luger, keeping it at hand.

They were stopped only once, at the edge of Brasov. Vlad Wallach's papers passed without comment, and from there they had an unimpeded drive. They had decided to begin their rebellious activities midway between Brasov and Ploesti, in a triangle of towns, Comarnic, Campina, and Targoviste, with a diversionary trip east to Valeni De Munte.

Multiple railroad lines ran north past these cities, carrying fuel, minerals, troops, and supplies for the soldiers gathering on the northern border, all in preparation for the coming invasion of the Soviet Union.

Lucille had a contact at the rail dispatch office in Bucharest who kept them informed about any potential targets for the Resistance, designating specific trains and cargo.

The first step was to acquire a new radio transmitter for the English spy. A communiqué was sent via Turkey, and an airdrop was arranged by the SOE.

A few days later, on a chilly night, in a vacant field of clover outside Pucioasa, Harker directed the others to lay out a line of cans filled with petrol. When the plane engine was heard in the night sky, they quickly put an improvised torch to the fumes wafting from the cans. The pilot used this line of flaming dots to drop a large package by parachute. Inside was a new wireless disguised as an ordinary-looking continental suitcase.

The Prince, not participating in the preparation of the beacons—it being too much like peasant work, he said—watched the approach and passing of the plane with unmasked awe. He trotted over to where the parachute had landed and examined the silk, totally ignoring the radio, fingering the cloth appreciatively.

"Such fine material for such a mundane task," he marvelled.

Harker gathered up his new transmitter like a woman reunited with her childhood doll. He showed the group how his SOE Camouflage Section had carefully aged the exterior of the luggage using spilled tea and sandpaper. The case was not light, weighing at least nine kilograms, but the radio did work. After the English boy made contact, another airdrop was made a few days later, this one containing more explosives and eccentric devices designed to cause mayhem.

During all of these preliminary preparations, the poor English lad constantly looked to Lucille for approbation. He was desperate for some kind of acknowledgement that the night in her bed was not an aberration. But Lucille was determined that her weakness on that lonely night was not going to be repeated.

She kept her emotions in check, purposely refraining from any encouragement for the suffering boy. Still her guilt was great, knowing that the raw wound in his heart was her fault, that she was the implement that caused him this pain.

She was also aware that she had begun referring to him, at least in her mental dialectics, as a "boy" although she was but three or four years older than Harker. Maybe it was his callow innocence in regard to war, his romantic notions of the forthcoming combat, his naivete and inexperience with women.

Possibly it was her instinctual rejection of that cow-eyed gaze she saw on his face every time she caught him staring at her. Like a lovesick adolescent in short pants.

It was depressing to see a poor fellow, whom you knew loved you honestly, going around looking all brokenhearted. This was a plight she had experienced ever since the first boy sent her a love note wrapped around a piece of Turkish Delight.

Finally Lucille could take it no more. Harker was at his radio, sending the intelligence he had gathered since his landing in Rumania. This took hours, transcribing his notes with his codebook then sending batches of transmission. He looked up at her when she stood next to him and she could see the hope in his eyes. Damn him.

"For the sake of time and to minimise your suffering, I think you should know that I—we—will not pursue our . . . intimacy," she said. "From now on I think it would be best if we maintain a purely professional attitude. I also hope we can find a way to be friends."

He stared at her for a moment, slowly assimilating her words and their meaning. There was the briefest flicker of pain across his face that he covered with the proverbial stiff upper lip.

"I see," he said, nodding. "I see . . . I'm sure we can manage an impersonal arrangement and continue our duties."

He turned away from her and resumed his radio procedures. Lucille knew he was hurt, and she tried to think of a way to leaven his pain, but nothing came to mind. Nothing ever had. She had been through this a multitude of times and had never found a way to reject a man's attentions without causing pain or anger. Or both.

They continued to work together, but it was a stiff and sometimes difficult exchange. Considering how dangerous things were about to become, she could only hope that their relationship did not become a hindrance.

With the upcoming peril in mind, Lucille decided to create a protective charm for each of her band. They were hiding out in an abandoned farmhouse. The farmer, a widower, and his sons had been conscripted into the military, leaving the buildings empty, the fields fallow. The inside had been cleaned and left neat as a pin. She hoped that they would live to return to what was obviously a place they loved.

Above the door to a chicken coop a rack of deer antlers had been mounted. Lucille sawed off the tips of six antlers, each the length of her little finger. Using a small knife she inscribed the Chinese character for *yongjiu* (forever), then carved a crude chrysanthemum on one side and a broadsword on the other, the Chinese symbols for immortality and the God of War, respectively. For extra good luck she rubbed cinnamon into her etchings.

She searched the nearby stream and found six stones, then scratched the Chinese characters for *longevity* on the smooth surface of each rock. After drilling holes into the deer horn amulets and the longevity stones, she threaded them into a length of rawhide and presented each of the men with the hexed charms. Horea, Crisan, and Closca, being the typical superstitious

Rumanians, accepted theirs with alacrity. Renfield allowed her to set the cord about his neck with no objection or even acknowledgement. Young Harker, brooding since her rejection of him, frowned, suspicious of her motives, but nevertheless, when she insisted, let her drape the charm around his neck.

The Prince refused her offer. "I put no worth in such beliefs," he declared.

"That is strange," she replied. "Since many would regard you with the same disbelief."

"True," he said, nodding. "And often I have relied upon just that. But, generally, superstition has been my enemy, not my ally."

Lucille could not help but compare the Prince with the callow Englishman. It was not just the comparative ages; she did not really regard the Prince as old. He was instead cultured, confident sometimes to the point of arrogance. But there was no denying his mystery, outside the legend and peculiarity of his existence. The stories he could tell, what he had witnessed through, what, centuries? How had he become what he was now? How had he lived? How many had he outlived, loved, lost?

She donned the Prince's charm herself.

I now have a transmitter and am finally in contact with my handlers and superiors. They are excited about our sabotage mission and welcome the intelligence about the Rumanian and German military movements and armament that I have forwarded.

I did not mention the vampire. For obvious reasons. They would think me dotty and thereafter view all of my intelligence with suspicion, I am sure. I am confused myself, this whole vampire business finding me well beyond my remit.

I have prodded the Prince with question after question about his encounters with my grandfather. His responses are terse, and I feel he is embarrassed by the experience, if not ashamed. Fair Lucy has had no more luck than I with her own inquiries.

As for her sudden turnabout in regards to our incipient romance, I am still bewildered. It really takes the biscuit. This cannot be happening. I am sure that she shares my feelings, that this rejection is a wily subterfuge to disguise our courtship and hide it from her comrades so as not to cause internecine disunity. Or she prefers to maintain a professional attitude during times of duress, as we are sure to sustain in the weeks ahead.

Whatever her reasons, I refuse to accept that our dalliance was nothing but that. I am convinced that we are destined to have a future together. My love is unabated.

And a sure sign of her thawing, today she presented me with a hand-wrought totem of friendship. I was wondering what she was toiling at in the corner of our hideout, and when she presented me with a necklace of her own design I was flabbergasted. She does care. And if I am not mistaken the deer horn is a symbol of sexual virility. She has not forgotten our night of lust! She's a corker, all right.

EXCERPTED FROM THE UNPUBLISHED NOVEL
THE DRAGON PRINCE AND I
by Lenore Van Muller

Damned Harker continued to be moon-eyed whenever Lucille found herself alone with him. He was indeed quite capable in many areas, but he seemed to find a variety of ways to vex her, among them his irksome habit of lecturing her and the others.

"Our mission is to undermine the enemy economy, disrupt their transport and communications, interrupt vital supplies and production, destroy them root and branch, and to deteriorate morale as much as we can," he told them, not twice but three times.

What did he think Lucille and her compatriots had been doing for the last year, playing Ring a Ring o' Roses?

The second airdrop delivered a pair of tubular containers almost two metres long, each hitched to a parachute. Renfield opened them like a child on his birthday. Besides the demolition supplies, he produced a bundle of pamphlets for the partisans to distribute among their fellows. Lucille inspected them, the writings of so-called SOE experts: "Art of Guerilla Warfare," "The Partisan Leader's Handbook," and "How to Use High Explosives." She laughed until her sides ached; the first two were handsomely printed in the Polish language and the third in French, all of little use to the Rumanian underground. The Prince was particularly amused.

But the pamphlets did prove to be very flammable and warmed them for a cold night in a damp stable. The team moved every day or so, trying not to spend more than a night or two in any one place. They slept in garages, basements, barns, and the homes of a few brave souls sympathetic with the cause. Lucille found herself in bed with a restless six-year-old one night, an incontinent octogenarian the next, then amid a clutch of chickens. She preferred the birds.

Quite often the unhinged Sergeant Renfield would choose to sleep outside. He could not bear to be enclosed in any place without light. Darkness made him craven and he would quake with alarm. A light had to be on at all times, or he insisted upon having the open sky as his roof. Because they rested in the day, this proved no great difficulty. But once, in the midst of a rainstorm, they took cover in a potato bin. When the lid was shut, turning the inside into a Stygian box, the Brit went into such a terror-stricken wail that they had to seek another form of shelter.

The airdrop contained the tools of Renfield's trade, more explosives and such. Lucille made contact with her Bucharest informant, and now that they were properly provisioned, it was time to act.

Their target—the rail lines.

DATED: 16 MAY 1941
TO: CSS REINHARD HEYDRICH, RSHA, REICHSFUHRER-SS
FROM: SS MAJOR WALTRAUD REIKEL
CC: HEINRICH HIMMLER, REICHSFUHRER-SS
(via diplomatic pouch)

MOST SECRET

STATUS COMMUNIQUÉ--Brasov, Rumania

I am happy to report that resistance activities around
Brasov and vicinities in the south of Rumania have
declined. For the most part, this subsidence is a
direct result of the rigid terms of our governance
and a few object lessons to demonstrate our intent: to
punish severely and without reservations any unrest or
sedition.

Certain suspicious individuals have been taken into
custody and interviewed. A variety of interrogation
methods have produced actionable intelligence and
provided the names of other members of the opposition.
They in turn have directed us to more such terrorists,
and we have been able to discover a chain of personages
who may be involved in a variety of rebellious
activities. Thusly we have been able to disrupt if not
destroy three of the cells in the terrorist hierarchy.
Regrettably at this point we have not been able to
follow this chain to the primary cell leadership.

By my honor, we will persist until every terrorist is in custody or has been punished for their transgression against our Fuhrer and the Reich.

We also assure you that we have been monitoring the reports from Ploesti and the municipalities in close proximity. Any attendant unrest in that area will have my immediate attention.

ATTACHED NOTE: (Handwritten on W. Reikel's personal stationery.)

W.R.

Eugene,

[Editor's note: Eugene was Reinhard Heydrich's middle name.]

Have you been to the opera as of late? The cultural activities here are puny and my only comfort is the recordings you send. Thank you for the Alfred Rosenberg article and the fresh copy of *New Nobility from Blood and Soil*. I have a promising Lieutenant who could use a dose of Darré. This same Lieutenant is also a decent hand with the foil and épée, but even more of a foe with the sabre. His attack is respectable, and our daily encounters help me keep in passable form. I entertain him with accounts of our bouts in the old days in Kiel. Of course these stories always end with you losing. You can tell your own lies to the beauties of Berlin.

Here I dwell at the hemorrhoid of Europe, attempting to sort out this Rumanian knot. I am using the old Night and Fog tactics we developed in Norway and France: Troublemakers disappear in the middle of the night, no witnesses, and vanish into the fog of war, no word, and no explanation. Maybe, if the family is lucky, they will receive a jar of ashes.

It is my opinion that this Rumanian rabble cannot be Germanised, no matter how hard we try. And these local agitators disgust me. I despise them all and will eradicate them. These are not soldiers like us; they have no more military conduct than a gang of children playing Shatterhand and the Indians. Well, I will teach them that this is no juvenile game dreamed up by Fenimore Cooper or Karl May. They will instead find themselves in a nightmare more suitable to Machen.

Give all my love to Lina.

Wally

P.S. Thank you for the kind word in Himmler's ear. Maybe it will be my ticket out of this backwater and into the real war. I owe you a drink. A bottle! A case!

Wally

FROM THE WAR JOURNAL OF
J. HARKER

(transcribed from shorthand)

Our first target—a railroad switching station, at a location that was a vital confluence of four rail lines from all four points of the compass. I conducted a brief recce of the crossing and then set to our preparations.

To everyone's surprise, including my own, Renfield came out of his somnambulant state and performed like the demolition master he was reputed to be. It seemed that if you put an explosive in his hands, he reverted to the professional he had been before his accident. And he was not shy about sharing his expertise with anyone who would listen.

Instead of the ribald ditties, we were privileged to receive an education in explosive ordnance.

"The Bickford fuse is a core of twisted hemp impregnated with gunpowder and coated with a waterproof material. This burns at a relatively constant rate of one centimetre per second, thusly culminating in a time delay between the lighting of that fuse and the ignition of the blasting cap at the other end, all depending on the length of your cord. Mind you, this gives your saboteur the chance of a safe getaway."

The proof of this lecture was put into play one glorious night at the switching station in Breaza. A few pounds of gelignite were laid under four sets of tracks and a few more placed strategically around the building overseeing the crossing. The fuse was lit by the Sergeant himself and then he ran giggling to the nearby culvert where we all had taken cover, telling us, "'Tis some dirty work at the bliddy crossroads, aye."

The blasts followed one another like a line of cannons firing a salute. We watched as the entire site was enveloped by a dense cloud of dust, bricks falling like rectangular hail. As the dust dissipated, we saw that the observations structure was no more and the rails were curled and bent into a steel tangle.

The sight was a demonstrative metaphor for the tangle of my emotions. Dear Lucy is maintaining her distance, and the chill I feel when I am around her wraps my heart in a cold grip. I do not see the fairness in her treatment of me. I gave her my all, my heart and soul. Still do so. Why does she deem to treat me this way? Do I deserve it? I say no. I do not know who is to blame for my torment. I have gone over my interactions with Lucy, every word and deed since we met. I cannot, for the life of me, find any reason for her displeasure. So, I must come to the conclusion that the fault is not mine. Could it be the influence of her father? I do not think he dislikes me, but then the protectiveness of a father cannot be underestimated. And I do not think I offended him in any way. Plus, he is not here with us and able to affect her. Nor is Lucy the type of woman to mindlessly follow her father's command if she should disagree.

Could the vampire be holding some sway over her? I see how they talk together, laugh, share opinions on the books he is always reading. Is he to blame for my misery?

But I refrain from assigning blame in a heedless manner. Mayhaps if I can find the source of our estrangement I can somehow combat what is now an invisible enemy. An enemy I am sworn to defeat. My happiness is at stake. My love.

My world is a contrast of dire proportions. The absolute joy of finally embarking upon a mission, to fulfill my promise to King and country. That is the bright side. In the dark, a deep, desolate, clouded gloom of my broken heart is Lucy's disaffection. I am torn between laughing and crying.

Oh, crikey, I am royally buggered!

EXCERPTED FROM THE UNPUBLISHED NOVEL
THE DRAGON PRINCE AND I
by Lenore Van Muller

Lucille was not as amazed as everyone else at the sudden lucidity that Renfield demonstrated whenever he was queried about his craft. She had witnessed his rational interludes in her basement.

What was surprising was the Sergeant's near adoration of the vampire. Renfield kept a constant watch on Dracula, attending his every move as a dog eyes his master at feeding time. Even when Dracula sat reading for hours, the poor, imbalanced soul would stare, a silent sentinel to the Prince's every move, even if that was only the turning of a page. Dracula bore this attention with patience and equanimity. And as before, whenever Renfield was required to utilise his craft, he transformed into the Scot demolition expert. "Aye, Cordex is a detonating cord with an almost instantaneous eight-foot-per-second burn rate."

As with the first attack at the rail switching station, the damned Brit Harker treated Lucille like a frail appendage to the mission, trying to protect her from any of the dangerous work. He took the explosive charge Renfield had provided right out of her hands.

"I'll handle this," he told her as if she were a child.

"Like hell you will," she replied, snatching it back with more vehemence than she wished. She thought she had proven herself more than capable, repeatedly, during her time with the partisans, ambush after ambush, battle to battle. She had to remind herself that the Brit had not witnessed any of this. Still, the kneejerk assumption by every damned male that combat was their domain and not the place for some weak female irritated her all to hell. That the Prince shared Harker's views only increased her pique. Closca and Crisan seemed amused at her current contretemps, and she shot them a look that wiped the grins from their faces.

Their next target was a bridge over the Lalomita River. While the rest of them stood guard, Renfield studied the structure for two entire days, staring at the beams and trusses with the concentration of a cat at a mouse hole.

The railroad bridge spanned the water with a gentle curve composed of wood and steel. The canyon it crossed was deep, two hundred metres, the sides steep and rocky. Access to the bottom was a narrow footpath that snaked back and forth across one side of the valley wall. Lucille's informant told her that the rail line was the main means of transport from the nearby oil refinery. Harker proposed attacking the refinery itself, and it was discussed. The final, mutual decision was that the facility was too well guarded and their team too small for a successful outcome.

On the night set for the demolition, the Prince approached Lucille and Harker. "It is time for my participation in your rebellion," he announced.

"You're coming with us?" Harker asked. Lucille could detect some fear in the Englishman's voice.

"No, I think not," the Prince replied. Harker seemed relieved at that.

"I could perhaps venture out on my own," the Prince offered. Harker instantly agreed and Lucille concurred.

The other members of the team were brought into the conversation, and Horea suggested that the vampire could target a nearby freight warehouse. The Germans had diligently looted and confiscated artworks from across Rumania, from churches, museums, and private collections—and the precious possessions of anyone arrested, be it Jews or "persons under suspicion."

These treasures had been gathered in the warehouse to be catalogued before shipping, per the usual Teutonic efficiency. A German staff of soldiers, Gestapo, and experts in art, jewelry, and antiquities were in the process of inventorying the stolen hoard. They had taken over a local hotel as their residence while working. Dracula would attack there.

This was not necessarily a formative military target, but if the Nazi guards could be eliminated the local partisans were prepared to remove the artworks and valuables. Nearby caves had been surveyed and considered large enough to hide everything from the Germans.

The Prince agreed to the assignment. Horea would drive and assist. Lucille thought the mission too dangerous for only two men and said so.

"But you are not calculating properly," the Prince replied. "It is one man and I."

"Maybe you overestimate yourself," she said.

"I doubt that," he said, his arrogance coming to the forefront once more.

"I say we let him give it a crack, old bean," Harker said.

Lucille relented even though she was afraid for the Prince. She had grown accustomed to allowing friends to put themselves in jeopardy for the cause. She wished the pair luck, and watched Horea drive the Prince into the moonlit night.

Then she and the rest of their force took the lorry to the bridge site where everyone—under Renfield's quite coherent instructions—set charges among the beams and supports. Renfield followed, wiring the explosives together. Once all the charges were in place they retreated to the western bank of the gorge, where Renfield attached an ignition switch to the ends of the wires.

Renfield gave the igniter a twist and the resulting blast was unimpressive. A short, sharp crack and nothing happened. Lucille's first thought was that they had failed.

She said so and Renfield responded, "You think I'm all fart and not shite? 'Tis not the size of the tool, lassie, but where you put it." He grinned lasciviously.

Then Lucille saw a great, centre support bend like a knee joint at the spot where the charge had gone off. Another small blast followed by a stuttering series of tiny explosions that spanned the entire construction, little puffs of spark and smoke like stitches in a quilt.

She watched the whole intricate structure bend slowly as if taking a stately, graceful bow. Then with a scream of protesting wood, the groan and squeal of tortured steel, and a thunderous crash, the entire bridge fell into the moonlit waters of the stream. Years of stalwart support were extinguished in but a breath as the massive framework surrendered to gravity.

She could not help but cheer, as did her comrades. She began to understand the complete atavistic satisfaction of destruction for its own sake. And it was obvious that the larger the object being destroyed, the more joy that accompanied the act. She was reminded of the first time she had fired a pistol and felt the sudden surge of power, a feeling she found nowhere else. Blowing up things magnified that same intoxication to an extent she had not thought possible.

They returned to the empty garage that had been their hideaway for the last two nights. It was a cavernous space, enough room for both the hearse and the lorry. Oceans of oil stains blotted the cracked concrete floor, auto parts were scattered about, fenders, doors, bumpers, wheels, and tyres stacked or piled along the walls. The wartime scrap drives had obviously skipped this place. It stank of oil and rubber, but the tattered vehicle seats made halfway comfortable beds.

Horea was waiting for them but the Prince was not. Lucille became instantly worried.

"Where is he?" she asked.

"He didn't show at the rendezvous," Horea reported. "He went in, there was a ruckus. I saw the hotel staff run out. Then there was a fire. I waited an hour past the designated time. Then I came back here."

Lucille nodded, knowing Horea had gone beyond what was safe.

"He'll be fine," Harker told her, laying a comforting hand on her shoulder. It was the first time they had touched since the night of her mistake. They both became acutely aware of the contact and he quickly removed his hand.

"But what if he uses this as an opportunity to run off?" she asked. "What if my father's worries were correct? Have we unleashed an unspeakable evil upon the world?"

Harker had no answer for her. She could tell that the same worry now dominated his own thoughts. He went to the Marx Brothers, who were passing a bottle of *palinca* around. Harker grabbed the bottle and took a hefty swallow of the twice-distilled brew. Soon they were all drunk, reliving the bridge destruction and their parts in it. Even Renfield was imbibing and began singing about a man who could pleasure himself in all holes. This went on until the balladeer was the only man still conscious.

The others collapsed onto their improvised beds. Renfield laid his blankets under the only skylight, where the stars and a half moon could be seen through murky glass.

Lucille would not sleep and spent the time tweezing splinters out of her hands. She had acquired them climbing the timbers of the bridge superstructure. A new thought had taken over her mind. Maybe the vampire had been caught, perhaps killed. She knew the Prince was immortal, or nearly so, but she still fretted. Was he immune to fire? What if he did not return by daylight? They were due to leave the next evening, as soon as the sun set. What if he wasn't back by then? Dare she delay their departure? They could not abandon him—correction, *she* could not leave him behind. But it would be most dangerous to spend another night here, especially after the commotion they had caused at the bridge.

She heard a rustle. The first time she thought it was one of the sleeping men. Or a foraging rat. Then she heard it again, in the opposite corner of their sleeping area, a dark recess, the shadows so deep and dark that nothing could be seen.

She approached cautiously, Luger in hand. The closer she came the more she could see. She made out crates of Coca-Cola bottles, stacked five high, an engine block, hollowed piston tubes, rusted and corroded, a black cloth-covered mound.

The cloth moved.

"Come out of there," she ordered.

The black cloth rose, slowly, like a plume of coal smoke. She raised her pistol. Then she recognised the figure: the Prince, his cape covering him like a shroud.

"Prince Vlad," she whispered.

He turned. She stepped back in shock.

His entire front was covered in blood and gore, the scarlet stain most visible on what once had been a white shirt.

"Are you hurt?" she asked.

"I am unharmed," he replied. Lucille could sense a forlorn quality to his voice, a profound sadness. She approached him. He immediately backed away from her.

"Do not touch me," he said. "I am an abomination."

"I don't understand," she said. "Please. At least let me find you a clean shirt."

"No! Leave me be!" He turned away from her.

"I don't think you need to use that tone of voice with me," Lucille said. "I'm just trying to help, trying to be . . . your friend."

"I deserve no kindness," he said, his voice soft. "No mercy. And certainly not any friendship."

"Why not?"

"Because it is true, what they call me. I am a monster." The defeat in his voice was pitiful.

"What happened?" she asked and stepped forward. He backed away but the wall prevented him from retreating any further. She placed herself so that she was face-to-face with him. He looked away from her probing eyes.

"What happened to you?" she demanded.

"I dare not say. You would abhor me as the world does. As I do. There was . . . carnage beyond your mortal imaginings. Blood and butchery."

"But have you not done this before?"

"Yes. That is the crux of my problem. I thought I had . . . more control, that I had come to grips with my compulsions. I have not. Far from it."

"Well, don't complain. Rather than whine about it, do something."

"This is not something to quibble about," he said, waving her to go away. "Please leave me to myself. It is not safe for you to be in my presence."

She reached out a hand to his face, made him look her in the eye. "I can help. We can overcome whatever problem presents itself. Together. You have friends here."

He flinched at her touch. "Go! Leave me be!"

She turned and walked away, jolted by the fierceness of his rejection. Retreating to her place across the garage, she sat and watched the Prince as he returned to his huddle in the dark corner.

It was difficult for her to contemplate, the powerful, noble character of the man she had begun to know, to admire, even have affection for—reduced to this aggrieved, miserable being. Even more grievous was that she was unable to do anything for him.

FROM THE WAR JOURNAL OF
J. HARKER

(transcribed from shorthand)

After our stupendous destruction of the Lalomita bridge and celebration of the same I slept until past noon. Upon waking I found the vampire in a distressed state, his clothes stiff with dried blood. Crisan went out for food and water and I gave him some money to purchase clean clothing for Dracula. Cleaning the garments was out of the question—we had neither the facilities nor the time.

Dracula reacted little to my offer to provend for him, no gratitude of any kind. It was as if he expected such service from us, his royal hauteur much in evidence at all times. He also seemed withdrawn, morose. So did Lucy. I sense some kind of disharmony between them. Dare I say, good show? Closca ventured out to the neighbouring hamlets to inquire about any heightened security or other consequences from the previous night's sabotage. He came back in time for a communal meal that Crisan had foraged from a local cafe. The gypsy chap never misses a chance to eat. While we fed he told us that the blown bridge was on everyone's lips and the local Rumanian police and military were still investigating the remains. There were whispers of sabotage but no particular alert. The other item of interest was the fire that had destroyed a certain hotel. None of the Rumanian staff had been harmed, but not one of the German residents had escaped the inferno, the cause of which was still unknown. The common theory was some kind of explosion that had rendered the victims into the charred bits and pieces that had been recovered. The curious part was that no concussion, the signature of any bomb, had been heard by any of the witnesses. Still there was no other explanation for the terrible state of the dead.

I tried to congratulate Dracula on the success of his first foray, but I was rebuffed with a sneer and a command to leave him be. His mood was not lightened by the gift of new clothes either, the ungrateful punter. Though he did change out of his ruined clothing, his bad temperament continued. I envy the beast. His raid was an unqualified victory. He is a one-man army. If I had his powers—what havoc I could, would, cause.

While we waited for nightfall I managed to find a moment when Lucy and I could be alone.

"Lucy, I was wondering if you and I, if it may be possible, for us, you and I, well, more importantly, if I could have another chance to, uh, pursue our association. As before, I mean."

"Association," she repeated with a slight smile. I was so glad of that beam of lightheartedness. It was like a ray of sunlight after a grim storm. Encouraged, I pressed my suasion.

"If you could just give me more time to prove myself," I said.

"Harker, please, don't," she said.

"Call me Jonathan. I'll do anything, Lucy. Anything. Just tell me where I am lacking and I will surpass your expectations, I know."

"Har . . . Jonathan, stop this. I thought we had resolved this matter. Let it be."

And she walked away from me.

The drive to our next objective was silent, none of us speaking. For once I longed for one of Renfield's vulgar tunes.

EXCERPTED FROM THE UNPUBLISHED NOVEL
THE DRAGON PRINCE AND I
by Lenore von Mueller

Lucille's spy had alerted her about a supply train destined for Germany. Over thirty boxcars filled with chromium ore, a prime material needed to make ball bearings.

As Horea said, "No motor runs without bearings, no car or truck moves without bearings. No boats or planes or tanks. No bearings—no war."

He had arranged for them to stay at a Masonic Hall. Crisan and Closca went into town to find an objective for the Prince who, despite his recent emotional turmoil, insisted that he do his part.

Lucille drove Renfield and Harker to reconnoitre the best location to attack the train. The Prince stayed behind, avoiding the daylight and seemingly deep into a book. Lucille knew he was not reading; he did not turn a page in the hour that she watched him.

Harker was sullen and withdrawn during the entire trip. Lucille wanted to chide him for this schoolboy pout but held back. She had done enough damage to what was obviously a fragile soul.

A suitable spot on the railway was found. It was far enough out of town that a derailment would not endanger any of the local inhabitants.

Upon their return to the hall Lucille checked, and it appeared that the Prince had read no further than when she left.

Horea laid out a table of meat pies and early tomatoes. Lucille ate while she walked over to the dark corner where the Prince had remained.

"You do not have to fight with us," she told him. "You could withdraw from the battle."

He gazed at her for a moment, pain evident on his face. "I am a weapon for you to use at will," he softly replied. "But be cautioned thusly, I am indiscriminate in my slaughter, and I do not want the killing of innocents on my conscience. The further killing of innocents. Not anymore."

"What happened last night?" she asked. "Tell me."

"It will change your opinion of me," he said. "And not for the better. And the loss of your esteem will cause me more pain than my deplorable act."

"Do you think that I have not done something in this war that I am ashamed of, that I regret with every part of me?" She gestured to the men gathered around and eating. "We have all committed acts that haunt us at night. Except for Harker, I suppose. But it will happen to him, if he lives long enough. Dastardly acts are part of war. Tell me what weighs so heavily upon you. If we are to be colleagues in this conflict, if we are to depend on each other for our very lives, if we are to be *friends*, we need to know each other."

She could see the Prince considering her words.

"There was a woman at the hotel, more of a girl, with one of the Huns, in his room, in the midst of coupling . . ." he began. "So young, thin, you could count her ribs . . . I was in a rabid fury, in no control whatsoever, and I attacked her."

His eyes bored into her own, challenging her, daring her to hate him.

"I feasted on her, just as I did on our enemy. I ripped her asunder. She was an innocent."

"Perhaps," Lucille replied. "But in some of the occupied countries, Rumania even, someone who cohabitates with the enemy is deemed a collaborator. And they are quite often punished. Even killed."

"And you approve of these reprisals?" he asked.

"No. But they happen," she said. "Everyone fights their own war, creates their own morality. If what you did is an anathema to you, do not do it again."

"You miss the point. If I could control myself . . . It is not that simple."

"Yes, it is. You are an intelligent man. Cultured and with some control over your . . . passions, or hungers, or whatever drives you in these moments. You have not attacked any of us."

"You do not know what I have wanted to do to you and your compatriots," he said.

"No, *you* miss the point," she said. "You have enough control to not rip us, as you say, 'asunder.' Try to do the same when you confront our enemy. War is not for coddling. Fight with us or go back to your tomb or prey on the innocents you seem to care so much about. You said before that you wanted to redeem yourself, that you would kill some Germans for us. Cry on someone else's shoulder. Now, come over so you can be briefed on your next assignment. Or don't, and I will find you transportation back to where Father found you."

She walked to where the other men were eating. The Prince followed. He made a slight bow to Harker.

"I thank you for the new wardrobe," he said to the Englishman. "Now, where am I needed next?"

Closca and Crisan briefed them about a telephone-switching centre a few miles away where a German Gestapo contingent was lodged. Phone calls from all across the country were being monitored by the Nazis.

"Gestapo?" Dracula asked.

"The Nazi intelligence apparatus," Harker explained. "A particularly nasty group of blighters, fond of torture, kidnapping, and assassination."

Lucille turned to the Prince.

"Are you game, Prince Vlad?" she asked.

"Indubitably," he replied.

When dark fell they went their separate ways. Horea once again accompanied the Prince. Before they left Lucy took Horea aside.

"Stay close. Don't just drop him off this time," she told him. "Make sure he attacks only our enemies. But do not put yourself in jeopardy if he . . . loses control. Understand?"

Horea nodded and she gave him a quick embrace, wished him luck, and joined Harker and the others. The drive was uneventful, nary a Rumanian military patrol in sight.

At the railroad tracks Harker put the tools of the saboteur's trade into Renfield's hands, and the demolition expert once again emerged from the daft balladeer.

"The pressure switch." At a rail siding Renfield showed them a little box with a prong standing out of the top. "Responds tae weight hitting on a hinged metal plate, striking and igniting the detonator."

A hole was dug and the unit set beneath the steel rail, the prong just touching the underside.

"Plastic explosive." Renfield held up a block twelve inches long, a couple thick, four wide. A pale yellow putty-like substance. "Unlike ammonium nitrate, 'tis safe tae store and handle."

Lucille was well versed in the use of ammonium nitrate, and how dangerous it was. How it caked in humid conditions and then became hazardous. One of her fellow partisans lost a hand when a caked portion spontaneously blew up while he was merely trying to carry it to a hiding place.

Renfield set a few pounds of the plastique under the rails some distance behind the pressure switch, then connected the two.

When the charges had been set, Lucille and the others lay in a potato field two hundred metres from the booby-trapped rail line.

In less than an hour the locomotive engine rolled across the booby-trapped spot and struck their mine. She heard a sharp blast and saw the engine leap into the air. It came down upon the gravelled siding. Sheer momentum propelled the iron beast across the ground, scouring the earth like a plow blade. With infinite slowness, the massive engine fell onto its side and came to a shuddering stop. The cars filled with chromium ore accordioned to a great cacophony of screeching steel and piled up upon each other like tin toys discarded by a petulant giant.

The locomotive's boiler blew, sending a fireball into the air and momentarily turning night into day. The concussion pounded through her body. Lucille watched the conflagration with her mouth hanging open, stunned.

She and the demolition team returned to their hideaway, and this time Harker refrained from the celebratory drinking. They found Horea and the Prince already returned from their own mission, the vampire peeling off another bloodied shirt. Lucille approached Horea, who was opening a bottle of *rachiu* he had found somewhere. He had a truffle hog's ability to sniff out alcohol.

"How did your visit go?" she asked.

"It was quick work for his majesty," Horea replied. "The Gestapo worked out of a private room. We caught them at the midnight shift change, herded both shifts into the eavesdropping room without being seen. While the Dark One went in to do his dirty work I gathered the telephone employees and sent them on their way. Once the Dragon was done, we blew up the entire switching station. Stuff old Renfield gave me. It was a merry blast."

Lucille left him to his celebration and walked over to where the Prince was sorting through his books. "I'm afraid I am running out of stories," he told her.

"We'll have to find a bookstore," she said. "So, how was this venture?"

"I seemed to have ruined another set of clothing," he replied.

"You know what I mean."

"I . . . I was able to restrain myself this time."

"Good for you."

"It was most difficult."

"But you succeeded," she said.

"Barely," he sighed. "I almost gave in to my more savage instincts. As I left I encountered a young man. An employee, I suppose, another innocent. I was in thrall of my bloodlust and . . . He was most . . . His pulse was like a siren song, I could hear his heart, I could taste . . . He was nothing to me but a surcease of my thirst, this hunger that overcomes, that rules me. I stopped but . . . I am afraid that I have lost any humanity that I may have possessed."

"I doubt that," she replied. "You take joy in literature, poetry. You seem to hunger for that as well. So there must be a sliver of humanity left somewhere in there."

She tapped him on his naked chest. He did not recoil from her touch.

"True," he answered.

"And there must be a few other random emotions flitting about inside you, no matter how dormant. You once felt love, if that novel was in any way correct. For Lucy Westerna and Nina Murray, as I recall."

"Not my proudest moment." He shook his head as if trying to dislodge the memory. "You remind me of a time when I lost control completely."

"But you felt something human," she said. "That was my point. Maybe that wasn't the best example. Tell me, when was the last time, before your dalliance in England, that you were in love?"

"You are most inquisitive," he said.

"Too much so?"

"No, no. I am not used to a woman so forthright," he said. "If you must know, my last great love died in my arms, withered and diseased with age, gasping for breath and cursing me for not aging with her."

"So, you felt sorrow and guilt," she noted. "A step in the right direction. Next thing you know you'll be telling bad jokes and farting out loud. You do—"

"Woman, you presume too much!" His anger was quick and then just a suddenly dissolved into a wide, wolfen grin. She laughed with him. Lucille saw Harker watching them and the distress on his face. She sighed; another wounded man she must deal with. Sometimes she felt more like a nanny than a warrior.

FROM THE WAR JOURNAL OF
J. HARKER

(transcribed from shorthand)

I think I have found the source of the disaffection between Lucy and me. For two nights I have seen her and the vampire in deep conversation, putting themselves apart from the rest of our merry band. They speak in low tones. I cannot hear the words, but there is an obvious intimacy between the two. Has that insidious creature been seducing Lucy all this time? The ruddy gall of the man. Has he mesmerised her? He is capable of such, this I know from conversations with Lucy.

What can I do about this situation? I am a clever man, top of my class in "Clandestine Manoeuvres." Surely I can figure a way to eliminate my rival without giving myself away.

It was my decision to drive to the next town in the daylight, the vampire ensconced in the back of the hearse, the windows blacked out. Dracula read, lying next to the comatose Renfield.

We had two objectives at our next location, a coming convoy that had originated in the south plus a synthetic rubber plant that was to be a target for the vampire.

"Rubber is vital to their war machine, all those tyres and other parts, gaskets and belts and such," I said. "That and fuel."

This factory was in the process of being disassembled, the machinery packed up to be sent to the Rhineland. I explained the reasoning behind the Nazis' actions to Lucy. The vampire listened from behind the partition that separated the front seat and the cargo section of the hearse.

"The Germans are removing all highly technical industries from their slave countries and plan to re-establish them in Germany so that the subjected peoples will become dependent on the benevolence of their German masters. Then the slave populations will produce the raw materials and labour to feed these industries and the food to feed the Nazi bastards. Rumania and countries like it will become only mining and agricultural communities forever under the yoke of Germany—and without the technology to ever rebel."

"Very clever of them." Dracula's voice could be heard from behind me.

"But we are smarter," Lucy said.

"So, this rubber manufacturing establishment, I am to eliminate the German supervisors, correct?" Dracula asked. "Where do they spend their nights?"

"They sleep on-site," I told him. "They have taken over the foreman's residence." Then I added, "I was thinking I could go with you on this one."

Lucy frowned at me. Perhaps she could ascertain my real motive: to probe Dracula about his intentions toward her.

"I think not," Dracula replied. "Horea will do. You are needed with the ambush unit."

I could not argue. Not without revealing my subterfuge. We arrived at our latest refuge, the grain warehouse of a local who was loyal to our cause—the German levies on his stocks (at below-market costs) most likely added to his justification to help us.

Leaving the vampire in the safety of the dark building, Lucy, Renfield, and I drove away to scout our next ambuscade. A land mine was put into Renfield's hands, and he became alive with excitement at the explosive possibilities before him.

On our return Lucy insisted on stopping thrice, once to purchase some new clothing for the vampire and again at a bookstore to replenish his dwindling stores of reading material. I could not help myself and was nearly overwhelmed by a wave of jealousy. The very vision of Lucy shopping for me, as mundane a purchase as a shirt, made my heart beat faster and my mind swoon with a paroxysm of intimacy. I had to stop this.

The third stop was to use a friendly phone to call her father and receive an update on the circumstances in Brasov. Most of her inquiry, though, seemed to be quizzing him about whether he was eating properly and not climbing a ladder to trim the roses on the cottage, not without having someone to spot this dangerous chore. There was a pause as she listened to something her father said.

"We are having great luck with our mushroom hunt" was her reply. Clever girl, knowing that the phone lines might be monitored. There was another pause, then, "Father, do not worry. We have been avoiding the poisoned ones."

Upon our return we feasted on a meal scavenged by the Marx Brothers, as Lucy refers to our compatriots. I do not know if my palate has been rendered numb by the repetitive diet or that the rations no longer have an alien enticement about them, but lately food has become nothing but fuel. No enjoyment there, either.

While we ate, consumed the better term, a middling wine, and yet another variation on cornmeal, I could not help but notice Lucy watching Dracula, the vampire deep into a copy of Whitman's *Leaves of Grass*. He reads all the time, like some dowager with nothing to else to do. I suppose if you do not sup, at least at mealtime, or sleep, then you must find a way to pass the time. Still he is an arrogant fellow, even asking me to dust off his sitting place once, treating us often like vassals. I have no patience with someone who thinks the sun surely shines out of his arse.

Lucy was trying very hard not to be observed watching the vampire, but I could discern her sidelong glances and peering over her cup of wine, the subject of her attentions clear to me.

I know better than to broach this with Lucy, so I instead sidled up to the vampire. I sat on a stack of rye grain, and Dracula put down his book.

"My grandfather knew you as his enemy," I said.

"He stood in the way of what I desired. At that time," Dracula replied. "I hope you do not see me as such."

"Oh, tish, we are allies, old stick," I replied. "For the moment."

"'For the moment'? You envision our affiliation to change?" He fixed me with an imperious gaze.

"No, of course not." I quickly left him to his books, feeling very much the coward. Why cannot I confront him on the subject so dear to me? Will we fight for Lucy's hand?

As the last rays of sunlight faded, Horea gathered his gifts from Renfield and drove away with the vampire. Lucy collected the rest of us around a map laid out upon a pallet of wheat sacks. She began briefing us on the route to our ambush site. The timetable for the convoy would put them due at around ten p.m. I pointed out possible escape routes, taking over the briefing. Lucy has a habit of assuming command even though she has no military training, not to mention her feminine shortcomings.

I would mention this to her, but we are on such tremulous ground lately and I am afraid I might make matters worse.

The drive to the location was difficult; the roads around here were not marked, and none of us were familiar with the terrain. I had driven during our recce, but everything looked different in the dark, and there was such an overcast that landmarks were difficult to discern. To my embarrassment we found ourselves lost more than once.

Finally, once there, Renfield dug into his kit and again assumed his schoolteacher role, the don of destruction.

"The pull switch." Renfield strung a wire from a telegraph pole to a tree trunk across the road, made it taut about a metre off the ground, and attached it to the pull switch. As usual he went on at length describing the particulars of this device. The sudden bouts of clarity were losing their charm.

The road was north of Gura Vitioarei, where intelligence had informed us that this Rumanian military convoy, carrying small arms and munitions to the Ukrainian border, was due. Closca waited in the belfry of a small church a quarter of a mile south of our ambush site. He was our lookout and early warning. The convoy was late. It was way past eleven when the church bell rang the once.

The rest of us all waited on the roof of a closed agricultural supply establishment so we could watch the oncoming cataclysm.

The first truck struck the wire, and the explosives we had buried in the road flipped the vehicle like a coin on a thumb. The gas tank blew with a great yellow billow of flame. The six trucks following skidded to tyre-burning stops. Then Renfield detonated the four other charges we had buried at five-metre intervals. Three of the vehicles suffered the same violent eruption of the first. Two of those were obviously carrying munitions as evidenced by the secondary explosions, artillery shells, and bullets popping and arcing into the sky, some with the neon trails of tracers.

These explosions engulfed the unharmed trucks and they, too, were soon ablaze and torn apart. Intermittent blasts continued the fierce destruction. At one point we had to flee the roof as rounds began landing about us. We dashed across the corrugated tin as bits of wood and metal rained down upon our shoulders.

The rest of the fireworks we watched from the safety of a hayloft half a kilometre away. I had become quite proficient at scouting our exit strategies, always planning at least two ways out of any situation we set up.

Returning to the warehouse we were all in a celebratory mood. But that joy was soon extinguished when we found Dracula, blood-drenched as usual after one of his outings, being guarded by a nervous Horea, who was pointing his pistol at the vampire.

"What happened?" Lucy demanded, standing over Dracula. The vampire refused to meet her eyes so she turned to Horea.

"He attacked me," Horea began. I could see that he was on edge, frightened even, the gun trembling in his hand. "He goes to where the Germans sleep. I go to set bombs on the telephone switching equipment, to destroy them, right? I come back. There is screaming from inside. From the Germans. The Rumanian guards hear this and come running. I hide. Dracula comes out, attacks the soldiers. Nothing like this I have ever seen. Nothing."

The poor man visibly shivered, then continued. "He kills them all. Maybe eight, maybe ten. I go to him. We must put the bodies inside and burn down the building, right? To hide what has happened. He attacks me. I shoot him. Nothing happens. Bullets do nothing to him. I, I am going to die, I think. Then he stops. Like he wakes up. I bring him back here. But I don't trust him. I keep a gun on him all the way."

"But you said bullets did him no harm," I said.

"What am I going to use?" he answered. "A harsh word?"

The vampire regarded us with a forlorn look. I could see bullet holes in his shirt, each circled by a black cloud of unburnt gunpowder. He had been shot at close range. And survived. There seemed to be no apparent harm to him. How was this possible?

"I am ashamed and bereft," Dracula whispered.

"Horea, go get something to drink," Lucy said, laying a hand on the man's gun arm. Horea put the pistol away and walked to the other end of the warehouse where Closca was opening the brandy.

Lucy turned to me. "Join the others," she told me. I acceded. But sipping my drink, I watched as she knelt at the vampire's side, speaking softly into his ear. Then she embraced him. I felt like someone had just kicked me in the chest.

EXCERPTED FROM THE UNPUBLISHED NOVEL
THE DRAGON PRINCE AND I
by Lenore Van Muller

The Prince's sudden relapse was a surprise. He usually appeared to be so much in control that it was difficult for her to imagine him losing his composure. Evidently he was quite shaken by this recent reverse.

"You lost control again?" she asked.

"One cannot lose what one never has," he told her. His defeat seemed total. She could not think of what to say, so she reached out and took him into her arms. He folded into her like a bereft child. She whispered into his ear.

"You wonder if you have lost your humanity," she said. "But your feelings now are evidence to the contrary. What you now feel, regret, guilt, sadness, defeat—all are human. At the core of us all. You are not so removed from us as you think."

He did not reply but also did not pull away. The next thing Lucille knew, she was waking, curled between two oat sacks, the Prince watching over her, book in hand. Mark Twain, *The Innocents Abroad*. She smiled at him and he smiled back. She had not had such a feeling of contentment since before the war.

Before she could relay the feeling to the Prince there was a commotion at the door. Lucille rushed over to find Crisan and Closca confronting a young schoolgirl, eight or nine, sporting a Catholic school uniform. Red-cheeked and big blue eyes under a fringe of dark brown hair, she wiped her nose on the back of her hand and insisted on speaking to Lenore Van Muller. Lucille introduced herself as that person, and the imp demanded identification. With some amusement for all, Lucille showed her fake papers and received a folded slip of paper in return. The child did a neat curtsy and ran away. Harker came over as Lucille read the missive to all.

Word had come down the partisan grapevine that it was time to move on. The local Rumanian Army detachment had organised a large unit whose sole mission was to find and eliminate the team that had ambushed their convoy and killed so many soldiers.

The team immediately packed the hearse and lorry to travel southwest, where they set up a new base. After calling for an airdrop, they began reconnaissance along the Arges River, studying the rail lines that ran along the waterway. This rail system was a major supply line from Yugoslavia to Northeast Rumania, where the Russian invasion was being staged.

It was soon apparent that the military had modified their tactics on rail transport, most likely the result of the recent sabotage by Lucille and her team. Search parties were being sent ahead of any important train, tasked to spot bombs or disturbances along the rails—or to get blown up instead of the more valuable train following. "Bait," Crisan called them. "Goats staked out to tempt the tiger." The enemy's cynical plan was to sacrifice a few men for the sake of vital supplies. Soon the soldiers assigned to this hopeless, suicidal job began to mutiny, so the army began to send a solo engine in front of the priority locomotive to detonate any charges laid down.

But the clever men had not counted on an even more clever group. Young Harker contacted his superiors and briefed them on the problem. The wizards at the SOE pondered and acted.

The next airdrop gifted their little sabotage team with a new pressure switch. This switch was activated after a designated number of train cars passed. These switches could be set for a number of car passings, up to eight. The pressure rod could even distinguish between axles or whole trains, indexed by a ratchet wheel on the side of the device.

Renfield used it to massive effect. At least a half-dozen supply trains were turned into twisted steel wrecks and their freight dumped into the adjacent river or strewn across fields.

Lucille took great delight at the results. Not only were valuable locomotives, cars, and their contents destroyed, but the massive wreckage had to be removed, a laborious process, taxing the enemy with a drain on their manpower. The tracks, curled and mangled, resembling noodles left on a plate to dry, had to be removed, the bed restored, new rails brought in, resulting in delays that left long lines of rail cars sitting on the tracks for days. And these stationary targets proved too tempting for the team to resist.

One such chain of cars, filled with diesel fuel, inspired the two British agents.

"A combined explosive-incendiary device," Renfield explained. "The explosive ruptures the tank. Another device placed in an opportune location explodes and disperses the diesel oil intae a fine mist that is henceforth ignited by the incendiary. And then just watch the bliddy fun."

Which they did as twenty fuel tankers erupted into voluminous gouts of fire. Columns of flame, swirling like tornadoes, leapt thirty feet, forty feet, into the air, the conflagration writhing like a living beast eager to devour the world. Night became day for miles around.

Gazing into the fiery maelstrom, Lucy thought she could see Satan. If he existed he certainly resided therein. This she related to Crisan, who replied, "You know there is no devil—just God when he's drunk."

The beauty of the balefire was profound, like malicious marigolds instantly blooming in the black night, something maybe only a madman like Van Gogh could render properly.

Nobody enjoyed the results of their labours more than Renfield, whose jubilance was vocal to the extreme. He squealed with delight, screamed in paroxysms of triumph. On more than one occasion his shouts of glee would draw the attention of the local gendarmes or soldiers responding to the calamity. At these times Crisan would clamp a hand over Renfield's mouth, stifling the shrieks of joy while Harker led them into the shadows and away.

After more than one narrow escape caused by Renfield's celebratory outbursts, Lucille started to administer a small dose of the tranquillizer to Renfield, after he had set his charges, of course, and this proved to be sufficient to calm the excitable bomb maker.

They demolished trains and railways in Titu, working their way north to do the same in Gaesti, Cateasua, and Pitesti, cutting telephone and telegraph lines whenever the opportunity presented itself. They blew up power stations supplying military bases and vital factories. Havoc was raised, as Harker exclaimed after every incident. And with every airdrop the SOE delivered a new bag of tricks.

And some of what they supplied proved to be just that, tricks. Lucille and Harker managed to close some of the emotional distance between them as they both took childish delight in various acts of minor sabotage. Particular pleasure was found tossing caltrops across the road; a caltrop was a tetrahedral-like instrument, small, sharpened triangles with knife edges, which when scattered upon a flat surface always presented a sharp point aimed upward.

Lucille and Harker would laugh like schoolkids pranking the teacher as they seeded the roads before a coming military convoy, watching as tyre after tyre burst, popping like balloons at their own private party. They told themselves that this was a ruin of precious rubber products, that this resulted in the enemy taking time and resources to repair or replace the tyres, besides the strike against enemy morale. But the truth of the matter was that it was simply outrageous fun.

The cunning explosives disguised as lumps of coal were tossed into barracks coal chutes by undercover partisan operatives. An even a more sinister explosive had been created to look like a dead rat. These remarkable facsimiles they placed in woodpiles, waiting for the natural human inclination to toss the horrid, deceased pest into the nearby furnace. The thought of bursting stoves and heating systems was enough to bring a smile any day.

One airdrop delivered a container of itching powder, and Closca scoffed at any possibility that the substance could be of any use. But Horea found a confederate working in an army uniform factory. She was able to sprinkle the evil ingredient (the barbed seeds of the Mucuna plant, dispensed in a talcum tin) onto the clothing.

Caught up in the mischief, Crisan sought out a contact who was employed in a factory manufacturing condoms. What Closca called "preservatives" and Horea "happy hats" were destined for troops along the Soviet line and also sent to the German Army occupying France. There seemed to be such a need in Paris that German manufacturers alone could not keep up with demand.

It was Crisan's brilliant idea to introduce the same irritant into the condoms. After that, the mere mention of the words "happy hat" was enough to produce childish chuckles from the entire team.

Harker's reports about these more mundane but insidious actions prompted the SOE to drop a shipment of something called carbachol, a powerful purgative. This was distributed by the team to others in the Resistance who then slipped it into the salt supplies at a variety of Rumanian military posts. The after-reports were vivid descriptions of Herculean bowel evacuations, another cause for amusement among the team.

Some of the tricks were not as successful, like the incendiary arrow, resembling a large safety match, eighteen inches long, a percussion fuse on the head, fired by a bow, supposedly with a range of fifty metres or so. The contrivance only worked half the time, and Lucille could throw the damned thing farther than the strongest man could fire it with the bow.

During this series of raids, sabotage, harassment, and hijinks, the Prince remained at their various base hideouts. He had not exactly refused to go out on his own missions, but no one had asked or assigned him one, either. The one thing Lucille knew was that Horea would never accompany the Prince again. He had told her this outright and had obviously been traumatised by his last encounter with the vampire.

Lucille wanted to comfort the Prince, help him find some relief from his turmoil, but he met all advances with a cold indifference. The intimacy of that one night in the grain warehouse was not to be repeated. And Lucille became so busy with their clandestine work that she had little time to coax him out of his doldrums. She was not the mothering type and felt that war was not a place for coddling.

And she had a feeling that such counseling was not something the Prince wanted. He was the type of man who needed to work out these internal problems for himself. And she was willing to allow him that privacy.

In the meantime, their efforts were proving to have a major impact upon military shipping operations in the area, which was demonstrated by the increased patrols—and those very patrols became targets for the team. Harker was also making regular reports to his minders—troop movements, manufacturing and utility locations to be marked for bombing at a later date—and any intelligence or rumour (denoted as such) was broadcast over his transmitter.

The nocturnal existence was taking a toll on them, the constant moving and the ever-present stress an exhausting strain on the entire team, that and living in each other's pockets. At the same time they knew they were making substantial contributions to the Resistance effort.

They decided to take a much needed rest at an old country estate presided over by a fascist-hating Grande Dame, one Zsusanna Karoli, a rather rotund little woman in her nineties, who insisted that everyone call her Tanti Zasu. She was much impressed by the courtly manners of the Prince and more so by his title. His solicitous attentions toward the dowager only gilded the lily.

On the afternoon of the second day of respite, Lucille came back from phoning her contacts to find young Harker on the transmitter receiving orders from his handlers in Britain. She watched him at his codebook, transcribing the message. His excitement grew with every word.

When he gathered the team together he could barely contain his joy.

"The German Gestapo have set up a training facility in Buzau. There they give instruction to specially selected Rumanians, teaching them the various methods of torture, censorship, how to search for Jews, gypsies, other enemies of the regime. Detention and deportation are also part of the curriculum. A school for cruelty and ethnic elimination."

"How many?" Crisan asked.

"Two dozen Germans," Harker answered. "They have commandeered a former girls' finishing school. Very small, two buildings. They reside in the attached dormitory. Out in the country north of the city. The big, fat fly in the ointment is that the entire place is surrounded by a Rumanian military camp, permanent buildings and temporary tent quarters."

"Dangerous," Lucille remarked. "Hard to get in, harder to get out."

"Not our kind of game," Closca added. "If we can't attack the oil fields, this is also beyond our scope."

"Just for a few bad Germans," Horea said. "Not worth the risk."

"There is something else." Harker's enthusiasm had not abated a bit. "My higher-ups have learned that the Gestapo have acquired the journals of a Rumanian physicist, a certain Demeter Olgaren. They would very much like to put their hands on those journals. What they contain could have a major impact on the war effort."

"What about the physicist?" Lucille asked. "Wouldn't they rather have him?"

"He died under questioning," Harker said.

"What's so important about this journal?" Horea asked after a proper moment of silence.

"Some kind of secret weapon that the Nazis are building," Harker answered. "The kind of weapon that could swing the war. There is some urgency to obtain these journals before they are sent to Berlin."

"Still sounds like a suicide mission," Crisan said and tossed his cigarette into the fireplace.

"Something for me then?" Everyone was startled and turned to find the Prince behind them. Lucille had not even noticed that he was listening.

"You?" Harker asked.

"I have an affinity for stealth," the Prince replied. "Which would appear to be needed in this excursion. I would be able to slip past the military encampment and into the training facility with some ease."

"Maybe true." Lucille turned to him. "But are you ready for another attack?"

"I am ready to earn my resurrection," he said.

"I'll go with you," Harker announced.

"It is better for me to operate on my own," the Prince said, looking pointedly at Horea.

"The purpose of this mission is not necessarily the elimination of the Gestapo," Harker said. "Though that would be a welcomed benefit, it is secondary. We need Olgaren's journals. You could waylay the staff while I find them. Two can be as surreptitious as one. And more efficient. I am not without my own stealthy capabilities. I have been taught by the best."

Lucille could see the Prince considering the situation.

"I'll go too," Lucille said. Both men turned to her.

"I do not think this is advisable," Harker told her. "It will be a most hazardous enterprise. For a woman especially."

"Will you please stop treating me like I'm one of your frail English country maids? Who, by the way, are most likely not as frail as you imagine." Lucille felt her anger rising. "This is not some Thomas Hardy novel. This is a goddamn war and I've been at it longer than you."

Harker sputtered a moment, taken aback by her vehemence. Lucille knew that she had trumped him.

"I will not have you with me," the Prince said. Lucille turned to him in surprise. She was about to protest when he raised a hand to silence her protest. "I cannot allow you to accompany us."

"You cannot?" she demanded.

"I will not," he said with determination.

"Because it is too dangerous for a woman?" She felt her face become hot. "You're as ignorant as this English twit."

Harker recoiled at the jibe.

"The mission is dangerous, agreed," the Prince said. "I am even more dangerous. I would protect you from a bullet, my dear Lucille. Thusly I would protect you from something even more deadly: myself."

She was too stunned to answer.

FROM THE WAR JOURNAL OF
J. HARKER

(transcribed from shorthand)

This is the uttermost despair. Now it is obvious that Lucy hates me. An "English twit," indeed. From love to loathing within a month. I do not, for the life of me, know how I have instigated such rancour. I had thought that these last few days of acting together on a common cause had united us, at least created a working relationship. But no, she despises me. And I am a miserable git.

I must put my personal turmoil aside and concentrate on the mission at hand. *My* mission.

During preparations Renfield constructed some of his devilish devices for the two separate excursions. But when we were about to leave, the Sergeant suddenly tried to join the Prince and me, even attempting to climb into the hearse. When, with much struggle on our part, he was pulled from the vehicle he confronted Dracula, going to his knees, begging, "Master, allow me to accompany ye."

He tugged at the vampire's coat, like a Dickens beggar: "Please, Master, please."

The Prince put a kind hand on the man's shoulder, and Renfield took this opportunity to lay his cheek against that hand, tenderly as a lover might.

"You must remain here," Dracula told his supplicant. "But I will return to you."

"Yes, Master." And to my surprise Renfield walked away without further complaint and busied himself with his kit as if this curious scene had never occurred. But I have seen this before. Whenever Renfield became caught up in one of his lectures or celebrated a demolition too loudly, all it took was one calming word from the vampire and the Sergeant settled. I was glad to turn over this command prerogative to the vampire, as when the birds in my Sergeant's attic begin to flit about, he becomes too much to bear, what with my preoccupation with Lucille and the business of war and all.

Closca drove the vampire and me to the outskirts of the Rumanian Army encampments. Horea refuses to be alone in Dracula's proximity, and even when all of us are gathered he edges as far away as possible from the vampire. When we needed someone to drive us to the drop-off point, Horea refused, and neither Closca or Crisan would volunteer. Obviously Horea has been sharing his experience with his fellows. Lucy was not speaking to us, so I had to make a command decision and order Closca to drive. I do admit that Horea's trepidation has made me insecure about accompanying the vampire on this raid. I will be alone with him and he will be unleashing his more beastly vices. I try to put these thoughts aside but they are there, lurking in the shadows like . . . well, like the creature at my side.

So, it was with some qualms that I watched the taillights of our lorry disappear down the dirt road. Would Closca be here upon our return? I could only hope. Would we return? Again, hope was my only refuge. That and the power of the vampire beside me—which carried its own threat.

Taking a heading from my compass, we started into the woods that bordered the access road. It was a dense stand of trees, mostly hardwoods, the branches overhead blotting out the feeble light from a half moon and the white splash of the Milky Way. I could not help bumping into trees and stomping on dry branches, making more noise than a herd of elk. So much for my lessons from the great Leatherstocking.

Dracula suffered no such clumsiness. He glided through the woods in absolute silence. Like a wraith he moved, weaving among the trees like the wind itself, with only the whisper of a rustle. He avoided every tree, every branch, as if he could see them, which was probably the case, considering his supernatural propensities.

Ahead of us there was light, silhouetting the forest before us. Once we had achieved the very edge of these woods, we could see the source of this false dawn. Great lights mounted on twenty-five foot poles ringed a temporary camp of Rumanian soldiers. Tents, large and small, were laid in military precision across a few hectares. The roads and pathways between were dusty and remarkably busy for such late hours, as we had arrived just past midnight. Notably there was no fence.

Dracula moved forward without hesitation, and I followed with some. I still did not have enough of the spy-actor in me to feel confident mingling with the enemy, my prey, despite my masquerade as a Rumanian Warrant Officer, a *maistru militar*. The uniform fit me well, Crisan having stitched up the trousers quite admirably, though the tunic smelled of tobacco, body odour, and a sickly sweet hair tonic. I added to my costume a holstered sidearm, a Ruby 7.5, and a valise. Dracula carried a larger briefcase. We both looked most professional. Just another soldier and civilian businessman intent on some dealings with the military.

Again, my fears were for naught as we walked through the camp without notice. Thank God Dracula had been convinced to eschew his cape. In his common attire he looked like just another civilian, if maybe with a more cavalier attitude than most.

Beyond the tents we came across newly built wooden structures, barracks, and command buildings. The activity here was less, with a preponderance of officers who paid us no more attention than anyone else. After wandering about the post for far too long, I realised that we were lost. I confessed this to Dracula.

"Then, we should ask for directions, should we not?" He asked as casually as if we had made a wrong turn in Picadilly Circus. He stepped up to the next man walking toward us. It was a Rumanian Colonel, a rather red-faced fellow with a preposterous mustache that extended past his jowls. I do not know if my misgivings rose out of my fear of being discovered or just habitual discomfort around superior officers. I managed a rather shaky salute.

"We are looking for the Germans," Dracula said. "Could you give us some guidance?"

"The Gestapo?" The Colonel took an involuntary step back.

"Precisely," I added, trying to do my part.

The officer gave us directions and within a few moments we came to the repurposed school building. It was a massive old stone structure, three storeys, an eighteenth-century mansion converted into a girls' finishing school some thirty years ago and now, once again serving a new function.

Within the vestibule squatted a varnished desk, situated to confront anyone who entered the front door. Sitting behind it a Rumanian Sergeant was sketching on a pad. His rifle leaned against the wall next to him.

As soon as we stepped through the door this gatekeeper pushed aside his drawing and snatched up the rifle. The Gestapo was apparently tough on their guard detail.

"Halt," he ordered without much enthusiasm.

Dracula walked up to face the man across the desk.

"Where do the Gestapo sleep?" Dracula asked.

The sentry seemed discombobulated by the question.

"This facility is closed," the Sergeant said. "Come back in the morning."

Dracula stepped around the desk, putting himself even closer to the soldier, who showed some concern. I could see him stiffening his spine, readying for a confrontation. Dracula was not intimidated. He made sure that the guard was meeting his eyes and waved his hand before the man's face.

"You will tell us where the Germans sleep," he said.

The man's face displayed no dazed look, no manifest evidence of hypnotism. He just answered.

"Third floor," he said.

"And the records?" Dracula asked.

"Second floor," the guard answered.

"What's on the first floor?" I asked. The guard did not respond, just kept staring into Dracula's eyes.

"What resides upon the first floor?" Dracula asked him.

"Offices."

"Is there a floor below this?" Dracula continued.

"Interrogation rooms. And cells for detainees."

"Ask him who is in the cells," I prodded Dracula.

"Who is in the cells?" he obliged.

"No one right now," the guard said. "They use them to practice. On privates and prisoners."

"Time for you to sleep," Dracula told him. The man smiled, set his rifle against the wall, and lay down on the floor behind the desk. Curling into a fetal ball, he was instantly asleep.

We walked past the desk toward the stairway leading up to the second floor. On the way I glanced at the sentry's sketchpad. It was not, as I expected, a crude nude so typical of soldiers but instead a rather finely executed drawing of a pair of horses frolicking. It was a bit in the abstract mode but you could feel the muscularity, the joy and freedom of the animals running wild. I was impressed.

On the way up the stairs I asked the vampire what he had done to the guard.

"He wanted to speak," Dracula said. "I just opened the sluice gates."

"With what?" I asked. "A crossbar?"

"A very strong suggestion."

We paused at the second-floor landing. I tried the door leading into the offices. Locked.

"Allow me," Dracula said as he grasped the doorknob with one hand, jamming his fingers into the gap between the hinges on the other side. There was a popping of steel and a cracking of wood, and without any effort at all he pulled the door out of its frame. He leaned the door against the wall and turned to go up the stairs.

"Time to feed," he said and began the ascent up to the next floor. "And to reduce the number of our enemy, of course."

I entered the offices. There was a main reception desk in front of me, then the room split into two wings, right and left. Each had a line of offices along the window side—the Gestapo like a view, I suppose. The only decorations were framed photos of the little man with the odd mustache and a large Nazi flag. On the inner side was an open area for secretaries' or assistants' desks, the wall behind them lined with file cabinets. I started with the files.

The Germans are an orderly lot—every desk in the office was as neat as a pin. The file cabinets were set up in a most systematic manner. I found Professor Olgaren's file almost immediately. But inside there was nothing more than a concise biography and a synopsis of the brief "interview" that ended in mid-sentence. I wondered what kind of interrogation led to a man dying before he could finish a sentence.

I quickly read the after-report on Olgaren's death but found no mention of the Professor's journals. Not finding the journals in the files, I then began searching the desks and offices. Most were locked. But I had thoughtfully packed a pry bar in my valise. I used it with abandon, ripping open office doors and tearing at desk drawers like I was a madman searching for the deed to my soul. When I was done, the offices on both sides were a shambles.

And I still did not have the journals.

I was just standing there, in the centre of my vandalism, trying to think of where else I could look, when Dracula strode in.

"I cannot find the journals," I told the vampire.

"I thought that might be a possibility," Dracula said. "So I brought someone who might be willing to help us."

He was carrying a man over one shoulder. He tossed the German into a chair. The fellow was in a dishevelled state, wearing only an undershirt and drawers. He was hugging himself as if against the cold, though it was exceedingly warm in the building. He didn't look at either of us but stared off into some distant place that did not contain a blood-splattered vampire.

"Where are the journals belonging to Professor Olgaren?" Dracula asked. The man did not answer, just sat there in his stunned state.

Dracula slapped him. The blow seemed a light one but it knocked the man off the chair. The vampire grasped him by a fistful of hair and lifted him back into the chair.

"Why not hypnotise him for the answer?" I asked the vampire.

"Some are resistant," he replied. "It may be that fear creates some sort of blockage." He returned his attention to the man in the chair. "Again, where are the journals?"

This time the wretch responded.

"Why should I tell you anything?" the chap mumbled. "You will still violate me like the others."

"No, he won't," I told the man. "I promise you."

Dracula peered at me. There was blood down his chin to his neck, dried clots clinging to his mustache. It was as frightening a visage as I have ever witnessed. But I had seen it before, after his other excursions, and I suppose I had become inured to it by now.

"Agreed," Dracula said. "You are safe from my predation. Now, as to the journals."

"They are in the courier's pouch," the fellow said. "Downstairs. To go out with the morning dispatches to Berlin."

"I believe you," Dracula said. And he snapped the man's neck with a crack that caused my sphincter to pucker.

We proceeded down the stairs and there it was, a canvas courier bag next to the door. It was locked, but I cut the bag open with the Ghurka service kukri blade I carried in my valise. Inside were three small journals, booklets filled with tiny writing and mathematical symbols. Inscribed inside the cover of each was the owner's name, D. Olgaren. I stuffed all three inside my Rumanian jacket and then, as an afterthought, the rest of the papers. Who knew the value of these documents?

"This is what we seek?" Dracula asked.

"Most definitely," I said. "Done and dusted."

"Then let us erase the evidence of my presence," he suggested and climbed back up the stairs. I followed him to the third floor. As soon as the door was opened the smell of blood hit me like a dank fog of death. I reluctantly followed Dracula inside a large room with two dozen beds arranged with a draughtsman's precision. My boots splashed across the tiled floor and I looked down to find myself ankle deep in a small pond of blood. I could barely hold back the gorge that rose in my throat and I turned away. But no place held any relief. The walls were splashed with arterial sprays that painted a portrait of violent death and agony. Bodies of dead men, their skin the white of their underclothing, were sprawled about in lifeless repose. Many had their necks torn into shredded meat. It was evident that Dracula's preferred method of execution was neck breaking, but many of the dead had limbs missing, chests ripped open, rib cages splayed like cracked walnuts. I will not enumerate the other brutal violations of the flesh I witnessed.

The lump in my throat could not be kept at bay and I discharged a volume of spew onto the floor and a severed leg. For some reason I felt some guilt at this offence to the deceased owner of this extremity.

During my momentary distress Dracula was walking around distributing the phosphorus charges that had been prepared for us by Renfield. Phosphorus burns at five thousand degrees Fahrenheit, destroying anything and everything it touches. As a result fire spreads quickly, incinerating, hopefully, any traces of our burglary—and what the vampire had wrought.

"I learned long ago not to leave any evidence of my presence," he had told us. "Such proof of my existence raises alarms and then opposition. Whereupon I find myself in much difficulty, and sometimes harm."

I helped set charges as he emptied his briefcase of the small bombs. They were each on a time delay so that we would have the opportunity to do the same to the file rooms.

Leaving the abattoir (in my case, gladly) and descending the stairs, we could hear voices below us. I do not know how our somnambulant sentry was awakened—the officer of the guard checking on his men, I supposed.

Whatever the circumstances when we came to the file room door we could see it was now occupied by two soldiers, our hypnotised sentry and an officer, searching the offices one by one. Looking for us, I reasoned.

"We must eliminate them," Dracula whispered to me.

"Couldn't you just hypnotise them both?" I asked. The slaughter I had just witnessed upstairs causing in me a reluctance for any more killing.

"They are too far away," Dracula answered. "I need proximity. And I do not think they will allow me to come close enough to be effective."

"True," I said, readying my sidearm.

"Leave me to deal with them," Dracula said. "I will meet you later at the rendezvous site."

Not waiting for an answer, his usual arrogance on display, he strode inside. I followed. I am not one to abandon a comrade.

The two soldiers saw us instantly and raised their weapons, the sentry's rifle and the officer's pistol.

"That's them!" the desk sentry cried out. Immediately the pair fired. Directly at Dracula, as I was three steps behind him.

To be honest, up to this point I had not believed Horea's tale about the vampire's invulnerability to bullets. I thought that Horea, caught up in the fury of combat, where confusion reigns, had misperceived the moment. Fear and the fever of the moment makes an unreliable witness.

Thus, when the two men fired and I saw the rounds strike Dracula, I expected the worst—for the vampire. Imagine my stupefaction when I saw two bullets exit Dracula's back and him still standing without apparent harm. Problematically one of the rounds hit me in the chest with enough force to knock me down.

From my prostrate position I watched Dracula attack both men. He grasped the desk sentry by the neck with one hand and squeezed, crushing flesh and sinew. The man's head popped off like a pea out of a pod. Dracula snatched the decapitated sentry's rifle from his dead hands before the body fell, then thrust the weapon into the officer's body, driving the muzzle through the man's solar plexus until the barrel came out of his back.

The astonished officer had enough strength left to fire two more bullets into Dracula before the man's eyes turned to look up to the ceiling, as if the answer to what had just occurred was written there, and life left him.

All of this happened in but seconds, the vampire moving so swiftly that his movements blurred in my vision. But then I was not in full use of my faculties, as I had been shot.

Having dispatched our enemy, Dracula rushed to help me to my feet, his grip lifting me as easily as if I were made of straw.

"Are you injured?" he asked. I was surprised at the concern on his face.

I quickly inventoried my body for pain, found none of consequence. I did discover a bullet hole in the front of my tunic. Was I so mortally injured that I was in shock, not feeling the wound that was about to kill me? I had heard of such. Was I going to die as puzzled as the officer I had just seen impaled by a Karabiner 98k?

Opening my jacket I found a hole in one of the journals, the bullet imbedded in the second.

"You are most lucky," the vampire remarked. I plucked the copper-jacketed slug from the notebook and pocketed it for future yarns of my brush with death. But as amazed as I was at my own close call, I was even more drawn to the four holes in Dracula's own chest. He seemed unperturbed, and there was no blood evident, at least any of his own. He turned away from me to scatter more of our incendiaries with not a hint of injury.

I followed his example, setting the phosphorus bombs upon file cabinets in the offices. When the last one was placed we left. During our fracas inside the offices the charges we had left upstairs in the slaughterhouse had gone off. As we exited the offices and walked down the hall we could hear the roar of fire above us as flame and smoke crawled down the stairs.

We hurried down to the first floor and sprinted to the front door. As I opened it I heard the charges we had planted in the second storey begin to fire off, a staccato of small pops like a string of firecrackers.

I rushed out of the building and into the cool night air. Dracula laid a hand upon my shoulder to slow me down, and, remembering my training, I began to walk as casually as I could manage. Dracula was hugging his arms to his chest as if against a chill but I knew he was hiding the ruination of his suit, German blood, and four bullet holes. I rebuttoned my own tunic, hoping the one small hole wouldn't be noticed in the dark. Halfway out of the encampment, at the boundary between wood and tent domains, we heard the clamour of a bell behind us, and I assumed that our pyrotechnics had been discovered.

We kept on walking without incident and easily entered the bordering forest at about the same point we had exited. The trek through the woods seemed shorter this time, and there was a brief wait at our rendezvous location. Crisan arrived on time, and the ride back was pleasant, the night air wafting through the open window of the lorry, dissipating the sharp tang of gunpowder and the copper odour of blood that clung to the vampire and most likely to myself.

Upon arriving at our hideaway I was in a mood to celebrate the success of our mission and my near-death escape, and to recount both to my comrades. Happily the Marx Brothers were infected by my exuberance and, truth be told, ever willing to open a bottle. Lucy, still of an ill humour, excluded herself from the merrymaking. The fair sex they are called, but so often they can be most unfair.

EXCERPTED FROM THE UNPUBLISHED NOVEL
THE DRAGON PRINCE AND I
by Lenore Van Muller

Lucille watched the men, her men, join in the hearty celebration of their survival. Harker was reliving his exploits to the others, while the Prince was more reticent. But even he joined in the merriment, poking a finger through the hole in the Englishman's jacket and recounting Harker's surprise when he realised he was still alive. Lucille was confounded at the pain their shared joy caused her. And as was her usual response Lucille turned that pain into anger.

She retreated to the front seat of the hearse and closed the door. Inside the quiet confines of leather and chrome she fumed. She allowed the indignation to stew for a while, willfully wallowing in her own sweet animus, working herself into a fine pique against the whole male kingdom. That was exactly what she faced, a reign of men, keeping women "in their place." That place created, defined, and enforced by those men.

Lucille took a deep breath and shunted her little mental tantrum to the back of her mind, where she kept the lifetime of offences against her and her sex. Then she proceeded to concoct a plan to prove herself, one more time. Once again she had to demonstrate her worthiness, her competency, that she was as good as any man. And at war, better than most.

At first light she bicycled to the nearest town and used a friendly phone to make a series of calls to all her contacts, seeking a target for another mission—a mission she would command.

By the time she returned to their hideout the sun was setting, sliding down behind the mountains. She found the men packing up the vehicles for the next move, to a sugar mill in Focsani.

"Change of plans," she announced and spread a map across the hood of the hearse. She pointed to Bacau.

"The German Army have set up an airfield just south of town," she began. "Rudimentary, a dozen planes, maybe to be expanded, but it looks like a refueling depot for bombers, most likely in preparation for the coming assault on Russia."

"Big target," Crisan noted. "An airfield."

"Most likely heavily guarded," Harker added.

"Not so much," Lucille said. "A Rumanian company. But their commanding officer loans them out to a cement block manufacturer in the daytime, and so a good many of them fall asleep at their guard posts at night."

"Why would he do that?" Harker asked. "Make them work for civilians."

"To make money," Closca answered. "Slave labour for the officer to get rich. And cement blocks are very much in demand by the Germans."

"They have these air machines?" Dracula asked.

"A half-dozen Arado 240s and a few old Heinkels," Lucille told him, then addressed everyone. "There are approximately thirty to thirty-five Luftwaffe pilots and support personnel on post. They have also taken over an off-post pub but always return to base by midnight as per standing orders."

"Capital! Sounds like a mission for us, right, stout fellow?" Harker tossed an amiable arm around the Prince's shoulder. This only irritated Lucille even more.

"And what do you intend?" Lucille asked him. "The two of you?"

"Kill some Germans." Harker grinned like a child excited about a visit to the zoo. "Destroy some enemy planes to boot."

"Sorry to rain on your parade, Leftenant," Lucille said. "But I think that this mission is too difficult for just two, no matter how formidable the Prince might be. I tracked down someone who has been there lately. They were able to draw this."

She laid a sketch on top of the map and continued. "As you can see, the aircraft are spread too far apart and too far away from the personnel to be easily sabotaged by two. And the German barracks, these five separate buildings, also are some distance from each other. You may be able to attack one, even two, but not without alerting the other barracks."

"Why are they so far apart, the planes and the barracks?" Horea asked.

"The plan seems to be common among the Nazis," Lucille continued. "Placing a great distance between aircraft and barracks makes it difficult to destroy the base with one air bombing attack."

"So, I take Horea, Closca, and Crisan with me," Harker said.

"And leave me behind with my knitting?" Lucille sneered. "I think not. I am leading this raid. Planning and leading it. Is this understood?"

There was quiet among the men. Harker opened his mouth to protest but Lucille stopped any utterance he could make with as harsh a look as she could manage. He swallowed and backed away, not able to meet her eyes. She turned to the Prince, who tipped forward at the waist in a slight bow to her.

"I am yours to command," he said.

She knew she would have no problem with her own men. The Marx Brothers were used to Lucille being in charge, and proving herself in combat. In more than one incident she had fought side by side with these men. She had saved their lives, and they had done the same for her. They would follow her anywhere, into any conflict, trusting her to bring them out alive.

When night arrived she sedated Renfield and they left. Dracula rode up front, Lucille taking over the driving duties to further miff Harker, who sat between them. The Englishman was silent the entire trip.

Surprisingly Dracula became extremely talkative. He opened his window and let the wind buffet his face and hair. He held forth on a variety of subjects.

"The night is misunderstood," he said, gazing into the dark rushing past. "Most think of the night tide as a black nothingness. But there is so much that is born once the sun abandons us and the moon reigns. Do you know how many creatures only begin to live at dark's falling? Creatures that disdain the day? More is out there than you can imagine. A whole world that most never see—or hear. The music of the night, the cry of predators on the prowl, the death whimpers of their prey, mating calls, the wail of loneliness—the wolf, for example. A plaintive song, is it not?"

He proceeded upon a long discourse on the nature and habits of the wolf, a creature about which he seemed most expert. This digressed into a discourse on the loyalty of the domesticated canine, then the Prince's abhorrence of cats, to a musing about rodents and how he had read that they had spread the Black Plague and so, on further thought, perhaps cats served a purpose after all.

"Imagine, a mite, the bathetic flea, able to exterminate so many," he marvelled. "Renders my lowly predation almost inconsequential."

"Almost," Lucille said, still holding some ill will against him. "Almost, but not quite."

He turned to her. "So, I have observed that the female is allowed to control these motor cars?" he asked.

"Oh, quite," she replied. "Between birthing and cleaning and servicing their husbands, we women find time to learn all sorts of handy talents."

She concentrated on the twin columns of light cast upon the road in front of her while the Prince reacted to her sarcasm with his own silence.

Once in Bacau they were given refuge by a motorcycle dealer, Edward Fejedelem, who was part of the underground network in that area. He was a tall, handsome man, with a jutting jaw and impeccable bespoke suit, a salesman of the finest ilk. He quartered them in the garage behind his showroom. His mechanic and other salesman were on a trip to Bucharest to collect a load of Polish motorcycles. This left the place to Lucille and her team until his men returned in four days' time. Fejedelem was not sure of his employees' loyalties or trustworthiness, so he advised the partisans to be out before their return. Lucille assured him that they would be gone.

He made an effort to flirt with Lucille, bragging about how great business was—as long as he could acquire product. Since the onset of gas rationing, motorcycles had become very popular, as they used much less fuel than autos. Lucille agreed with his point; she had seen people riding them even in winter, during blizzards, the temperature below zero, snow blasting riders bundled like Eskimos.

Fejedelem waxed ecstatically about how rich he was becoming, how he had a beautiful chateau a short distance away, that he would be glad to show her.

Lucille fended off his advances and sent him home to his wife and kids. He left her a key to the garage and a wink. Before the rest of her team could settle, Lucille insisted that they venture out immediately to scout their target.

They left the Prince behind as dawn was beginning to glow on the horizon. After an hour's drive she parked and led them on a short walk through forest that bordered a checkerboard of farmland, fields of new hay and corn. The woods were green pine punctuated by vertical slashes of white birch. By the time they arrived at the outskirts of the airfield, there was enough light to observe the layout of the buildings and the dispersal of the aircraft. From the safety of the hedgerows they reconnoitred the target. Lucille's intelligence proved to be true, as it was evident that a good many of the Rumanian guards were still asleep at their posts.

The Germans, she had to admit, were very clever. Each plane was protected on three sides by sandbagged walls with an overhanging net of woven rope. Sheaves of wheat were entwined in this web, making the planes invisible from the air. From high up it would appear to be just another patch of farmland. Workshops and fuel dumps were also housed under the same kind of camouflage, interspersed among the line of aircraft.

These structures were spread some distance apart along a narrow lane, just wide enough for the plane to taxi to the runway. The runway itself was a wider road, this one paved. Alongside this road were five buildings where the pilots and maintenance crews lived, plus a command office, a few outbuildings, and a long structure open on one side that sheltered three lorries, a fuel tanker, a fire engine, and a command car. All of these buildings were constructed to look like weathered farm sheds, chicken coops, and barns.

From the air it would seem to be just another farm. It would be nearly impossible to recognise this as an aerodrome, to spot the pockets of planes and workshops. And with everything so spread about, the whole area could probably be bombed heavily without considerable damage.

With the sentries asleep, it was a simple matter to slip through the hedgerows and observe the entire layout. While they were watching, there was a sudden burst of static, and a loudspeaker mounted on the outside of the command office blared and reveille was called in German. Sleepy-eyed men stumbled out of the three barracks and found their way to what Lucille assumed was the mess hall. They wore Luftwaffe grey, and Lucille counted thirty-one of them. Considering the number of late sleepers and men stationed in the headquarters building, Lucille assumed that her informant's count had been accurate.

Renfield was alert and took a moment to sketch the layout of the hangars and buildings—a quite accurate and skillful sketch, Lucille noticed; the engineer in him had come forth. He counted the number of explosive charges he would need and mumbled to himself the size and type while he drew. When he was satisfied they hurried away as the sentries began to wake. They slipped past the guards and into their vehicles. Again Lucille drove back to the motorcycle garage. There she created a mock-up on the floor using matchboxes and some yellow chalk she found on a workbench. She laid out her assault plan, ran through it three times. The last run-through she had everyone recite his role back to her. Then she told everyone to catch some sleep. Harker was sullen during her presentation and retreated to an overt sulk as he went to nap in the lorry bed, curled up inside a blanket like a child after a scolding.

The Prince, besides insisting on assaulting one of the barracks without assistance, watched her lay out the strategy with a bemused smile that irritated her. Afterward he walked away to immerse himself in his latest book obsession, the works of Jules Verne. He was halfway on a journey to the centre of the earth.

Lucille was not tired, her usual state before combat, and just studied her plan, going through every step, over and over, trying to imagine what could go wrong, what *would* go wrong. She knew very well that every plan fell apart once the shooting started.

The others couldn't sleep, either, the tension of the coming fight acting as a stimulant. Crisan sidled up to Renfield, who was prepping his demolitions. The Rumanian had become the Scotsman's pupil, discussing the arcane craft like art students deconstructing Cubism. Once, when Renfield lapsed into a serenade of a crude tune, Crisan taught him a roughly translated, equally dirty gypsy ballad.

Horea and Closca spent a bottle of wine arguing the benefits/depredations of Communism versus the same for Catholicism, enjoying the discourse as if it were a meal itself. Their sustenance was argument, and it seemed to bring the two men closer than a married couple. In fact, the constant back-and-forth reminded Lucille of many a bickering couple who fought day and night but loved each other to the grave.

When it was suitably dark outside, Lucille ordered everyone into the vehicles and they headed out of Bacau. Lucille drove again. She could hear Renfield humming a jaunty tune in the back of the hearse. His devilish devices were stored in the bed of the following lorry. On the way they ran into a thunderstorm. The rain pelted her windscreen so hard and so fast that Harker had to shout to be heard.

"Rain!" He leaned across the Prince to bellow at her.

"Ever the master of the obvious, Leftenant," she replied.

"Perhaps we should turn back," he said. "Try some other evening when the weather clears."

"The Leftenant doesn't have the clandestine experience to know that rain is the saboteur's friend." She knew she was lecturing him like a proctor would a student and took some pleasure in it. "Rain masks the noise of our approach. If a sentry is awake and alert, the leaves and foliage underfoot will be wet and not crack or snap to betray our movements. Plus visibility is reduced. The guards will seek shelter and reduce or neglect their patrols. Everyone stays inside where it is warm and dry. Unless you think you will be too uncomfortable to participate . . ."

He swallowed any reply. The downpour subsided to a drizzle and she turned down a side road about a half kilometre from the airfield. Lucille parked in a clearing made by woodcutters, trimmed branches and pale piles of woodchips laying about the stumps. The hike through the forest was as expected, wet and uncomfortable. The Prince strode through the rain, past the pine and birch without hesitation, striding tall, never ducking the branches but somehow bypassing them. The rain made everyone else look like a wet cat. But the raindrops cloaked the Prince in a fairy-like sheen. When they reached the airfield perimeter Lucille took Harker aside.

"Tonight you will be required to engage the enemy," she told him. "The first time for you, I suppose. Man to man, as they say."

"I am sure I will account myself to your satisfaction," he said. "As I did the other night. I was shot, you know."

She turned to the others.

"My friends, are you ready to eliminate the guards?" she asked her three guerillas. "As you know, silence is imperative."

Crisan pulled a length of wire from his pocket, draped it around his neck. Lucille had watched him make the garrote. They had been camped in the ruins of an old mansion where in one corner leaned the guts of a piano, looking like an ugly harp. The rest of the instrument had been chopped up for firewood. Crisan scavenged the remains of a mahogany leg out of the fireplace, cut himself two fist-long pieces and secured a metre of thin piano wire to each chunk of wood. He had found no reason to use it, thus far.

The other two held up their daggers, the blades painted black for night work. All three men smiled at her, looking more like pirates than partisans. These were times that required pirates.

"Rejoin us when you are done," she told them. "See you at the rally point."

They pulled their watch caps down and adjusted them so that they could see through the eyeholes Crisan had stitched into them. He was quite handy with needle and thread, once hand-stitching a leather shoulder bag for Lucille as a birthday gift.

"Good hunting," she said and they slipped into the woods, disappearing instantly into the shadows. Harker nudged her.

"What was that wire Crisan put about his neck?" He asked.

"Something better seen than described," she replied. "On second thought, maybe the other way around." She led them toward the runway. At the edge of the forest, across from the buildings, they set down the heavy satchels of explosives that each carried and waited for the Marx Brothers to return.

"I could have helped them," Harker said.

"They are excellent at this kind of work," she replied. "No offence, but you would be a hindrance. As would I."

He had no answer for that. The four of them waited. Lucille could not help but notice that the Prince was watching her like one studied a creature one has never seen before. As she had first studied him. Surely he was curious about this side of her, an aspect he had never witnessed. She could feel the pressure, mostly fed by her own insecurities. How was it that she felt so vulnerable to his opinions and expectations?

There was a rustle from the shadows, and Lucille's hand went instinctively to her Luger. She stared off into the trees, trying to separate tree from whatever hid in the black beyond.

"It is our comrades," the Prince whispered. Lucille could not see what he did and kept alert. Then a whistle pierced the dark, a whippoorwill. Lucille answered in kind. Harker had his own weapon, an American Thomson machine gun, raised and aimed into the woods, his finger on the trigger. Lucille reached out a hand and pushed the barrel down.

The three Marx Brothers emerged from the shadows. There were smiles on their faces and blood on their clothes.

"Whippoorwills are not night birds," she told Horea. "Use the nightjar, or an owl."

"I can't do a nightjar," Horea answered, somewhat sheepishly.

"And his night owl sounds like a sheep having an orgasm," Crisan said and everyone laughed, softly. She turned to Renfield, who was standing still and paying no mind to the rain spattering him.

"Are you ready, Renfield?" He smiled, hefted his bag of bombs.

"Ready tae raise a bliddy ruckus," he said, and she knew he was in enough possession of his faculties to perform.

"Go to it," she ordered. "Remember, give us enough time for a getaway. A half hour at least."

"Thirty minutes, on the jot," he said and gave her a jaunty salute. Then he gathered the satchels of charges everyone had been carrying for him and trotted off toward the line of aircraft. Lucille waited until he was out of sight.

"All right, gather around," she told the others. "One more time. Here's how we do this. Horea, you're with me at the far west barracks. I'll take the front door, you the back. The middle barracks is for Harker and the Prince, Harker at the back door. Crisan and Closca take the east, Closca at the front. At my signal we in the front toss in a grenade."

"Or two." Closca grinned. "Just for grins and giggles."

"Or three," she added with her own smile. "Followed by the front man entering and shooting anything that still moves. The man at the back door is there only for any Germans that manage to escape that way. You do *not* enter the barracks. You'll just get shot by your own side. Not a way to die. And watch out for bullets and shrapnel going through the walls and windows."

"What about the Command HQ?" Harker asked. "It appears that the Commanding Officer resides there. Also there is probably a Duty Officer to contend with."

"There is no back door to the HQ," Lucille told him. "And I had Renfield fix us up something special for whoever might come out when they hear us at work at the barracks."

She pulled it out of her own satchel and led the team to the compound. Sprinting across open ground gave her a gut-wrenching moment of nausea, but the crossing went unnoticed. There were lights on inside the HQ hut. Peering through a window, Lucille could see that the place was divided in two; a wall and door separated the front office from a probable billet to the back where the Commanding Officer slept. Harker was right—there was a Duty Officer visible in the front office, sleeping at a desk, his Luftwaffe jacket unbuttoned, a half-empty wine bottle in front of him.

With her foot Lucille drove a wooden stake into the ground in front of the door. She attached Renfield's device to the stake. It was a chunk of plastique backed by a broken shovel, the front embedded with roofing nails and screws. She planted it so the hardware faced the door then strung a wire from the explosive detonator to the doorknob. As soon as the door was pulled open the charge would be ignited, launching the various bits of steel at the speed of a few thousand feet per second toward whoever was unlucky enough to be in the doorway.

She tested the tension on the wire and turned to the others watching her. "The bliddy pull switch," she whispered with an exaggerated brogue, and they all smiled at her, even the Prince.

After setting her booby trap, Lucille led her team toward the barracks. The three buildings were lined up with the usual military precision, each structure as uniform as the next, despite the farmhouse camouflage. The mess hall was an identical building. All were dark.

Lucille checked to confirm that everyone was in position. She knew Harker had taken umbrage at being designated a back-door man and not a front-door attacker, but she had put him there for a reason—exactly to put him in his place.

Taking her own position at the entrance to the eastern barracks she saw Closca and the Prince watching her, each standing in the shadows. The heavy mist hung in the light like a silver cloud.

She pulled a grenade out of her ammo pouch, held it up for them to see. The Prince gave her one of his wolfish smiles. Closca grinned, and she could see a dental glint of gold as he raised his two grenades. She pulled the pin on the grenade, held down the ignition spoon as she turned the doorknob, and slowly eased open the barracks door.

Nodding to the Prince and Closca, she tossed in her grenade, shut the door, and hit the ground prone.

The following explosion blew out the windows, and she could feel the concussion through the mud. It was followed by two more explosions and a ragged, shrill scream. She paid it no mind and stepped inside. As she did so she heard another, duller, bang. The Command HQ. Somebody had opened the door to his own death.

In the barracks a few bunk beds were toppled, feathers floated in the air, the residue from a ripped pillow. Bodies were splayed about the wreckage, but only in the front of the room. With the white fluff wafting in the air it looked like a souvenir snow globe celebrating the seventh level of hell.

In the rear a half-dozen men were rousing themselves from the shock. She shot them. The man going for the gun hanging from his bed was her first target. Then the others as she strode down the middle aisle, shooting the stunned, dazed, and wounded. There was no opposing fire. She opened the back door and Horea stepped inside. He glanced about the room with a nod of appreciation. She reloaded and the two of them shot each of the soldiers in the head.

Stepping outside, into the cleansing rain, she reloaded again. The Prince was just exiting with Harker, Closca, and Crisan coming out of the eastern building.

The Prince quickly went into the HQ building, stepping over the body hanging over the threshold. There was another scream, cut off in mid-howl.

Everyone gathered in front of the HQ. The Prince stepped out to join them, and as usual, he was soaked in blood. Lucille glanced at his newly ruined clothing saturated in crimson.

"Maybe we should provide you with some sort of work clothes that we could toss afterward," she said to him, then turned to Harker. "Do you want to do a quick search of the HQ for any valuable intel, Leftenant?"

He nodded.

"And be sure to leave a few of Renfield's presents to destroy any evidence of the Prince's handiwork," she added.

Harker reached into his own demolitions satchel and extracted a pair of incendiary devices. Lucille opened the HQ door for him as Crisan and Closca hauled the dead Duty Officer out of the way. Looking inside Harker could not hide his instant revulsion at what he saw. Lucille could see a splash of blood on the wall.

"Do you need any help?" she asked, as she moved to enter behind him.

"You don't want to see this," he told her as he blocked her passage.

"Thank you for preserving my fragile sensibilities," she said with as much sarcasm as she could muster, pushing him aside to enter.

Then the Prince put a restraining hand on her shoulder. It was as if she had been gripped by a rock. He leaned over to speak into her ear. There was no breath, just his voice.

"I would rather you not witness the clutter from my efforts," he said. She stepped back and Harker proceeded alone.

Lucille turned to the Prince. "Are you also trying to protect my delicate nature?"

"It is more like trying to protect my own discomfort," he replied.

"We are both too sensitive for these times," she said and received a smile from him.

Harker stepped out of the HQ. Behind him there was a burst of light as the incendiaries ignited.

"Mission accomplished," Harker announced as he stuffed a stack of papers into his satchel. "Done and dusted."

"Congratulations," she told him, this time without the sarcasm. She surveyed the team, taking a head count. "Where's Renfield? He should be back by now."

"I'll go fetch him," Harker volunteered.

"No." Lucille shook her head. "That's my place. The rest of you go to the vehicles. We'll meet you there."

She could see that Harker wanted to protest, but to his credit he swallowed it and joined the others as they jogged away.

Lucille crossed the runway and headed down the aircraft access road, passing the bunkered and camouflaged hangars. The rainfall had ceased, but the mud underfoot was a thick pudding clinging to her boots, making them heavier with every step. Her clothes had become sodden, clinging to her, producing a chill that seeped into her bones. Clearly the adrenaline that had been fueling her so far was abating. At each of the sandbagged hangars she searched for the lost Renfield, calling his name. She thought she saw something behind the fourth hangar down, a movement in the dark.

She raised her pistol, finger on the trigger, trying to make out the moving figure. Then it suddenly burst into view, Renfield on a bicycle. He skidded to a stop next to her, like a kid showing off. He beamed his idiot grin.

"Look what ah found!" he exclaimed proudly.

"We were waiting for you," she chided.

"Ah found something else," he said. "Aye, an ammo dump. Big bliddy boom coming."

At that moment the first airplane blew up. The aircraft must have had a full fuel tank, evidenced by the large orange-and-yellow marigold of flame that blossomed in the air. Wheat-bundle torches and airplane parts flew into the sky.

Then the next one exploded, another blossom of fire equal to the first. The third outdid the previous two, the air conflagration full of leaping barrels, most likely a fuel cache. The ball of fire roiled and climbed into the night sky, sandbags flew like clumsy swallows, wheat sheaves flared and burned, sparks floating to earth in a fiery parody of snowflakes.

Lucille was rooted to the spot, waiting for the next eruption. That was why she did not see the approaching car. It was then that she remembered the vehicle shed. On the reconnaissance the day before there had been six vehicles: three lorries, the fuel and fire trucks, and the staff car. Tonight, as they passed the shed she had noticed only five, the trucks but no car. Her mistake.

And now it occurred to her that she had not gone into the buildings to count heads. She had no idea how many Germans were dead or, more important, missing.

She cursed at herself as the car came into the blazing light cast by the burning planes. Lucille could see Nazi officers hanging out of all four windows, gawking at the billowing flames. Probably returning from a birthday party, a promotion, one of them clearing a case of gonorrhea. It did not matter. She should have checked the local pub the Germans had taken over.

These thoughts raced through her brain and froze her for a few seconds. She remained that way until she saw the flash of gunfire from the car speeding directly at her and Renfield.

If they were drunk before they saw their aircraft blowing up, they had sobered up quickly, and now they were aiming their sidearms at the only targets available—the woman and man standing before them, brilliantly lit by the burning airfield.

Bullets splashed up mud around Lucille and Renfield. With one hand she shoved Renfield behind her, raised her pistol with the other, and took aim at the car speeding toward her. The three passengers and driver had guns out the windows. And those guns were spitting bullets at her.

Good God, man, but she is a stunner. I've never seen the like on God's green earth. She is an astonishing specimen. Of late I have been a bit peeved at her, I admit, for a variety of slights and transgressions on her part. But after witnessing her actions on that blasted airfield my affections for this woman, no, for this WOMAN, have increased manifold.

We were on our way back to our vehicles as suggested by Lucy (I can no longer apply the term *dear* or *sweet* to her name; a new appellation must be found). When our hearse and lorry came into sight, my reservations about leaving her alone to find the tardy Renfield built up to the point where I drew myself to a halt.

"I'm going back," I said to the others. "Renfield is my responsibility."

"I will accompany you," Dracula volunteered.

I turned to Horea. "Stay with the vehicles. We'll be back in two shakes." He nodded, and I turned back the way we had come.

As we approached the airfield an explosion was heard. The billowing flame put the forest in front of us in stark relief, the black trunks of the trees silhouetted against this premature dawn.

Then another booming blast that was immediately followed by a much larger explosion. There was no cause for alarm thus far, as I expected them, the blasts being the result of Renfield's craftwork. But then the sound of gunfire erupted. This was enough to spur me on and I began to run. The vampire passed me instantly and I had to press myself to catch him.

He stopped where the woods ended and the land had been cleared for the taxi strip. There was another explosion as a plane blew up and I saw a tail piece tumbling through a cloud of flying sandbags.

But the focus of our attention was drawn to Lucy, standing in the midst of the taxi lane, aiming at a grey German staff car racing toward her and Renfield, who stood at her side gawking at the conflagration he had created. Four arms protruded from the open windows of the car and four pistols were firing at Lucy like a scene from some Yank gangster movie.

But she stood her ground, the bright fire from the burning airfield bathing her in a yellow, flickering illumination. She did not flinch as a fusillade of bullets struck the mud and punctured the air around her. Calmly she aimed and fired as if the bullets buzzing about were mere raindrops.

She shot and the staff car windscreen shattered. The driver was obviously hit as the car swerved, canting into a sideways skid, speeding directly at Lucy. She never faltered, rather used the opportunity to shoot the two passengers on that side. The vehicle slid to a stop. Then with supreme self-composure she reloaded a fresh magazine, walked around the car, and shot through the rear window, killing the remaining Nazis.

This extraordinary event was followed by a massive blast, behind the aircraft and fuel bunkers. Tracers arced into the air, and there was a popping of small-arms ammunition and larger eruptions as bombs cooked off.

Dracula and I ran across the field to join Lucy and Renfield. Over the thunder of ammo explosions and the remaining aircraft and fuel salvos she shouted into Renfield's ear. He responded by tossing a charge under the staff car. As we walked away the auto blew up behind us. We were so inured to the ongoing cataclysm that we did not even glance back. Well, except for Renfield, who always dawdles to watch the fiery results of his craftsmanship.

At our hearse, Lucy was greeted by her three comrades as the returning hero she was, indeed. Her face was blackened with smears of gunpowder and soot, her hair a wild tangle, wet and glistening, giving her the appearance of a ferocious Amazon. I was never more enamored of this magnificent woman, excuse me, as I said before—WOMAN.

Renfield climbed into the rear deck of the hearse with some reluctance. "Ach, cannae we dally a bit and watch the show?" he asked.

"Sorry," Lucy told him. "Time to go before the local militia take notice and arrive to spoil our little excursion."

Lucy took the driver's seat, I the passenger side, with Dracula between us. She drove away with the remains of the airfield ablaze behind us. I could not help but look back to the merry mess we had created, and with some satisfaction. Imagine, our little party destroying an entire airfield. A small one, but still. The boys back in London were certainly going to have to give me proper respect after this exploit.

Dracula was examining Lucy as if she were some rare botanical specimen he had just discovered—which was not far from the truth.

"Are all modern females similar to you?" he asked her. "Or are you an exemplary exception, like Catherine the Great?"

"You've read about her?" Lucy asked.

"She and I were . . ." Dracula paused. "We shared a convivial relationship. She was a redoubtable woman, in all manners and ways. As you evidently are."

Lucy could not contain her delight at his approval, and I could not hold back the jealousy I felt at that moment. We did not return to the garage but travelled through the night, much to my regret, as I was looking forward to examining the motorcycles in the showroom. I have a particular fancy for that type of transportation. But we needed to put as much distance as possible between us and our raid.

Dracula rode in silence, reading a book. His vision must have been phenomenal, as the dash light hardly gave any illumination, at least for reading. I kept to my own thoughts, renewing my decision to find a way to sway Lucy to my affections, and her attentions to me.

We are the perfect match.

EXCERPTED FROM THE UNPUBLISHED NOVEL
THE DRAGON PRINCE AND I
by Lenore Van Muller

As tired as they might have been, the residual thrill of escaping death made the morning after each and every attack a period of insomnia, since the saboteurs were too full of residual energy to sleep.

As for Lucille and Harker, if they had not found rapprochement they at least had reached an emotional stasis. His longings were kept at bay, and she made her own compassionate concessions, treating him with a brotherly affinity. At least that was what she thought up to this point. But, no, the English boy was thick as a brick.

On the drive to their next refuge, Harker found a moment when they were refueling to take her aside. He was in a fervour and told her that he found Lucille never more beautiful than when, her hair in a mad tangle, her face smudged with a dusting of cordite, her eyes burning with a fierce anger, she showered the enemy with bullets from her long-barrelled Luger. She could only answer with a sigh and he did not speak for the rest of the trip.

The next night as he scribbled away in that damned diary with those hen scratchings he called shorthand, Lucille heard him say the words out loud as he was wont to do when making entries, "She is a true girl and improves under strain that would kill a weaker nature."

Still Lucille's boundaries of no physical contact were maintained. When they had arrived at this new next hideout Harker attempted to congratulate her success at the airfield with a quick embrace. "Well done! Oh, I say that was splendid," he declared.

Lucille immediately pulled away and there was an uncomfortable look from the Englishman, his hurt-puppy gaze making Lucille feel guilty. And angry, at herself more than at Harker.

She had thought that they had finally found a working relationship that was satisfactory for both, devoid of any emotional bother. They were two adults and were supposed to act as such. She had thought the matter had been settled once and for all. But the Englishman was an obtuse pup.

All in all, the six of them had created a redoubtable team and were causing much hardship against their enemy, a source of happiness for all. The only shadow over their work was the messages for Harker attached to the drops. The English officer had a mate on the other end who would leave notes (in code, of course). Messages from home, much of it concerning the German bombing of his native land and sometimes naming mutual acquaintances who had died in "the blitz" or "the good fight."

Despite their mutual peace accord, Harker still found new ways to irritate her. The lectures on warfare she finally terminated by one day asking him how many men he had personally killed, face-to-face. His answer was grim silence.

The latest irritants were his constant inquiries about her father. One question after another concerning "the Professor," and it was evident that the Englishman's focus was on the days recounted in that damned novel.

His curiosity mirrored her own, but she gave him scant information and rebuffed most of his queries. Even though she had hectored her father for years on the same subject, she was reluctant to give away what she knew. She felt obliged to guard her father's privacy as diligently as did the old man. Anything she would have told Harker would seem some sort of betrayal.

The first night after the airfield attack, his badgering became too much and she fled to the roof of their current hideout. They were ensconced in a top-floor apartment of an office building in the centre of town. It was the former residence and headquarters of the Walnut King of Rumania, a Hungarian named Ferenc Dezso Blasko. His was the second highest structure in town, six precise inches lower than the spire of the Catholic church two blocks away. An architectural concession negotiated with the local diocese.

Below the apartment were six floors of walnut industry offices. Blasko, a vocal anti-Fascist, had seen the coming cataclysm and sold everything, fleeing to Grand Rapids, Michigan, of all places.

Local partisans had offered the old apartment as a temporary refuge. It was beautifully appointed in all walnut parquet floors, floor-to-ceiling walnut paneling, ornate walnut ceilings, and, yes, every stick of furniture was hand-carved wood—walnut.

In comparison to their other safe havens it was quite plush, better than many of their previous residences.

Lucille had confronted Harker, telling him to go to her father for answers and to leave her alone, for God's sake. He retreated to transmit his nightly radio posting. Every night he submitted reports to his SOE handlers: local war preparations, military movements, troop armament, intel gathered from other Resistance cells as well as from their own observations. This time he was relaying what they had found at the Luftwaffe HQ. So, for now, he was busy enough to leave Lucille to her own devices. She was going to query the Prince, who had ensconced himself in Blasko's library and was cherry-picking a stack for his own amusement. She watched him peruse the shelves and saw the joy in his eyes. She decided to not bother him and went back to the others.

But then the Marx Brothers began loudly arguing over whether the Americans would enter the war. Desperate for some peace and quiet, she had taken the stairs to the roof.

Renfield was already there, having rejected the apartment because all that dark wood bothered him. He had set his bedding under the stars, and Lucille envied him. It was a balmy night, the whispered breath of summer in the air. A few small clouds ambled across an otherwise clear, starry sky.

In the kitchen of the apartment Lucille had found a delicate white porcelain cup and made herself a pot of tea. She took the pot and cup onto the roof with her. She offered to fetch another cup for Renfield, but he was in one of his non-communicative fugue states. Stepping away from him, taking a corner of the roof for herself, she poured a cup and drank the contents in one quick swallow. It was hot but she managed.

Then she stared into the cup to read the leaves, as was her habit. All she saw was a dark clump on one side. Tea reading, as taught to her by an Irish hag from Dalkey, was driven by the reader's interpretation of the pattern made in the bowl. There were certain images, symbols formed. Birds meant good news. But the other forms, cats, dogs, kites, snakes, were all free for explanation by the reader. The symbols could be created by the dark matter, the leaves against the white background, or seen in the reverse, reading the white space.

She saw neither here. Just a dark lump of no defined shape. She thought the error was in her technique and tried to relax, let her mind open itself to the spheres around her.

She dumped the leaves and poured another cup, this time slowly sipping the drink so as not to disturb the serene receptiveness she needed to be able to read. Lucille was careful to read from the present, starting at the handle and following the symbol downward in a clockwise spiral. And again she saw nothing but a dark lump gathered at one side of the cup. She focused on the congregation of damp leaves. Nothing.

Lucille tried to remember the teachings of the Irish hag, a tiny, toothless woman whose accent was so thick Lucille had asked her to repeat things three, four times. What had she missed in the lesson?

She made another attempt. Renfield was watching now, so she turned away from him. Lucille had always been shy about demonstrating her abilities, knowing she could face either derision or fear.

Pouring another, this time draining the tea into her saucer, since drinking more liquid would only lead to frequent visits to the loo, she concentrated on the results. A repeat of the amorphous mass, facing a different direction from the handle but still unreadable. At least for her.

Then she caught herself. At each reading the clump had been on a different side of the cup. Did that mean anything? She whished she had spent more time with her teacher. But the witch also read the Tarot, and Lucille had been in a hurry to study the cards so she could foretell the future of her relationship with an English opera baritone.

What was she missing? Suddenly the insight came to her. At every reading the collection of leaves had been on the east side of the cup, no matter her position. Lucille walked to the eastern side of the roof, peered out into the night.

The small town was spread before her, so peaceful looking. The only hint of war was the blackout curtains that had turned the windows into neatly lit outlines of squares and rectangles. She thought about how behind those windows people were going about their mundane lives.

She was not so naive that she thought they were ignorant of the death and destruction gathering about them. But she did envy their momentary solace of family and friends, lives of order and comfort. She longed for even a brief respite from the stress, the killing.

She was wallowing in this rare moment of self-pity when she saw a whole section of the city suddenly go dark.

Serendipity. Janos had a phrase: "Serendipity, I lean on it." It was his word for luck. Lucille didn't believe in either. Not in war.

But the fact was if she had not argued with Harker, if she had not had her fill of the Marx Brothers' interminable quibbling, if she had not turned away from Renfield, if she had not decided to read the leaves on this very night, if she had not stood there mooning over the life she did not have . . .

Serendipity. Maybe her beloved Janos had not been off the mark.

The lights flickered back on. A small section of town, only four or five blocks, at some distance from her perch. A possible power outage?

But then another section went black. An area of about six square blocks adjacent to the previous area. She stared at the great swath of black until the muted lights returned. And then another bit of the city lights went out, again next to the previous and this one closer, only three blocks from their hideout.

This last event turned her curiosity to alarm.

"Renfield! Grab your gear! We have to go!" She helped him gather his pack. "Forget the bedding! Go!"

She pushed him to the roof access door and they ran down the stairs. Leaving him in the vestibule she burst into the apartment. Harker was still at his radio transmitter, tapping out code. She yanked the earphones off his head, ripped out the improvised antenna, tore the power cord out of the wall.

"Cut the transmission!" she yelled into his astonished face. "They're on to us! We have to run!"

The three Marx Brothers stared at her dumbfounded.

"NOW!" she screamed.

And then the lights went out.

Lucille cursed. They all quickly collected their weapons and belongings, fumbling in the dark until Horea located his flashlight. The Prince calmly stuffed a handful of books into the valise he had commandeered after the Gestapo raid. Harker closed up his transmitter. Lucille grabbed her own duffel and they hurried to the stairs.

Renfield was waiting on the landing like an abandoned child, rooted to the spot until someone fetched him. Lucille took him by the hand as they rushed down the stairwell, Horea lighting the way.

On the way she told them what she had witnessed on the roof.

"I don't understand," Horea said. "So some people lost power. Happens all the time in my neighbourhood. Wiring's a rat nest."

"Somebody was turning the power off in a systematic way. One quadrant at a time," she told them.

She explained that this was a method the Army and Secret Police used to seek out clandestine radio transmissions. She had heard of it as a Gestapo tactic used against the Resistance in Paris. Once they discovered a suspicious signal they turned off the power in designated areas. If the suspicious transmission ceased at the same time, that meant the radio resided within that location. If it remained transmitting, they moved on until they pinpointed the right section of town.

That was what was happening right now. And the horrendous coincidence of the lights going out just as Lucille had stopped Harker from sending had given away their location.

"That is a most clever stratagem of the Hun," the Prince said.

"And deadly," Lucille answered.

They made it to street level and stopped at the door. It was a lesser dark outside than in the stairwell but not by much.

"How can they find us?" Closca asked.

"House-to-house searches," she replied. "They were probably stationed at the border of each designated zone. As soon as the signal stopped they would begin their search."

This was instantly proven correct. As they made their way up the sidewalk to the first intersection headlights were seen down the right hand street.

"Trucks!" Crisan yelled. The vehicles were three blocks away. Then headlights splashed the corner to their left, two blocks away. The headlights were half-masked for blackout purposes, giving the trucks a sullen aspect, even evil.

Their hearse and apple truck had been stationed in an old auto repair garage three blocks from the hideout, straight ahead. Harker was leading them in that direction, keeping to the deeper shadows. They cautiously but hurriedly made their way up the block.

Lucille's Luger hung from a lanyard around her neck and she flipped off the safety, held the gun waist high, ready.

As they approached the next corner they hugged the wall. Crisan, the stealthy one, made his way up front to see if the going was clear. Lucille heard him curse under his breath as he quickly pulled his head back.

"Sentry," he told them.

Lucille and Harker took a peek. Yes, one lone Rumanian soldier standing, smoking, his rifle at his side. Harker reached for his pistol and Lucille put a restraining hand on him.

"A gunshot will just draw the others to us," she warned.

Crisan pulled out his garrote, eyed the sentry, and then turned to Lucille for permission. It was evident that Lucille had deposed Harker as leader, and the partisans once again looked to her for major decisions. Harker had not complained and seemed to accept the turnabout. Maybe he would grow into a decent commander.

"Allow me," the Prince whispered. She nodded to the Prince. He stepped around the corner and casually walked toward the guard.

"Halt!" The guard snatched up his rifle and aimed at the vampire. But by then the Prince was only six feet from the soldier. Raising a hand the vampire fixed his eyes upon the man.

"You have checked our credentials, found them in order," he said to the sentry.

"You may move on," said the hypnotised soldier. Lucille and the others began to move out of the shadows.

"What's this?" A voice was heard and another soldier, buttoning the fly of his trousers, appeared and walked up to the Prince. Lucille's heart sank. Amazing, Lucille thought, captured because some Rumanian private had stepped away from his post to piss. She quickly tapped Crisan on the shoulder.

He moved immediately. Three steps, quick and quiet as a cat, and he was behind the second sentry. Crossing his arms he looped the wire over the man's head. Lucille doubted the doomed soldier ever saw it. What, a silver glint that whipped past his eyes?

Crisan yanked his arms akimbo, which closed the piano wire loop with one powerful pull.

It cut through the man's neck like a wet knife through cheese. There was a click as wire bit through neck vertebrae. The head tumbled down the man's chest. Crisan kneed the body away from him. The neck stump pumped blood with the last few beats of the failing heart, one, two, three scarlet spurts, then ceased.

Lucille heard Harker's whisper. "Blimey . . ."

At the same time the Prince closed in on the sentry in front of him. The man was shaking his head, as if coming out of a dream, but in an instant the Prince had grasped the man by the neck and one arm. With no evident effort the vampire threw the sentry into the air, as high as the second-storey windows. The body arced across the street and landed headfirst upon the cobblestones with a wet thud. Horea rushed forward to make sure the man was dead.

Harker, mouth agape, was still staring at the disembodied head propped on the cobblestones, the grey face staring up at them, cigarette still glowing between the grimaced lips.

The air was thick with the smell of blood, and Crisan stripped the headless body of its tunic as Closca separated the head from the helmet. Lucille took the man's rifle. Horea rejoined them, wiping his dagger blade. "Harker, lead the way," Lucille ordered, breaking him out of his shock. He moved across the intersection. Lucille and the others followed, Crisan pulling Renfield along.

Lucille was worried that Renfield might burst into song any minute and give them away. She was not sure what she would do if he did. Would she slit his throat? To save her team, the mission? She hoped she would not have to make that decision.

The next intersection was guarded by two Privates and a Corporal. All three sat on the hood of a parked car and smoked cigarettes. Their rifles leaned against the fender. Lucille would never let her people be that far from their weapons.

Harker retreated to the shadows. "Too many for the Prince, I'd say."

He and Lucille turned to the vampire.

"I cannot assure you that one will not get off a shot and alert the fellows gathering around us," he said.

"I agree," Lucille said. "I say we try playing soldier."

She turned to Closca, who was already donning the sentry's tunic and helmet. She gave him the rifle. He pointed it at her back and she raised her hands in surrender. Horea and Crisan followed suit. They had used this pantomime before. Harker shrugged, hid his gun under his coat, and followed with the Prince close behind.

They marched in front of Closca and crossed the street.

The Corporal saw them and slid off the car.

"You need help there, comrade?" he asked Closca.

"No," Closca said. "Just hauling them in for questioning."

"What did they do?" the Corporal asked, frowning and peering through the dark at Closca's boots. The footwear was not exactly military issue. But then the Rumanian Army was notoriously lax about its uniform policies, especially with the shortages lately.

"Damned if I know," Closca replied. "I just follow orders."

Closca kept walking, prodding Lucille in the back with the rifle.

"Where the hell are you taking them?" the Corporal demanded as he reached for his own weapon. "The collection point is at the fire station."

Closca had no choice. The ruse was foiled. He swivelled the rifle away from Lucille and shot the Corporal in the chest.

The rest of the team scrambled for their guns.

The two privates went for their rifles. The Prince crouched, ready to pounce. Before he could leap the rest of the team fired their guns.

It was difficult to tell who killed which soldier with the entire team firing as one. The car and the two soldiers were perforated. The air filled with the stench and blue smoke of burnt gunpowder. Renfield stepped into the cloud and took a deep breath through his nose as if he were testing perfume. He grinned in pleasure, oblivious to the carnage that had just occurred.

The Corporal was trying to crawl away, a slime of glistening blood trailing behind him. Lucille walked over and put a bullet into his skull.

Harker gave her a brief look of disapproval. Then he wiped it from his face.

"No witnesses, I know," he said by way of apology.

She nodded at him.

"Now we have to hurry," she said.

They could hear shouts echo down the street. Headlights appeared, turning a far corner.

Harker led the race to their vehicles, but the Prince passed him easily. At the garage the vampire did not hesitate or wait for the key Lucille carried. He simply wrenched the door off its hinges. Lucille ordered that the two vehicles should attempt different routes out of town, making the odds better that one of them escape. A rendezvous was hastily agreed upon, a secluded vacation spot outside a tiny village north of town. Lucille demanded that each man repeat the time and place to her out loud. Then they immediately drove their separate ways.

It was a harrowing night as they wandered the town in the hearse. Harker was driving, his knuckles white on the steering wheel, as they tried to find an escape route.

Over and over they saw roadblocks ahead and had to turn down some side street. The Rumanian Army had locked up the entire town.

The danger of running into an army blockade became so dire that Lucille repeatedly had to step out of the hearse and walk to the next intersection, checking to make sure that they were not making a turn directly into an ambush.

The sun was nosing over the mountains and Lucille cursed her luck, aware that one of their best weapons, the Prince, was now rendered inoperative. She noticed that the morning traffic was beginning to back up at the checkpoints.

Lucille ordered Harker to join a queue. Her theory was that the guards would be so hard-pressed to clear the traffic that their hearse would be able to pass through with but a cursory glance.

It was a tense half hour, inching ahead, horns honking about them, drivers and passengers yelling at the roadblock soldiers. By the time it was their turn the harried soldiers weren't even bothering to ask for papers and merely waved them past with a disgruntled gesture, like fanning away a bad smell.

Curiously, Renfield slept through the entire episode, thank the gods, as she had left his tranquillizers behind. Prince Vlad lay in the back immersed in the travails of Tarzan.

The hearse was the first to arrive at the designated meeting site, a lakeside picnic area, sunny and bucolic. They waited, Lucille watching the dragonflies skim the still water as Harker scribbled in his diary. Their frightening and bloody breakout seemed a million miles and a millennia away.

She was startled out of her reverie by the arrival of the lorry. The Marx Brothers leapt from the truck and embraced Lucille, Harker, and Renfield. The Prince was safely in the shadowed interior of the hearse, and Closca thumped the roof, receiving a "Welcome back" from within.

Horea told Lucille that they had stopped in the village for fuel and, of course, food. There they made contact with a local partisan who relayed a message from her father. With some trepidation Lucille unfolded the note.

It was typically concise and clear: "Come home—immediately."

DATED: 27 MAY 1941
TO: CSS REINHARD HEYDRICH, RSHA, REICHSFUHRER-SS
FROM: SS MAJOR WALTRAUD REIKEL
CC: HEINRICH HIMMLER, REICHSFUHRER-SS
(via diplomatic pouch)

Three items worthy of your attention—

1) Our confinement quarters are proving inadequate and a number of our detainees are soon to be sent to the <u>Konzentration-slager</u> in Neuengamme. We are attaching locomotive transport cars to an aero-fuel shipment already destined for Berlin. Most of those arrested so far have been Jews, gypsies, Communists, degenerates, and a small number of Jehovah's Witnesses. Sadly, we have lost more than a few of them as they have died during the vigorous interviews.

2) We think we are closer to capturing the English spies. I have put every man I can spare on this search, but as of yet we have not apprehended anyone who can shed any further light on their whereabouts. But be assured that we will pursue this line of inquiry with extreme diligence. As soon as we have a single foreign agent you will be notified.

3) We are honored to have the SS Reichsfuhrer take an interest in our work here in the hinterlands. We realise he has many other monumental tasks in front of him, and we appreciate his attentions. The reports concerning our interrogation techniques that he requested will be

forwarded in the near future. I am sure that we have
found some very effective procedures that will benefit
all.

Heil Hitler.

FROM THE WAR JOURNAL OF
J. HARKER

(transcribed from shorthand)

As soon as we arrived at the Van Helsing residence the Professor quickly ushered myself, Lucy, Dracula, and Renfield into the house. The vampire had to be escorted across the sunlit yard with Lucy and me holding a spread jacket over his head for shade against the deadly daylight. The Marx Brothers were dismissed with grateful thanks and they drove the hearse and lorry away. I was sad to see them go, as we had shared so much together down south.

Inside the Van Helsing parlour that toad of a woman, Anka, was waiting with her associates Pavel and Farkas. Lucy hurriedly drew the curtains so that Dracula could enter. I was tired and stiff from the strain of our escape and the long ride. I wanted nothing more than a bath, a cuppa, and a bit of food, but the imperious troll, Anka, insisted we immediately get down to brass tacks.

"Our people are in great danger," she announced with vehemence in her eyes. "The Nazis are deporting all of the people they have kidnapped and imprisoned, shipping them to the death camps in Germany."

"When?" Lucy asked, her own fatigue disappearing from her face.

"Tonight," Anka said. "Leaving at eight ten. Attaching cars to a train from the south."

"How do we know this?" I asked.

"We have our people among the cleaning crew at the castle," Anka said. "They hear and read things. They saw the order for a truck transport to the rail station."

"And four local trucks have been requisitioned," Farkas told us. "Fuel has been confiscated from the Rumanian Army depot."

"The destination is Neuengamme," Pavel added.

"Neuengamme . . ." Lucille nodded, turned to me. "This is not a death camp as such. It is a labour camp, but no one ever leaves."

"They work the prisoners to their deaths," Anka spat. "So it might as well be a death camp."

"Exactly," Van Helsing agreed.

"We must stop these trucks. If not the trucks, the train," Lucille said, her face set in grim determination. I had seen this look before during our southerly exploits.

"If we act, there will be reprisals." Anka shook her head. "The truck transport is too close to home."

"True," I added my two pence.

"But we cannot just stand by and let them take away our people," Lucille said.

"Tin-a-ling, goddamn, find a woman if you can.
If you can't find a woman, find a clean old man.
If you're ever in Gibraltar, take a flying fuck at Walter.
Can you do the double shuffle when your balls hang low?"

It was, of course, Renfield, grinning like the village idiot and singing at the top of his lungs. None of us could disguise our irritation at this tomfoolery interrupting such a dire discussion.

"Do your balls hang low? Do they wobble to and fro?
Can you tie 'em in a knot? Can you tie 'em in a bow?
Can you throw 'em o'er your shoulder like a Continental soldier?
Can you do the double shuffle when your balls hang low?"

There was the sudden sound of hands clapping together and we all turned our attention from the barmy sergeant to Dracula, who was applauding the vulgar chantey.

"Well sung, Chanticleer," Dracula said.

"Thank you, Master," the Sergeant replied.

Then the Prince directed his attention to Anka. "The solution to me is simple. We intercept the railway transport several miles away from here, far enough not to arouse any reprisal against the locals. And you wish that attack not to appear to be a Resistance operation. Is this not correct? This would deter suspicion from yourselves, would it not?"

"I was thinking along those same lines," Van Helsing said.

"How do we do that?" Farkas asked. He and Pavel had retreated against a far wall, putting as much distance between them and the vampire as was possible without leaving the room.

"Leave that to me," Dracula told them.

"Boom," Renfield said. Again, he had our attention.

"Boom?" Dracula grinned, flashing those canines. "I like this. A man whose talents can be defined in one word. *Boom.* Yes, my good friend, there will be an opportunity for your 'boom.'"

Renfield beamed like a dog given a scrap from the master's table. Dracula turned to the rest of us. "Can anyone provide a map that describes the route this railway follows?"

Maps were brought forth and studied. Dracula pointed to a spot he knew and asked if the train still passed through this point. This was affirmed by Pavel. The others debated the logistics, how to transport ourselves to the location the vampire had chosen, and then the subsequent transport of the passengers when and if Dracula was successful. The vampire was not forthcoming about the particulars of his plan. Anka, thus far the Prince's archenemy, suddenly agreed to his participation, most likely out of desperation. Once certain details had been decided, the rest of the council exited to make arrangements

That left us time to catch a few winks. Dracula secluded himself in the Professor's library. Lucy went upstairs to her bedroom. I watched her go with a forlorn regret. After a three-hour rest, I brought this journal up to date, foraged in the Van Helsing kitchen for some lunch, woke Renfield to feed him and myself. After, the Sergeant quickly went back to his bunk, and I used the cipher book to create a message for my superiors in London. I had not finished this when I heard the sound of car engines, joined by the raucous clatter of a motorcycle two-banger. I peeked through the coal chute and was relieved to see Anka and Farkas stepping out of their vehicles. Pavel was the one who arrived by two wheels. I also saw that it was near dusk.

I tapped Renfield to consciousness and helped him load a satchel with plastique explosive and pencil fuses. I armed myself with a few extra magazines and grenades.

Outside, I helped load the vehicles with the machine guns and ammunition. Then we became entangled in one of those mundane squabbles that can drive a man as batty as Renfield.

"I will not ride with that," Anka declared, glaring at Dracula, who had stepped out into the twilight.

"Nor I," Farkas declared.

"Such petty prattle," the vampire mused. "Are we at war or not?"

I thought the same. Here we are trying to do our bit to save the world and these lunatics are bickering about who rides with whom like it was some family outing to the beach.

"The Count, sorry, Prince rides with me." Van Helsing sighed. "Now, about the roadblocks. Pavel?"

"There is but one. I will take care of it," Pavel said as he brandished the bottle of cheap wine that the Professor had given him. He stuffed it into the saddlebag of his motorcycle, then roared away.

Van Helsing tapped me on the shoulder. "You drive," he told me. "Once we get north of Brasov proper it is easy. The road follows the rails."

I drove with Dracula sitting in the passenger seat next to me. I wondered if Van Helsing had arranged this on purpose to keep the vampire and his daughter separated. In the back seat Van Helsing and Lucille bookended Renfield, not a bit cramped due to the spaciousness of the Bentley's interior.

I took the opportunity to engage the vampire in small talk. I had discovered that he, too, was a student of languages, speaking fluent German, Hungarian, Slovak, Serbian, Wallachian, and Romany, plus his English. We traded phrases and it was as comfortable as talking to a schoolmate. I was sorry that my jealousy had prevented me from a more convivial relationship with him. I vowed to pursue this new amity.

A dense fog hung in the occasional low spot, and I had to turn on the windscreen wipers to clear the heavy mist. This piqued the vampire's curiosity about the car, and he began to disport himself with every switch, dial, and button on the Bentley's dash panel. He investigated the glove box, turned out my headlights. I had previously explained the functions of the speedometer, odometer, and fuel gauge. This time I gave a brief explanation on the workings of the brakes and clutch.

"Modern transportation," he marvelled. "Genius. And you have said that the common man has been trained in the use of such mechanisms? If I had not seen it in our travels I would not have believed it."

We passed the roadblock Pavel had informed us about. A guard shack had been erected, but the four Rumanian sentries were slumped inside and out, unconscious, Pavel's wine bottle lying at the feet of one.

"Poison?" Dracula asked.

"A strong sedative," Van Helsing answered.

"In some large cities there are thousands of automobiles on the road at the same time," Lucy addressed the Prince. "So much so that there are massive delays as vehicles crowd each other—sort of travelling self-created roadblocks."

"Thousands at once . . ." Dracula contemplated the image I had seen so many times in London that it was mundane to me. "I would very much like to observe such phenomena."

"It isn't a phenomenon so much as a pain in the arse," I remarked.

"Can you do the double shuffle when your balls hang low . . ." Renfield belted out the beginning of another piece of drivel.

"Renfield, please," Dracula addressed him and as in times before, the Sergeant ceased instantly. As many times as I had tried to silence him, he had not acquiesced once. Another reason for me to resent the vampire, I suppose. But no, I had sworn to stop this kind of thinking.

"How fast do we travel?" Dracula asked as he unwound his window and stuck his arm out and began to glide his hand in the slipstream much like I had when I was seven or eight years old. I shook my head at the preposterousness of the act and I could hear Lucille's chuckle behind me.

"Fifty-two kilometres per hour," I told him.

"Genius," he said again. It was his favorite word, as of late. He wound the window back up and shook the moisture from his hand.

There was silence in the car, just the Bentley's engine purring beneath the hood and the drone of the tyres on the road. Van Helsing broke the quietude.

"So, Prince Vlad, my daughter has told me that you have struggled and succeeded in tempering your more sanguine tendencies," he said.

"I do strive for such control," Dracula said.

"I hope so," Van Helsing said. "Still, you cannot blame me for having doubts. The last time we met . . ."

"I had little control over my desires," Dracula acknowledged.

"But you do now, you say," Van Helsing said.

"I do. I think I do," Dracula said somberly. "Try to understand. When a young boy comes of age, his senses overwhelm him with certain primal urges."

"Sex," Lucy offered.

"Lucy!" Van Helsing exclaimed.

"The forthrightness of your daughter no longer offends me," Dracula went on. "She is blunt, but yes. The juvenescent male has little control over his own body; his senses are ruled by his lusts."

"Women feel it, too," Lucille interrupted. Her father's sigh could be heard all the way up front.

"Then you know of what I speak," Dracula continued. "In England, that unfortunate incident with the poor Miss Westerna and young Harker's grandmother, I was not in control of myself. I was ruled by my monstrous desire."

"Lust." Lucy brought the discussion to a point.

"Yes. For blood. Bloodlust," Dracula said. "And something more. Survival, I suppose."

"It is still lust," Lucille countered.

He looked back at her and I checked her face in the rearview mirror. Did this conversation have an undercurrent to which I was oblivious?

"Yes, you are correct." Dracula turned his gaze back and peered through the window into the endless dark outside the car. "When I was in my tomb these last forty years plus, I had much to think about."

"You were conscious?" Van Helsing was horrified. "All that time? Lying there in your coffin?"

"I was," Dracula acceded. "After all, I am the un-dead. At first I thought that I would go mad. But instead I began contemplating my past, my metamorphosis into . . . what I am, what you see before you. And I decided if my mortal being can transmogrify, then I can do the same with my thoughts. Now I feel I have accustomed myself to my state. And I am in control. At least more so than ever in my past."

"We shall see," Van Helsing said.

"Yes," Dracula concurred. "We shall see."

During my unconventional warfare training at the SOE's graduate school at Beaulieu Manor in the Hampshires, I had an instructor who was a veteran of the Burmese Shoe Question conflict, and one day between sessions, having a smoke behind the old mansion, he gave me a bit of advice.

"Know your area of operation," he told me. "Always get yourself a map. Even if all you have is one of the buggers made by the bleeding Geographical Society, study it. Don't be mucking about. Use your own blooming eyes, take note of your bleeding surroundings, and make a blooming map of your own. From memory. Compare the two, yours and the official. Then do it again. Do it until you know your way around like it was your girlie's drawers."

I took his counsel to heart. In our southern sojourn I studied local maps, then, as instructed, paid mind to the roads and landmarks every time I travelled about. Every day I would draw a map of my own, from memory, repeating the process over and over until I knew my area of operation as if I had been born and raised there. With these maps I plotted our egress strategies.

This day I had taken what I knew of Brasov from map and memory and drawn a path to our destination for tonight. So, this time I needed no directions and was able to find my way to the road that paralleled the railway angling northwest.

The tracks were to my left and the mountains to my right. On the other side of the rails a river coursed along the valley, where mountains rose into a vertical wall. At a point several miles from town, at least two hours' drive, the road veered right as the rails passed through a gap only wide enough to allow the river and the rail line through.

The obstacle was a tower of basalt a few hundred feet high called by the locals "the Devil's Tooth." The road circled the base and returned us to the rail line on the other side. Here there was a wider valley that crossed the road at an angle, creating a flat area of a few acres.

This was to be the location of our interdiction with the train.

Three lorries waited and two more cars were parked near the tracks, hidden by another rock outcropping the height of a London double-decker bus. Anka and Farkas waited next to the vehicles with three lorry drivers and the Marx Brothers: Horea, Closca, and Crisan. I was quite happy to see my comrades-in-arms again.

The group was smoking and conversing like all soldiers before battle. All were heavily armed, sub-machine guns and bandoliers filled with magazines. The gypsy, Crisan, had decorated his vest with six or seven grenades, which hung on it like ornaments on a Christmas tree.

I parked and climbed out, arming myself with my own machine gun and bandolier. Then the vampire made his appearance, stepping out of the Bentley like King George from his carriage.

All conversation ceased as the three drivers stared in awe and fear. One man's mouth actually dropped open and his cigarette fell off his lip, the ember a tiny meteor falling and exploding as it hit the ground.

Lucille chambered a round in that archaic, long-barrelled Luger. Seeing that Van Helsing was unarmed, I offered him my Browning, but he declined with a quick jerk of his head.

"With my shaky hands I would be more of a danger to my colleagues than the enemy," the old man said with a smile. "I am here only to observe and advise. This operation belongs to the Prince."

And he turned to Dracula, who gave him a small, Old World bow of thanks. Everyone watched the vampire as he craned his head skyward, glancing at the moon, which at the moment was hiding behind a nimbus of wispy cloud. He surveyed the valley, the mountains to the north, the Devil's Tooth rising in a straight vertical until the top disappeared into the darkness.

"First we must stop the locomotive," Dracula intoned.

"Aye, with a boom!" Renfield grinned his lunatic simper. Then his face changed and he once more transformed into the demolition expert. "Ah can blow the tracks. Ah can blow the train. Timed or direct detonation—your choice, Master."

"No, no, my friend." Dracula frowned at the tracks bending around the Tooth until they disappeared. "This cannot appear to be a partisan attack."

"Ah could create an avalanche!" Renfield was getting excited now. "One carefully placed wee charge and Ah could bring down the whole bliddy mountain. Ach, but how ye get up there Ah have no idea."

"No," Dracula repeated. "That would harm the prisoners being transported. I have a role for you and your deadly contrivances, but later. I will stop this locomotive myself."

"How?" Lucy and I asked simultaneously. I smiled at her. She did not return it.

Dracula didn't have a chance to answer as Pavel roared up on his motorbike, coming to a stop with an eruption of gravel and sand.

He lit a cigarette off Farkas's as we gathered around him.

"After giving the sentries their bottle . . . By the way, what was that stuff, Professor? It put them out quicker than a hammer to the head." He grinned through the smoke wafting from his mouth.

"Chloral hydrate," Van Helsing replied.

"The old Mickey Finn." Lucy laughed. When a few of us showed a lack of comprehension she explained. "An American idiom. Continue, Pavel."

"Right. After putting the soldiers to bed I rode to the train depot, climbed onto the station roof. There I can see the Germans herd the prisoners aboard cattle cars. People beg, want to know where they go, but only get kicks and gun butts for answers. The Nazis rob some, some are stripped naked, clothes ripped off their backs. Especially the women. The rat bastards burnt the pile of clothes after, so it was all for sport." He spat onto the ground for punctuation.

"Did you see our people?" Anka asked.

"Many of them," he reported, listing a dozen names unfamiliar to me. "And the gypsies. Maleva, remember, the girl who walks the tightrope, swings in air in tight clothes? She was singled out by a German officer. Separated from the others. There are two cars of these Nazi officers, coming from Bucharest maybe. Maleva's father, Ouspenkaya, the fire-eater? He fought the Germans, to protect his daughter, but he was beaten to his knees, thrown into the cattle car."

"What happened to Maleva?" Lucy asked.

"She was thrown into one of the officers' cars. A luxury car, red velvet curtains, chandeliers even. Full of German officers, drinking, smoking cigars. They watched the beating of the prisoners as if it were performance at a private theatre. I heard the bastards laugh. The girl Maleva was brought to this car, tossed at their feet like meat for a hound."

"How many Germans on the train?" Van Helsing asked.

"I count ten officers in one car, fourteen in the other," Pavel replied. "At each luxury car is one guard. That is two. Two guards on coal car behind the engine. Now four."

"Just those four cars?" Anka asked. "Two luxury cars, two cattle cars?"

"A coal car," Pavel said. "Plus five oil tanker cars towed at the rear."

"How far behind you?" Dracula asked.

"Ten minutes, a little more," Pavel answered. "I am a fast rider."

Dracula turned to me. "Quickly, you must drive me." He headed toward the Bentley, shouting to the others, "The locomotive will stop here. Be ready to evacuate your friends. Keep your weapons at bay, if you will."

I heard Anka murmur something about who is giving orders now. Jumping behind the wheel as Dracula slammed the passenger door shut, I heard the thunk of another door close and glanced into the rearview mirror to see Lucy sitting in the back seat.

I was about to object, but the look on her face disposed of any such action.

"Drive back the way we have come," Dracula ordered, and I sped away. I rounded the Devil's Tooth, and when we reached the other side where the road rejoined the rail tracks, he told me to stop.

As soon as I brought the car to a halt he threw his door open and stepped out of the vehicle. Lucy and I rushed to his side as he stared up at the vertical cliff. The sheer rock was studded here and there with mountain ash and thorn, roots anchored in the cracks and crevices of the stone precipice.

"Go back to the other side," Dracula said. "I will meet you there."

Then, to my astonishment, he flexed his knees and made a great leap up, twenty feet or so. His fingers made purchase upon the ragged rock and he began to climb the sheer face of the mountain.

Once, on a summer jaunt with my parents, we travelled across northern Italy and into Switzerland. On a lazy Saturday morning, dining alfresco at our chalet hotel, I watched in amazement as three men climbed the mountain across the valley from us. The ping of their hammers pounding against their pitons echoed across the canyon. They made their way slowly up a sheer wall of basalt. During our entire meal I don't think they managed to climb but thirty feet.

But Dracula scampered up the rock with exceeding alacrity. I admit I stared, gobsmacked at this remarkable athletic demonstration. I turned to Lucy, who was as stunned as I.

"'For the dead travel fast,'" I murmured to myself. *"Denn die todten reiten schnell.'"* Lucy turned to me with a frown. "Gottfried August Burger's 'Lenore,'" I attributed, but she just shook her head in annoyance.

Dracula sped up the cliff a hundred feet in a matter of seconds, just as a lizard skitters up a wall. He then performed an even more singular feat. He stopped, clinging to the rock face by his bare hands, and reversed his position, hanging upside down. His cape fell over his face with a flash of the scarlet lining, and then, to our mutual amazement, he released one hand from his grip on the wall of stone and brushed the cape away so that his view was unobstructed. He was clinging to the cliff with but one hand and his feet.

I was about to declare my stupefaction to Lucille when I heard her say, "The train."

And then I heard it, too, the unmistakable, rhythmic grind of a locomotive echoing through the canyons behind us.

As the black steel beast came into view the din increased, smoke billowing from the engine.

I looked up and saw Dracula perched high above the tracks, like a bat hanging from a cave wall. At that same moment he jumped. Too soon, I thought. The train was still a hundred metres from the cliff. He spread his cape into wings and glided down. It appeared that he would plunge short of the locomotive and, if nothing else, be run over by the engine. I held back a shout of warning. It was too late for that.

But, no, he flew right into the white worm of steam and disappeared for a brief second.

The next time I saw him he was standing in the middle of the coal car, having landed as lightly as a crow upon a telephone wire, moving toward the two guards sitting on the front edge of the car.

They had their backs to him, but something roused their interest and they both turned to gaze upon the vampire, his cape billowing behind him like the smoke from the engine stack. One of them was too stunned to move, this sudden apparition standing before them. The other reacted a bit faster, stood, and raised his MP38 sub-machine gun. He fired a burst at the vampire. Dracula was staggered by the impact. Despite the monstrous noise of the train passing, I heard Lucille gasp next to me.

But I was intent on the vampire as he charged that guard, made a spear point with his fingers, and plunged his hand into the man's chest. The guard's scream was cut short and he looked down in time to see his heart plucked from his rib cage. I doubt he lived long enough to realise what had just happened to him.

The other guard wisely turned to run, but Dracula was upon him in one long leap, his fangs sinking into the man's neck. The poor fellow struggled like a fish on a line, his arms flopping in the air as though he were attempting to fly away. The motions slowed, then his arms fell limply to his side and Dracula tossed the drained carcass far out into the river that ran along the tracks.

This whole Mephisthophelean scenario I glimpsed in pieces as the billowing steam from the engine swirled and danced around the figures like lace curtains in a demonic wind.

The train disappeared around the Devil's Tooth.

"We must go!" Lucy yelled into my ear, and I was suddenly aware that she was clutching my arm with such power that she was actually causing me pain.

We sprinted to the car, and I sped back to where the others waited.

What happened on the train while it was out of our sight I learned later from the devil himself.

When Dracula finished with the two guards, he approached the engine compartment, where two men minded the boiler, a large man stoking the fire with shovelfuls of coal and an old engineer casually monitoring his gauges, both unaware of the coming threat.

Dracula jumped from the coal car into the open engine compartment and the man with the shovel stopped, his huge frame backlit by the fire from the boiler's open door. He stared at the vampire.

"What are you doing here?" he demanded in German.

"Stopping this train," Dracula calmly replied. He stepped between the two men to examine the dials and levers that operated the locomotive.

The stoker raised his wide shovel and charged the vampire.

Moving with blinding speed, Dracula stopped the shovel's downward arc with one hand. Stunned that he had been interrupted in mid-strike, the sweaty stoker strained, muscles bulging, putting his massive body and both hands behind the contest with Dracula's one arm. And the stoker was losing.

Dracula pounced, bit. The brute struggled under him, futilely. The vampire drained the man, then, surging with a new power, snapped the giant's neck and dropped him. The behemoth hit the floor like a sack of old rags.

Dracula turned to the engineer, who cowered in a corner of the compartment.

"Don't hurt me," the old man pleaded. "Please."

"Are you not German?" Dracula asked, perceiving a familiar accent in the man's voice.

"No. Rumanian. From Slobozia. Don't kill me."

"Slobozia . . ." Dracula considered. He was still not confident in the rules he had agreed upon. Was he only to kill the German enemy, or were Rumanian collaborators fair game? He decided that because of his earlier transgressions he ought to err on the side of compassion. "Not Transylvanian, but . . . you are free to go."

"Go?" The old man rose to his feet. "Go where?"

"Out," Dracula said and grabbed the old man by the collar with one hand, by the belt with the other, and threw him into the dark night like a sack of mail tossed to the depot. The engineer sailed into the river with a splash.

Then Dracula pulled the long brake handle.

Lucy and I arrived on the other side of the Devil's Tooth just as the train began screeching to a stop, a keening of steel against steel that hurt the ears. Sparks spewed between rail and wheel.

I parked with dispatch. Lucy and I ran to join the other partisans. The train was stopped with only the engine and coal car past the Devil's Tooth; the rest of the cars reposed alongside the great rock.

I watched as Dracula leapt back up onto the coal car and strode into the cloud of steam roiling over the top of the train.

The next car was the first of the luxury carriages, brilliantly lit from inside by cut-glass chandeliers, full of unsuspecting Nazi officers singing along with a piano being pummelled by a drunken Captain, all boisterously drinking. A few peered out the windows to see why the train had stopped. Most ignored the scenery. All they could see was a wall of rock on one side or the river on the other, and continued their revelry. What had they to worry about? They were destined to rule the world.

The partisans charged precipitously forward along the narrow gap between train cars and rock face. I gave chase, trying to stop them. A guard in the vestibule of the first luxury car saw them and turned, his Schmeisser sub-machine gun swiveling with him.

I saw Pavel aim his rifle at the guard and was about to shout Dracula's order not to shoot, when the vampire appeared out of the cloud of steam, hopped down to the vestibule, and, with one swipe of his hand, ripped out the man's throat.

Then Dracula entered the car.

Pavel and Farkas moved to follow.

"No!" I grabbed Pavel and whispered harshly into his ear. "Leave them to the Prince."

"He might need help," Lucy said, and she, too, moved toward the car, but her father held her back.

"We should all witness this," Van Helsing said. "Watch the monster take precedence over his mortal soul."

After one step into the luxury car Dracula paused to take in the scene. The car was panelled in dark wood and red velvet curtains with gold brocade trim all about. The bright lights sparkled off the chandeliers, and a haze of blue cigar smoke hung in a dense overcast. Brass ashtrays and dark brown leather chairs were arranged along the walls. Most of the men, wearing their dress uniforms, had a glass in one hand with a cigar or cigarette in the other. A small, polished wood bar crouched in one corner; a collection of liquor bottles replicated themselves in the mirror behind.

One of the Germans, a red-faced man wearing pince-nez, was brandishing a small black box with a short barrel protruding from the front. He would aim this box at one of his comrades and that man would become animated, most attempting some caper. Dracula first thought it might be some kind of new weapon, but then, when the Nazi aimed it at him, he saw the glass eye and realised it was some sort of camera.

One of the officers, wearing a very nicely tailored uniform, beautifully designed, walked up to him. Dracula did not recognise the rank, not that it mattered.

"Why have we stopped?" the officer demanded in the tone of one who was used to command. "Who are you?"

"Wrong questions," Dracula told him. The officer frowned, focusing on the bullet holes in the vampire's shirtfront, the splatter of blood from feasting on the stoker and guard.

"What would be the right question?" the officer asked, swaying a bit against the tide of inebriation.

"Why are you still alive?" Dracula said as he reached out one hand and snapped the officer's neck. Dracula dropped the dead carcass and the resounding thump of the falling body attracted the attention of the nearest Nazis. Guns were drawn from polished holsters.

From outside the luxury car, all we saw were the flashes of gunshots. We heard screams, guttural howls of terror, and the lachrymose wails of dying men. I saw a frightened face thud against a window, the eyes begging for mercy, mercy that was not forthcoming, and then the horrid visage disappeared, pulled from the glass as if it never had been there at all. Then blood splatters of bright sanguine crimson splashed across the windows like paint thrown about by a mad artist.

We were all transfixed, staring at this Grand Guiginol being performed before us.

"Come," Van Helsing ordered. "Remember our mission!"

Our trance interrupted, we followed the Professor past the two luxury cars, carefully crouching beneath the windows. The second car was oblivious to the carnage occurring next door, the general revelry drowning out the noise of Dracula's rapacious plunder. Pavel attacked the locks on the livestock cars with a pair of long-handled bolt cutters.

We heard a crash behind us. A German officer had been hurled through a window of the first luxury car. Shattered glass and a dead body fell onto the coarse gravel of the siding.

I noticed that Renfield had lingered and was still watching the mayhem with undisguised glee.

Inside, Dracula walked the length of the first car, slaughtering as he went. A few of his victims he feasted upon, ripping into their necks.

Another guard stepped through the rear vestibule. He raised his Schmeisser and fired a burst at the blood-drenched specter before him. Dracula took the rain of bullets in his chest and solar plexus. The impact forced him to lean back, but nothing more. Then he was upon the poor guard faster than the man could react, a blur in the fellow's vision. By the time he knew that the vampire was only a foot in front of him Dracula had ripped off his arm and used it to swat another German. Both officers hit the floor, where Dracula crushed their throats under his heel as if they were vermin.

Dracula held the dead man's arm, the hand still clutching the Schmeisser. The vampire disengaged the hand from the weapon, tossed aside the arm, and, in the midst of all his self-created chaos, examined the Schmeisser MP38 as if he were thinking of purchasing one.

"Genius," he mused. "Remarkable progress." He laid it upon the bar, peered behind the curved counter to see if anyone was hiding there, surveyed the car to confirm that there were none left alive, and exited.

The sharp, distinct report of the vestibule guard's Schmeisser on full automatic was enough to alert the officers in the second car that something untoward was occurring. At least some of them. As Farkas slid open the cattle car door I glanced into the second luxury car and saw a half-dozen Germans draw their side arms and cautiously approach the vestibule.

Lucy was at my side and also took notice. "Too many guns against him," she muttered. "Are we going to let him fight them all by himself?"

She raised her Luger and charged toward the car.

I, of course, followed.

Entering the other side of the car, we were witness to a grim spectacle of drunken louts passing a young girl from man to man, each one stripping off a bit of her garments. So preoccupied were they with this perversion, coupled with the drunken sing-along, that at first they saw nothing of what was happening at Dracula's end of the car.

When Dracula entered, covered with blood and gore, a few of the officers discarded their amusements and paid attention. They had further reason to pay heed as he waded into the midst of the officers and began killing. Again, a few he feasted upon, ripping into their necks with his fangs. He became a beast, governed only by his lust for blood and death, unleashing an uncontrollable rage and desire. As I watched this tableau of horror I could think only of Van Helsing's warning. The monster's mortal soul was not much in evidence.

But this was no time for rumination, as the Nazis on our side of the car armed themselves. One fool shot himself in the thigh as he drunkenly drew his Walther from his holster. Besides this wounded tosspot, Dracula was now facing over a dozen armed men. The bullets might do no harm in twos and threes, but enough firepower could possibly shred his flesh in ways I did not think he had even imagined.

So I shot one of the Germans. In the back, yes. I am not proud, but we were outnumbered, and to give our enemies a timely warning would have been folly.

My gunshot was accompanied by Lucy's Luger. We both cut down five or six of the Nazis before they turned on us. Some of the men were only wounded and fired back even as they fell. I had yet to learn my lesson—a wounded man is as dangerous as a live man. Shoot to kill.

Dracula, too, was a victim of this dictum. One of the Germans in the first car survived his attack and surreptitiously came up behind him.

He felt a sharp pain, snapped a hand behind him in reaction, fumbled, and found the hilt of the knife imbedded in his shoulder. Yanking the blade out, he turned to face the young, blond Lieutenant, whose blue eyes were wide, standing there holding an empty scabbard in a trembling hand.

"You think that does not pain me?" Dracula asked the young soldier and plunged the dagger through the top of Nazi's skull.

Another rushed the vampire, bringing up his weapon. Dracula did not wait for this one to fire his gun. He merely grabbed the soldier by his coat front and, with one hand, slammed the man against the top of the mahogany bar, upside down, pounding the soldier's head into the hardwood as if he were driving a nail, over and over, until the man's cranium merged with his shoulders, just a bloody smudge.

While Dracula laid waste to German after German, Lucy and I committed our own version of slaughter. Later, when I had the time to think about it, I decided I was caught up in the derangement of what occurred in that car. Was the bloodthirsty butchery of Dracula's melee any different from what Lucy and I brought upon our enemy? One attack was a bit more ferocious and perhaps somewhat untidy compared to our more efficient methods, but the results were the same—a carload of dead men.

Dracula ceased his rampage, looked around the car. There was blood everywhere. Nary a body stirred. The stillness and the mephitic reek of death filled the railroad car. He looked at us with red eyes, bloodshot to the point of opacity. The glare was so fierce and inhuman that I took Lucy's arm and led her out of the abattoir. She did not resist, being as awestruck as I at the demonic presence. So bestial was his apparent state that I was certain Dracula had lost control and would attack us without a thought. This was her first glimpse at his brute butchery.

Left alone, Dracula espied a stirring behind the bar. He bared his fangs in a feline snarl, hissed, his primal wrath still driving his actions. He reached down, filled his hand with a fistful of hair, and hauled the human out of hiding.

It was the gypsy girl, covering her naked breasts with crossed arms, staring at the bloody creature in abject terror. I am ashamed to say that, in my haste to leave, I had forgotten about the captive girl.

Dracula felt bloodlust blur his vision, overtake his reason, his mental acuity. Everything was meat, was blood, all was prey. He felt the heat of the girl's body, heard the pump of her heart, saw her pulse throb, all with a keen perception beyond ordinary senses.

He could taste the sweet blood that was in the offing. Then he perceived an itch at the back of his mind, like a lost memory, teasing at his brain, a whisper of conscience, the tiny voice of what was left of his humanity. The atavistic beast that now inhabited his body roared, drowning out that small plea.

He bent the girl's neck, exposing the vein that pulsed with such a siren call. She, frightened to her core, offered no resistance.

Lucy and I had gone to assist the other partisans as we evacuated the prisoners from the livestock car and into the lorries. Many had to be carried. I helped an old woman—I swear she didn't weigh more than a large cat—and she gaped at me as if she were in the arms of the Christ himself.

The screams and sounds of battle emitting from the luxury cars had ceased. Nothing but the hiss of the river's rapids. We all seemed to turn at the same time to witness Dracula stepping down from the car, the girl in his arms. She was wrapped in his cloak.

Dracula's face was not a sight for those with a weak constitution. It is only when a man finds himself face-to-face with such horrors that he can understand their true import. His visage was still contorted with bloodlust, his eyes ablaze with a demonic fury, his mouth, hands, and shirtfront covered in crimson gore and blood from his hideous repast. His entire appearance was terrifying to behold.

As a youth, preoccupied as I was with the lurid tales of my grandfather, I became a devourer of strange fiction, especially the imaginative stories in the pulps. My treasure was a near-complete collection of *Weird Tales*, a Yank publication of varying quality. But some of the stories had the power to make peaceful sleep impossible and caused me, in one influenza-induced fever dream, to murmur, much to my parents' consternation, *"Tekeli-li! Tekeli-li! Ia! Ia! Cthulu! Yog-Sothoth!"* None of those hellish, nightmarish yarns could have prepared me for the sight of the vampire stepping out of that hemic carnage.

The gypsies about us went to their knees as one. He gazed down upon them with an imperious stare; his eyes were positively blazing, and the red light within them was lurid, as if the flames of hellfire blazed behind them.

"Drakul," a chorus of gypsies murmured in hushed awe. Lucy's face showed her shock at the sight. I saw fear and dread fall across Van Helsing's face.

The gypsy girl's father rushed forward to gently take his daughter, for this must be the aforementioned Maleva, from the vampire's arms. His joy was discernable behind the mask of his bruised and swollen face.

"Thank you, my Prince," he whispered in his mother tongue, Romani. "I, Ouspenkaya, am eternally in your debt." The reverence in his voice was profound.

Dracula nodded. The rage in his countenance dissipated before our eyes. Lucy approached him, observing this segue from savagery to refinement.

The vampire glanced at her, then down at the ruins of his blood-soaked clothing, the bullet-shredded shirt. From his own wounds, a dark ichor leaked.

"I'll need a new shirt. Could another trip to the tailor's be in the offing?" He strode over to the river, tearing off the ragged remains of his shirt. He rinsed the tattered cloth in the swirling waters at the bank and wiped his face, his chest, cleaned his hands as if it were an ordinary morning toilet. As I watched I was amazed to see his wounds heal before my eyes; they closed, scabbed, then became shiny pockmarks, then disappeared. The process gave me a deep sense of wonderment, and I suddenly understood how truly alien he was.

The partisans and the freed prisoners still gawked, but Pavel and Farkas, not unfamiliar with the vampire, herded them to the lorries. Van Helsing walked with Ouspenkaya to their transport, at the same time tending to the girl huddled in her father's arms.

"She seems unharmed" was Van Helsing's diagnosis. "Take your people into the mountains. Hide as best you can."

"My people have been hunted before," the gypsy leader said. "In our mountains, not even God can find us."

"Can you take the others with you?" Van Helsing asked, pointing to the Jews and other prisoners.

"Of course. All who are under the iron fist of the Boche are now kin."

I went back to survey the results of Dracula's predations inside the luxury cars. I was not eager for the duty, but I thought the officers might have been carrying some kind of documents of value to our intelligence section. Stepping into the first car, I was struck by the odour of the slaughterhouse, blood and offal. There was absolute carnage, parts of men lying about, some I could recognise, some I could not. The dead lay slack with stricken faces, open-mouthed and with wide-eyed stares of pure horror.

It was all I could do not to gag at the sight and stench. For some reason, my attention was captured by the shined boots of one of the victims, a man dressed in an immaculate uniform from glistening black heel to the Iron

Cross on his chest—First Class, a hero—all perfect as if for inspection; the only deficit was the mess he was from the neck up, no head. I know I stood there and stared at this abomination for a few seconds.

Turning away, I could see Dracula and Lucille through a crimson-smeared window. She had taken the rag of his shirt and was cleaning his face with a tenderness that made my heart stop. I could hear them through the shattered window next to me.

"I did tell you not to interfere, did I not?" Dracula said to her. "Why did you attack?"

Lucy took umbrage at the question.

"They were shooting at you," she said, her anger rising.

"They could not kill me," he stated with not a hint of braggadocio.

"But it hurt, didn't it?"

"It did."

Hearing a buzzing sound, I spied an object on the floor, a small sixteen-millimetre camera, its crank still rotating. I picked it up and tossed it out the shattered window toward the river. Who knew what it had recorded? But I was not really as focused on my recce as I was on Lucy and the vampire. I hurriedly left the car, intent on interrupting this tender tête-à-tête.

"Maybe I welcome the pain." Dracula gazed into Lucy's eyes.

"Possibly as a recompense for your sins?" I asked, joining the conversation. Dracula turned his eyes on me, and I found myself suddenly very afraid. There was a chilling threat in his stare.

"You cannot dare to understand what I may feel or think, sir."

My jaw wobbled as I struggled to find a reply. But then Renfield saved me as he brushed me aside and accosted the vampire.

"Master! Master!" Renfield bounced around the pair like a puppy begging for a biscuit. "Ye said Ah wid have a go! Aye, ye said Ah wid have a go! Master?"

"Yes, my friend." Dracula turned, put his hands on the shoulders of his eager acolyte. "Here is what I would like you to do. Can you improvise a device to make the oil in these container cars blow up?"

"Aye." Renfield grinned. "Easy-peasy."

"But can you make it happen when I deign it to occur?"

"Ach, when ye want it, she'll blow," Renfield replied.

"Excellent." Dracula nodded. "Then this is what I desire. *Festina lente.* Make haste slowly."

We gathered close as Dracula laid out his plan. And as he did so I noticed something remarkable. It was a cold night; we hugged our clothes close, and every exhaled breath formed a white cloud in front of everyone's faces. Everyone except Dracula. He alone made no such mist.

What follows is conjecture on my part, pieced together from eyewitness accounts, secondary sources, and a clandestine visit to the site:

Due to the persistent sabotage by the local partisans, the Brasov railway station was under Rumanian Army control, the security detail billeted in an old warehouse adjacent to the tracks. A transportation unit with a large motor pool resided directly across those tracks. It was usually devoid of vehicles, as the Rumanian General Suciu had a very profitable lend-lease program with area merchants who might need a lorry for business purposes.

Dawn was quiet at the rail terminal; the Commanding Officer was not an early riser and, since he led by example, reveille was determined by the severity of the Sergeant Major's hangover.

On this particular morning, the sentry at the station ambled about the rail yards, awake for once. He had fallen asleep in an old comfy chair inside the ticket master's office and awoke to a lap full of squirming rats fighting over the bratwurst he still clutched in his hand from his usual midnight mess. One of the rodents mistook his thumb for sausage and the bite woke him with a jolt. After an impromptu dance, feet futilely trying to stomp the fleeing creatures, complete with a vigorous waving of his arms attempting to dislodge the rat still clinging to the tasty thumb, the sentry gave up on any more sleep for the night, much less the near future, and decided he might as well make his rounds.

The yards were quiet. A low mist hovered over the ground, and the rails were shiny with condensation. The sun was just hinting at a rise in the starlit sky. There being not enough light as yet, the sentry carried a kerosene lantern to see his way through the tangle of rails. He sipped from his flask, an armour against the morning chill and most likely the reason his sleep was sound enough to allow five filthy rats to climb his legs and nest in his crotch.

As he high-stepped across the rails (a previous stumble had split his lip and swollen his nose), he heard a sound that stopped him. He froze, listening. What was it? Then, as the noise became louder, he recognised the unmistakable mechanical churning of a locomotive. Nothing unusual in that at a train station.

But he glanced at his watch, an old-fashioned chunk of Hungarian silver, big as a turnip. His eyebrows gathered together and he gave a little shrug of his shoulders. Curious. Nothing scheduled. His months of night duty, due to an inebriated altercation with his sergeant, had made him very familiar with the arrival and departure schedules. But trains had arrived unannounced before, the vicissitudes of war and the incompetence of governmental bureaucracy prevailing. For example, the special train that had stopped here at the beginning of his watch and took on two cattle cars before departing an hour later than usual.

For some reason, this new arrival made him uneasy, and it took him a second to comprehend the reason—the rhythm of the oncoming train's engine was not diminishing. Even trains that passed through Brasov without stopping had to slow down. This locomotive was not slowing at all. In fact, judging from the sound, it was moving faster than any train in the sentry's experience.

He peered down the tracks. Usually he was able to see quite a distance, three miles down the line on a clear day before the dual strands of steel curved out of sight.

But visibility was only a mile or so on this dim, foggy morning and, when the sentry finally spied the engine and cars headed his way, the sight struck him with cold fear.

The train was speeding toward the station backward. And the cars he saw first were tankers—full of aviation fuel. He had watched them leave only a few hours before his dinner and nap. Aviation fuel. Thousands of gallons.

And this train was not stopping.

He decided to run.

He barely made the little brick shack used by the rail workers before the runaway train slammed into a file of boxcars waiting on the track.

Here was where the particular genius of Sergeant Renfield came into play. He devised a simple plunger detonator attached, not to the first, but to the last fuel tanker's coupling. As soon as the coupling encountered any resistance it would depress and ignite the fuse. Then the Sergeant placed his charges, and this was where his prodigy further expressed itself.

He had clambered atop the tanker car and released the catches that bound the two-foot-wide hatch, flipped it open.

"The most important aspect of igniting any petroleum product is tae remember that 'tis not the liquid that burns, but the gas emitted from the fuel's exposure tae the air," he lectured like a Cambridge don, his madness once again put aside for his favorite subject—blowing things to smithereens. "The more gaseous ye can make the fuel, the bigger the detonation. So, we put a charge inside the tank, immersed in the liquid. It will detonate first, vaporising the fuel, and then a split second later this charge, set above the fuel, will go off, igniting the vapor. Ach, a bliddy grand explosion follows."

He wired the charges, one immersion device and one on top of the tanker, linking one car to the next and finally to the plunger attached to the coupling.

"Always wire the ignition device tae the charge last," Renfield cautioned. "Some fool may accidentally activate the igniter while ye are setting up the explosive or the igniter may be defective and set off the charge prematurely. Aye, you work the other way, from yer explosive toward yer ignition system. Maind ye, ye could ruin yer whole day."

He obviously took pride in his profession. I always tried to assist when possible, and it was a pleasure to watch his hands make such quick and tidy work.

When he was finished, he rushed to where Dracula waited. The vampire was now dressed in an old sea coat Lucy had found in the trunk of the Bentley. It was too small and made him look not ridiculous, but oddly vulnerable.

"'Tis done, Master," Renfield reported.

"Cease calling me Master," Dracula protested. "Someone should remove the bodies killed by Miss Van Helsing and Mister Harker. Those with bullet holes. It would spoil our subterfuge if they were found."

Pavel volunteered that there was an old quarry nearby, the waters unfathomably deep. He and the other partisans quickly went about gathering up the pertinent corpses.

Dracula leapt up into the engine compartment, and I helped him shovel coal into the fiery maw of the boiler. I was hard put to match his pace; he tossed three, maybe four, times the shovelfuls that I could manage.

At one point he turned to me and thanked me for assisting him in the luxury car. I knew that my assistance was of minor consequence, but the acknowledgement was a gentlemanly act, and my opinion of the man rose another notch.

Once the boiler was as full as possible Dracula engaged the gears, putting the locomotive in reverse. As the great steel wheels spun, striving for some grip upon the rails, we leapt from the engine and watched it return the way it had come, gaining momentum with every chug of the massive engine.

So eventually, when the poor sentry at the Brasov station saw the train approaching, the locomotive engine was rolling at full speed toward him. As he sought sanctuary in his tiny brick structure, no larger than an outdoor privy, the train cars collided with one of the stationary cars parked on a siding. A few thousand liters of aviation fuel ignited instantly.

The explosion was unprecedented. It shattered windows over a mile from the station, completely demolishing the ticket office and brick terminal building, which were blown apart like stacks of sugar cubes. Rails were bent into twisted curlicues as one idly bends pipe cleaners. Brick and steel rained upon the adjacent army barracks, penetrating the corrugated tin roof, injuring many a soldier and leaving the structures unlivable.

Railway cars were tossed airborne a hundred metres and came crashing to the ground like the sky was raining houses. In all respects, it was a most satisfying end to our mission.

My only regret was that I and, most importantly, Renfield, could not have witnessed the results of his handiwork.

By the way, the sentry was found unconscious under a pile of bricks that had once been vertical.

On the drive back to town none of this was known to us. It was quiet in the car for some time, then Van Helsing spoke.

"I was witness to your engagement with the German officers." The Professor addressed Dracula, who sat in the back with Lucy and Renfield. "That was no simple attack. That was . . . slaughter. Butchery. So much for controlling your bloodlust."

"My endeavour toward personal improvement is still in the embryonic stage, I suppose," Dracula answered coolly.

"You unnerved me," Lucy told him.

"At times I frighten myself," he replied.

"The creature who impaled twenty thousand Turks as mere warning is not that far under the skin, perhaps," Van Helsing said.

"I suppose not," Dracula agreed. He was not his usual poised self, seeming uncomfortable with the admission.

"That could be said for all of humanity," I interjected. "As much as we pride ourselves on our so-called civilised ways, we repeatedly seem to revert to our more atavistic selves, hence the war we find ourselves fighting now."

I do not know what prompted me to defend the vampire, but there it was, and I did not regret the outburst.

"I have a question for you, Doctor," Dracula addressed Van Helsing. "You knew how to destroy me, not the stake, but completely. But you did not do so. Why did you refrain?"

"I am puzzled myself." Van Helsing shrugged in that vague Continental manner. "In my younger days, after receiving my degree, I lived for a while in Bavaria, a village that is now a small city. I remember walking those woods, taking respite between writing chapters of my first book. The forest was dark, inhabited by bear and wolf. I loved those ambles. It was like entering a Musaus fairy tale, full of shadows and the possibility of monsters, dragons or witches, ogres and gnomes, but with a happy ending, as I always found my way home, back to damned civilisation."

"I have experienced many of the same emotions since you woke me," Dracula remarked, "stepping into this new world where creatures such as I should not exist."

There was a moment of silence.

"But I interrupt. Please continue," Dracula told the old man.

"Yes, well, one day a bear killed a breeder's horse and the townspeople armed themselves and invaded those woods," Van Helsing said. "They hunted and killed each bear in that forest. Slaughtered every one of the beasts and their cubs. Plus what wolves they found for good measure."

"That is barbaric," Lucy said.

"This is what humans do," I said.

"I walked in my woods but one more time," Van Helsing intoned sadly. "It was not the same. We need bears in our woods. And wolves. As we need ogres and dragons."

"The dragon is my family signet," Dracula commented. "The derivation of my name."

"This we know," Van Helsing remarked as his attention was drawn away from the conversation and out the window.

Ahead of us lay Brasov. The warm grey of the quickening sky was smudged by an inky blot rising from the town. A black column of smoke, expanding as it rose, appearing very much like the dire tornado that snatched away Dorothy in *The Wizard of Oz*.

"Renfield's work," I commented.

"Indubitably," Van Helsing added.

"Boom," said Renfield as he stared at the results of his work, grinning like a child presented with a birthday cake.

"Boom," we all chimed in and erupted in laughter together. Even the vampire could not contain his delight.

DATED: 19 MAY 1941
TO: CSS REINHARD HEYDRICH, RSHA, REICHSFUHRER-SS
FROM: SS MAJOR WALTRAUD REIKEL
CC: HEINRICH HIMMLER, REICHSFUHRER-SS
(via diplomatic pouch)

MOST SECRET

Regarding the destruction of the Brasov railroad
terminal:

The wreckage is extensive. Buildings, rails, and
various locomotive materials are a complete loss. The
experts brought in from Bucharest estimate five to six
weeks for enough repairs to allow trains to pass through
here again. From my experience with the Rumanian work
ethic I would expect these repairs to take five to six
months, if not years.

Until then rail transport to and through Brasov is
impossible; we will supply ourselves by road convoy.

As to the cause of this destruction: Upon my arrival
at the Brasov terminal, I witnessed a great desolation
of the property. Whole train cars had been scattered
all over the area. There were large fires amid the
ruins fierce enough to melt rails and steel cars.

There was but one eyewitness to the conflagration,
a Rumanian Army Corporal who was on guard duty and
described the source of the incident--a runaway train
that had left the station earlier that same night. The
evidence that he was correct came in the form of two
passenger cars containing German officers on leave to

the homeland from the Ploesti oil field security, the
Brandenburg Battalion. There were also two cars filled
with prisoners destined for Neuengamme and three tanker
cars of aircraft fuel.

The explosion of that selfsame fuel left little
but kindling and molten steel, so the exact cause
of the detonation may never be known; the combustive
properties of the fuel itself, plus the collision,
might have been enough to ignite the gasoline. The
train was apparently returning to the station at an
extremely high speed when it crashed into the terminal.

The next question is why the train was put into
reverse and accelerated back toward the station.
One of the passenger cars was found halfway intact,
more exactly, half of the car had landed in a nearby
strawberry field at least a hundred metres from the
rail yards. That this heavy unit had flown such a great
distance demonstrates the power of the eruption of the
fuel tanks. But this was not the only remarkable aspect
of this artefact.

Entering the car was like walking into a
slaughterhouse. Blood was everywhere, the floor, the
walls, even the ceiling. Dead German officers, and
parts of these men, lay strewn amid the wreckage. There
was evidence that these men had obviously been killed,
not by the collision, but by some unseen hand. These
men had been torn apart, throats and bellies ripped as
if by claws, limbs rent from their sockets, and their
faces frozen in a rictus of abject terror. The last
sight those dead eyes witnessed froze their visages
into masks of horror.

Some of the investigators, after examining the
carnage, have proposed that this is the result of a
bear attack. I asked what kind of bear could cause
a locomotive to reverse its engine and received no
coherent answer. Plus, we found no remains of the
prisoners occupying the other two cars--not a remnant
of one. They could not all have been vaporised by the

fire and explosion as we assume the rest of the German
victims were consumed. Could they have escaped from
their car and created this animalistic slaughter?

I ordered a party out to search for the place where
the train had stopped. One of my Lieutenants proposed
that the train may not have done so, and I had to
remind him of the simple physics: For it to reverse, it
had to stop. This and the fact that the prisoners most
likely did not leap from a moving train, especially the
old and infirm among them. I ordered the rail line to
be walked, a step at a time until they find the precise
location where this incident began.

I had the sole surviving rail station guard brought
to the castle, where he was interrogated vigorously.
No more information was forthcoming.

By the time that interview was terminated, I received
a report from the field that the site of the attack had
been located.

Because the road parallels the tracks for a good
part of the way, I decided to lead a small convoy to
the location, some 87.3 kilometres north of Brasov.

Surprised at the speed of the discovery, I was
told that an enterprising motor pool Sergeant had
commandeered a gasoline-powered railroad cart used
for rail inspections and they had driven the distance
slowly and with an eye out for any anomaly.

This patrol discovered the bodies of two members of
the train's security detail lying alongside the track.
Further along, past a peculiar mountainous outcropping,
there was a sandy open area where the search party
found another pair of bodies, German officers, slain
in the same manner as those found at the terminal. An
amputated arm was also discovered, plus a smattering of
broken glass most likely from a passenger car window. A
few weapons of German issue lay alongside the tracks,
some of which had been fired, their magazines empty or
near empty.

Another unit searching by foot spotted a body tangled in the debris alongside the river, apparently the corpse of the civilian fireman, a rather large man, bearing the same animal-like marks as had the other victims, a few of which had exhibited a rather horrendous tearing of the flesh at their necks.

I searched the sand for vehicle tracks, but our own made a jigsaw of any that might have been left by the perpetrators. Of this I am sure: There were more tracks than could have been made by our own transports.

Hearing a cry from one of the search parties, I was alerted that a living survivor had been found on the opposite bank of the river. This was the engineer of the train. He was in a much-weakened state, old and nearly drowned. When asked what had occurred here, he had a one-word answer.

This answer was so outrageous that I concluded that he was either in shock from his ordeal or was lying, and I had him escorted back to the castle for some medical treatment, enough to make him viable for an interview.

Walking the river's edge, deep in thought, focusing on this puzzle and the engineer's most mysterious explanation, I spied an object that did not fit among the rounded stones: a black enamelled square box. A moving picture camera, one of those with a crank at the side that winds the mechanism like a clock. The kind of object favored by our more affluent officers, hobbyists who need more than a still photo.

I ordered one of my men to take this camera into Brasov to the local photography shop and have the film developed immediately.

While the engineer was being questioned (see attached transcription), the processed film arrived, along with the photography shop proprietor, who brought his personal projection equipment.

I viewed the footage alone--the proprietor operating.

I will not explicate what this viewing revealed. If I were to put what I saw into words, you would be as disbelieving as I was of the engineer. I myself had to view this film a number of times for the inevitable conclusion to sink into what, I am proud to say, is a rational mind.

View it yourself. It is indeed a documentary of what happened in that passenger car.

I do have to say that what it reveals is far beyond my experience as a professional soldier, and I eagerly await your instructions as to how I should proceed.

P.S. The projectionist has been rendered silent.

ATTACHMENT TO COMMUNIQUÉ

INTERVIEW CONDUCTED BY MAJOR W. REIKEL, INTERVIEW SPECIALIST CORPORAL SCHRECK. (Also present is your company scribe.)

INTERVIEW TRANSCRIPT:

The Subject, one Bogdan Stelymes, is a Rumanian male, fifty-three years of age, from Slobozia by way of Bucharest, employed as a locomotive engineer for the Rumanian Transportation Corporation. A background check is being pursued by the Gestapo at this moment.

Subject is in third hour of interrogation. Subject so far has withstood mild physical intimidation. A member from our medical staff revived the Subject at three different intervals during the initial interview. The fourth time, the Subject was discovered to be feigning unconsciousness and was mildly punished for the ruse. This led to another call for the medic to keep the Subject alert for the next round of questioning.

The Subject's recalcitrance forced the initial interrogator to resort to more aggressive techniques.

The Subject was passed on to Corporal Schreck.

Corporal Schreck took the Subject to his private interview chamber. The Subject was secured to a wooden chair by leather restraints binding the Subject's wrists, ankles, and chest to the chair. This protects the Subject from any undue injury.

The chair was built to Corporal Schreck's specifications. The arms of the chair are made of oak or a comparable heavy wood, as are the legs and back. (There is a tendency to use pine for easier driving of the nails, but any abrupt movement by the subject may crack the boards. Oft-times the struggle is enough to render the pine chair useless.) The hardwood pieces are screwed together so that each piece can be removed and replaced when distressed because of repeated use. A one-kilogram-weight hammer is recommended, though Corporal Schreck uses a two-kilogram sledge with a shortened handle.

MAJOR R.: Again, who attacked the train?

SUBJECT: I told you. Over and over. A vampire.

MAJOR R.: A vampire?

SUBJECT: Yes, yes!

A brief cessation of the interview was given. Major Reikel gave Corporal S. the order to proceed with a more vigorous method of questioning. The hammer was procured from the Corporal's tool chest, also a box of nails, 100 millimetres in length. (Dual-headed carpentry nails are preferred, to ease removal later.)

Corporal S. secured the Subject's right hand with a strap placed upon the chair arm for this purpose, positioned the nail at the joining of the scaphoid and os magnum bones, and fixed the Subject's hand to the wooden arm of the chair with one stroke of his hammer.

The Subject's response was vocal and vigorous, but non-verbal.

MAJOR R.: Who attacked your train?

SUBJECT: I said before. I say it again. The vampire.

The Subject's other hand was similarly attached to the other arm of the chair. Again, only one blow of the

Corporal's hammer sufficed. The Subject responded the same as previously, though with decidedly less vigor.

SUBJECT: Please, no more. Tell me what you want me to say.

MAJOR R.: Who attacked your train?

SUBJECT: Who do you want me to name? I will name them. Please . . .

MAJOR R.: Intelligence gathered this way is never reliable.

It is not known whether this statement was directed at the Subject, the Sergeant, or your humble scribe.

MAJOR R.: A couple more nails and toss him into a cell with some other prisoners, as an inducement to those about to be interviewed.

SUBJECT: Please, no.

MAJOR R.: A vampire . . . These people are tough, but creative.

At this point the Major exited the interview room and, though more hammering commenced, your humble transcriber exited with the Major. From all reports, nothing more of consequence was communicated by the Subject.

END OF TRANSCRIPTION

ATTACHED PERSONAL NOTE

Eugene,

How is the glamorous life in glorious Berlin? Here the food is abysmal, not fit for goats. The wine tastes like the stale piss of a dead man. (Do not ask how I know this. Haha.) And the women—there is a joke: If I had a dog as ugly as a Rumanian woman I would shave its ass and teach it to walk backward.

Actually, not all is bad, but everything rankles when I know that we are on the verge of a great battle, a battle for the history books, to reclaim the land stolen from us by the Tsars. My whole life has been dedicated to the Fatherland, to be a soldier of service to our Fuhrer. I yearn for a proper battlefield, to lead men into the face of death, to prove myself to my father, to my comrades-in-arms, to my Fuhrer—not play hide-and-seek with peasants.

Fear not, I will do my duty here to the fullest extent of my abilities and complete the task laid before me, but I want to be a part of the coming fight, a war that will be written about for ages. I mean to make my own mark upon that history.

I will finish my labours here as Hercules cleaned out the stables.

Then be advised I will pressure you on every level, professional and personal, to relieve me of this dismal assignment. Be assured, I will be as relentless as I was against your sabre.

Give my regards to Lina.

Wally

EXCERPTED FROM THE UNPUBLISHED NOVEL
THE DRAGON PRINCE AND I
by Lenore Van Muller

After the rescue of her compatriots from the Nazi train, Lucille and the others returned home just in time for the vampire to avoid the sunrise. She was curious about this aspect of the vampire's physiognomy, a lone weakness in what she assumed was unbridled power. She had so many questions, but every time she found herself in Dracula's presence and the opportunity for inquiry arose, she balked like a horse at a fence.

Upon arrival at the house, Dracula went immediately to his curtained room. Her father looked haggard, and Lucille sent him to bed with a glass of warm milk. She feared for his health. The long days and nights, the expenditures of his energy, and the stress put upon him by his role in the Resistance leadership was just too much for a man his age.

She waited for him to drain the glass of milk. She had dosed it with a mild sedative. She was, after all, a doctor's daughter.

"Who's the child here?" he asked, detecting the drug's presence and twisting his mouth in disgust.

"Neither of us," she answered. "We just watch over each other. Like soldiers and families do."

"Then I would be remiss if I did not warn you once more." Van Helsing gave his daughter a tired smile. "Be careful around him."

She did not reply. Kissing the old man's forehead, she turned off his light and left. He was snoring before she closed the door.

Downstairs, washing the glass in the kitchen sink, she encountered the Englishman dallying for no reason at the cupboard. She was so tired of his constant pursuit of her. Why was she unable to put a damper on his misplaced ardour? She had been able to close many a door to men just like him. The type who jumped from dalliance to marriage with nothing more than a kiss, a dance, or a mere wink from across a smoky nightclub, and the next day were naming their children. And every one of these misguided men had finally listened to reason and stopped pursuing her. Well, some had left with angry, expletive-laden tirades, and some sent awful, heartbroken letters. Still, the unwanted attention ended. But this one . . .

As she washed the glass she studied Harker. The new regimental mustache did nothing to belie his youth, actually emphasised his boyish appearance. He looked like an adolescent in a school play with an eye-pencil line across his upper lip. His eyelids drooped at the outer corners, a slight epicanthic fold that gave him a melancholy aspect. The effect was not so much that he was sad but that he shared your sadness.

"That was a bit of all right," he said, as she set the glass on the counter. "Tonight. The train. We make quite a team. You and I."

"Look, Harker," she began.

"I keep telling you, call me Jonny."

"Jonny is what you call some urchin hawking the *Times* in Picadilly Square," she said. "Now Jonathan is the name of a soldier, a spy, someone to reckon with. I shall call you Jonathan."

She tried a smile, but he was not charmed. "Look, Jonathan," she began again. "I know that you are perturbed that our, shall we say, moment of intimacy was never repeated."

"Not the lack of repetition, madam," he replied. "But, shall we say, the bloody cold shoulder afterward and acting as if it had never happened."

"That is what I am attempting to correct. If you will let me." He nodded and she continued. "I fell into bed with you. One time. And because it did not become a nightly affair, your pride is hurt."

"Not my pride."

"What then? I want you to know that the subsequent rejection of your affections was in no way caused by anything lacking in your performance that night."

"Why, thank you so very bloody much. That's jolly decent of you."

"Don't get huffy. The event was more than satisfactory."

"More than satisfactory! I'll get that embroidered on a pillow."

"Let me explain." Lucille knew that she was just digging herself a deeper hole with this approach. "That night was a momentary lapse on my part. I was, for the moment, requiring some physical succour. Some companionship beyond the casual embrace. And you filled that vacuum."

"Oh, I see," he pouted. "I fill a vacuum like some kind of mattress stuffing."

"There's that huffiness again. Not a very attractive trait at all, if I may say so."

He looked abashed, and she continued, "I just want you to understand. That night was an aberration and will not happen again. What I am hoping is that this momentary lapse of mine will not stand in the way of us being able to work together and maybe even become friends."

"We already work together," he retorted. She could see he was in pain.

"But this cloud hangs over us and I would like it to be gone," she said. "So, can we try this? Just wipe that night from our memories? Can we?"

"The problem," he began, "is that, for me, the evening under discussion, your 'lapse,' was quite memorable. Quite."

He looked at the floor, avoiding her eyes.

"I am sorry," she said.

"Do not be." He raised his eyes to meet hers. "In fact, it was and is one of the most memorable nights of my life, and I suspect it will be the last thought that passes through my brain at the moment of my death."

His face was contorted with emotion, his eyes filling with tears.

"I suppose I should be flattered," she said softly. "Are all of you English such romantics? Don't answer, purely rhetorical. What we need to do is get beyond this impasse and be able to work together. Is that possible in the least?"

"I suppose we must." He tensed his mouth, raised his chin. The very illustration of the proverbial stiff upper lip.

"We must. You are a kind man, heroic, and good-looking, Jonathan. You will find the right woman. And she will be a very lucky girl."

"The song sung to every poor fool in love with the wrong woman," he said sadly and left the kitchen.

Lucille sighed heavily and called after him, "As you gain experience, Jonathan, you will discover the vast gulf that lies between love and infatuation."

But he was gone and she was speaking to herself: "As I, myself, have learned so many times."

She went to her bedroom, tried to sleep. Failing that, she attempted to read, but the usual post-mission energy was still coursing through her system. Added to that was her inability to escape the images of what she had seen through the train windows. The vampire in full siege. The power unleashed, the brute, atavistic dominion of the vampire over so many men, armed men. And then when she washed the blood off him at the river's edge. She watched the bullet wounds heal before her eyes. Lucille had stared at the shiny new scars in wonder. This was true magic, strong magic, nothing like her crude, weak dabbling in the occult.

In the past, when she was this agitated she would find surcease in some libidinous exercise. But that was what had put her in such complicated muddles as Janos and the damned Englishman. No, no relief of that kind, thank you very much.

Lucille found herself knocking at Dracula's door.

"Enter," he said.

He was lying upon the red horsehair chaise, a book in his hand, the lamp next to him casting his face in a golden glow on one side, into shadow on the other. The yellow light erased some of the paleness of his countenance.

With an air of propriety, he stood when she entered.

"Miss Van Helsing." He gave her that short bow. "Shouldn't you be sleeping?"

"It eludes me after nights like this," she explained and smiled at him. "But you never sleep at all? There are reports that you slept in a coffin."

"You mentioned this before. I have at times used one for transport. Travelling in daylight can be hazardous to me, and Customs Inspectors are not surprised to find a dead man in a casket."

"But don't you need to remain in contact with your native soil? You put dirt in the coffin, right?"

"You think I lie in dirt? Where do such ideas originate? Your father?"

"No. As I have said, he would never speak to me about you. It comes from that book about you."

"The vaudevillian's account. My purported history?"

"Not really. It was sold as a fiction, but it is, more or less, about you and my father in England. Mina. Lucy Westerna. Harker's grandfather's adventures here in Transylvania."

"Mina and Lucy . . ." Dracula gazed into the shadows. "As I said, I was a different man then. After you live too long you become . . . bored. Supremely bored, and the next stage is what some philosophers deem an existential nihilism. It was such a state that ultimately led to my depredations in England."

"And at what stage are you now?" she asked.

"We shall see," he replied. "The search for a reason to live is a difficult quest, and there are myriad paths on which one can become lost."

"I, too, am on this same pilgrimage."

They were silent for a moment.

"I understand," Lucille said. "Really I do. I had my days of unbridled adventures. As soon as I was of age I fled this house. Call it adolescent rebellion; two people too close for too long. But Brasov seemed too small for what I wanted, so plebeian. Rumania itself was too paltry a playground."

"Now you risk your life for it."

"Irony gets you every time, don't it?"

"Where did you go?"

"All the hot spots: Paris, Berlin, London, New York City, California, Hong Kong, India . . . It was a time of . . . Before the war it was a time of experimentation. Not just me. It was the twenties . . . The youth of the world went on a bacchanal. I went a little wild myself. There was . . . excess. I finally came home to put myself back together and to warn my father that the Nazis were kicking up their jackboots. I was hoping he would decide to move to Australia. But then the Japanese are building a fire in that part of the world, are they not? There seems to be no safe harbour from this war."

She shrugged, leaned forward. His eyes examined her face, her eyes, the auburn tresses like a painter's sable brush.

"The point in all this is, I do understand your attempt to control yourself," she told him in a whisper. "I understand lust."

She moved closer, sat upon the chaise. Their faces were inches apart. She lowered her lips toward his. Dracula abruptly pulled away.

"Thank you for your understanding," he said rather formally. "So, this bit of fiction—I would be interested in reading this tome."

"There's a movie, too," she said, putting some distance between them, a bit embarrassed, but covering.

"A movie? Ah, yes, the moving pictures you spoke about. This cinema."

"We should go!" She jumped up with sudden enthusiasm. "Oh, there's a good one playing now in Brasov!"

Dracula was struck by her childlike joy. All presumptions of sophistication, any worldly airs, disappeared, and before him he saw a little girl excited about sharing an enthusiasm. And for that same moment he forgot his own dire history and had a vision of his little brother's delight at finding a newt in the garden.

"We have to go!" she exclaimed. "We must go!"

"Now?"

"Tonight," she declared with a dip of her chin. "It's a date. Oh! And I'll get you the book."

And she dashed away to the library. There she found a volume, the spine announcing the title in gilt letters: *Blood Diseases of the Oceanic Tribes*. It was a mask, being only the dust jacket of that volume wrapped around a copy of The Book.

She rushed back up the stairs to Dracula's room. He was patiently standing where she had left him.

"My father had many a copy sent to him." She handed the book to him. "Once the author presented it to him at a conference in Malta. I don't think Father ever read it. I do know he burned it in the fireplace. A most extreme act for a man who worships literature in any form. Too painful perhaps."

"Painful for everyone involved," Dracula answered.

"I found this when I was nine. Stole it."

He hefted the volume in his hand, examined the cover. It was a simple declaration, the title at the top—*Dracula*—and below it, the author's name. He thumbed through the pages, not looking at her.

"So. Tonight." She backed to the door. "A date!"

And she was gone. Dracula listened as her footsteps receded, still bemused at her many forms: terrorist leader, vagabond, nurse, bibliophile, and now excitable maiden.

Back in her room, Lucille lay in bed staring at the ceiling, amazed at the boldness of her overture toward the vampire, embarrassed by his rejection. It was these thoughts, plus the anticipation of the promised engagement later, that threw her mind into a vortex that finally sucked her down into a delirious sleep.

The trip from home to the theatre had been an adventure. Lucille had forgotten that the summer days were longer now and the sun was still above the mountains as the showtime neared.

"We'll miss the movie," she had mourned. Weekdays, the Brasov cinema played their feature only once a night, and there would still be light in the sky past the starting time. She explained this to Dracula.

"Let us try," he said.

"But you cannot go about in the daylight," she protested.

"I can with precautions," Dracula told her. "Briefly. The sunlight is perilous to my skin and my eyes."

"So you can cover up?"

"I have done so successfully."

"Excellent." Her childish enthusiasm had returned.

She searched for and found the pair of darkened glasses she had repeatedly tried to make her father wear, to no avail. They made the vampire seem even more exotic. That effect was instantly ameliorated by a scarf knitted by a grateful patient who apparently couldn't stop her runaway needles, creating a swath of wool nearly three metres long. She wrapped it around his neck a few times until his face was totally obscured.

Next came a pair of leather gloves and a broad-brimmed hat Lucille wore while gardening. He looked ridiculous, but in the end not an inch of albino skin could be seen. She decided that Dracula now bore a resemblance to Claude Rains in *The Invisible Man*.

As for herself, Lucille wore a dress for the first time in months. Before the war she had pursued style and fashion like men chased riches. But the pragmatic matters of war had changed her focus. These days she wore her father's discarded shirts and worn-out slacks cinched with a tie or a belt a sailor had gifted her in hopes of a kiss. She had gotten the better of the deal, the belt macraméd from knotted fishing line, a sturdy old sailor's craft. It was beautifully made and would most likely outlast the memory of the kiss.

Eschewing practicalities tonight, she had found a soft, slinky dress that clung in the right places. She had shaved her legs and even dabbed on the slightest bit of makeup. For good reason: She was going on a date! With the most unique man on earth!

She drove into Brasov, the roadblock guards just waving them on when the car was recognised. She and the Prince walked two short blocks to the cinema, making it in time for the cartoon. Dracula was beguiled by the old black-and-white antics of Bugs Bunny and Elmer and laughed out loud when the rabbit declared, "Of course you know this means war." During the newsreel she tried to explain that the cartoon rabbit was quoting from the Marx Brothers film *Duck Soup*, but the vampire shushed her. He was engrossed in the footage of the little man with the ludicrous mustache.

And then *King Kong* began and there was no talking to or among anyone. Just shrieks and gasps at the travails of the tragic monster and his blond love.

Sitting next to each other in the dark, she found herself watching the vampire more than the feature up on the screen.

Dracula's gaze was fixed upon the images that floated before him, spellbound by what was projected through a column of light onto the silver curtain.

He was riveted to his seat, stunned at the magic before him. How did the photographs become animate, so fluid, so lifelike? Where did the music come from? He saw no hidden orchestra. But the questions quickly evaporated as he was lost in the thrall of the story. And when the characters landed on Skull Island, he was swept away to that mysterious land.

Lucille saw the reflected light dance across his pale face. His emotions, so far mostly hidden behind a regal facade, were now fully displayed upon his face, naked for her to see. He gasped, laughed, stared in awe, ducked once, gaped as the Max Steiner score soared, thundered as the beast approached the walls, the anticipation building to a point of unbearability. He held his breath as the fair maiden was offered as sacrifice, twisted and turned as though he were battling the giant lizard himself.

The scenes in New York fascinated him. He scooted to the edge of his seat, leaned toward the screen as the giant gorilla escaped his captors, ravaged the elevated train, and then climbed the skyscraper.

And when Kong fell, as the beast lay bleeding on the street and Denham intoned his elegiac "It was beauty killed the Beast," Lucille saw a tear flow from the vampire's eye, a pinkish droplet slipping down the chalk-white cheek.

Lucille wondered if he identified with the poor creature, so powerful and yet so tragic. An outcast, alone, maybe the only, if not the last of his kind. A king without a kingdom. She watched his rapt attention and studied his face. Could the Prince relate to the mighty Kong falling in love with a mortal woman?

She reached for his hand, offering comfort, and he took it into his own, clasping his fingers around her palm. His skin was cool to the touch.

As soon as the lights came up he began questioning her. He asked if such a beast had really been discovered and was sorely disappointed when she said it had not. He queried her about the newsreel, with its litany of German triumphs and the prodigy of Hitler. Dracula commented, "So that is the little man causing all this grief."

It was fully night when they left the auditorium. Dracula, now free of his bundling, asked how cartoons were made. He especially admired the music behind Bugs and Elmer, the "hyperactive muscularity of the orchestral score."

She asked him how he liked the movie itself.

"Genius," he said. "Extraordinary. I would say even profound. And you say there is one of these photodramas about me?"

"Yes," Lucille took the crook of his arm as they walked into the lobby. "You wouldn't like it. It's a bit hammy. The actor who plays you is short and creepy."

"'Creepy'... He creeps?"

"A bit of slang. It means 'unpleasant.' You can skip it."

"'Skip it'?"

They passed through the cluster of people milling outside the theatre entrance. A few of them stared at Dracula with more than idle curiosity and a modicum of fear. She was sure that they could not recognise who or what he was, so she suspected the reaction must have come from a more primal level. He was oblivious.

"More slang. It means 'forget it.' But wait until you see Fred Astaire dance! Poetry in motion. Oh! And Buster Keaton! Another poet of the physical. And *The Wizard of Oz*. You will be ... when the house lands and the screen goes from black-and-white to ... I don't want to spoil it. *La Regle du Jeu*! *Snow White*! *The Thirty-Nine Steps*!"

Dracula slowly shook his head in marvel. "Every time I think that this world has been reduced to barbarism, that the human creature is but another soulless animal, something alters my opinion. A bit of music, a line of poetry or literature, something sublime as this magnificent work you just shared with me, something as inspiring as this gives me hope."

Lucille shook him out of his reverie by nudging his elbow with her own, bringing his attention to the truck filled with German soldiers that rolled to a stop in front of the theatre.

The Nazis leapt off the vehicle and waded into the crowd, some invading the lobby and auditorium to roust those still lingering inside.

The familiar Lieutenant Guth stepped out of the truck cab shouting, "Everybody out of the theatre!"

He stood in front of the crowd, fists on hips. "This establishment is closed. Assemblies in Brasov of more than four individuals are now forbidden."

Cesar Tirlea, the proprietor and projectionist, and his wife, Vasilica, ticket seller and usher, were forcibly dragged out of the theatre and the doors locked and chained.

The SS used their rifle butts and a few kicks from their boots to hurry the crowd away from the building. An old woman was given a brutal shove and she fell into a child, both tumbling onto the pavement.

Dracula was incensed and stepped forward, intent on some kind of intervention. Lucille pulled him back, impelled him to turn away, walked him into the shadows.

Behind them they could hear the Nazis shattering the windows of the ticket kiosk.

There was a scream from Vasilica. Dracula turned back at this and Lucille vainly tried to restrain him, but it was like attempting to pull down the Empire State Building with her bare hands.

She leaned into him, put her lips to his ear. "Don't make yourself conspicuous. Leave, to fight another day."

She could not believe that she was repeating what her father had cautioned so many times. Advice she had defiantly dismissed, over and over.

"I would rather fight now," Dracula said fiercely.

"So would we all," Lucille whispered, matching his anger. "We choose our battles."

He allowed her to walk him away from the commotion.

"Another day," she said.

"Another day," Dracula repeated. "And soon, I hope."

EXCERPTS FROM UNIDENTIFIED DIARY
(translated from the German)

[Editor's note: Despite an extreme effort we have not been able, at this date, to authenticate beyond all doubt that this is in fact Adolf Hitler's personal diary, written by his own hand. We still are pursuing all means to verify its authenticity.]

May 20

Herr Wolf cannot sleep. His Mind is a waterwheel spinning with the planning of the coming Operation Barbarossa. And this Hess farce—What was he thinking? Surely he is deranged.

Herr Wolf has tried to read, finishing the Hemingway novel _Fiesta_. Romantic balderdash full of Communist bickering. The hero, a misnomer, is a perfect metaphor for the Americans. Impotent. Much like the Cripple who leads them.

HH is relentless with an annoying demand to watch some film he has obtained from the Balkans.

Does he not know that the Soviet invasion is our opportunity for Lebensraum? Herr Wolf imagines a place for Germany to expand, like the British into India, a colony for Germans to establish handsome, spacious farms, marvelous lodgings that Herr Wolf has designed himself (often drawn during those dreadful meetings where his Generals give all the reasons not to do what must, will, and has been done). They tell Herr Wolf that Russia is too big, that the engagement will take too long, and we will find ourselves stuck on the tundra in the blasphemous Russian winter like Napoleon. They lack Vision. Herr Wolf has a Vision, one that has Conquered every obstacle before us thus far. If he had listened to the Generals we would still be negotiating with the French. It is a test of Willpower between the Generals and Herr Wolf, one which they will lose. Herr Wolf's Iron Will prevails, as always.

These new lands will have government offices like palaces, honoring the glory of our Fatherland; it will be a closed Society, a bulwark against the corrosive influences of the Russian barbarians, none of the degenerate miscegenation that the emasculated British are prone to indulge in.

The postponement of Barbarossa, due to the unreasonable and unexpected duration of the Jugoslav liberation, has put Herr Wolf on edge. He is impatient for the Seeds to Sprout, the plant to bloom, the bloom to fruit, the fruit to ripen, and finally for that first bite, the first bite always proven to be the best. Molotov is drawing out the talks of an accommodation with the Communists that will never be found. Stalin has been warned by Churchill of our intentions, but Stalin does not trust the English, suspecting them of trying to trick the Soviets into declaring war on us.

Herr Wolf has spies in Stalin's command and . . .

[PAGE OR PAGES MISSING]

. . . and the Americans have frozen all German assets in the United States. This was expected, a typical weak-kneed response by the Cripple and his Jews in America, solving their problems with their weapon of choice—Lucre.

Advisors have talked Herr Wolf out of his intention to ban this disgusting habit of smoking, cigarettes and pipe, especially cigars. The entire country is in the clutches of this irritating custom, even the female populace have fallen under its destructive spell. Herr Wolf's suggestion that, in lieu of a ban, every packet be emblazoned with a death's head, to remind the user of the consequences, was also discouraged. Herr Wolf would prefer that soldiers not be issued this vile product, maybe issue chocolates instead of tobacco, but he was warned that there would be a rebellion among the military. This is how pernicious the habit has become.

Besides these thorns in his side, Herr Wolf's new suits do not fit properly. Herr Wolf has an indisposition to close-fitting jackets. He needs to move his arms! He thinks some sort of sabotage lies behind this problem. It will be investigated.

Joke of the day—courtesy of HH. How do you make a Jew crazy? Ham at half price. Very funny. Haha.

Herr Wolf was examining the latest communiqué from Egypt. King Farouk states he will welcome us if we guarantee the expulsion of the British from his country. This was when HH interrupted once more about this damnable film. Ten minutes was all he requested, then begged.

Herr Wolf relented. As a Leader, one must respect the opinions of those he has chosen to Command. If HH declares something important, then Herr Wolf must acknowledge that concern or unduly weaken the man in sight of his fellows. A Great Leader must be aware of these protocols.

Herr Wolf allowed himself to be led to the small private theatre where coffee and carrot cake were provided. The previous evening, Herr Wolf had enjoyed another showing of <u>The Lives of a Bengal Lancer</u> in this theatre. Another film to be shown, the new Greta Garbo feature, was declined as Herr Wolf was indisposed—stomach pain of uncommon strength.

In the theatre waited the other H. Reinhard. He explained: this film came from an event in Rumania that had occurred four days previous, a raid upon a train transporting some of our officers on leave. A great loss to the Fatherland. One of these brave men carried with him a motion picture camera. What followed would be footage shot during that raid.

HH nodded to the projectionist in his booth and the lights dimmed. The white light leapt from the booth portal and onto the screen.

Herr Wolf watched as German officers gambolled in what was obviously a railroad car. They drank and laughed and sang—all silently, there being no sound, the camera work very shaky and, well, amateurish, though the footage was in colour, a comment on the cinematographer's dedication to his hobby. There was one amusing moment when a rather fat Lieutenant demonstrated the unique ability to draw deeply from his pipe and blow smoke out of his ears. Herr Wolf did not know this was possible.

Outside that one jape, Herr Wolf was growing bored, hinting that he had more important matters before him, witnessing a soldiers' drunken frolic not his priority despite the love for his soldiers in the field.

HH begged for a little more patience, explaining that they had not time to edit the film and, in fact, the context was important to prove that what he was about to see was not fakery.

So, Herr Wolf watched the incipient Fritz Lang dwell, for far too long, on the new Emil Jannings, who was entertaining one and all by putting his cap on backward and rolling his eyes independent of each other, another feat Herr Wolf had not seen before, when the camera swung violently away from the clown to witness the entrance of . . .

Herr Wolf was fixed to his seat for the rest of the film, until the end when the camera, lying on its side on the railroad car floor, recorded nothing more than the still, dead face and eyes of the man Herr Wolf assumed was the camera operator.

The only movement in the frame was a spray of blood that landed on the lens and slowly dripped until it obscured everything in a pink curtain.

The film ran out into stark black. Herr Wolf stared at the brilliant white of the still-lit screen until his eyes began to pain him. Could this be?

— Play it again, he ordered.

They did. No one spoke a word while the film was re-wound, re-threaded, and shown again.

And Herr Wolf watched the remarkable footage five more times. Now the jovial antics of those poor soldiers created a grim dread in Herr Wolf's soul.

After the last showing Herr Wolf turned to HH and RH.

The questions were simple. To RH's credit so were the answers.

— Who has seen this?

— Here, just the three of us and the projectionist.

— In Rumania?

— The SS officer in charge and a projectionist, who has been silenced.

— Could it be faked?

— We suppose so, but it is a very elaborate and difficult process. When the arm comes off . . .the throat torn out . . . I do not know how you would do that. I could consult with some of our motion picture professionals.

— Then again there is the question: To what purpose would such faking be? I cannot come up with any viable answer. (This was RH positing.)

— Forget the professionals. Herr Wolf ordered, we must limit the exposure. Who sent this?

— Major Waltraud Reikel in Rumania. A very trusted SS officer. Not one for pranks.

— He and I were on the Olympic fencing team together, RH vouched.

— From Rumania, you said?

— Yes. Transylvania, to be exact.

Transylvania. Herr Wolf contemplated this fact, then gave his orders.

— Send our projectionist to the Russian front lines. As an infantryman. Tonight. He may speak to others, but no one believes a mere Private. As to . . . the personage on the footage, capture him. Alive. Or un-dead. Herr Wolf laughed at his own pun. Whatever its state, preserve it.

EXCERPTED FROM THE UNPUBLISHED NOVEL
THE DRAGON PRINCE AND I
by Lenore Van Muller

After returning from the theatre Lucille and the vampire conversed through the night. She told him about her trip with her father to the Paris Art Deco Exposition in 1925. She was fifteen and very impressionable. The first sight of the Lalique fountains at night, lit from within by neon, set a romantic ideal that was matched with every event, every vista.

They visited the Galerie Pierre and viewed the first group show of surrealists, works by Paul Klee, Hans Arp, Man Ray, Miro. At her insistence, they went back repeatedly, and Lucille decided to be an artist. She was not sure of her medium—photography, sculpting, or paint and canvas—but she was determined that the life of an artist would be her destiny.

Then they went to Coco Chanel's shop, and for two days she thought that high fashion might be her metier.

She remembered the first time she saw an advertisement for a performance of *La Revue Negre* with Josephine Baker. The posters were everywhere, on every lamppost, vacant wall, and pissoir. She wanted to be like, no, wanted to *be* this exotic woman with the slicked-down coiffeur and spit curl on her forehead. Her father refused to allow her to attend what was considered a risque show, and this only added to the allure. Still she imitated the look with her own hair for at least a year after. Until her Greta Garbo phase.

After they returned home she became a fanatical Francophile. Not necessarily the country. Her fixation was on the doings of Paris. This was the golden age of literature and art in the City of Lights, and this made her all the more aware that she was mired in what she considered a rural backwater. She made her father's life miserable with constant hectoring about her wretched, sequestered life.

She made him subscribe to all of the Paris magazines and journals: the *Transatlantic Review*, *Gargoyle*, *Tambour*, *Transition*, *Vogue*, the *Chicago Tribune* (Paris Edition). She kept track of the exploits and accomplishments of Hemingway, Dos Passos, Pound, the Fitzgeralds, Joyce, Picasso, and Chagall, who, to the delight of the teenage Lucille, painted in the nude. She knew what Diaghilev was up to with the Ballets Russes, pestered her father for the latest Stravinsky record, followed the existentialists like her girlfriends followed the dating habits of their peers. Gertrude Stein had named her two-seater auto "Godiva," so Lucille gave her bicycle the same appellation.

She was a Communist for a month or two, a Socialist for less, an anarchist for an entire winter.

Her father bought her the silk stockings, Ambre perfume, and Fleur de Peche she had read about. She ordered crushed-almond skin cream and began to smoke evil-smelling cigarettes with a long, ivory holder. She felt as much an expatriate as any of the Americans.

As soon as she left her last finishing school, she picked a fight with her father and packed a case for Paris. But five years had passed since first love, and the creative fire that had ignited so many talented people had dimmed to dirty embers. The days of wine and absinthe and cocaine had claimed too many victims. She would sit with the pimps and street girls at the club Le Rendevous des Mariniers on the Quai d'Anjou and the scene made her sad, not a bit of romance to be found.

She would go out at night to dance at the jazz clubs. She met Hemingway, an angry drunk with a fragile ego. Her idol Zelda was in an asylum. She bought a year's subscription to Shakespeare & Company, spotted Sylvia Beach bringing tea to Sam Beckett and Jean-Paul Sartre. She ambled through the stacks so she could overhear the two. They spoke no great thoughts, but merely complained about the rain. Lucille was too embarrassed to announce her own recent ambitions to be a novelist.

She dallied among the colony of the third sex and found herself in the arms of a penniless drinking colleague of Henry Miller and Anaïs Nin.

After a short time she came to the conclusion that the parade had passed, the streets were filled with nothing but has-beens and never-bes. The golden age had turned to brass, and tarnished brass at that. She heard a bearded young piano player say that the lost generation, generation *perdu*, had become the *fichu*—ruined—generation. Sadly she realised that Paris had become less an island of artists and more a conclave of tourists and posers.

She sipped onion soup at Le Chien Qui Fume in Les Halles, overheard the reporters describing the savagery of the Nazi party in Munich. She decided to abandon the rotting fruit of Paris and try Berlin.

After a brief interlude and debauch in Berlin she headed west to England, then the United States, reading as she went, e. e. cummings on the Isles, John Steinbeck in the Americas. In the Orient she read Fei Ming and Kawabata.

But even there, the clatter of sword against shield was increasing in volume. Despondent and depleted in her mind and soul, she decided to return home and warn her father. But first she stopped in Berlin to confirm the rumours of war. The city had changed dramatically in the few years she had been travelling the globe. During her first visit it was known as "Wicked Berlin," a city determined to break every social convention. Provocative behaviour in the extreme had been the rule and the raison d'etre.

The Friedrichstadt quarter had teemed with prostitutes in the thousands, so many that the whores were divided into categories, any act to fit any depravity. It seemed colourful at the time, the streetwalker specialties given various sobriquets: boneshakers, grasshoppers, boot girls, woodchucks, half-silks, gravelstones, Kontrol Girls, and Nuttes.

Gigolos and pretty boys prowled the tourist hotels and downtown pensiones, their faces painted with rouge and mascara like toddlers raiding their mother's makeup case.

To Lucille, this city of iniquity fascinated and titillated her. Children hawked dirty postcards on the streets like newspapers. Dark cabarets were host to drug parties and nude dancing—by the patrons! There were naked boxing and wrestling arenas, private torture chambers, and pornographic films depicting Gymnasium masters and nannies humiliating their naked charges with a variety of objects.

Berlin had been a constant, almost hysterical, bacchanal as the German people tried to erase the monstrous horrors of the recent lost war and the daily tragedy of massive unemployment and unparalleled inflation. It was an economic nightmare where a wheelbarrow of marks might purchase a mealy loaf of bread.

And Lucille dipped her toe in the shallow end of this polluted pool. She was sucked into the seductive maelstrom of dissolution and desperate thrills.

She spent a wicked weekend with a degenerate adventuress, an aging flapper who strutted into parties with a terrified spider monkey clinging to her neck, the monkey clothed and the woman wearing nothing but a thigh-length mink coat and a brooch packed with cocaine.

Lucille partook of a bizarre concoction of white roses dipped into a potion of chloroform and ether, then consumed the frozen petals. She woke the next morning amid a half-dozen other naked bodies, in an apartment she did not remember travelling to, her body spotted with bruises, smears of lipstick, and a cigarette burn. She had no memory of the night.

She fled the city the next day and began wandering the globe searching for *experience* and herself.

Her return found a completely different Germany. At first the newly cleansed Berlin impressed Lucille. The Nazis had brought a certain order and prosperity to the city, and thus a comity she had not seen before. But behind this sedate curtain she discovered a new hysteria rising.

She was witness to a woman being thrown from a trolley, her head shaved, her beaten and bruised face distorted by fear. This desolate creature lay in the street and was kicked by ordinary citizens just passing by. Lucille hurried to the woman's side and helped her to her feet. That was when she saw the placard hung about the poor woman's neck, "Consorted with a Jew." Lucille suddenly realised that what before had been a whisper was now a scream.

Virulent anti-Semitism was evident in the movies, the radio; and the newspapers fuelled the fire. There were book burnings and demonstrations where speakers spewed hate and vitriol. Brownshirts cruised the streets beating Jews while the legitimate police just watched. Cabaret comics were imprisoned for telling mild jokes about Hitler and his cronies. American jazz and modern art were condemned as degenerate.

And the little Corporal with the Charlie Chaplin mustache gave belligerent rants, inciting the populace into a national fervour exalting the purification and glory of war.

The *Berliner luft*, the idea that the air in Berlin made the residents excited and full of life, that intoxicating atmosphere, had turned poisonous.

The tipping point where unease turned to fear came on a cold November night. The brownshirts and their thuggish sympathizers attacked nearly every Jewish store, house, and synagogue in Berlin and, as she learned later, across Germany. They set fire to Jewish buildings except when that conflagration might threaten an adjacent non-offending Aryan structure. In those cases, instead of torching the Jewish building they demolished it with sledgehammers and axes.

Storefronts were smashed until the streets were carpeted with broken glass, giving the rampage the name "Crystal Night."

Lucille wandered the cold city witnessing the brutal destruction of Jewish property. That night police and fire departments stood idle and watched the violence. Fashionably dressed women clapped their hands in excited applause as Jewish hospitals were ransacked and the patients tossed from their beds to be kicked and beaten.

Mothers hefted their babies over the heads of the crowds so that the infants could see synagogues turned to rubble, and encouraged their older children to fling those very stones and bricks through the windows of Jewish homes.

Lucille despaired at the sight. What had happened to these people?

Thirty thousand Jews were arrested that night and sent to Dachau, Buchenwald, and Sachsenhausen. A thousand synagogues burned, seven thousand Jewish business destroyed. No one was sure how many Jews were beaten to death. And in the aftermath, to add perverse insult to disgraceful injury, Jews were fined a billion dollars to repair the damages. Jewish businesses and properties were seized to pay the bill.

She hurried home to warn her father.

Lucille had never told anyone the details of her travels across the globe, and she had no idea why she was opening her heart to this strange man. And it was not just a recitation of her personal history. The Prince interrupted the narrative to ask questions, offer opinions. It was a conversation in which he shared only a little of his own history, exploits, and embarrassments.

The discussion became heated at times, neither of them taking offence at the other's opposing viewpoint. Sometimes the debate sank into argument for argument's sake, a verbal conflict that both of them engaged in with equal enthusiasm, point-counterpoint, sparring with words like two fencers, thrust and parry, no concessions, no surrender.

They even fought over the movie they had just seen.

"I love the movie, do not doubt that," Lucille said. "But it is yet another example of some male fantasy of a woman at the mercy of a domineering male."

"And you do not think this is also a female fantasy, to be carried away by some strong male?"

"I will concede this trope, but only because women have been indoctrinated by a male ruling class to think this way," she countered. "But it is still woman as object."

"An object of beauty and desire, an age-old theme for poetry, literature," Dracula argued. "Why not these same themes for this new form of story?"

"Still an object. Not an equal," she said. "Another victim from another male-dominated industry in a male-dominated world."

Lucille was surprised at her own vehemence and had not realised that she felt so passionately about the subject. During her world travels she had witnessed the subjugation and drudgery that most of her sex experienced, but she'd never felt she was one with them and part of their struggle. She was sensitive to the fact that she had always been separate, different. Maybe it was her intelligence; she knew she was smarter than the average person, much more educated. But her individualism was more than just her brain; it was the way she looked at the world, somehow outside it. She was always the observer, no matter how much she participated, alien to the rest of mankind. She didn't bemoan the fact; she was just aware of it and accepted her plight as she did her red hair.

She was alone, and her state of loneliness was as much a part of her as her dislike of squash and peas.

"I think," Dracula said with a smile, "that you have let your modern way of thinking intrude upon what is but an entertainment, a remarkably effective one, one that may transcend its mode. Still I admit my experience is limited in this form."

"That's right," she interjected, teasing. "I am arguing with the uneducated. You are woefully unqualified for this debate, sir."

"Agreed." He met her grin with his own smile. "Let us look at the story from the point of view of this gentleman, Doctor Freud. I read his book, and it seems to me that the symbolism of the giant male, of dark nature and complexion, taken from the wild continent and introduced to the modern world, the great metropolis, then attacking the mechanised beasts of that city, climbing to the highest pinnacle, an evident representative of the male member . . ."

Dracula's rumination was interrupted by the entrance of Professor Van Helsing and the young Harker.

"Lucille." Her father kissed her on the forehead. "Did you not sleep?"

She glanced at the clock and was astonished at the time. It was an hour past sunrise.

"We were talking," she explained.

"Ah, talking through the night," her father said while examining Dracula with acute scrutiny. "A pastime I indulged in many a time."

"Me, too," Harker interjected. "School days, uh, nights. Solving the problems of the world over a pint. Or two." He grinned at Lucille. "Or three, even."

"So, Doctor Van Helsing, I read the book you gave me. What do you think of this Freud?" Dracula asked.

"Let us have some breakfast first," her father said and led them downstairs.

"Hokum," Harker declared as they descended the steps. "Freud. A pseudo-scientific sham."

Lucille helped with the cooking, Harker getting in the way. Dracula sat at the table, awaiting further discussion.

"Some of his theories, I admit, seem to be a mite outre," Van Helsing said. "But the idea of exploring the human psyche as a scientific pursuit is one that I endorse. It is comparable to our own explorations of the far reaches of the Amazon, the depths of the ocean, our solar system, worlds of which we are ignorant and that wait for us to divine with every tool at our disposal. The human mind is one of these dark, mysterious lands where we should begin some kind of mapping, even if some spaces have the legend 'Here there be monsters.'"

"'There are more things in heaven and earth, Horatio . . .'" Dracula began.

"'. . . than are dreamt of in your philosophy,'" Lucille finished.

She and Dracula shared a look and a laugh. The Englishman did not share the humour, but instead frowned at the pair.

"How you two carry on," Harker remarked. "You would never think that you were separated by five hundred years or so."

"Miss Van Helsing has a very old spirit," Dracula said, more to her than anyone else in the kitchen.

"Call me Lucille, please," she told him. "And Prince Dracula is open-minded, not calcified in the old, restrictive, and oppressive ideas that dominate our era."

"But he is still a killer," Harker said flatly. The statement put an instant damper on the conviviality. Lucille turned on Harker, her lips in a thin, hard line.

"It is a time of war, Lieutenant," she stated. "We are all killers. You as well."

"But we kill out of necessity," Harker countered. "The Prince takes life to maintain his own vitality, for, shall we say, sustenance. And at times, for what he admits is bloodlust. It is not exactly the same."

"Not the same?" Dracula asked. "Have you not enough war experience to witness the occasional bloodlust of your fellows in battle? Do you not kill to perpetuate your own existence? And have you not killed or had killed an assortment of animals for your own sustenance?"

"You are comparing human life to that of dumb beasts, cows and sheep?" Harker asked brusquely. "Of course you would. Because you are not human. You are some kind of beast yourself. A simulacrum of a human being."

"Similar enough to feel anger at your tone, young sir." Dracula eyes were alight with anger. He stood and faced Harker. The Englishman could not help but quake at the vampire's puissance.

Lucille sought for a way to ease the tension that had suddenly arisen.

"Father," she said rather loudly. "Any word regarding the Nazi reaction to our little foray the other night?"

Van Helsing was more than glad to take the baton. "It seems we have confused our enemy," he said. "Or, rather, the Prince has done so. I would even say we have planted some seeds of fear among our occupiers. There are rumours of a bear attack upon the train, other tales of a wolf pack, even mountain lions. Or worse."

"Magnificent," Lucille said.

"German troops stationed in Ploesti are declining home leave unless they can get there by plane. We may not have the numbers or weapons, but we can scare the enemy into paralysis."

"Which we are doing," Harker said, turning from the vampire. "Fear, a few well-placed bombs, a dash of perspicacious sabotage, and we are able to cripple them. For the moment. But what next?"

"As to that, I serve up more than eggs this morning. We have the possibility of a new errand for our merry band," her father said, motioning for Harker to sit. Lucille provided a plate and Van Helsing dropped a perfect omelette before the Englishman. Her father was as exacting a cook as a surgeon, and his food always looked as if it were made for illustration. He broke eggs into a bowl for Lucille's.

"An old Tatra auto fender factory in Sfantu Gheorghe has been recently converted to make artillery shells," Van Helsing continued.

"This is the place using slave labour, correct?" Lucille asked. "I thought it was too well-guarded for us to even think of attacking."

"It is," her father agreed. "And heretofore the end result of such an assault, a momentary cessation of their armament production, was not worth the potential cost to us, in people and possible retaliation upon the local citizenry.

"But while the price of the endeavour may not have decreased any, the prize has grown in value," her father said. "Twofold: One, the German authorities have established an intelligence-gathering operation inside the factory, a cooperative group comprised of Gestapo and Rumanian Army Intelligence officers, taking advantage of the complex's protective capabilities."

"The purpose of this operation?" Harker asked.

"They are tasked to create a list of Rumanian undesirables," Van Helsing told them.

The weight of that statement hung in the kitchen like smoke from the stove.

"Files on everyone with Jewish blood, genealogies going back four, five generations," Van Helsing continued. "Lists of gypsies, homosexuals, Communists, leftists, and some certain individuals whom your government either think a threat, just dislike, or merely desire their estates."

"And, in time, these people will be collected and sent to the camps, I assume," Lucille said. "Never to return."

"You said twofold," Dracula said. "What is the other value at this factory?"

"They have begun manufacturing a shell for a new artillery piece," Van Helsing replied. "A version of the Great War's Big Bertha. Called the Schwerer Gustav and the Dora. Siege guns. A cannon, the biggest ever. So large it can only be transported by multiple railroad cars. A super-heavy howitzer shell able to penetrate seven metres of concrete, one metre of armoured steel. Range anywhere from thirty-seven to fifty-five kilometres."

"You could fire such a gun across the English Channel into London," Harker said with some alarm.

"Two types of shells are being made in Gheorghe," Van Helsing continued. "A seven-ton and an eleven-ton projectile. Devastating weapons."

"So the artillery production must be stopped," Lucille summarised, "and the list destroyed."

"But as was stated before, the plant is impregnable," her father added.

"Then we must have a plan," Dracula said.

DATED: 22 MAY 1941
TO: CSS REINHARD HEYDRICH, RSHA, REICHSFUHRER-SS
FROM: SS MAJOR WALTRAUD REIKEL
CC: HEINRICH HIMMLER, REICHSFUHRER-SS
(via diplomatic pouch)

MOST SECRET

Received your communication. Am proceeding with dispatch and my utmost to capture the aforementioned. The local rebel forces have at least one spy in our headquarters; the intelligence concerning the departure time of the intercepted railroad shipment was known only by my office. Rather than immediately root out this leak, we have, instead, put this awareness to our own use. I have put forth memos and orders establishing an operation centred at the Sfantu Gheorghe munitions manufacturing facility. This operation, plus the production of the munitions plant, should be enough enticement to flush out the seditionists and our primary target. In addition to the falsified written documents, I have given verbal orders regarding the decoy operation. These conversations were intended to be overheard by as many personnel as possible.

Adding to the fable, an office has actually been set up inside the factory, staffed with a motley squad of Rumanian military under the supervision of one of my trusted Lieutenants. Even he is unaware of the ruse. He sends me daily complaints detailing the incompetence of his charges.

Three Gestapo cadres from Ploesti and a security detail from my own unit have been dispatched to the Sfantu Gheorghe factory.

The security unit has been briefed by me personally with the threat of the firing squad if any of this information ever goes beyond the unit.

I am confident that this is sufficient bait to lure our adversaries and their latest recruits, the English spies and the one you seek.

I will keep you updated on our progress.

Heil Hitler.

FROM THE WAR JOURNAL OF
J. HARKER

(transcribed from shorthand)

MAY 23, 1941

I am a blithering fool! I do not know what possessed me. I suppose that when I walked into the kitchen and saw them conversing, laughing with such intimacy, I immediately felt like an interloper and something came over me. I do not know what.

Yes, I do. It was jealousy that thoroughly put my nose out of joint. Simple, ugly jealousy. The problem is that I like the man, correction, the vampire. He is personable, intelligent, and seemingly honourable. Or has been so far. I have attempted to overcome my feeling for the fair Lucy, to forget that one night of bliss, but I fall short. I fail miserably. I am not that strong.

And so I made a complete botch of things. My father once told me that many a man has been led astray by thinking not from above the neck, but from below the belt. He forgot to tell me about the space between, the heart. That is where this uncouth behaviour has been born; that is where my pain dwells.

I must seem desperately sad and broken to her. And I must admit my stalwart manhood seems to have shrunk somewhat under the strain of my much-tried emotions. This has been a bitter blow, and I am reminded of my mum's admonition that oft-times we have to pass through the bitter water before we reach the sweet.

But I must soldier on. What is at stake is more important than my emotional straits: the upcoming mission and the eventual world conflict that will inexorably roll toward us when Russia and the recalcitrant Americans summon up the mettle to join the good fight.

I have been deceptive in my postings to headquarters and this has given me further dolor. I have made no mention of the vampire in my dispatches to my higher-ups, neither his participation in the jaunt down south nor in the rail rescue. I am convinced that if I did, the believability of my bulletins would suffer. I know what they would think if I reported whom I was working with—a mythical creature, much less Dracula himself—it would be met with incredulity and cause some doubt as to my sanity and thus my ability to conduct my mission. They would think me barking mad. At minimum I would be called back to England. And I do not want to abandon this unique opportunity, or leave dear Lucy. So, I push on with the sin of omission.

So far, on my return to Brasov, I have still been unable to rouse the local partisans into a more aggressive effort of sabotage and harassment. I made an appeal to Anka, Pavel, and Farkas at the railroad rescue, but the fear of extreme reprisals holds them at bay. And I do not reproach them, as the Nazis have a history of committing one monstrous act of revenge after another. After all, it is their families and friends at risk. I try to think what I would do if this were happening in Great Fransham, Norfolk, or Monk Sherborne, Hampshire. Would I risk the lives of my fellows and relatives?

But this "undesirables" list, as it is called, should be a worthy target and, again, it is far enough from Brasov to not cause any local retaliation. Yes, the Germans will be able to reassemble such a census again, but our raid will stall such efforts, and we will be able to alert those on the roster. Plus I must do something, anything.

Each day I hear about the despicable bombing of my country and the bravery of the British airmen as they defend our homeland. I want to do something to help. For King and country and all that. This long-distance artillery shell being manufactured at the prison factory is an imminent and immediate threat to my own home and hearth. I must do what I can to eliminate this threat.

In case we are successful at Sfantu Gheorghe, I have been working on an escape route to transport any of those on the list out of Rumania to Istanbul and Odessa. Using the local cell and some SOE assets in the neighbouring countries, a series of friendlies will harbour the fugitives and move them on to the next haven, then from station to station until they are free of Axis control.

But more than delaying the Nazi operations, this raid will be seen as a statement against the German-Rumanian rule, a banner the partisans can hold high. It can help attract more people to their cause and possibly lead to the more aggressive activities frequently and forcefully recommended by the Home Office.

Now if only the easement of my personal problems was as hopeful.

EXCERPTS FROM UNIDENTIFIED DIARY
(translated from the German)

. . . and so the noise about Poland will be blown away like wheat chaff in the wind. Who remembers the extermination of the Armenians? No one. If Herr Wolf can send the Flower of the German Nation into the Hell of War without the smallest pity for the spilling of precious German Blood, then surely he has the right to remove an inferior race that breeds like vermin.

May 25

If Herr Wolf is destined to Rule the world, any act that advances that rule is justified. Rule or Perish—the only outcomes worth consideration.

[Editor's note: The word "rücksichtslos!"—"ruthless!"—has been scrawled across the entire page.]

Herr Wolf cannot sleep. He thinks he has cancer. He is a constant victim of Headaches. Dizziness. Pains in his gut and lower intestines. Oft-times after a long bath the symptoms recede. He paces through the day. The possibility of the existence of this Creature has him, despite his ailments, in a fervour of mental intoxication. If this legendary being exists, then we will silence our critics, the unbelievers.

Ever since the early days in Vienna, Herr Wolf had been a reader of Ostara, the publication wherein the mystical theorist Lanz von Liebenfels put the Occult in concordance with modern Science. Herr Wolf has since been a Believer.

Herr Wolf has hoped that the search for and acquisition of the Spear of Destiny would be enough to quiet the doubters, but a thorough examination of the object found no magical properties or emanations. This artefact is either a fake or not actually the true lance of Longinus.

And Otto Rahn's search for the Holy Grail, fabled to hold power of indescribable magnitude, produced only what seems to be an ordinary wine cup. Whether it was used in the Last Supper or not, the item has no occult properties at all. In fact, the vessel hardly holds water.

The expedition in North Africa for the Lost Ark has provided even less-satisfactory results, as has the investigation in Tibet concerning a certain elixir of Eternal Life.

Herr Wolf is aware that this interest in the Supernatural is mocked. But even the haughty British have allowed the Coventry Witches to create a magical Circle of Power around their cherished island in hopes of preventing an invasion. They even subscribe to the notion that we did not follow Dunkirk with an invasion due to the success of this conjury.

Herr Wolf's bombers defy that ring of thaumaturgy every day.

HH believes. He is a devotee of Clairvoyance, Faith Healing, Sorcery, and attempting to produce gold from base metals. He assisted Herr Wolf in enabling Hanussen to bring back the mandrake root from the butcher's yard in Herr Wolf's birthplace to eliminate any hindrance to Herr Wolf's ascendancy.

Herr Wolf's investigation into what some may call the Fantastical is based on pure Scientific Principles. Does not every facet of our world require proper and equal examination? Some folk remedies have been proven to be as efficacious as modern drugs.

Lately our scientists have been able to transform a physical material called Uranium into a completely new element, Plutonium. They are very enthusiastic about the process and promise it could even lead to a new weapon of some consequence. So the mythical Philosopher's Stone becomes real and the Alchemists' dream, the transmutation of the elements, becomes fact. Most of these investigations into Myth and Magic will prove false, but how many attempts failed before man flew like a bird? Another feat deemed impossible until it was accomplished.

Thus Herr Wolf's consulting of an Astrologer or a Numerologist and exploring the possibilities that other Extraordinary Phenomenon might have merit is no more futile than assuming a blind Corporal might some day become Fuhrer.

There are things that one cannot understand and yet which are. Ah, it is the fault of our Science that it wants to explain all; and if it explains not then it says there is nothing to explain: corporeal transference, materialisation, astral bodies, reading of thought, hypnotism. There are things done today in electrical science which would have been deemed unholy by the very man who discovered electricity—who would himself, not so long before, have been burned as a wizard.

Now we will have scientific proof of what was previously thought as fantastical. Already the victims of the train assault (or bits of the victims) are being examined by an associate of Dr. M. This man, a Baron von F. exploring the possible existence of Dippel's Oil, an Elixir of Life, is now studying the blood of ones bitten and hopes to discover some clue to their predator's corporeality.

Meanwhile, Herr Wolf's mind spins with the possibilities of this new find. He has read up on this legendary being. This foul thing of the night has the aid of Necromancy. It can direct the Elements, the storm, the fog, the thunder. It can command the meaner things, the rat, the owl, the bat, the moth, the fox, and the wolf. It can become small, grow, vanish. It can translocate upon moonlight rays as elemental dust. It can command The Dead!

We must capture the Creature! We must!

FROM THE WAR JOURNAL OF
J. HARKER

(transcribed from shorthand)

MAY 27, 1941

Our preliminary reconnaissance of the munitions factory brought back bad news. The entire complex has been walled in with a fourteen-foot-high construction of corrugated steel and iron stanchions topped with barbed wire. The area inside the walls is patrolled by guards. In the enclosed area, crude barracks have been erected to serve as quarters for the slave labourers while newer construction houses the guard unit. The workers are supervised by armed guards day and night. There is but one entrance, a broad gate wide enough to allow lorries to enter, delivering materiel and new prisoners to replace those who have died on the job. The product of their labours exits from the same gate.

The production lines work twenty-four hours a day, seven days a week. If one of the labourers drops from exhaustion or starvation they are shot on the spot. Some workers die at their station. The bodies are thrown into the smelting furnaces. I saw this with my binoculars. My surveillance perch was the roof of a tall office building across the street from the factory.

The roof of the factory has a row of narrow windows near the peak that are permanently louvered open, allowing a release of the fetid air and, in the day, light to work by. These openings gave me a clear view of the interior. It is a view into hell. Smoking, steaming machines of every variety, among them huge ten-ton presses that shake the earth with their incessant pounding. Dirt and grime coat the apparatus and the workers. Steel shell casings are being stamped, welded, milled, loaded with gunpowder, and capped with the projectile itself.

The product of this malefic operation is artillery munitions. The shells are uncommonly large. I thought it was a matter of my inclined perspective, but I was able to do comparisons of adjacent familiar objects and realised that each shell was approximately five metres long.

I reported my recon to the partisan leadership cell. They were all sitting around that scarred table in Mihaly's basement. Dracula stood off alone in a shadowed corner. I noticed that Lucy sat upon stacked bolts of cloth in close proximity to the vampire.

I was glad that I had to concentrate on my presentation. The others examined the map that I had drawn with the help of Renfield, who had accompanied me on our recce. He proved to be an excellent draughtsman.

"Guards inside the factory itself?" Farkas asked.

"Above and below," I told him. "They patrol a catwalk above the production line and walk below among the workers. All armed. The guards on the floor are meant to keep the labourers' noses to the grindstone. If a prisoner slows or falls, he is beaten. There are fewer guards at night than in the daylight hours."

"Where do they keep the gunpowder stores?" Van Helsing asked. Renfield's ears pricked up at the question, happy that we were finally discussing something he had an interest in. He stepped to the table and pointed at the proper place on the map.

"A series of berms behind the factory proper," I elucidated. "Not as far away as they should be for safety, but the re-tooling of the factory allowed only so much distance. They also store the finished shells in the same area. Here and here. Stacked in pallets waiting for transport."

"Ach!" Renfield exclaimed. "All that boom together."

"Yes, Sergeant." I patted him on the shoulder. "You are going to have an opportunity to use your toys."

"Where is the list being compiled and kept?" Anka asked.

"Here." I pointed. "In an office on the second floor of the factory proper. It overlooks the factory floor with windows allowing the shift foreman to observe the production lines."

"Right in the centre of the complex," Pavel noted. "Surrounded by a wall, a factory, and all of the guards."

"This is a very dangerous operation we contemplate," Farkas said.

"I think it is impossible," Anka declared. "Tell the English to bomb it with their planes."

"Not possible without killing the workers," Lucille said.

"They are doomed either way," Farkas replied.

"So we have to find a way inside, take possession of the lists, and destroy the records, then find our way out without harming any of those poor people," Van Helsing summarised. "Not an easy task."

"Actually," I added, "I think we should free the prisoners." And I described the exit route and strategies for evacuation I had prepared for those on the lists.

"Donae forget the boom," Renfield said with a bit of worry in his voice, like a child reminding his parents they promised him a sweet.

"A boom would be nice," I said. "A very big boom to destroy the munitions. But only after we are able to evacuate the labourers." I could not get the images out of my mind, those poor wretches slaving over their machines, the brutality of their minders, the degradation and pure misery I had seen during my recce. I had to do something to rescue them from that debased life. Something, anything, or their plight would surely haunt me.

"I do not like this. Twenty-four-hour military sentries, three layers, four layers deep. It is a death trap," Anka said and brushed aside my map as if it were a soiled napkin.

"I think I may be of assistance in this venture." It was the first time Dracula had spoken.

Anka glared at the vampire. "We had a meeting and have made a decision regarding your participation in our fight," she announced. "We will no longer ally ourselves with such an ungodly monster."

"When was this meeting?" Lucy asked. "And why was I not told?"

"We knew you would object," Anka replied. "It is final. We will not associate with this beast." She gave Dracula her baleful best.

"Even if it means the Germans win?" Lucy asked. "Don't be childish."

"This is unholy!" Anka spat.

"Superstitious claptrap," I said, surprising myself by again defending the Prince.

Anka shot me that same baleful glare. "It would be best for you to remember this, young Englishman," she said with some vehemence. "We are in Transylvania, and Transylvania is not England. Our ways are not your ways."

I withdrew from the circle for the moment, properly chastised, knowing I had stepped outside my bailiwick.

"What happens when the Nazis are defeated?" Farkas asked. "Then he will turn on us for his abominable desires."

"A bit melodramatic, don't you think?" Dracula commented drily. "Are you sure you know me well enough to predict my behaviour?"

"We all saw your behaviour on the train," Pavel murmured.

"My grandmother knew you well enough to have a stake driven through her heart," Anka said through gritted teeth. "My grandfather was the one to cut off her head. He never recovered from that dreadful act. The stories he told . . . This monster took our children; babies were lost to the godless beast."

"Babies?" Dracula's brow furrowed. "Where did this nonsense originate?"

Anka stood up and stepped toward the vampire, her face twisted with vehemence. "We will not abide you, demon!"

"Father." Lucy turned to her father to intercede. He was closest to the stout woman. But Van Helsing shook his head.

"I've argued myself hoarse," he said. "I am but one vote. I cannot force anyone to do anything, as much as I think they are wrong. So very wrong. "

"We will manage," Anka said. With that Anka requested that Dracula leave the meeting.

The Van Helsings, Renfield, and I left with him. On the street, walking to the car, the silence was broken by the vampire.

"They will be slaughtered if they attack the munitions factory, will they not?" He addressed me.

"I am afraid so," I told him. "It is heavily fortified. And the only tactic I have ever heard from any of them is the frontal attack."

"They will have the element of surprise," Lucy offered.

"Surprise is of little advantage if you are outnumbered," Van Helsing countered. "Plus, the enemy is firmly ensconced. Lives will certainly be lost."

"Perhaps an intercession on my part might save their lives," Dracula said.

"You alone?" I asked.

"I'll help you," Lucy responded immediately.

"And me, Master," Renfield chimed in.

"I will, of course, assist in any manner possible," I told them. Surely if a woman and a mental defective could enlist in this suicide mission, I had no choice but to throw my hat into the ring.

"But just the five of us?" Van Helsing frowned. "Impossible."

"I have an intimate acquaintance with impossibilities." Dracula smiled.

EXCERPTED FROM THE UNPUBLISHED NOVEL
THE DRAGON PRINCE AND I
by Lenore Van Muller

Lucille and Dracula strolled alongside the wall that surrounded the munitions factory. It was a long walk. The facility occupied four large blocks of the neighbourhood. The neighbouring structures were mostly other, smaller industries and office buildings.

The night was quiet, the other businesses closed, even the clothing factories. Only the muted rumble and clatter of the machines beyond the wall accompanied Lucille's footsteps upon the concrete walkway. The vampire's tread was as silent as a cat's.

Lucille could almost pretend that rather than conducting a reconnaissance, she and the Prince were on a lover's amble under the half moonlight. They even held hands to maintain the romantic masquerade for any observers, casual or otherwise. His hand was cool in hers, but she was now accustomed to the chill of his touch, even welcomed it. The contact gave her a sublime sense of intimacy with him.

Dark, rolling clouds overhead gave the air the oppressive sense of incipient thunder.

They completed one circuit of the entire complex, finally meeting young Harker waiting where they had started their walk. He was leaning against the wall smoking his pipe, dressed as a hobo.

"All quiet?" Harker asked.

Lucille nodded.

"Same here," he said.

"Well, this seems to be as good a spot and time as any," Dracula said, eyeing the top of the wall eight feet above their heads.

"Shall we commence with some mayhem?" Lucille asked. "Here, boost me up."

"Boost?" Dracula looked puzzled.

"Help me over the wall," she explained.

"The plan, as articulated by your father," Dracula said, "is for you to attack from the outside."

"It's not a wise idea," Harker chimed in. "To deviate from the mission plan at the last minute."

"As usual, it appears that I am outnumbered," she replied. "Three men against one woman."

"Equal odds," Dracula said with a smile. "If you are that woman."

"I'll give you a hand up," Lucille offered with her own wry grin and cupped her entwined fingers. The vampire ignored the offered assist, flexed his knees, and leapt straight up to land deftly atop the wall, standing on the narrow support post as easily as a squirrel on a telephone wire.

Lucille stared up at him. Then she and Harker shared a sigh. She turned her head back to Dracula.

"Show-off," she said.

The vampire reached down and stretched a hand toward Harker.

"You can change your mind," Dracula offered the Englishman.

"A Harker never shrinks from duty," the young man said and nodded to Lucille. She again cupped her hands and he put his foot in the maiden-made stirrup. With a heft from her and a leap of his own, Harker was lifted high enough for Dracula to grab his outflung hand.

Dracula pulled the young man to the top of the wall as easily as hoisting a baby. Harker's pant leg caught on the barbed wire and tore, but he was otherwise unharmed.

The vampire turned to nod and smile at Lucille, then leapt to the other side and out of sight. Harker followed.

Her part finished, Lucille hurried away from the wall, remembering that smile.

FROM THE WAR JOURNAL OF
J. HARKER

(transcribed from shorthand)

Dracula swooped down from the wall, landing as gracefully as a ballet dancer after a majestic leap. He held his arms up to me, and I bounded down from my precarious perch. He caught me easily, like a fireman catches a baby, and set me onto my feet. For a moment I felt the steel-like sinews of his arms. It was as if the man were made of cast iron.

We started for the factory. To get there we had to pass the quarters for the workers and security personnel. The eight barracks were of wooden slat construction, built a foot or two above the ground. There were gaps in the siding where the wood had warped, probably green when they built the structure, revealing a cheap and hasty construction. The factory and the various outbuildings were comprised of brick and cement block; the smaller structures, ugly utilitarian rectangles, mostly single-storey. The plant itself was three storeys at least, a quarter of a mile in length. The peaked roof had a line of windows running down the centre, some of the panes hinged open to vent the fetid air that accumulated inside. The glass was grimy to near opacity. In fact, everything about us was coated with a century of soot and grime that painted the whole landscape with a drab greyness. Under the pale moon, the world resembled a black-and-white photograph. Even the newer barracks were already dusted black, making them appear as old as the rest. A heavy rain had fallen a few hours before, turning the ground into a muddy wallow, but the buildings looked as if they had never been washed by anything but a chimney sweep's broom.

My relief at the ease of our intrusion into the enemy's perimeter was precipitously interrupted with the sudden appearance of two sentries. They were being towed by a pair of giant Rottweilers as they emerged from around the corner of one of the barracks.

At seeing us, the dogs immediately began to whine and snarl, straining at their leashes, giving the handlers almost more than they could manage.

"Bismarck!" shouted one sentry, calming his instantly obedient beast.

"Krupt!" yelled the other to the same effect.

I then realised that the guards were wearing German uniforms. My previous reconnaissance had revealed only a Rumanian guard detail. And no canine patrols.

"You there!" one of the Nazis bellowed at us in German. "Halt! Now!"

I stopped in my tracks. But Dracula kept walking, nonchalantly striding across the grounds as casually as if taking a Sunday stroll. I guess you can maintain that kind of attitude if you are immortal. I, on the other hand, mere mortal, paused. Dracula, though, walked directly toward the pair of dogs and men.

"Halt!" The order came again, directly aimed at the vampire, as both guards unslung their rifles.

My hand slipped to the sling of my own sub-machine gun, a Thompson that I had acquired by airdrop. American-made, the .45-calibre weapon favored by gangsters and FBI agents. A fine gun that did me no good hanging on my back and under my coat. An unconscionable blunder. I knew I could not bring it to bear before one of the guards fired.

Dracula ignored the command and waved at the men. The dogs were in a restrained frenzy now, fangs bared, spittle flying from growling muzzles.

The sentries reached down and let loose their hounds from the leashes. The two animals sprung forward, a few hundred pounds of teeth and claws launched directly at Dracula. I reached behind me for the Thompson, but the two guards raised their rifles to their shoulders and put me in their sights. I froze my hand.

The Rottweilers were only a few metres from Dracula when he raised one hand, palm toward the beasts.

And the canines stopped dead, paws skidding in the mud, eyes fixed upon the vampire.

Dracula pointed his index finger to the sky and gave it a slight twirl. I was astonished to witness the slavering curs make an obedient about-face as if they were on a stage in Picadilly. And then I was even more dumbfounded— as were their masters, I assume—as the animals charged their handlers.

The two guards abruptly had to turn the aim of their rifles from me to their own dogs.

"Bismarck! Halt!"

"Krupt! Halt!"

The animals ignored the order. They pounced on the men, tearing at their throats in a mad mutilation. There was a ghastly sound of men wailing, a gnashing of teeth. I heard a wet tearing, guttural howls, and screams so animalistic that it was difficult to tell if the origin was man or beast.

Dracula paid little mind to the mayhem and continued on his original path to the factory. I followed. Glancing back at the two sentries, I saw that the men's bodies were still and the beasts were feasting, their muzzles bloody with gore. I was suddenly reminded of Dracula, covered in Nazi blood. I shook my head, dismissing the vile picture, and hurried after the vampire, glad that he was on my side.

Our path took us between the shoddy barracks. I trotted past the windows, mostly broken, some stuffed with newspapers or rags. An odour wafted from these sad domiciles, a distinct tang of sweat and misery.

We crossed the open field that separated the barracks from the immense manufacturing building, the black mud sucking at our boots, a wet gasp with every sticky release. There were no more encounters with any guards.

When we made it to the factory wall, Dracula once again crouched and jumped. This flight sent him up onto the roof. I sprinted along the wall, bent down to keep my head below the windows, until I found a door. It hung open, and I was able to peer through the gap between the hinges and observe the factory proper.

A great din rolled into the night air, metal against metal, the clatter and clang of hammer and anvil, the thunderous boom of the gargantuan presses and every clangorous racket in between. There was a keening cry of the lathes peeling steel, the occasional great bellow of a furnace belching flaming gouts of fire into the air. Steam billowed under ochre lights, and the labourers toiled over their oily, glinting machines. Some of the men were stripped to the waist because of the wet heat, their bodies shiny with sweat.

Overhead, two guards patrolled the catwalk thirty feet above the assembly line. The moon was barely perceptible through the dirty strip of windows that ran across the ceiling. Looking up, I thought I saw a shadow flit across the sulphured panes.

The catwalk ended at an office with a stairway to the floor below. Large windows lined the office to allow the occupants easy viewing of the workers. Situated below the office was a tool room, labelled as such with a sign over the half door. There labourers had their drill bits sharpened, tools supplied or replaced.

Upstairs, the office lights were on and I could see four men playing cards at a desk, smoking and laughing. Two wore the distinctive uniform of the Gestapo.

On ground level, four guards ambled among the workers. They, like the catwalk soldiers, were Rumanian Army.

I stole inside, backed into a deep shadow behind a huge chunk of iron and steel, what appeared to be an abandoned piece of equipment. I brought up my Thompson and followed the catwalk sentries with my front sight. I had fired the Thompson once, as part of my weapon familiarization training in England. It was not an accurate gun, but what it lacked there it made up for in volume, spitting out bullets at a rate of 720 to 850 rounds per minute, depending on the model. And the bullets were of the formidable .45-calibre, powerful enough to knock down an ox.

One of the catwalk sentries reached the far end of his scaffolding and was about to turn around and repeat his route when Dracula slipped down through the canted window like he had been poured through it. The sentry stared for a moment, most likely briefly stunned by the apparition. From what Dracula told me later, the guard was even more astonished than I supposed. The vampire had mesmerised the man into believing that it was not a man but a mist that floated through the window opening.

The guard peered through the roof window aperture into the clear night. There was no fog out there. Where did this crawling mist come from?

He approached the cloud with a tentative step, bent his neck, and squinted his eyes to inspect the phenomenon a bit closer.

Totally in the grip of the hypnotic spell, the guard stared in amazement at what he, in his mesmerised state, saw as mist formed into foggy hands. One floated toward his groin while the other wrapped misty fingers around the guard's neck. Both vaporous hands suddenly gripped crotch and throat, and miraculously lifted him into the air.

At this point he awakened enough to scream.

Too late. The man's body was brought down sharply, slamming his back onto the catwalk railing. I could hear the crack clearly, even above the mechanical cacophony. The dead guard was flung over the side and landed in the maw of one of the growling machines below, and was subsequently chopped into stew meat.

Dracula started down the catwalk toward the second guard, who turned in time to see the vampire and aim his weapon.

A certain Sergeant Major Sadler taught me how to be effective with a sub-machine gun given its poor accuracy and limited range. "Pretend it's a bleeding garden hose, aim low, and walk the stream of rounds up into your target. Not very efficient, but bloody effective." To achieve this he taught me to load a tracer round every third shell in the magazine, then one could watch the trajectory as an orange trail arcing toward the target. So, being the proper pupil, I now aimed at the catwalk below the sentry. The first bullet struck the wooden planking, sending a shower of slivers into the air. As I elevated the muzzle, the bullets climbed and the fifth or sixth round hit the guard in the chest. The big slug blew the man right off his feet, and he plummeted to the floor below. There was no notice of this on the ground floor or in the office. Thankfully, the scream and machine-gun fire were lost in the din of factory noise.

It was at this time that I heard a tremendous crash and felt the floor jolt under my feet. I turned to see a great steel plow blade come to a shuddering stop inside the factory, the remains of the wall cascading around the steaming grill of a lorry. Van Helsing and Lucy had arrived.

Dracula nodded a thanks to me and began striding to the office. But a floor guard below had nearly been crushed by his fallen comrade and was instantly alerted to something amiss above him. He looked up and aimed his shotgun at the vampire. He fired. The shotgun pellets splattered against the steel catwalk supports, blowing a hole through the wooden planking and shredding the hem of Dracula's cape.

I searched for the shooter, but he had ducked to safety behind a lathe.

EXCERPTED FROM THE UNPUBLISHED NOVEL
THE DRAGON PRINCE AND I
by Lenore Van Muller

Lucille hurried from the wall, sprinting down the street to where her father waited behind the wheel of a stolen truck. They had parked a long block away from the factory. She climbed into the cab. Her stomach was churning with worry for the two men she had just helped step into the mouth of the beast. She checked her Luger, confirming that a round was chambered.

Renfield sat next to Van Helsing, the English soldier's knees nervously vibrating up and down like pistons. He clutched a large satchel in his lap, knuckles white and eyes wide with excitement.

Her father kept his gaze on the factory gate some two hundred metres ahead of them. The road where they had parked the truck led directly to the factory entrance. The kerb was lined with a few other trucks, so their vehicle did not draw any untoward attention, just another hauler.

"They are over the wall," Lucille informed them. "Anything here?"

"Still much the same," Van Helsing told her. "But don't those guards seem to be preternaturally alert for such a late hour?"

She squinted through the night at the guards. Four men in Rumanian uniforms flanked the closed wrought-iron gate, two to a side. Their rifles were slung, but their posture was not that of tired, bored men. During her tenure in the Resistance she had spent many a tiresome hour observing guards. It was past two in the morning now, and men who had been on guard duty this long were generally fighting off sleep and tedium.

"They do appear to be more vigilant than routine and monotony would imply," she noted. "But that has no bearing on our plan. Shall we?"

Her father had thought about adding his voice to the other men asking his daughter to withdraw from the coming fray, but he knew it was a moot discussion. This was a debate the two of them had circled repeatedly, ad nauseam. He just felt the catch in his heart at the thought of her endangering herself or, God forbid, being harmed.

But he knew how headstrong she could be, and so he swallowed his protest, stomped on the clutch, yanked the truck into gear, and pressed the accelerator.

The engine growled and the truck rolled forward, gaining speed with every rotation of the immense tyres. It was not an ordinary lorry they had stolen. The vehicle had been specially constructed to plow snow-drifted roads in the winter. The six giant wheels grabbed the pavement, and a huge V-shaped steel blade fronted the entire hood, angling past the width of the cab.

Van Helsing had raised the blade, not so far as to make the engine vulnerable, but high enough to protect the cab occupants. He peered over the blade and aimed at the gate.

One of the gate guards heard the rumbling engine and aimed a spotlight at the truck. Another shouted a "Halt!" that could barely be heard over the engine noise and coughing muffler.

Van Helsing paid no attention to the order, just pressed his foot upon the gas pedal until he felt the floorboard. The vehicle increased speed. The other two guards now joined in the shouting, their voices unintelligible as the engine whined at full exertion.

The four guards pointed their rifles, two kneeling, two standing behind. The thought struck Lucille: These were not humdrum factory guards, these were professional soldiers, disciplined and prepared.

They fired at the onrushing truck. Bullets pinged off the plow blade. Two shattered the windshield. Lucille turned to her father in alarm, but the old man merely brushed the broken glass from his face and kept driving. She used the barrel of her pistol to clear the rest of the glass from the window, aimed at the guards, and emptied her entire clip at the four men. Next to her Renfield giggled.

The guards leapt away from the gate, just as the truck struck the wrought iron.

The plow cut into the gate with a great crash. The truck slowed as it dragged the wrought iron across concrete. There was a horrendous grinding, and sparks flew from the contact.

Lucille was able to reload, lean out the side window, and shoot the two guards on her side of the cab before the men could regain their feet. She put all her bullets into them.

Renfield tossed a grenade past Van Helsing's nose. The grenade landed in the lap of one of the guards. Lucille did not see the explosion—the truck was through the gate by then—but she heard the eruption behind her, felt the concussion.

Up ahead was the factory. A ramp for loading and unloading machinery inclined toward a wooden double door that led into the plant floor. The door was not wide enough to allow the plow truck through.

Van Helsing never wavered. The truck shot up the ramp, and the plow plunged through the doors. Wood shattered under the impact; bricks were torn from the support columns. The truck exploded into the factory itself. The motorised monster shuddered to a stop, body halfway inside, steam belching from under the hood.

Lucille leapt from the cab, surveyed the scene. She heard gunfire, saw the source: Harker shooting up at the ceiling. She followed his aim and saw a guard fall from the catwalk.

And across that same catwalk strode Dracula, his goal a glass-enclosed office at the end.

There was a booming sound. Lucille recognised the report of a shotgun and saw Dracula's cape whip as if by a sharp wind. She sought the source and spied a crouching floor guard chambering another round, taking aim again at the vampire.

She ejected the empty clip from her Luger and reloaded.

Dracula was but a few steps from the office when two German officers stepped out to meet him on the catwalk, drawing their pistols. Some kind of challenge was issued, but I could not hear it over the noise of machinery and the gunfire on the floor.

With amazing speed Dracula rushed at them, grabbed each man by his Sam Browne belt, and, with an astonishing display of strength, lifted both men over his head and slammed them into each other. Their heads met and crushed each other's skulls.

Dracula hurled them to the floor below as casually as discarding an empty cigarette pack.

I began moving toward the guard wielding the shotgun at Dracula, but I heard gunfire and saw the man duck down. Searching for the source of his diffidence, I saw Lucy firing her Luger at him.

Van Helsing was firing a carbine through the open window of the cab, using the plow as cover.

Every floor guard sought cover behind some machine, and we found ourselves in a full-fledged gun battle.

The workers scattered to hide from the gunfire. I manoeuvred toward the guard with the shotgun, who fired another round at the vampire. The glass in the upper office fractured and rained down like icicles from a roof, shattering into glittering fragments on the floor.

Dracula ignored the windowpane waterfall and charged into the office. One Nazi stepped forward and aimed his pistol at the vampire, ordering him to surrender. Whether the German was foolish, brave, or an imbecile, it mattered not to Dracula as he seized the obstreperous fellow, forced the head to one side, and feasted on the vulnerable throat.

He drank. The German raised his pistol, trying to shoot Dracula in the head. I uttered a warning, knowing it could not reach the vampire's ears.

Dracula suddenly pulled away from the man in revulsion.

"Diseased!" Dracula hissed, spat out the blood, and snapped the victim's neck before he could pull the trigger on his Walther. The vampire turned to face the other German, who fired his PPK. Four rounds, directly into Dracula's chest. The vampire leaned back, driven by the power of the bullets. He winced, but that could have been from the noise for all the harm the bullets did him.

The shooter could see the hunger in Dracula's red-shot eyes, the blood dripping from his fangs, smeared across his mouth. The man put the Walther to his own head and fired the one shot needed to avoid the fate before him. Dracula shook his head, at the waste of blood, I suppose.

Below the office, the tool room door flew open and five men hit the stairway at full gallop. I recognised the uniforms. Waffen SS!

I sprayed slugs from the Thompson at them. Two fell; two sought refuge behind a drill press. The fifth man tripped, tumbled, his weapon falling from his hands. I fired a burst at him, missed. Using all four limbs, he clambered up the stairs toward the office.

Dracula was opening the file cabinets and dumping the contents onto the floor. He didn't see or hear the SS soldier come up behind him. But he saw the shadow loom over the wall in front of him and turned just in time for the Nazi to stab him in the chest.

Dracula gasped, yowled in pain like a wounded animal. His hand snapped out and grasped a fistful of the German's jacket, pulled the man toward him, and bit, drinking deeply. The soldier writhed futilely, hands flapping, feet dangling, kicking, the struggle growing weaker by the second.

EXCERPTED FROM THE UNPUBLISHED NOVEL
THE DRAGON PRINCE AND I
by Lenore Van Muller

Lucille was stunned to see another half-dozen well-armed German soldiers suddenly rush into the factory from a back door. Where were all these damned Germans coming from?

She had seen the SS pour out of the tool room. Although she was gratified when Harker cut down most of them, the presence of the German soldiers momentarily dumbfounded her. Harker had not reported any Nazi presence in his reconnaissance, much less an SS contingent. Harker had detected only the Gestapo staff creating the "undesirable" list. These reinforcements could only mean that this was a well-planned trap.

She recognised one of the SS men, a tall Lieutenant with a severely pocked face. He had manned one of the roadblocks in Brasov. What was he doing here?

Lucille emptied a clip from her Luger at the new assailants. They sought safety behind a bin of raw steel parts. She reloaded.

Meanwhile, her father fired from behind the plow blade. Renfield reached into his satchel and withdrew another hand grenade.

"No!" Van Helsing ordered. "Too many innocents!" He had to shout over the gunfire. Renfield reluctantly put away the grenade.

"To the office!" her father ordered him. "Fire the records!"

Renfield grinned, slung his sapper satchel, clambered out of the cab, and sprinted across the factory floor, dodging and weaving through the machines. She was impressed by his sudden agility, as nimble as a football player dancing through a field of defenders.

Lucille and her father kept shooting, keeping enemy heads low so that the mad sergeant could dart from one point of cover to the next.

Lucille took aim at the tall Lieutenant, who was edging his way along a stack of raw steel, heading for the office stairs. Her finger began its squeeze on the trigger when she was abruptly pulled onto her back.

One of the Rumanian guards had jumped her. The Luger was flung from her hand as she wrestled under the weight of her attacker. A labourer hiding under the assembly line rushed to her aid, but was knocked back by a bullet fired from some unseen shooter. The other workers reacted by crawling deeper into the recesses of their hiding places.

Her father was encountering his own difficulties. His weapon, an old French MAS 38, jammed and he was trying to clear it. Two SS, realising he was not returning their fire, rose and rushed him. He was a dead man.

They quickly made it to the truck, flung the doors open, and aimed their weapons at the old Professor, who dropped his. One of them spoke: "He is the one we are to capture?"

"No," said the other, checking a photo. Van Helsing caught a glimpse of a grainy picture. Dracula on the train.

"Then I can kill him, yes?" the first soldier asked and raised his gun to Van Helsing's head. He never had a chance to pull the trigger.

Workers appeared behind the two Germans, labourers gripping pipe and steel rod cudgels. They swarmed over the SS and beat them beyond death. It appeared to the Professor that the workers had a surfeit of anger.

Lucille was fighting for her life. The guard had her throat wrapped in his hands, squeezing until she could not draw a breath. Her lungs burned, her vision began to dim. She struggled with all her waning strength and was able to gain her feet.

They staggered in a crude dance until Lucille was backed into the immense tower of thundering steel that was the ten-ton press.

The machine was still pounding away, great, deep, booming clashes of steel upon steel. Usually sheets of brass were fed into its oily maw to be bent into large tubes. Now it pounded only air, shaking the factory floor with small earthquakes every time the dies slammed together. With her hips pressed against the base, Lucille felt the rhythmic cataclysm through her entire body.

No matter how hard she fought against him, the guard was pressing her backward, her spine curling and her head being forced under the press. The back of her skull hit the hard metal die and that was enough to give her the impetus to fling herself out of danger. She threw out a hand, fingers scrambling like a crab on a rock, blindly feeling about for any kind of weapon. Her fingers found a wrench and hefted it, swung it at the head of her attacker, attempting to brain the lout. He knocked the wrench aside with an upthrust elbow. The wrench flew out of her hand, landing in the mouth of the press. One great stamp and the wrench was flattened instantly.

Lucille saw this and knew that her skull would be crushed even easier.

With a hand under Lucille's chin the guard was slowly but surely forcing her head toward the meeting of the press dies. Her senses were painfully acute, the acidic sting of solvent in her nostrils, the heavy odour of lubricating oil, a tinge of ozone, in her ears the explosive concussion of the press slamming steel against steel. She was going to die.

With a surge of strength the guard pushed her head onto the press platform. She could look up and see the ten tons hurtling toward her face. With a sudden increase of will, she lunged out of its path at the last second. The steel dies collided inches from her nose. She felt the rush of air propelled out of the gap, like foul breath blown into her face.

The press rose again to ready another descent. The guard changed his attack. Letting loose of her throat, he put both hands on her waist and lifted, thrusting the upper half of her body under the press. He held her there.

She panicked, watching her death dropping from above, struggling with every bit of her strength. She saw the upper die rush toward her face.

And was unexpectedly pulled out of the way. The press chomped down like the gates of hell slamming shut.

She looked away from the press and found herself in Dracula's arms. Arm, for he was using only one. She looked into his pale amber eyes, then back at the site of her near destruction. Six inches of her hair lay upon the bottom die of the press, as neatly clipped as if by a barber.

She turned back to her saviour. "I owe you my life," she said, her voice hoarse through her tortured throat.

"Hold on to it," Dracula said, "for it is precious."

And he turned to face the guard who had been assaulting her. The man was sprawled on the floor where Dracula had thrown him. The Rumanian rose, snatching up a pry bar, and charged the vampire. Dracula caught the steel bar in mid-strike and tore it from the man's grasp, then flipped it in his hand and hooked the guard under the rib cage, hoisted him like a fish on a pike, and hurled the body into the jaws of the ten-ton press.

Lucille turned away so as not to witness what occurred next. But her ears heard the wet mashing. Dracula held her close and she wrapped him in her arms, clinging to him as if to a floating timber in a stormy sea.

FROM THE WAR JOURNAL OF
J. HARKER

(transcribed from shorthand)

I stood there impotent, powerless to do anything as I saw Dracula tear Lucy from the peril of death. I had tried to get to her as she battled the guard, but a withering crossfire kept me back. Dracula had seen the same fight at the ten-ton press and just leapt from the catwalk, flying down thirty feet or more. With his tattered cape billowing behind him, he looked like nothing more than a great crow descending onto his prey. He threw the Rumanian soldier away from Lucy, snatched her from the mouth of the machine. When she gratefully embraced him my heart stopped still in my aching chest.

But gunfire interrupted my selfish contemplation and I saw Renfield trying to climb the stairs to the offices, but driven back repeatedly by enemy gunfire. I let loose with a salvo of my own, and the soldiers ceased firing for a moment, long enough for my Sergeant to achieve his goal.

Inside the office he set his incendiary charges and timer. I loaded a fresh clip into the Thompson, preparing for a new volley from the SS soldiers.

But once again the labourers responded, as they had with the salvation of Van Helsing. They attacked the soldiers with every sort of tool: wrenches, screwdrivers, pry bars, and any improvised bludgeon, venting a fulsome store of animosity accumulated during their forced servitude. The soldiers were rendered dead and more in seconds.

Renfield climbed down the office stairs without incident. I met him and we joined Van Helsing at the truck, where Dracula and Lucy were already waiting. Renfield was tossing timed blocks of gelignite about the factory, next to fuel and oil barrels, alongside ovens glowing red hot, one atop a fat pipe that had stenciled warnings on the tube. He was sowing mayhem like a farmer tossing turnip seeds into the loam.

"Time to absent ourselves," Van Helsing said. "How long do we have, Sergeant?"

"Fifteen minutes," Renfield responded.

"We need to hurry if we are going to take care of the bunkers and munitions," I said, trying to ignore how Dracula and Lucy still held each other.

"Aye, the rest of the charges are pre-set," Renfield told us, in his rational mode. "Just dump 'em and pop 'em."

"I'll help you," I volunteered. "Lucy, you and your father evacuate the civilians. Dracula, watch their backs?"

"That I will," the vampire answered.

Then the office burst into flame with one great explosion of fire.

Renfield giggled.

I checked my watch and glared at him. "Fifteen minutes, my arse."

He shrugged. "Ach, lowest government bidder" was all he said.

EXCERPTED FROM THE UNPUBLISHED NOVEL
THE DRAGON PRINCE AND I
by Lenore Van Muller

With her father, Lucille hurried the workers out of the factory. Some of them informed her that there were more soldiers occupying a barracks next to their own domiciles.

She was surprised that these had not been awakened by the battle inside the factory, but obviously the routine manufacturing clangour had masked the gunfire.

Dracula went directly to the building indicated. He entered the barracks and she heard the same bloody havoc that echoed the slaughters in the railroad car and at the airfield.

The workers meanwhile commandeered the various trucks and military vehicles inside the compound and loaded them with their compatriots. Some of these poor people were so weak from overwork and malnutrition, mere skeletal figures, that they had to be carried.

The two Englishmen ran among the pallets of completed artillery shells stacked in the yards behind the barracks, dispersing explosive charges like boys delivering newspapers.

They did the same among the bunkers, where gunpowder was stored for the making of the shells. Then they joined the Van Helsings at the ruins of the front gate.

"Aye, 'tis going to be a bonny boom." Renfield beamed. "A splendid show. Pretty flowers of flame. A bouquet of boom. Pity we'll miss it."

They waited for Dracula, who soon arrived, drenched in blood. When Lucille went to him she inadvertently clutched his limp arm and he winced.

"Let us remove ourselves," Van Helsing said and led the way out of the compound. "I fear that we were expected and our enemy may have reinforcements nearby."

"'Twill be a most exhilarating cataclysm, Master," Renfield said to Dracula. "The best I ever rigged. Cannae we tarry and watch?"

"No tarrying," the vampire replied as he held his injured arm, flinched. Cars and trucks rushed past as the workers fled, some of them yawping at Dracula.

Lucille saw two Rottweilers sprint out of the gates and down the street, their claws clicking on the bricks like high heels on terrazzo. The dogs ran with their mouths agape in what could only be described as joy, a jubilance known only by those who face freedom for the first time after a life of indenture.

The Van Helsing Bentley was up the block. The group ran across the brick-paved street to where it was parked. Midway Dracula staggered and fell. Lucille and Harker were instantly at his side, helped him to his feet, and carried him to the Bentley.

Van Helsing held the car door open so that the vampire could be deposited into the back seat. Van Helsing sat himself behind the wheel, and Lucille took the back seat alongside the Prince. Harker was halfway into the car when he stopped to look around.

"Where's Renfield?" he asked.

"He was right behind us," Lucille said. She searched the street, but there was no sign of the British Sergeant.

"We'll go back for him," Van Helsing suggested.

"Father," Lucille said. "There is something wrong with the Prince."

"No," Dracula protested. "Find the Sergeant."

But it was evident that the vampire's strength was failing. The cause of his sudden weakness Lucille could not imagine. Wasn't he immortal, shrugging off bullet wounds as though they were mosquito bites?

"You push off," Harker said. "I'll find Renfield. I have an idea where he went."

He leaned into Lucille. "See to the Prince. I'll meet you in Brasov. Go before the explosions alert every soldier in the area."

And he ran back toward the factory.

The Professor started the car and drove away. They had not driven a mile when the concussion of an explosion made their car shudder on its wheels. Lucille glanced back through the rear window and saw the bright, early dawn that had been created by the missing Sergeant.

FROM THE WAR JOURNAL OF
J. HARKER

(transcribed from shorthand)

My original reconnaissance was from the roof of a six-storey office building just to the north and across the street from the munitions factory. From that height we had a clear view of the entire prison compound and a glimpse of what the factory roof windows allowed. Renfield had accompanied me on the earlier jaunt to recce the targets for his own specialty. We spent an entire day and much of a night watching the location through our field glasses.

I now assumed that the barmy Sergeant had returned to our roost to watch the spectacle he had wrought. A box seat for the best show in town.

The front door was ajar, its glass shattered, glittering shards scattered across the vestibule. Renfield had obviously broken in. He was here. I entered the building at a full sprint, climbing the stairs two and three at a time.

I was on the third floor when the first explosion blew out the stairwell windows. I threw myself to the floor. Broken glass rained down upon me. I pushed myself back to my feet, gingerly brushed the splinters from my clothes, and looked out the empty pane. I saw a series of massive explosions as the factory was torn apart before my very eyes. Bricks flew into the air and rained down like stony hail. Debris pelted the street, the barracks, and outbuildings.

This conflagration was followed by secondary explosions as gas lines blew, spewing flame as if from a dragon's mouth, accompanied by a deafening roar.

Then the pallets of shells began to go off. One pallet of artillery went up in a cataclysm of flame and shrapnel, then another and another in a chain reaction of phenomenal proportions, some shells arcing into the night sky like Jubilee rockets.

I could not pull myself away from the pyrotechnics, hoping that Renfield was enjoying his handiwork. I thought I heard his childish laughter from somewhere above me.

Then a low rumbling was added to the boom and tumult of the unending eruption outside. It took me a few seconds to recognise the sound, footsteps in the stairwell below me, a great many feet pounding the steps.

I popped through the third-floor access door, closed it behind me, and found myself in a dark hallway lined with offices. Cracking the stairwell door once again, I was able to look down and see a dozen SS troops hurrying up the stairs, guns at the ready. They raced right past my floor and to the roof. I closed the door and took a deep breath and tried to assess the situation.

Obviously I could not go up or down. I hoped I was in error about Renfield's destination. This hope was proved wrong in a short time as the Nazis descended, at a slower pace this time, two of them dragging an unconscious Renfield between them.

My hand went to my machine gun, but no further. I knew that any action would be suicidal. Nevertheless I felt ashamed at my timidity. Ashamed and a coward.

Then I heard a German voice boom in the stairwell. "Search the building! Find the others! Search every floor!"

TO: CSS REINHARD HEYDRICH, RSHA, REICHSFUHRER-SS
FROM: SS MAJOR WALTRAUD REIKEL
CC: HEINRICH HIMMLER, REICHSFUHRER-SS
(via diplomatic pouch)

MOST SECRET

In regards to your last communiqué, I will respond to your questions in the same order they were asked.

1) We _were_ prepared for the assault. It was expected that the enemy would attack at night and in a clandestine manner. But the actual incursion was prosecuted by a much larger force than expected. According to the men present there were fifteen to thirty aggressors, armed with mortars and machine guns in an organised and formidable assault. It was only due to our preparation and vigilance locating the enemy's reconnaissance post, plus constant surveillance, that we were rewarded with the capture of our prisoner. To be fair, we underestimated our foe and their commitment to the raid. We will not do so again.

2) The goal was not to defend the factory or to protect the list. They were only decoys, bait for our trap. The destruction of the munitions is regrettable, but I remind you that the Fuhrer himself gave the order to capture this entity "at all costs."

3) No, we did not capture the object of this operation. My failure. If someone must be punished then I am that person. I am ready to accept my reassignment. Send me to the Russian Front.

4) We <u>did</u> lure the one you want into our snare. Evidence of the entity's predation was found on some of our dead. (The corpses were in poor condition, due to the ravages of the fire and explosives. We were left with little to examine.) So the entity <u>was</u> among the raiders and participated in the attack. On this level, our plan was efficacious. We did draw out our quarry. We can do so again.

5) The personage we did capture will lead us to our prey. I am confident in this. He is obviously one of the British spies rumoured to be operating in our area. As such, he must be in contact with and even be a member of the underground leadership. The capture and death of these terrorists will be a great triumph for us. I am sure that the original object of our ambuscade is close to their inner circle. We will proceed to interrogate the captured individual (who is shamming a mental deficiency at the moment. See attached transcript). He will be broken. They all break.

If he does not know the information we seek, he can be used as bait. If they will risk so much for a mere list, they will risk even more for one of their own. And this time we will be even better prepared.

Heil Hitler.

EXCERPTED FROM THE UNPUBLISHED NOVEL
THE DRAGON PRINCE AND I
by Lenore Van Muller

The ride from Sfantu Gheorghe was perilous and distressing in so many ways. At their first attempt to flee the city they found roadblocks no matter which way they turned. But the local partisans had prepared for just such an eventuality. All Van Helsing had to do was look for chalk marks.

Hastily sketched arrows on the corners of buildings and light poles showed him where to turn or not; etched swastikas warned of a German roadblock ahead. These guiding marks finally enabled them to escape Sfantu Gheorghe.

Once outside the city limits they thought they were free, but then the Professor spied chalk on a concrete kilometre marker, the crudely drawn face of a pig. He slowed, confused.

Then Van Helsing drove on. He and his daughter were debating the significance of this symbol, whether it even had any relevance to them, when their headlights illuminated a farmer standing at the side of the road. The man was accompanied by a great spotted sow tethered to a rope. This most unusual apparition in the middle of the night, plus the previous curious marking, convinced Van Helsing to stop their car.

"A beautiful evening," Van Helsing said through the car window. "Walking your pig?"

"She has trouble sleeping when the army trucks make all that noise setting up roadblocks and all."

"Roadblocks?" Lucille asked, turning from Dracula, who lay limp and unmoving.

"On the road ahead of you," the farmer said, a lean, weathered man with silver whiskers and rheumy eyes.

"I, too, am annoyed at the sound of army trucks," Van Helsing said. "I wish there were a way to avoid the nuisance."

"Follow me and Pippi then," the farmer advised. "And turn off your lights."

Van Helsing flicked off his headlights and used the pale hindquarters of the sow as a pink beacon to guide him down the dark dirt road.

The path was barely two ruts between freshly plowed fields. Pippi had a saucy stride that shimmied like a Paris streetwalker. Though malapert, the pig's gait was hardly speedy, and Van Helsing had to keep the car engine barely above an idle.

Lucille turned back to Dracula, who was slumped against the seat, eyes closed, mouth open as if in the midst of a silent scream. He was obviously in pain, his strength fading, such an uncommon feeling that he found no way to fight the wave of nausea and vitiation that was overwhelming him.

Lucille was equally overcome by a sense of helplessness. She had spent enough time assisting her father and absorbing his medical tutelage to qualify as a nurse, but that knowledge was inadequate to the uniqueness of this man. He was cold to the touch, but he was always cold, and she did not know what to do to make him comfortable.

She had to face the fact that he was not human and, therefore, the usual remedies would not be effective. How were she and her father to find a way to heal him?

"Father, we must hurry," she said once again. She tried to keep the fear out of her voice, but failed.

Van Helsing poked his head out of the window and addressed the farmer. "Sir, is it possible that we could put Pippi in the trunk of our vehicle and move a little faster?"

"Pippi's susceptible to sickness when she rides in motorcars," the farmer explained. "Not much farther, though."

They finally came to a ramshackle shed at the junction of two dirt roads. The farmer brought his pig to a halt, leaned into the car.

"Take this road to the left here. Follow it until you meet up with the paved road again," he instructed. "That will put the roadblock behind you. From what I hear, it is clear sailing from there."

"Thank you, sir," Van Helsing said. "And I hope Pippi has sweet dreams."

The old man raised his right arm in a *bras d'honneur*, flexing his elbow while clutching his bicep with the other hand. Not the Nazi salute, but one Lucy had seen many a partisan use.

"Fuck Hitler!" he announced smartly.

The old man grinned, showing more gums than teeth, and then walked back the way he had come, his sauntering sow following.

It was a slow two kilometres farther down the designated road, if it could be called such. Still circumspect with his headlights, Van Helsing had to lean forward, hunched over the steering wheel, to make out the ruts he was following. After an interminable drive the car lurched onto pavement again.

Lucille glanced out the back window, and she could see the military vehicles a half kilometre behind, their headlights illuminating the soldiers. They were stopping every car and truck leaving Sfantu Gheorghe. Van Helsing waited until they crested a hill and were securely out of sight before he turned his headlights back on. Then he was able to speed up, and he did so with fervour.

Feeling his daughter's distress and impatience, he pressured the gas pedal and sped toward Brasov.

The rest of the ride was uneventful. Lucille's concern for the weakening Dracula predominated her thoughts. She watched over him, keeping his head in her lap.

He lay in a near swoon, his mind floating in and out of focus as the poison spread through his body. He tried to fix on to something, anything to maintain some hold on reality, struggling to remain conscious.

He concentrated on the woman hovering over him, her face wrought with concern. Who was this charming but formidable creature? So fearless and deadly, so fierce a beauty with moments of childlike enthusiasms and joy. How all of these contradictory aspects could be contained in one woman was amazing to him. And a godsend. If anyone was to shepherd him into this astonishing new world, it was she.

If he survived.

Finally they reached their home, and Van Helsing moved to help Lucille carry the vampire into the house. The Prince surprised them by pulling away from their aid.

"I can walk," he gasped. His words were in stark contrast to his abilities as he immediately fell to one knee. There were no more protests as father and daughter returned to their burden.

Van Helsing steered them to his clinic, the section of the house he used for visiting patients.

Once there they set Dracula in the examining chair. While Lucille turned on the lights, the Professor cut away the vampire's shirt to reveal his wound.

"Can you tell me what your distress is?" Van Helsing asked. "I am not edified in your . . . the specifics of your physiology."

"I was stabbed," Dracula said. He craned his head to examine the wound. There was a seep of dark fluid, not quite blood, a darker, more viscous liquid.

"Indeed, there is a small puncture in your anterior thoracic region, between the pectoralis major and the latissimus dorsi." Van Helsing probed the area. "But that is mostly thick muscle. No vital organs."

"You have been stabbed and even shot before and bore no permanent damage," Lucille said. "I have seen this."

"I think the blade might have been made of silver," Dracula said. "Why that would be, I do not know. Silver cannot keep an edge and serves badly as a blade."

"Some of the ceremonial daggers that the SS carry are made of silver," Lucille explained.

"Silver is detrimental to you?" Van Helsing asked.

"Extremely," Dracula answered. "It is a poison to me."

"Interesting," Van Helsing mused, poking the cut with his scalpel.

"Is there some kind of antidote?" Lucille asked.

"None that I know," Dracula said. "I am not that studied in my own physiology, actually."

"Fascinating," the Professor exclaimed excitedly. "This was why I left you alive. There are so many questions to be answered about your species."

"The most important one right now is how we heal him," Lucille chastised her father.

"Of course, of course." Van Helsing turned a gooseneck lamp to shine on the wound. There were faint scars from the recent bullet wounds, already healed. But there was also a raw, blackened rip in the vampire's pale flesh, and poisonous tendrils emanated away from it under the skin. Lucille could see them growing as she watched, tiny tributaries branching away, spreading across his chest.

"The poison is spreading rapidly," she told her father.

"I see it," the Professor said. "But I do not know how to stop it. Antibiotics, maybe?"

"There must be a bit of the evil metal still within me. You must excise it." Dracula winced under the prodding of the scalpel as Van Helsing probed the wound.

"A bit of silver in the wound, you say?" Van Helsing asked, frowning.

"Yes, quickly please," Dracula hissed between gritted teeth. "And you must also remove the diseased flesh."

"Much like cutting away gangrene or rotted tissue," Lucille said. She went to the operating tray, filled it with her father's instruments. She dipped each one in alcohol, not wanting to waste time heating the autoclave.

"The wound does not bleed much," Van Helsing observed.

"Blood is something I take, not easily grant," Dracula told him.

"Are you sure this is a recent wound?" Van Helsing asked. "The necrosis is at an advanced stage."

"Necrosis?" Dracula asked.

"Dead tissue" was the answer from Lucille.

Dracula laughed. "I am, after all, the walking dead," he said. "Excise the silver, please, before more of my flesh is poisoned."

"First some anesthesia," Van Helsing proposed.

"Anesthesia. Another new word for my vocabulary," Dracula said. "Explicate, please."

"A pain-killing drug," Lucille told him and went to the cabinet where they kept the vials under lock and key.

"I am immune to such." Dracula shook his head. "If pain mitigation were possible for me I would have succumbed to such a long time past. Please, cut out the corruption. I can feel it proliferate as we speak."

And the poison was doing just that. Lucille could see the black spider veins coursing under the calcimine-like derma.

"Ready?" Van Helsing asked the vampire.

Lucille offered her hand to Dracula, who took it in his own. Dracula nodded to the doctor.

Van Helsing took up a pair of forceps and inserted the tip into the wound, probed. Dracula set his jaw and did not protest, though he was in obvious pain. Lucille marvelled at how steady her father's hands were, even at his advanced age.

"Got it," Van Helsing announced and withdrew a small triangular bit of white metal. He dropped it onto the tray and picked up the scalpel.

"Now, excise the dead tissue, you say?" he asked the vampire.

"The necrosis, if you please. The dead tissue is me." Dracula managed a smile.

The scalpel slid into the skin around the wound where the black had not reached yet. Dracula's face contorted with pain.

TO: CSS REINHARD HEYDRICH, RSHA, REICHSFUHRER-SS
FROM: SS MAJOR WALTRAUD REIKEL
CC: HEINRICH HIMMLER, REICHSFUHRER-SS
(via diplomatic pouch)

TRANSCRIPT OF INTERVIEW (01/06/41)

INTERVIEW CONDUCTED BY MAJOR W. REIKEL AND INTERVIEW SPECIALIST CORPORAL SCHRECK. Also present is your Company scribe.

Subject is restrained in the Corporal's specially designed interrogation chair. Subject bears bruises and abrasions received in capture and earlier undocumented interview.

MAJOR R.: Who do you work with?

SUBJECT: Caviar comes from virgin sturgeon / Virgin sturgeon's a very fine dish. / Very few sturgeon are ever virgin, / That's why caviar's a very rare dish.

Corporal S. gathers up his tools: mallet and nails.

MAJOR R.: We could save us all a lot of uncomfortable time if you would just give me one name. Just one. That's not so difficult, is it?

SUBJECT: Oysters they are fleshy bivalves / They have youngsters in their shell. / How they diddle is a riddle, / But they do, so what the hell.

MAJOR R.: You ARE going to tell me who you are collaborating with.

Corporal S. was commanded to remove a tarpaulin in the corner of the interrogation room. Under it is a body, badly burnt. Even though the remains are charred, it is discernible that the throat of the corpse has been torn out as if by an animal. (The scribe had to remove himself for a brief moment to take advantage of the facilities.)

SUBJECT: The other night, dear, as we lay sleeping. / I could not help it, I lost control./ And now you wonder, just why I'm leaving; / You will find out in nine months or so.

Corporal S. is given a nod by the Commander. A small nail (30 millimetres) is inserted between the Subject's middle knuckles of the first finger on the left hand. The Subject responded vocally, none of it transcribable.

MAJOR R.: A name. One name.

SUBJECT: R. M. Renfield, Sergeant, Royal Engineers.

Major R. gives another nod. Another nail is inserted and secured in the same manner, this time in the second finger of the same hand.

SUBJECT: They shan't murder me by inches! Ah'll fight for my Lord and Master!

FROM THE WAR JOURNAL OF
J. HARKER

(transcribed from shorthand)

After hearing the order to search the floors, I sprinted down the hallway, frantically testing every door. I behaved much as a rat does in a trap, desperately searching for a way out of my predicament. Left and right, every door to every office was locked. I now wished I had paid more attention to the lock-picking course at Beaulieu Manor, but I happened to be hungover that day after a post-cricket celebration.

I thought of breaking a window in one door, but soon dismissed the idea; the broken glass would be a definite red flag for anyone searching, as it had been for me at the entrance.

Finally a door gave way to my panicked push. As soon as I entered I knew, by the pungent effluvium, that I was in the loo. I soon deduced that it was not even the men's water closet, this conclusion reached by the absence of any urinal and the presence of a dainty rattan settee painted white with faded, stained pink cushions. The toilets were stained yellow with age, and the once-white octagonal tiles that lined the floor were cracked in a variety of places, each irregular cleft blackened with years of grime. The air was heavy with dank moisture, redolent with the musk of stale cigarettes and sickening-sweet perfume.

Frantically I looked everywhere, desperate for a place to hide. But there was nothing, not a vent or crawl space. The lone window was high off the floor and decidedly too small for me to get through. It looked as if it had not been opened since Napoleon's time. The place was sealed as tight as a submarine, which probably had something to do with the smell.

I pressed my back against the door and could hear the rattling of doorknobs and shaking of doors in the hallway, the same procedure that had led me here. I peeked out into the corridor and saw a lone soldier checking the offices one by one.

This Nazi bastard was about to discover the same thing that I had found. Only one door would open. The one I was huddled behind. I had seconds until I was discovered. The beating of my own heart and the blood surging through my temples pounded like blows from a hammer, so loud that I was sure my pursuer would be able to hear.

Setting aside the Thompson—one burst from the machine gun would alert the whole building—I withdrew the .32-calibre silenced Welrod that I had carried for much of the southern campaign. I had found no reason to use it then, only fired it a few times. It was not very accurate beyond five paces, but the loo was a tiny room. This kill would be close. Thank the Lord, as I have proved to be a terrible shot with the pistol, not able to hit an elephant in the ass if I was holding his tail.

My fingers curled around the pistol grip, squeezing much too hard, the long tube that covered the barrel resting against my leg.

The door eased open. A German soldier wearing the ubiquitous muted grey tunic stepped inside.

The curious paradox of war that I had never dwelt upon was the fine line between killing and murder. How a civilised man, a religious man taught to abhor homicide, intellectually and morally, indoctrinated by our laws, religion, and family mores that it is resolutely wrong to kill another human being, can, abruptly, with the flip of a mental switch, rationalize that the assassination of his enemy is not only required, but proper. And often glorified.

Up to this time I had indeed killed my enemy, in our southern actions, at the railway car, in fact, had slaughtered more than my share at the munitions factory less than an hour before. But they were all at a distance, just targets that fell; their ultimate terminus noted but not dwelt upon. Once removed in deed and mental rationalization, shall we say. In a kill-or-be-killed situation, the act was performed and all other thoughts became muted by the sheer relief that one was still alive.

But the most salient quality of this orthodox murder was the remove from the target.

This man who stepped through the door was instantly close enough for me to detect the onion and paprika on his breath. Close enough to see the pinkeye that had swollen one lid, making it appear as if he were winking at me. Close enough for me to see the sunburnt skin and abnormally low widow's peak plunging down from the brim of his cap. He reminded me of my uncle Clive.

It was not the memory of my uncle that gave me pause (he was a prat), so I suppose it was the proximity of the soldier and, there is no other word that serves, his human-ness that caused me to hold back my murderous impulse.

I reversed my grip on the Welrod, grasping the fat barrel instead, and clubbed him on the head. The blow knocked his field cap askew and he looked nothing if not startled. But, unlike Bulldog Drummond's opponents, he did not fall to my feet unconscious.

I responded to his lack of pulp novel cooperation by pounding on his skull a few more times. This still did not produce the hoped-for outcome. In fact, one of his hands darted toward the Schmeisser machine gun slung over his shoulder. The other arm shot out and grabbed me about the waist to steady himself, I suppose, as my repeated pummeling began to have some effect.

He sagged to one knee and pulled me down with him. We tumbled to the floor; the Welrod flew from my hand and skidded across the tiles with the grinding sound of steel against stone. We rolled across the floor, grappling at each other, me trying to keep him close so he could not wield the Schmeisser, and he attempting to drive me away. The odour of violet brilliantine from his hair tonic was strong enough to make me cough.

Again, during my warcraft training, besides the use of the pistol, rifle, and other killing instruments, I was given some lessons in hand-to-hand combat by a little Welsh fellow, Sergeant Charlie Hall, who edified us college boys with constant thrashings. He had a variety of techniques, from back-alley fisticuffs to an oriental pugilistic approach of throws and counter-throws. These were taught us in a ritualistic fashion of poses and attacks, more ballet than brawl.

In no manner did the soldier I wrestled in that ladies' loo attend to any of Charlie's choreography. He gouged at my eyes, bit, clawed, and kicked. I responded in kind, fighting as a berserker. It was a barbaric struggle, both of us subsumed to our bestial antecedents. Holding him close, I was subject to a vicious pounding upon my back. He also kneed me in the groin. I let go of his torso and wrapped my hands about his throat, drove my thumbs into his larynx until I felt the cartilage break like chicken bones. After that his breath came in wheezing gasps. But he persisted in his assault with even more vigor. And I held my own and more, I must admit.

I kicked, I clawed, I used my teeth, battling for survival like a beast in the wild. Finally I was able to place a knee into his chest—or was it his knee in mine, I do not know, being caught up in the frenzy of the melee— but suddenly one of us kicked off and we were flung apart. He stood and scrambled for his machine gun, heretofore pushed to the small of his back. I crawled to my pistol.

I aimed as he aimed. I fired. The pistol spat and the Nazi flinched, a hole appearing above his right eyebrow, not a bad shot considering the circumstances and my heavy breathing. I think I was as astonished as he. The rise of his Schmeisser paused. The Welrod being a single-shot weapon, I prepared to bludgeon him again.

The man sighed deeply, and his shoulders shrugged as if he were at the end of a long day. Then he found a residue of strength and raised the gun barrel toward my face. I watched the slow rise, knowing that just a faint pressure on the trigger would send a fusillade of bullets my way.

Then he stopped, raised his other hand to his sweaty forehead as if to scratch the itch the .32-calibre bullet had caused.

He fell, a slow sideways subsidence, like that of a great, cut tree.

I fell back against the wall and slid to the floor, trying to get my breathing under control, gulping great swallows of air, waiting for the rest of the Germans to burst through the door at any second.

EXCERPTED FROM THE UNPUBLISHED NOVEL
THE DRAGON PRINCE AND I
by Lenore Van Muller

Lucille was coming back to the clinic with a fresh bottle of carbolic when she heard voices inside. Her father and the vampire were conversing. Something made her stop outside the door to listen.

"You must understand this, Prince," her father was saying. "My daughter is God's gift to me."

She heard Dracula moan as the doctor cut the damaged tissue from around the wound.

"Do you cause me pain to warn me away?" Dracula asked.

"I can give you more than pain. I can cease it altogether. Forever," Van Helsing warned. "I conquered you once before. But I appeal to you, gentleman to gentleman. When I settled here in Transylvania, after our encounter, I was already an old man. I met a woman, a blessing, and then we had a child. It was beyond me why I should deserve such happiness."

"A karmic reward for defeating me, perhaps?" The question was followed by a hiss of pain.

"You could look at it like that. I worshipped my wife, my child. I lost my wife, God rest her tender soul. Then Lucille became my all. Sad to say, as she grew into a woman I still treated her like a child, hence the rebellious streak."

Another muted moan of pain from Dracula.

"What I am trying to say is that I would gladly lay down my life to keep her from harm. Do you understand?"

"I do," Dracula replied. "And you should be aware that in the short time I have been of her acquaintance, I feel the same, would do the same."

Lucille felt her heart stop beating and she caught her breath, still as death for a brief moment. The irony did not escape her.

There was quiet in the room, and Lucille chose that moment to enter. She poured the carbolic into a basin, soaking the needle and suture in the chemical. The silence continued as her father proceeded to sew up the gaping wound.

When he was finished, Lucille daubed the stitching and the area around it with iodine and helped her father bandage the vampire. She carefully avoided both men's eyes.

Her father spoke first. "I think I have excised all of the tainted flesh. I have no idea regarding your recuperative faculties, so I suppose we shall just have to wait and see. Now to bed." He turned to Lucille. "Both of you."

"The doctor should take his own prescription," Lucille said. His eyes were heavy and the lines of his face drawn long.

Dracula swung off the lounge, then staggered. Lucille was immediately at his side.

"I'll help you to your room." And she supported him out of the clinic as her father began to clean up. "I'll tend to that later, Father. Please," she begged.

"First I'm going to check to see if the two Englishmen have arrived back," her father said. "I will make some inquiries."

"Where would they come but here?" she asked. "Go to bed and we will deal with them after we have rested. Until then there is nothing we can do. If they are here when we wake, then it is a moot point."

Her father agreed and followed her and Dracula up the stairs, the old man's tread slow, weary. She paused to make sure he entered his own bedroom and then helped the vampire into his, assisting him to bed. She had to remove a pile of books to make room for his legs.

He eased himself back onto the pillow and she fussed with the covers a moment.

"I have no further need of your ministrations," he told her.

"I know," she replied. "You are the fearless monster."

He smiled, emitted a short laugh that caused him some pain, and he involuntarily clutched at his wound.

And at that moment, upon this most vulnerable moment, Lucille saw not a myth, not a historical figure, but a man. The man that he was before he was a vampire, even before he was a Prince. Maybe she even saw a hint of the boy before he became a man.

And she was struck with a profound empathy for him. A sense of his loneliness, an isolation forced upon him by his singularity. He was a being set apart from the rest of the world and had no companion, no equal, no one who understood, no one with whom to share this uncommon life.

Lucille felt an acute affinity with the Prince, this creature, this man. She was him and he was her.

After the brutal and exhausting battle in the ladies' loo, my escape from the building itself was relatively simple. I wrestled the dead man out of his uniform and slipped it over my own hobo mufti. Conveniently, he was a large man, so the fit was passable.

Discarding the Thompson was a difficult decision, but I did so, slipping it under the settee, taking my late opponent's Schmeisser instead. The spoils of war and all that. The body I left where it lay, not knowing how or where to hide the bloody thing. Actually there was little blood, the hole in his head leaking but a dribble.

From then on I just walked out of the loo, that first step a chill-inducing move. But the hall was empty. I had another moment of pause at the door to the stairwell, checking my disguise one more time. Pulling the cap further down my forehead, I opened the door and walked into the chaos of soldiers hurrying down the steps.

"All clear." I heard this call repeated up and down the stairs by a variety of voices. Taking my cue, I repeated the phrase in my best Low German to the SS Sergeant at the landing above and joined the exodus of descending Nazis.

Outside the German troops were milling along the kerb, muttering and smoking, laughing in the manner of all soldiers given a brief respite between orders. I mingled, but slowly made my way to the periphery of the crowd, desperately trying to fight the rising urge to flee from this smoky pit of enmity.

Here, thank the Lord, my training took over as I heard the voices of my instructors at the school of dirty tricks. They had drummed into my brain that only a guilty man runs; an innocent man acts naturally, blends with his surroundings. Under this dictum, I bummed a cigarette from one Nazi, a light from another, who used the ember from his own ciggie to fire mine. It was a chore to keep my hands from trembling. I admit I had to stifle my cough as the harsh tobacco scoured my throat like sandpaper. During this masquerade, I sought about me for a sign of my Sergeant. To no avail, as Renfield was nowhere in sight.

By this time I had made my way to the fringe of the group and found myself only three steps from the corner of the building under assault. With some sly back-stepping while facing the gaggle of Germans, I was soon there and, when I thought no one was observing, I took the paramount final step around the corner and out of sight.

Glancing down this new street I saw no Germans and began to walk as casually as I could manage, just a lone soldier taking a smoke and a stroll. If confronted I would plead the woolgathering of a typical dunderhead. My ears were attuned to any shouts behind me. It was a tense walk but my ruse went undetected.

Halfway down the block, I spotted a car at the kerb. Checking for any observers, I tried the door. Locked. I could see why. This was a Lagonda Le Mans Coupe, a marvelous streamlined triumph of car craft. Hating myself as I did it, I used the Schmeisser to smash the side window. There was no notice of this sacrilegious vandalism, so I reached inside and unlocked the door, slipped into the seat, and climbed over into the driver's side.

Using another lesson from my SOE mentors, I ripped the ignition wires from under the dash so I could see them and, after a couple of unsuccessful combinations, was able to make the engine turn over. A further manipulation of the choke made the car purr to life, and I drove away.

Stripping off my former foe's tunic and cap, I tossed them out the window a few blocks away. I stashed the Schmeisser under the passenger seat. My immediate concern, now that I had accomplished my escape, was to warn Lucy and, of course, the rest of the cell, that Renfield had been captured. It was manifest that he would be interrogated and, if the intelligence from SS headquarters was true, tortured until he gave up everything he knew. His current dementia notwithstanding, the common credo that "everyone talks" had to be assumed. Everyone he had come into contact with needed to be alerted. My personal concern was with the Van Helsings, but everyone in the Resistance was in danger.

The Lagonda drove like a dream car, the twelve cylinders responding like a lion after a gazelle. If only the boys at Shrewsbury could see me now.

One problem quickly presented itself. As I approached the outskirts of Sfantu Gheorghe I could see a roadblock ahead. Making a quick turn, I proceeded down another boulevard and found this route, too, was blocked, a squad of Rumanian soldiers monitoring anyone leaving town, by foot or vehicle.

Changing my course once again, I parked a few blocks away so that I could ponder the situation. It was likely that every avenue out of town was similarly guarded. The question for me was whether my identification papers, so well counterfeited by the gnomes in the Forgery Section, were good enough to get me past what must be a super-vigilant perusal. It had become evident to me that the Germans and the Rumanians had been lying in wait for us. They had prepared their ambush and now were blocking any egress in an attempt to capture us. I could only hope that the Van Helsings had escaped before the roadblocks had been established.

I decided that I could not chance my documents. My own capture was not my primary worry. It was how my capture would be a hazard to my comrades. I was desperate to get word of Renfield's apprehension to the partisans in Brasov. My mind was in torment at the image of Lucy in the clutches of the reprehensible Major Reikel.

The sun was beginning to lighten the overcast sky. Clouds were rolling in from the east and bouncing the unseen sun's light into the houses and streets before me. Time was fleeting. I drove on, testing my theory about the roadblocks, hoping against hope that I was wrong. It did not make me happy to be proven correct—roadblocks were at every Sfantu Gheorghe exit.

Parking once more, I was trying to decide whether to finally risk my phony credentials, angry at myself for my waffling, when I saw a storekeeper setting out the tiny tables and chairs of an outdoor cafe.

I immediately rushed out of the car and approached him, a tubby little man with a mustache that curled to spiky tips.

"Sir, do you have a phone?" I asked. He murmured an assent. Digging into my pocket, I rummaged for the handful of leu I was carrying, but found nothing except a scattering of tobacco and a box of matchsticks. It dawned on me that I was still wearing the britches of the man I had killed. I renewed my search, this time reaching into the pants underneath the outer pair.

The cafe proprietor openly gawked at what most likely appeared to be a man fumbling inside his underwear. His yawp quickly transformed into a yellow-toothed grin as I foisted the cash upon him. He directed me to the phone, and I immediately had the operator connecting me to the Van Helsing line in Brasov. But all I heard was a curious humming through the earpiece with sporadic eruptions of static. Finally the operator told me that she was unable to make the connection. The only other number I knew was Mihaly's Tailor Shop, which functioned as a clandestine message centre for the leadership cell.

But that connection, too, failed. The operator was perfunctorily apologetic and told me that the lines to Brasov must be down, even though there was no storm, that being the usual cause, maybe an accident at one of the poles, that had happened in '32. She prattled on and I hung up, thoroughly despondent. What was I to do? The proprietor presented me with a cup of coffee and a slice of lemon cake. I thanked him and sat at one of the outside tables, using the modest repast as a chance to think.

What to do? The alarm had to be sounded or the whole partisan effort would collapse. My compatriots would face a grim fate. And I could not deny the fact that their jeopardy was my fault. I was Sergeant Renfield's senior in rank. He was my responsibility, and I had come a cropper in my wardship, to him, my comrades in war, and, ultimately, my mission in Rumania.

I am not one to wallow in self-pity and guilt, not for long at least. My next thought was how to rectify my failing. The roads were blocked, so I could not get to Brasov that way. Communication lines were down, whether by chance or on purpose mattered not. I did not know any members of the Sfantu Gheorghe underground; Van Helsing had made the local contacts, so I could not just pass on the warning to someone else. I was stymied. So I sat there cursing myself in frustration.

Finally I decided at least to get on my feet and start walking, any forward movement better than just sitting on my bum. I thanked the proprietor for the coffee and cake and returned to the Lagonda. It was difficult to abandon that beautiful machine, but I feared an alarm was out concerning its disappearance. I wanted to retrieve the Schmeisser, reasoning I might have use of its firepower.

I was having some difficulty hiding the machine gun under my jacket, the weapon being a bulky item, and was thinking of leaving it behind when a motorcyclist sped past. The motorised bike was stenciled with various military designations and the rider a soldier in uniform. Obviously this was a Rumanian Army vehicle. Judging from the fat satchel hanging from his neck the motorcyclist was most likely a courier.

It took but a moment's thought that the motorcycle would be a much better escape vehicle than the ostentatious Lagonda. If I somehow could obtain the bike and, even better, the courier's uniform I would be able to pass through any roadblock. So I followed him in my stolen car.

But then the sudden impetus to do so began to lose its shine. This fellow on two wheels was just going to lead me into the midst of some Rumanian Army command post, where my chances of survival were less than that of a snowflake in a teakettle. As I shifted from first to second gear, so did my brain. What was my plan? Shifting from second into third, I flailed about for some kind of stratagem. Force him off the road? Could I do that without wrecking the motorcycle? Pull ahead, block the road with my car, wave him down? Use the machine gun as a motivator?

But then the gods smiled on me as the rider turned down a dirt road byway and stopped in front of a cottage that had seen better days: walls crumbling, windows missing and patched with tar paper, the porch leaning. As he dismounted, the front door opened and a young woman, still wearing her nightdress, rushed into the motorcyclist's arms. They entered the cottage together.

I parked the Lagonda and walked down the dirt road to the motorcycle. It was a Polish Sokol 1000, not a beauty like the Norton Manx I rode during a summer jaunt across Spain, but it seemed a very pragmatic machine. I glanced at the cottage, searching for any observance, and saw none. From inside I could hear a rhythmic thumping, a sound reminiscent of a headboard banging against a wall. Not that I have a surfeit of experience in such activities. Good for you, courier boy. Rolling the Sokol off its kickstand, I walked the bike down the road a quarter mile before I kicked the motor to life. The accompanying bellow was loud enough for me to glance back at the cottage in paranoia, but no one stirred and I rode away.

Since I did not have the camouflage of the courier's uniform, the roads were still a problem for me. I decided I would avoid them and strike out cross-country. And the Sokol was the perfect transport to do just that.

DATED: 2 JUNE 1941
TO: CSS REINHARD HEYDRICH, RSHA, REICHSFUHRER-SS
FROM: SS MAJOR WALTRAUD REIKEL
CC: HEINRICH HIMMLER, REICHSFUHRER-SS
(via diplomatic pouch)

MOST SECRET

The presumption that the vigorous physical aspect of interrogation is the only method that extracts results is a fallacy.

Physical intimidation is only a first step toward a successful interview. As much as it weakens the resolve in some, such methods can also strengthen another subject's defiance. Either case has its own reward--the cries of protest and pain from the subject do more to debilitate the prisoners in the adjacent cells than weaken the subject at hand.

In reference to the subject we captured in Sfantu Gheorghe (R. M. Renfield, Sergeant, 6th Royal Scot Fusiliers, as he has repeatedly told us. And I do mean repeatedly, as it is his prayer to a deaf God), he has resisted all efforts to extract any clear intelligence under the craft of my chief interrogator, Corporal Schreck.

The Corporal has been with me since Poland, and his work has proved to be most efficacious. He is an expert at Verscharfte Vernehmung [sharpened interrogation] and the use of a variety of techniques: electrodes, rubber nightstick, genital vise, soldering iron, water and ice. I assure you that he can squeeze any man or woman dry within twenty-four hours.

My first step was to confine our prisoner in isolation, giving the subject some time to contemplate our next level of inquisition. His cell was one specially constructed to admit no light, as black a jail as can be made.

The door was shut upon the Brit, and he was left to the terrors of his own imagination. In less than three hours, he was begging for some surcease. His pleadings were interjected with declarations and promises of cooperation. Anything for a bit of illumination. The subject, truth be told, was, in fact, near hysteria when finally released. He was trembling, cowering in a corner, ready to give me an answer to any questions put to him.

As our mentor Heinrich Himmler once remarked, ofttimes the most effective inducement is not physical, but mental torment.

We have our terrorists.

EXCERPTED FROM THE UNPUBLISHED NOVEL
THE DRAGON PRINCE AND I
by Lenore Van Muller

On Lucille's first visit to Paris alone she became infatuated with a young Russian surrealist painter. His oeuvre was dominated by a lot of trains going into tunnels a la di Chirico. His artistic focus was a bit obvious, but it was her first time alone in Paris and her first artiste and he was sexy in a scruffy, alley-cat way. The attraction may have been abetted by the fact that she could only understand one word in ten that came out of his bearded, petulant mouth.

One day she decided to embrace the free love movement espoused by the Russian and his coterie of low-rent hedonists. She purchased a black silk peignoir, handmade lace from the Netherlands, and had her hair cut into a Theda Bara bob, which she thought at the time was very vampish.

The whole romantic encounter disintegrated into a comic embarrassment as her beau fell into an opium-and-absinthe-induced somnolence. She went home and sheepishly stashed the tissue-wrapped negligee in the corner of a drawer like it was an old maid's keepsake. The scrap of filmy material followed her in her travels, still wrapped in the tissue. And sadly she never found an appropriate occasion to unpack the fragile garment.

This night, she gently retrieved the peignoir out of the drawer where it had been preserved like an old memento. Feeling the silk caress her skin as it slid down her body was like a lover's kiss. She performed a slow pirouette in front of her mirror. The silk was transparent, a gauze revealing hints of her nipples, her mons, the wink of her navel. It had been a while since she had regarded her naked body, and she noted that she was no longer the thin waif she had been in Paris, or even last year. That bony form of a girl had been transformed; she now wore the curves of a woman.

The trouble began when she entered Dracula's room. She posed next to the door, knowing the lamplight would only add potency to her libidinous display. The vampire paid scant notice of her brazen theatrics. He merely glanced up from his book, set it down, slipped a thumb inside to mark his place, and cocked his head like a dog examining a squirrel.

She approached the bed, hoping that her physical proximity or just a closer look would inspire the expected reaction.

"I've come to check on the patient," she said, realising that she had just become a character in a bad sex romp.

He at least smiled at her sham. She lifted the bandage from his chest. The only sign of any recent wound was the black whiskers of stitches astride a shiny scar.

"Amazing," she said, leaning over him. She caught him peering down the neck of her negligee where her breasts hung free. So he was not totally immune.

"Look at that," she said, half-teasing.

His eyes met hers, his smile making its way there.

"Like it happened years ago," she remarked.

"A testament to the calibre of my physician," he said. "And his nurse, of course."

"My father would give his eyeteeth to know how your biological systems work." She took the book from his hands. It was the Bram Stoker opus. Plucking a hair from her head she marked his page, set the tome upon the nightstand. "How do you like the book?" she asked.

"Somewhat lurid and histrionic," he said.

She sat on the edge of the bed and he slid over to accommodate her.

"Was the author a Catholic, by chance?" he asked.

"I do not know. A theatrical agent, I think."

"Ah, that makes sense."

"You will not like the ending." She leaned back onto a pillow, toed off her slippers. She stretched out upon the silk comforter without touching his body with her own. "Would it be out of bounds to ask some questions concerning your . . . condition?"

"Not in the least. I am in your debt and at your service."

"Intimate questions?"

"How intimate?"

She moved closer until her skin almost touched his. "Your lust . . . is it only for blood?"

He did not move away. "How do you mean?"

"You know exactly what I mean."

"Are all the women of this age so forthright?"

"Just answer the query."

He paused a moment, turned his gaze to her face, exploring her features the way a lost soul beholds the sunrise, finding hope in a new day.

"My desires are manifold," he said as he took her into his arms.

FROM THE WAR JOURNAL OF
J. HARKER

(transcribed from shorthand)

JUNE 2, 1941

My way out of Sfantu Gheorghe was through a bean field, the green foliage strung upon a straight line of wire and stick supports that ran for acres. I must say it was quite the achievement, guiding the Sokol between the narrow rows, bent low over the handlebars, keeping my head below the crop so as not to be seen from the roads that bordered the fields of beans. I would stop at the end of each tillage to search for any observers, then, seeing none, cross to the next field.

I drove from bean field to apple orchard to blackberry hedges, the latter's thorny vines tearing at my clothes and skin. But I did not slacken my speed or determination. It was likely that Renfield would have cracked by now. Lucy and the Resistance were at extreme risk, and I was the only man able to save them. If I could just make it to Brasov in time.

I have to admit that my focus was oft-times interrupted by the event back at the lavatory. I had killed a man in close quarters. His face kept popping into my mind like a catchy tune you cannot banish from your brain, a horrible, wretched melody; his sweaty face, the bloodshot eyes, his mouth twisted in hate or fear, maybe desperation. The same desperation most likely reflected back at him by my own visage. I remembered something from Kierkegaard: "There is nothing of which every man is so afraid as getting to know how enormously much he is capable of."

The nightmare images of the dying Kraut almost led to my own death. My attention strayed while I was speeding down a dry irrigation ditch, sixty kilometres an hour or more, and I suddenly saw a concrete culvert ahead of me. I slewed the motorcycle up the bank, nearly flipping the damned thing, then sailed over the cow path and back down before I knew what I was doing.

Once past the roadblocks, or the mere possibility of them, I tacked to the main road to Brasov and opened up the throttle on the motorcycle. The bike proved to be quite the corker. The speedometer needle leaned into a hundred kilometres per hour for most of the way.

On the outskirts of Brasov, I began recognising various landmarks and was able to avoid the permanent roadblocks I knew were in place. I had to ride straight through town to reach the Van Helsing home. As I passed Mihaly's, I was stunned to see an SS lorry drive up to the storefront and discharge six storm troopers, who broke down the front door.

I kerbed the Sokol down the street and turned to watch the haberdasher's.

Mihaly was popular among the Nazis, at least the officers, as he catered to their affectation for smartly tailored uniforms. Besides being a meticulous tailor, he kept his prices exceptionally low for them, doing the work below his own costs. What he lost in revenue, we partisans gained in intelligence. As women gossip with their hairdressers, men banter with their tailors: officers bragging about their promotions or grumbling about a transfer, all sorts of military intelligence tidbits and rumours. And Mihaly was cunning at wheedling out the details behind the more useful fragments.

"What kind of lining would the Lieutenant desire? Hot weather, cold? It makes a difference in the cut. North African silk or Russian Front wool?"

The answer would quite often come with embellishments, the division, the locale, dates, and names, all to be passed on to London by my transmitter.

So the sight of Germans at the shop was not unusual, but they did not generally break down the front door. Soon after this brutal entrance, I was witness to Mihaly being dragged out of the store, his face bloody from a scalp wound. He was tossed into the back of the lorry. From the store came the sound of smashing furniture and glass, followed by the Nazis carrying out the weapons cache. I knew that the basement hideaway had been discovered.

Renfield had talked.

And Mihaly had been exposed as a partisan. Who else? Lucy? I started the motorcycle with an urgency that made my heart pound, my hands fumbling, and in my haste I almost tipped the bike over. As the rear wheel caught, the front wheel leapt into the air. I finally managed to get the bike under control and sped toward the Van Helsing home.

EXCERPTED FROM THE UNPUBLISHED NOVEL
THE DRAGON PRINCE AND I
by Lenore Van Muller

Once, while accompanying her father to a medical conference in Venice, Lucille succumbed to a bout of influenza. She lay in that strange bed with a fever that none of the consulting doctors her father brought in could abate.

When they left her alone she found her own palliative. Stripping herself of her nightdress and underwear, she would lie prostrate upon the marble floor, letting the cool stone soak the heat out of her fevered, naked body.

This was how she felt lying in the vampire's arms, allowing his chill temperature to absorb the fire that raged through her body after they had coupled.

She gently tugged at his stitches, slowly drawing them out like pulling threads from a sweater.

"Does that hurt?" she asked.

"Not enough for me to leave your side."

"How long has it been?" She looked into his amber eyes. "Since you succumbed to . . . this other form of lust?"

"What century is this?"

"That is so sad. Truly sad." She gave him a teasing look and received one in return. Good, he was feeling better.

During their lovemaking Lucille could feel him holding back; his power, the astounding strength that could crush her, break her so easily. What did it say about her that she found the incipient violence as a mighty aphrodisiac? She had been infused with a matching feral ferocity, energised as never before, and she was suddenly overcome with visions: of old worlds, people in costumes she had seen only in ancient paintings. She saw lives taken, absorbed, subsumed. She felt herself die—and then reborn, again and again.

He reached out a cool hand, ran it lightly down her ribs, along the dip of her waist, along the gentle ridge of her hip.

"I would say it was worth the wait, but you might take the compliment as mere flattery," he said.

She rolled atop his body, feeling the length of him. It was like embracing a marble statue, the flesh so cool, so smooth to the touch, hard on the surface, but pliable, so pliable.

"Tell me, do you receive a thrill when you bite and feed?"

She bit his neck, taking the white flesh between her teeth with just enough tension to pull at his skin. He was not immune to her attentions; she could feel his interest rise betwixt their bodies.

"When you bite," she persisted. "Is it as good as sex?"

"I don't remember."

"Then we must jog your memory."

And she kissed him. Deeply, pressing her lips fiercely against his. He took her face in his hands, pulled her to him. They rolled over, he atop her, both of them striving to meld their flesh into one body, one being, consuming each other.

He ran a palm across her breasts, and her nipples responded instantly. The hand slid lower and she shivered, but not from the cold.

She gasped for air as they merged. They moved, against and with each other, passion ruling.

Dracula caressed her with his eyes, her face encouraging him, urging him on, her lips, swollen, bruised from desire, her neck, a graceful curve of pale flesh. Where the major artery, a blue line under the fair skin, pulsed with the rhythm of her heart, the rhythm of their congress.

He became fixated on that vein, riveted on its promise, the promise of blood, the throb of life . . .

Lucille noticed the focus of his thrall.

"Do it!" she cried in the throes of her carnal erotomania. "Bite me! Take my blood!"

He succumbed to her entreaties, lowered his head as his fangs extended. His mouth hovered over her throat, feeling the heat of her flesh on his lips.

"Do it," she whispered, her voice husky with desire.

Lucille tilted her head, readied herself, eyes closing in pleasured anticipation.

"Bite me, dammit!"

Abruptly, she felt him pull away from her, peel his body off hers. She opened her eyes to see him sitting at the edge of the bed, his back to her. Abruptly he strode all the way across the room, as far from her as he could manage.

"I cannot," she heard him say. "I will not."

Lucille gasped for air, so suddenly was she pulled back from the precipice of desire.

Dracula walked back to the bed, under control now, the fangs retreated. He began to dress, aware that Lucille was hurt, angry. This only made his anger rise.

"I am no trifle for you to salve your curiosity," he said.

"I was not playing. I was serious."

"Serious or not, you do not want what you ask for."

"I do," she said fiercely.

"No." He shook his head. "Mine is not an existence to envy or desire."

"So say you. Maybe it is the way you manage that existence."

"Possibly." The admission put a damper on his ire. "But mark my words. You do not want what you ask for."

"You said that." She turned to dress herself, lifted the negligee, then bitterly tossed aside the fribble with some vitriol and, instead, wrapped herself in the coverlet. She put herself in front of him, looked him in the eyes.

"You've had power, in one form or another, most of your life. You also know what it is like to have no power at all. I refer to your imprisonment under the Turks. In my world an intelligent woman is no better than a horse that can talk or a dog that dances. We are treated as an accessory, a trinket for some man. Even you regard me as a 'mere' woman when it comes to 'manly' things like combat."

"I did n—I regret that."

"But you and every other man believe it. I receive no respect for my mind, my innate talents. That changed with the war. That changed the day that I first held a gun in my hand. The first man who saw me point a weapon at him, I saw the respect in his eyes."

"Might you have mistaken fear for respect?" Dracula asked.

"Fear suffices. But this regard will end once the war does."

"There is always another war," he said

"No doubt. But I have seen how men appraise you. They see your power. You receive respect," she said.

"Again you err. It is fear! And disgust."

"As I said, I'll take the exchange." She stepped into his chest, bared her neck again. "Bite me."

She leaned into him, close, her breath a sirocco on his face. He stared at the exposed vein, ran his fingers along the blue tributary, felt the thrumming pulse under his thumb.

Lucille held her breath in suspense as he wrapped one arm about her waist, pulled her tight against him; the other hand cupped her head, and fingers snaked into the tangle of her hair.

The bedroom door flew open. Her father rushed into the room.

"Lucy!" he cried. "Prince!"

"Father, I am of age and—"

Van Helsing saw the embrace, his daughter wearing only a blanket. It gave him pause, then he remembered his mission.

"The Germans!" he spat. "They are at our door! We must flee!"

He dashed back out the door. Dracula and Lucille followed.

She darted into her own room, snatched her dress and shoes, dropped the coverlet, and slipped the garment over her head on the run. The cloth momentarily blinded her, and she almost collided with the banister. She paused on the stairs to slide into her shoes.

Her father and Dracula were at the front window. There was a loud clatter and clank outside, melding with an engine's roar.

"The SS are here," her father intoned. "They are—"

He was interrupted as the adjacent wall exploded inward with an eruption of brick, mortar, and lath. The front end and cannon barrel of a tank protruded through the debris.

Dracula suddenly found himself bathed in the blazing sun. He recoiled, fell to the floor as his skin smouldered, protecting his eyes with his forearm.

Lucille and her father gripped him by the arms and dragged the vampire out of the light. They weaved around the wreckage, broken furniture, and rubble. Plaster dust hung in the air like a fog.

Behind them, soldiers began clambering over the tank and through the breach in the wall. Lieutenant Guth led the charge, pointing at Dracula and shouting, "Get him!" Dracula, revived enough to help the Van Helsings reach the clinic, slammed the door behind them.

Inside, the vampire shoved a heavy cabinet across the entrance with such ease it might have been a shoe box. Lucille and her father pushed the chaise to block the door to the anteroom.

Lucille turned to the Prince, examining his face, its skin burnt and blistering. "Does it hurt?" she asked. He shook his head, but it was a lie.

Her father rushed to his desk, put a shoulder to it, and rolled it to the wall on its casters. A trapdoor was revealed underneath.

"Hurry!" the old man commanded as he tried to lift the hatch. Lucille lent a hand, and the door flopped open.

The clinic door rattled with a pounding from the other side. Dracula helped Lucille to the stairs that gaped under the trapdoor.

The anteroom door gave way with a crash, fell onto the chaise. Five German soldiers scrambled over the door like it was a bridge.

Dracula charged the invading SS with open arms, driving them back. He glanced back at the Van Helsings.

"Run!" he shouted. "Now! Go!"

Lucille hesitated, but her father dragged her down. She fought her father and started back up the stairs, but Dracula kicked the trapdoor shut on top of them. The falling door struck Lucille in the head and knocked her unconscious.

The soldiers massing against Dracula had swelled in number. A dozen men tried to push their way into the room, packed together like a rugby scrum.

The vampire was being forced back, his feet finding no purchase on the floor, skidding across the hardwood. In an instant, he was overwhelmed. The soldiers piled upon him and he was buried under the dozen bodies.

With a surge of strength, he lifted the entire Nazi mob and scattered them about the room like tenpins.

Dracula rose from the floor, eyes becoming bloodshot, fangs growing. He stood before his enemy in all his fiendish glory, ready for carnage.

As he stepped toward them the clinic wall suddenly caved in. A half-track leapt into the room with another avalanche of brick and plaster.

Sunlight fell upon the vampire once more. He screamed in pain, curled into a protective fetal ball.

A steel net was hauled out of the bed of the half-track and thrown over Dracula's prostrate body, his skin smoking and burning. They rolled him in the mesh over and over until he was barely visible amid the tangle of steel cable.

Guth climbed onto the vehicle and shouted orders. His men scurried to bind Dracula in the net. It took the twelve and more to hoist the heavy steel cocoon and toss it into the rear of the half-track.

The smell of burning skin permeated the air.

"Cover it with the tarp," Guth instructed. "Orders are not to kill it."

This was done. The half-track backed out of the demolished house and drove across the yard to the road. The vampire's howls of pain and outrage could be heard over the metallic chatter of the vehicle's treads.

Lucille and her father watched this from a gazebo that fronted the yard across the street and a few houses down from the Van Helsing home. They were crouched under the gazebo floor, peering through the latticed slats. She could only watch helplessly as the damned Germans destroyed her home and captured the Prince. For a moment she even mourned what she had angrily fled so many times. This had been her home.

After Lucille had been rendered unconscious, her father had carried her halfway through the escape tunnel until she awakened enough to walk on her own. She tried to go back to help Dracula, but a breathless and fatigued Van Helsing had already collapsed the tunnel behind them with previously rigged falls.

The pursuing Germans were at this very moment in disarray as they found their passage blocked. They assumed that the tunnel ran true, and once aboveground, they drew a straight line from that assumption and raided the abandoned barn directly across the street from the Van Helsing house. But her wily father had designed the tunnel so that it angled after the collapse and led to a nearby property.

The Germans swarmed over the house, searching and finding weapons but also carrying away the van Helsing possessions like thieves. After a while the soldiers gave up and left two guards behind. Lucille helped her father crawl out from their hiding place. They crept through the neighbour's yard to the nearby garage where they kept a getaway car.

During their entire escape, Lucille's thoughts focused on the plight of Dracula, the man she now thought she loved.

FROM THE DESK OF
ABRAHAM VAN HELSING

(Translated from the Dutch)

My initial and worst fear was that the Prince might assault my dear daughter as he did poor Lucy Westenra. But as life has taught me repeatedly, your worst fear can metastasize into an even more tortuous nightmare. I think that Lucille has become attached to, no, is infatuated with that devil. Nothing has been said, but I have eyes and a father knows. And it vexes me in the extreme. True, he has proven himself not to be the bloody butcher I encountered before, well, except when unleashed upon the Germans. Around our circle of conspirators he has behaved like . . . well, a human—a rather erudite, engaging gentleman of culture and probity.

Still, a relationship with my daughter, in any form, is an anathema to me. It cannot continue. It must not. But I cannot broach the subject with Lucille. I know my daughter. If I forbid their communion she will defy me just out of spite.

This is all a moot point, of course, if we do not free him. I am torn about my duty here. Do I rescue the vampire? Where is my responsibility? As of this moment I am only going through the motions, and I think Lucille suspects my lack of dedication to our cause.

Oh, what have I wrought?

FROM THE WAR JOURNAL OF
J. HARKER

(transcribed from shorthand)

JUNE 4, 1941

Only resolution and habit can allow me to make an entry in this journal tonight. I am too miserable, too low-spirited, too sick of the world, including life itself; I would not care if I heard this moment the whispering wings of the Angel of Death. Lately she has been flapping those grim wings with success all over Europe, and I can feel her dark shadow pass over my soul.

I watched the half-track rumble away from the ruins of the Van Helsing residence, then the much slower tank followed by a lorry full of SS. I knew Dracula was in the half-track, bundled in some net-like material. I had seen his capture. But of Lucy and her father's status I was woefully ignorant. I can only assume they were carried away.

I had failed.

Riding the Sokol to within sight of the Van Helsing home, I had seen the arrival of the German Army vehicles and the encirclement by the soldiers. I parked the motorcycle and dismounted to watch from behind a copse of dogwood.

Cursing myself for my tardy arrival, I could do nothing to help the dear Lucy. Or her father. Or anyone else, for that matter. I was a complete failure. If I had not spent so long at the cafe vacillating, been so dilatory in my progress. If I had just ridden faster. If, if, if . . . What was I to do now?

I sit here in a dank grain storage silo, my only companion a pair of bold rats. My misery envelops me just as the fog blankets the farmland outside this pitiful sanctuary.

Too late. Too late to save Renfield. Too late to warn Mihaly. Too late for dear Lucy. Too late, too late, too late. Is this to be my sad epigram?

DATED: 4 JUNE 1941
TO: CSS REINHARD HEYDRICH, RSHA, REICHSFUHRER-SS
FROM: SS MAJOR WALTRAUD REIKEL
CC: HEINRICH HIMMLER, REICHSFUHRER-SS
(via telegram)

MOST SECRET

WE HAVE IT STOP.

FROM THE WAR JOURNAL OF
J. HARKER

(transcribed from shorthand)

JUNE 5, 1941

What follows I either saw for myself or I was able to gather from eyewitnesses:

Pavel was working at his garage. I was not aware of his civilian occupation, but it appeared that he operated an auto repair service with his uncle. He was under an old Citroen, removing the oil pan, talking to the owner of the ancient car, a Frantisek Zeklos, who was recounting the small avalanche that had ruined his undercarriage. He had been coming around a mountain curve and suddenly encountered a suitcase-sized chunk of granite. The choice of a fifty-foot drop on one side of the road or a collision with the mountain wall did not sit well with the driver, so he tried to straddle the rock and, in doing so, cracked his oil pan, leaving a black snail track all the way into town.

"Like Hansel and Gretel laying out bread crumbs," Pavel commented from under the vehicle. When he received no reply, he glanced to where the shoes of old Frantisek had been. Instead he saw the black boots of an SS soldier. Turning his head, he could see three other pairs of the same boots. They surrounded the car.

In anticipation of this very eventuality, Pavel made a habit of hiding a pistol in the undercarriage of any vehicle he worked on. First thing he did with every job. He reached for the Belgian pistol he had stowed atop a leaf spring. Hands gripped his ankles and yanked him out from under the Citroen. Before he could raise the pistol, one of those boots stomped on his gun hand.

There followed a succession of kicks and blows that left Pavel bloody and unconscious. He then was shackled and taken to Bran Castle.

Pavel's comrade, Farkas, was working a huge pillow of dough at his brother-in-law's bakery, cutting and setting yeasty lumps into bread pans. His job also provided useful intelligence for the Resistance, as his in-law was one of the local provisioners to the SS unit at the castle, plus the Rumanian garrison in Brasov.

At that moment a fat Rumanian Corporal was stuffing *gogosi* into what seemed to be too tiny a mouth to feed such a massive bulk.

"So, how many soldiers in this new gun battery?" Farkas asked.

"Who cares?" *Gogosi* number fourteen disappeared into that bottomless gastronomic pit.

"I can maybe help you out, slice the bread a little thinner. Fewer loaves used. Maybe some left over to do with what you like, sell, eat, barter. Another *gogosi*?"

"Don't mind if I do." His reach for another was interrupted by the sudden crash as the front and back doors of the bakery simultaneously flew open.

Farkas knew what was up and dashed for the side door, threw it open. An SS trooper stood in the way. Farkas darted back into the bakery, knocked one German against an oven. The soldier howled with pain as his face met hot steel. Two soldiers came after Farkas. He shouldered one to the floor, gave the other a swipe of his forearm. This man stumbled and fell against the upright mixer. As one arm became jammed into the giant bowl, the spinning hook snatched the Nazi's arm and pulled the rest of the man into the bowl, where his head was instantly crushed, cutting off his unearthly scream.

Farkas sprinted for the front door, where the passage had been momentarily left unguarded.

But more Germans were waiting outside and quickly leapt upon him. He was summarily beaten and hauled away.

Anka, the despotic grande dame of the partisans, spent her days on her hands and knees before the men she held in contempt. She had finagled a job at the castle with the cleaning service hired by the Nazis. While feigning that she had no understanding of the German language, every day she scrubbed floors, keeping an ear out for any intelligence she might overhear. Dipping her scrub brush into her bucket, manning a mop or dusting rag, even cleaning the toilets, she listened to orders, gossip, and cross talk among the clerks, officers, and underlings. She emptied wastebaskets into bags that she carried to her flat in town. There she perused them at her leisure with a glass of middling cognac.

This day she was listening to a young Lieutenant bemoan his fate here in the arsehole of Rumania while his sister's boyfriend was assigned to a cushy posting in Nordhausen, guarding prisoners at an A4 rocket plant.

"What is an Aggregat Four rocket?" his typist asked.

"Part of the Vergeltungswaffen" was the answer.

Anka turned to her fellow washwoman, Dumitra, and they exchanged glances, both noting this bit of information.

Anka heard the click of boot heels on the tiled floor before she saw them, two SS ruffians striding down the hallway toward her. Something about their demeanor aroused her sense of paranoia. The jackbooted feet came to a stop inches from her bucket.

"Anka Pascu? You are under arrest. Stand up."

She nodded obediently, having perfected the obsequious manner of the servant class, set her brush back into the bucket, and slid her hand deep into the grey water. And drew it out holding a Walther PPK.

Two shots. Two dead men. Just like she had practiced on scarecrows out at Mugur's farm. Head shots instead of pumpkins.

She ran. A startled armed guard at the end of the hall raised his rifle. She shot him on the run and leapt over the falling body.

Once outside, she ran across the courtyard. She was sprightly for an old woman. Four years before she had won second prize in a Budapest jitterbug contest. A courier returning from the rail station on his bicycle was just entering as Anka ran to the gate. She shot him, snatched the bike before it fell to the ground, and pedalled away before the other German soldiers in the courtyard could respond. Guns were fired, she felt a slap on her upper arm, but she soon disappeared down the road and around the bend.

Vehicles gave chase, and they found the bicycle, a trace of blood on the handlebars, a half mile from the castle, tossed into a ditch. An extensive search found no trace of the crack-shot scrubwoman in what must have been a total embarrassment for the commanding officer.

I did not witness any of Anka's exploits. I did see the capture of Farkas, another event where I was too late to warn or help. It was becoming a dreadful habit.

Parking the Sokol in a narrow alley, I had walked three blocks to the bakery. When I saw that the Germans had already arrived, I posed as a customer at the cobbler's across the street, tarrying at the window as if I were interested in a new pair of brogans, even pretending to examine the heels of my own shoes. I had a leg cocked back and was doing just that when the Germans not occupied in the pummeling of poor Farkas began to round up the various onlookers, including me.

"You!" One of the Jerries pointed at me. I acted as though I did not hear or see the Kraut and started walking away as nonchalantly as I could manage.

"Halt!" was the next command, but by then I was already turning the corner. As soon as I was out of sight I ran, hearing a lot of German shouting behind me. I dared not glance back, and I felt the muscles between my shoulder blades tighten in expectation of a bullet.

Coming to the next corner, I shot a look behind me and saw two Nazis running after me, both armed. There were a few more shouts of "Halt!" I responded by increasing my dispatch, ducking into the next alley. My motorcycle was two blocks away and I was far enough ahead to give myself the confidence that I would make it in time to escape. Except for unforeseen impediments . . .

By turning my head to check on my pursuers, I did not spot the loose cobblestones in my path and an abrupt twist of my ankle sent me sprawling. I scrambled back to my feet, but my ankle instantly proved weak, unstable, and most painful. I saw that I had lost my advantage on the Jerries. They were almost upon me. And one was raising his rifle. There is nothing more dispiriting than seeing the business end of a gun's sights aligned upon one's face.

The two Krauts were only a few metres away, one of them keeping me dead in his sights, to use a phrase. My thoughts turned to capture, name, rank, and so on, meeting up with my old mate Renfield, maybe, seeing Lucy once more before my execution, all that romantic tommyrot.

These were my defeatist thoughts, when the angled door of the coal chute that the Jerries had just passed eased up and opened. A figure stepped out into the alley and aimed a ridiculously long-barrelled pistol at the backs of my pursuers. Lucy!

The surprise must have been evident on my face, as the Kraut aiming at me began to turn. Lucy simply put the gun to the back of his head and whispered in German.

"Drop your weapon."

Which he did. The other German stopped in his tracks. He whirled about, went for his own gun. Lucy shook her head at him.

"Do not move or your friend here has his brains scooped out with a nine-millimetre," she told him, and he let his rifle clatter to the pavement. "What do you think, Jonathan? Did that sound like Cagney or Bogart?"

She laughed, and I chuckled to myself as I scurried forward, limping only slightly, all my pain forgotten at the sight of this brave, brazen woman. I picked up both rifles; neither man was carrying a pistol.

The rifle that but a few seconds earlier had been trained on me was now pointed at my enemy.

"Lucy . . ." I began. "I'm so . . . relieved to see you."

"Not now." She prodded one German and gestured to the coal chute door with her gun. "Down," she ordered.

One Kraut moved quickly to obey. The other was a bit recalcitrant and I gave him a little incentive with the butt of my rifle. *His* rifle, if you want to be picky.

Professor Van Helsing was waiting at the bottom of the stairs that ran next to the chute. He also was armed, and he kept a vigilant eye on our captives as they descended. The basement was clean, smelling of mould and tobacco. Old furniture and a dusty glass display case lined one wall.

I shut the door behind us. Lucy and her father made the Jerries strip out of their uniforms, and I tied their hands and feet with some lengths of curtain cord found in a pile of mouldy draperies lying in a corner.

"Thank God you're safe." My excitement was barely containable. "I thought you had been captured. Or worse."

"We're not safe yet," Lucy said.

"We have to leave town, double-quick," her father added.

A bit of the drapery material was used to gag the Krauts, and we secured them to a support beam.

"Now it is but a matter of waiting for dark and slipping out of here," Lucy said.

"Dracula was captured, was he not?" I asked, knowing the answer.

"Yes." I could hear the defeat in Lucy's voice.

"What do you think we should do to correct that?" I asked. Lucy was silent, deep inside herself. The Professor answered me.

"We will free him," Van Helsing said. "And our comrades. But first we must recruit some assistance."

"We will free them," Lucy whispered, swearing an oath more to herself than to us.

The silence that followed was interrupted by muffled shouting and the slamming of doors. This agitated our prisoners, and Lucy tapped one on the head with the butt of her Luger while I went to the coal door and eased it open to peer outside.

The SS were searching the alley, checking every back door. Lucy appeared beside me. We both saw our predicament. We were minutes from being discovered.

"Looking for these two, I suppose," she said, putting it succinctly.

"This way," Van Helsing said, heading up the basement stairs.

"The Germans were out front, too," Lucy cautioned.

"Hold on," I said. "Might we use a diversion?"

Digging into my pockets I found the leather case in which I carried a half-dozen pencil fuses, selecting the shortest one, a thirty-second timer (the device was coded black, nominally a ten-minute time delay, but some rather awkward field experiences had taught us otherwise). From another pocket I withdrew a pocket incendiary, replaced and inserted the new fuse.

I had Lucy nudge open the coal door, made sure that the Nazis were preoccupied, cracked the fuse glass, and tossed the device across the alley onto the roof of a garage. The explosion quickly followed. Not loud, but enough to focus our enemy's attention. Flames immediately leapt into the air, black smoke joining the conflagration. I thought how that old sod Renfield would have enjoyed this moment.

Putting that melancholy reflection aside, I locked the coal door behind us and followed the Professor and Lucy up the stairs. The door at the top opened into a tobacconist's shop. The proprietor, a tiny, swarthy man, was at the establishment window on the lookout.

We joined him. The squad of German soldiers on the street was in a state of perturbation, accompanied by a measure of shouting and confusion. Then, en masse, they all followed a Sergeant as he led them around the corner and out of sight.

"You go now!" the tobacconist whispered urgently.

And we did just that, fled out the door, across and down the narrow street to where the Van Helsings ducked into a snazzy Polish Fiat 508 that my old flatmate, Wyndham Standing, would have given his clock weights for.

And now we had a new problem. How to get out of Brasov? We knew an alert would be out and the roads heavily guarded, and the soldiers would most likely have our names and descriptions in hand. We were in a bit of a pickle.

. . . his unfortunate Private Life. EB wants to marry. Herr Wolf tried to explain to her that he has another wife—Germany! But EB wants children. Herr Wolf would rather not, especially if they have a chance of taking after their mother. She is as malleable as wax and Herr Wolf can shape her at his Will, and she is amenable to this, desires it even. Dear Tschapperl is a fine Companion, but her blood should not be passed on. And Herr Wolf is sure that his own is contaminated by that encounter so long ago that left him with the scald.

June 6

Herr Wolf needs more anti-gas pills and Neo-Balestol. Must remind CS.

Joke of the day—courtesy of HL. A rabbi and a Catholic priest live across from each other and are very competitive. One day the priest buys a new Mercedes 260. The rabbi sees this and sells his Ford and buys a new Rolls-Royce. The priest sees the Rolls and invites his congregation over and they parade around the Mercedes three times and sing chants for an hour. The rabbi calls the synagogue, gathers his people, and they march around the Rolls five times and they sing for two hours.

The priest watches this and blesses his Mercedes with holy water.

So the rabbi cuts three inches off the Rolls' tailpipe. Hahaha. Very funny.

Must find a more suitable mate for Blondi. JT's Shepherd has shown no interest after Blondi bared her teeth at him upon his first approach.

D presented Herr Wolf with a new painting by von Stuck. Very evocative and stimulating.

Last night another private screening of Snow White and the Seven Dwarfs. What this Disney fellow does with his animation! It far outperforms what actors can communicate. The Dwarfs—nothing but outstanding! One can only wonder what

Herr Disney could do with <u>The Nibelungenlied</u> . . . Siegfried . . . –Must tell J to enlist the man in such an endeavour after the war) Herr Disney must have Teutonic blood. I will have HH do some research on the man.

The preparations for Barbarossa proceed with dispatch while the under-equipped Brits fall back in Syria and Iraq. Bloody little battle after bloody little battle. The Drunkard C's hegemony in the Middle East is dissipating. The Japanese are keeping the Americans busy looking across the Pacific, diverting a good many resources away from Europe to our benefit.

But behind the progress of the war, Herr Wolf has a Shadow looming over his shoulder, awaiting news from Brasov.

Herr Wolf cannot concentrate. His mind is in Tumult over the capture of the Creature. This lack of Focus has become a handicap during the vortex of activity surrounding him. The possibility of the Creature's actual existence staggers the Mind that such Supernatural Beings still exist among us Mortals. Could there be more? Not of the same Species necessarily, but other Mythical Entities. There may finally be Proof that the ancient Gods of the North actually walked the earth. To think that mighty Thor is not just a tale told to children, but as much our history as Chlothar, Odilo, and Otto the Great.

"What demon's art lies hidden here? What store of magic stirred this up?"

But Herr Wolf is presumptive. A study must be made, a strict examination to validate the authenticity of our discovery. Orders have been issued to do this and the results of this analysis to be forwarded with dispatch.

Still . . .

EXCERPTED FROM THE UNPUBLISHED NOVEL
THE DRAGON PRINCE AND I
by Lenore Van Muller

The horse was old, swaybacked to the point that its belly nearly touched the ground. It slowly trod forward with plodding steps. There were bald spots where the poor beast's hair had fled, possibly to get somewhere, anywhere, faster than this hoofed snail. The pitiful beast walked with its head down, weary, nearsighted, or bored with the route it had shambled along hundreds of times.

The farmer matched his horse, bent over, neck craned so far down that in order to see what was ahead he had to peer through a thicket of eyebrows, the grey hairs like a pile of steel shavings. The lump between his shoulders only emphasised the curve of his ancient spine.

The horse placed one deliberate hoof in front of another. When it was creeping through Brasov to make a delivery, children would dart around and around the wagon, circling the driver and his motley old nag, mocking both. The old man did not mind; these were the children of the farmers and vendors where he delivered his potatoes every week, and his customers were the only family he had left, besides his loyal nag.

His was a slow journey, but he and the horse completed the trip and that was all that mattered. Potatoes do not go sour or melt in the sun. A few hours one way or another made no difference to the tubers. Besides, the cycles of nature were also slow and steady, as every man who tilled the land knew.

Farmer Volara was a familiar sight to the Rumanian Army sentries stationed at the outskirts of town. It amused the old man that none of the soldiers were a bit curious as to why a potato farmer was leaving town with a full load of potatoes rather than an empty wagon. If stopped, he had a ready lie in his back pocket: seed potatoes, the eye sprouts poking out of the grey-brown heap like yellow-green porcupine quills.

The trip into town from farm to market or back took his old mare, Cincinel, three hours. Sometimes more.

The entire ride was misery to Lucille and Harker. So, when the rattletrap wagon finally came to a stop next to the old and equally swaybacked barn, both of them sprang out from under the pile of spuds like clowns out of a dual jack-in-the-box.

Both were covered in dirt, looking like chimney sweeps, joints aching from having to lie inert for so long. It did not help that the cart's springs had been wrecked since the horse was a colt; every pebble and crack in the road had bruised and battered them. Her equally filthy father had to be helped out of the wagon. He could barely walk, and Harker supported the old man like one aided a drunken friend.

"I'll never look at potato pierogis the same way again," Lucille declared.

As they were brushing themselves off, Anka stepped out of the barn. She had one arm in a makeshift sling.

"Good," she said to them. "You made it through the checkpoints."

She turned to where the sun was riding the crest of the mountains, ready to dive out of sight for the evening.

"As soon as the sun is down we have someone to take you to the Black Sea. From there you can proceed to Russia."

"We're not running away," Lucille said with some finality. "We're going back. To the castle."

"Why would you do this?" Anka asked.

"To rescue our compatriots," Van Helsing said. He moved to examine Anka's arm but she pushed him away with a scowl.

"I have to free Renfield," Harker added.

"The monster also?" Anka asked.

"He fought with us," Lucille told her. "For us."

"Not for me," Anka said.

"We were hoping you would assist us," Van Helsing told Anka. "With men, weapons."

"Not for the vampire. As for the rest, it is hopeless." Anka was adamant.

"What about Pavel, Farkas? They're your people," Harker confronted the woman.

"They knew the risks." Anka turned away, not able to look them in the eye.

"Well, Sergeant Renfield is my responsibility, and I intend to remove him from that prison." Young Harker set his jaw, not appearing so boyish anymore.

The old farmer drove his wagon into the barn and unhitched the ancient nag.

Anka led Lucille, her father, and Harker into the adjacent house. It was a tiny stone cottage that seemed to be only one room, the iron stove squatting on one side, the bed against the other wall. Through the murky window Lucille could see the privy in the backyard.

Her father confronted Anka. "I know you have a personal antipathy toward Prince Dracula," he began. "But can you not put that aside long enough to fight a greater enemy? Use him like you would a rifle. You hold no animus toward any bullet that kills a German."

"Don't try to befuddle me with your philosophies," Anka told him. "He is an abomination to man and God. Let him rot in the castle he built."

"Then we will get help somewhere else," Lucille said. But where that help was, she had no clue. She felt hope leave her like water down a drain.

"Where?" Harker, ever the master of the obvious, asked.

"I have an idea on that," Van Helsing said. Lucille and Harker both turned to him with hope in their eyes.

DATED: 10 JUNE 1941
TO: CSS REINHARD HEYDRICH, RSHA, REICHSFUHRER-SS
FROM: SS MAJOR WALTRAUD REIKEL
CC: HEINRICH HIMMLER, REICHSFUHRER-SS

MOST SECRET

INTERVIEW CONDUCTED BY MAJOR W. REIKEL, INTERVIEW
SPECIALIST CORPORAL SCHRECK, & LIEUTENANT GUTH. Also
present is your Company scribe. A military cinematographer
with 35mm camera records the proceedings.

INTERVIEW TRANSCRIPT:

The Subject is secured to the wall of his cell with
large railroad spikes driven through the palm of each
hand, thus suspending him off the floor. As a further
precaution, his feet are shackled together and secured
by a chain to a ring bolted to the floor.

This was done while the Subject was unconscious,
presumed a result of his exposure to the sun.

A small wooden platform forty-five centimetres high
has been constructed and set in front of the Subject.
This allows access to the hanging body and close study
of the Subject. Burnt skin hangs from the Subject's
face and the parts of the body not covered by clothing.
Strips of this epidermis have been removed, along with
an equal sample of living tissue. These samples have
been forwarded to Berlin for analysis.

The Subject regained consciousness during this last procedure.

MAJOR R.: It is difficult for me to believe that you are what they say you are. Perhaps a test?

CORPORAL S. is cued by the Major and leaves the interrogation room.

Major R. makes an attempt to pry open the Subject's mouth to examine the teeth using the handle of his SS dagger. The Subject resists--successfully.

MAJOR R.: I see no fangs. Are you able to transform yourself into a bat? I have so many questions. And we will have them all answered. Eventually.

The questions are from a list sent from Berlin.

MAJOR R.: But first the test.

Corporal S. enters, dragging one of the captured local insurrectionists behind him. This prisoner identifies himself only by the appellation "Pavel." This man has undergone intensive interrogation and is physically debilitated, losing one eye in the process of his interview. That aperture appears to have been cauterized. Despite this, he still maintains a veneer of defiance.

MAJOR R.: (addressing the Subject) Legend has it that you have a taste for blood.

The Subject does not respond. Major R. passes his SS dagger to Corporal S.

The Subject struggles against his restraints, cries out in protest. Non-verbal grunts.

Corporal S. takes in one hand the hair of the man calling himself "Pavel" and stretches the man's head back, baring the throat.

The prisoner "Pavel" has his throat cut. Exsanguination proceeds. Corporal S. holds the prisoner upright by the hair on his head. The blood is caught in a tin receptacle by Lieutenant G. The prisoner's blood more than fills the cup. The bleeding continues for a brief moment until the cessation of life. The corpse is dropped. The receptacle is passed to the Major.

Major R. steps onto the wooden platform and holds the receptacle of blood in front of the Subject's face. Major R. orders the cinematographer to come closer. The cinematographer suggests switching lenses instead. This is agreed upon.

The Subject rears away from the container of blood. But it does demonstrate an involuntary reaction. The Subject's eyes become bloodshot, caused by a sudden swelling of the eyeball capillaries. The Subject's eyeteeth--cuspids, or upper canines--lengthen into fangs by three to five centimetres; a proper measurement was not possible at the moment. This seems to be an extrusion from the alveolar and not a growth.

The Subject tries to rear away from the goblet, struggles against his restraints, loosening one of the spikes holding him to the wall. The left.

MAJOR R.: Well, mirabile dictu, a true vampire. The Fuhrer will be pleased.

Major R. steps off the platform. Corporal S. is ordered to reset the loosened spike. Corporal S. ascends the wooden platform with hammer in hand.

With a loud, somewhat animalistic outcry, the Subject wrenches the left-hand spike out of the wall, brings it around in a backhanded manner, and inserts selfsame spike into the right eye socket of Corporal S.

Corporal S. reacts with his own very loud cry, covers the wound with his hands, and drops his hammer in the process.

The Subject shakes loose the spike and uses the now-free hand to pull at the other restraint holding his right hand to the wall.

Your Transcriber observed what follows from a viewing point outside the cell.

Major R. steps to the opposite wall of the interrogation room and opens the shutters recently constructed for just this eventuality.

Sunlight floods the room. The Subject is bathed in the glare. The Subject recoils, cries out in what appears to be pain, covers his eyes with his free arm.

Major R. picks up the discarded hammer, retrieves the loose spike. With the assistance of Lieutenant G. and much exertion, he tears the Subject's free arm from his face and pins it to the wall. The cinematographer is also called to assist, and after repeated orders from Major R., he does as ordered. Major R. proceeds to impale the Subject's hand with the spike and secure it once again. With vigor.

Once the Subject is immobilised, the shutters are closed.

The Subject's skin is charred; smoke is observed.

Corporal S., still screaming, is removed from the room. The cinematographer, who abandoned his camera, returns to his filming position. Major R. orders the filming to cease.

MAJOR R.: (addressing the cinematographer) Develop that film as quickly as possible. Do it personally. No one else is to know of this. No one. Anyone who breaches security will suffer the fate of that one.

The corpse of the one calling himself "Pavel" is indicated.

MAJOR R.: (addressing the transcriber) Have the film sent to Berlin immediately: the negative and one copy of the transcription. One copy will be given to me. And your notes are to be destroyed in my presence. Understood? Do your job well. Remember, the Fuhrer will see this. Hitler himself.

The corpse is withdrawn. The room is locked.

FROM THE WAR JOURNAL OF
J. HARKER

(transcribed from shorthand)

JUNE 11, 1941

The beldam Anka relaxed her rigid opposition to our mission enough to help us obtain transportation. This time we travelled by tractor and wagon. As comfort comes, it was a step up—we weren't buried under a pile of potatoes, and the tractor was much faster than the farmer's glue pot candidate. Van Helsing would not tell us our destination, but having no plan myself, I went along.

We came to a stop at the base of the looming Carpathians, where another stone cottage huddled under a bluff, the back half of the house residing inside the mountain. There, we were provided with hiking packs, sturdy boots, and the proper clothing for mountaineering. Also provided was extra ammunition for Lucy's Luger and a new Thompson for me to replace the one I abandoned in Sfantu Gheorghe.

A meal was supplied by a round little woman with apple cheeks and a nimbus of white-blond hair, her age an indeterminate place between twenty and forty. I had forgotten how long it had been since I had eaten, and I ate more than my share of lamb stew and consumed most of a bottle of sour wine. We were shown blankets on the floor next to an iron stove that emanated a comforting heat. Sleep fell upon me like the flicking of a switch.

My dreams were of a man's face twisted with rage as he tried to strangle me. I awoke repeatedly, sweating, but not because of the stove. After every nightmare I slipped back into a deep sleep again and repeated the grisly cycle over and over until the morning glare of sunlight stabbing through a window rescued me from myself.

A cold breakfast was given to us by the cherubic woman, and we set upon preparing for the journey ahead. As we left, the matron of the house trotted outside and foisted onto each of us a small flour sack filled with victuals for our hike.

"There is some dried fruit, some cake, a cheese," she told us.

"Thank you so much," Lucy said. "I don't know how to repay you."

"Just stop this war before they kill my son." The vehemence from that angelic face surprised me. "God bless you," she added without irony.

And she planted a kiss on each of our cheeks. Then we were off, following a path that curled around one side of the cottage and up into the talus that skirted the towering mountains.

DATED: 13 JUNE 1941
TO: CSS REINHARD HEYDRICH, RSHA, REICHSFUHRER-SS
FROM: SS MAJOR WALTRAUD REIKEL
CC: HEINRICH HIMMLER, REICHSFUHRER-SS
(BY COURIER)

MOST SECRET

<u>SECOND INTERVIEW TRANSCRIPT</u>

INTERVIEW CONDUCTED BY MAJOR W. REIKEL, INTERVIEW
SPECIALIST CORPORAL SCHRECK. Also present is your
Company scribe. A military cinematographer with 35mm
camera records the proceedings.

The Subject's restraints have been upgraded. A chain
across his chest bolted to the wall at each side. A
shackle on each wrist, also chained and bolted to the
wall. Like a fly in a web of linked steel. In answer to
your question about security: Access to the Subject's
cell is limited, and most of this unit is not even
aware of the existence or presence of the Subject.
      MAJOR R.: Corporal, you may be excused from this
one. I know that you are still recuperating. And the
infringement on your sight from the loss of your eye
is reason enough for you to take a respite.
      The Corporal has taken to wearing a grey swath of
cloth over his wound.
      CORPORAL S.: I only need one eye to do my job, Sir.
And I am eager to help. Very eager.

The last is addressed to the Subject, who appears haggard but defiant. Since the Subject's last exposure to sunlight, the Subject has acquired a white streak in his hair, like a lightning bolt in a night sky. The Subject does not respond to the Corporal's taunt/threat. Only his eyes following our every movement give credence to his cognizance.

MAJOR R.: (addressing the Subject) Higher authority has requested more tests. I hope you don't mind. That was a lie. Actually I hope you do mind, for the Corporal's sake if nothing else.

From a satchel Major R. withdraws a garland of garlic. The garland is thrust into the Subject's face. The Subject does not respond.

MAJOR R.: Garlic does not have any effect on you?

SUBJECT: A peasant superstition. Save it for your goulash.

Major R. discards the garlic. From the same satchel he extracts a wooden crucifix, a crude hand carving of the Jesus of a light-coloured wood, affixed by brass nails to a cross of darker wood, approximately twelve centimetres by thirty.

This object is also put within a hand's breadth of the Subject's face. The Subject calmly examines the object.

SUBJECT: Would it be blasphemous to suggest that I, in my current circumstances, have a wealth of empathy with the poor fellow?

MAJOR R: So the Cross of Our Saviour does not strike you with fear and revulsion.

SUBJECT: Only the bearer of such. Another superstition disproved, I'm afraid. Created by a church attempting to demonstrate a power over something which they have absolutely no control. Their usual modus operandi. Anything to salve the fears of the multitude they cannot help.

MAJOR R.: Then I assume holy water would also produce none of the expected results.

With this statement Major R. tosses water from a vial into the Subject's face.

SUBJECT: Refreshing, but nothing more. If you could gather enough to indulge me in a bath I would appreciate it.

MAJOR R.: Interesting . . .

The Major studies the Subject for approximately three and one half minutes.

MAJOR R.: All these legends . . . tell me, can you turn yourself into a mist, seep under doors, and through the slightest crack of a window in that state? Transform into a bat and fly away? I suppose not. Otherwise you would have surely done so by now and escaped.

SUBJECT: Might the case be that I linger to enjoy your exalted company?

MAJOR R.: There are other stories. That you are immortal. Immune to bullet and blade.

MAJOR R. draws his dagger from the sheath. With his other hand he draws his pistol, a Mauser Schnellfeuer M712.

MAJOR R.: Which shall we test first?

CORPORAL S.: Let me! Sir, let me. Please, Sir, I beg of you this boon.

MAJOR R.: I suppose it would only be fair. All right. But do not become too enthusiastic. It may be another romantic fable, and our orders are to keep him alive.

CORPORAL S.: Pain only, Sir. Pain only, I swear.

Major R. turns the blade and pistol over to the Corporal. Corporal S. approaches the Subject, steps onto the wooden platform, raises the dagger to the Subject's eye. The Subject involuntarily draws away until the Subject's head strikes the wall.

MAJOR R.: Not the eyes, Corporal. I understand your urge to even the score but . . . the limbs, if you will.

Two gunshots. In quick order. Two stabs with the dagger. Equally distributed among the limbs. Right arm--stab wound in biceps area between shoulder and elbow. Left arm--bullet wound across forearm. Right leg--stab wound, upper thigh. Left leg--bullet wound, into calf.

Subject responds with a stifled cry.

Major R. studies the Subject's face.

MAJOR R.: It suffers pain. Good to know.

Inserting a finger into the wound holes made in the Subject's clothing, Major R. rips the fabric around the injured flesh.

Major R. motions the cinematographer to come in for a close recording of the affected areas.

The wounds do not bleed as such. A slight issue of a dark red, almost black, viscous fluid seeps from the holes. The wounds quickly close and seem to heal immediately. This takes approximately forty-seven minutes. Another twenty-three minutes for the scar tissue to form and disappear. The cinematographer is heard murmuring a prayer as he changes magazines.

MAJOR R.: Are you getting this? Are you? The Fuhrer will be very happy. Very happy, indeed.

The Subject glares at the Major with what could only be described as fury.

NOTE FROM MAJOR REIKEL:

In answer to your question in your last missive about the Creature's transformative powers: I think if the vampire could turn itself into a bat it would have done so and flown away by now, the windows and even the bars of the cell proving no impedance to such a creature.

Also, as per your query, continuous observation has found no instance of any alimentary processes, urine or otherwise. But time may tell.

FROM THE WAR JOURNAL OF
J. HARKER

(transcribed from shorthand)

JUNE 13, 1941

This journey through the mountains was a mite more manageable than my hike with Renfield and that cumbersome transmitter case after our calamitous parachute drop into Rumania. Van Helsing was a superlative guide, having explored the Carpathians for his research into the alpine flora used in various folk remedies. Every few yards on the mountain slopes, he managed to discover a plant worth mention. Above what he called the juniper belt, he pointed out the rose bay, lilies of the valley, pigeon chins, bird's eye, and something called pursuance.

He might have been fifty or sixty years older than I, but his eyes were as perspicacious as any youth. Spotting one bird after another, having to point them out because my own eyes had not noticed the creatures. And Lucy proved to be quite the ornithologist, recognising and naming every fowl. Thusly I became acquainted with the local titmouse, woodpecker, plover, lark, and possibly a majestic mountain eagle that sailed the air currents far over our heads.

The Professor craned his neck to marvel at the gliding birds of prey. "In the days when I was young and spry," he told me, "it was my habit to wander these mountains for amusement and edification."

"If the pace you set when you are old and infirm is any indication, I would not have lasted a mile with you back then," I commented and I meant it. My ankle was still paining me from my stumble in the Brasov alley, but I did not voice my discomfort. It would be unseemly for a young man to complain while a woman and an old man stoically pushed on.

We rarely paused for rest, ate and quenched our thirst on the trot. But the higher we climbed, the thinner the air became, and soon even the hardy old man began to seek out a spot to shelter for the night.

I had been pestering the Professor concerning our destination and our mission, but he was closemouthed on the subject, saying only that we were seeking assistance to mount a rescue. Where we would find confederates in these desolate mountains, I had no idea.

Our camp for the night was a slight declivity in the side of a cliff face with a shale overhang. We made a small fire and lay out our blankets. Van Helsing amused us with a tale of his search for Attila's tomb, the Hun and his treasure supposedly buried in these mountains, the gravediggers executed to conceal the burial place. The Hun was rumoured to have been entombed in three coffins, one of gold, one of silver, and the last of iron. A most tempting lure for treasure hunters and historians. They never found it and he seemed still intrigued about the possibility of its existence. He gave us a short biography on the man called the "Scourge of God," who delighted in war.

Lucy had been silent during the whole climb, strangely silent for such a usually forthright and voluble woman.

We supped on the contents of the flour sacks the beldam had provided. The cake, a heavy lemon affair, was delicious, moist with just the right balance of tart and sweet.

The old man ate and fell immediately into a dead sleep, snoring with a sonorous rattle that reminded one of a foraging animal. The worry that some other creature of the night might mistake it for a mating call was voiced by me, but Lucy did not bite at my conversational bait. So, I sidled over to her as she nibbled on a bit of dried fig that her father had foisted upon her. I knew what was weighing heavy on her mind.

"You are worried about him," I said.

"I know my father," she said. "By the morning he'll be marching us into the ground again. He used to tell me that the reason he married my mother was because she was the first woman who could keep apace with him when he walked down the sidewalk."

"You know who I mean," I persisted.

"My concern is not your concern."

"Ah, but it is. Since the day I met you," I said. "I would not worry too much. He is, after all, immortal."

"Not entirely. Just ask my father. And I think immortality is not necessarily an advantage under torture."

"Point well taken." This led to thoughts of what the Jerry bastards must have done to Renfield in order to make him talk.

"I'm sorry," I said.

"You have nothing to be sorry for. The fortunes of war and all that shit."

"Yes, I do," I said. "I should have kept a better eye on poor Sergeant Renfield. His capture was under my auspices, the poor daft sod."

"On a mission to rescue my people." She laid a hand on mine. "I learned a long time ago that in fighting a war, people will be lost. And one mustn't let that loss stop the fight. You cannot save everyone, and if you try you will be feckless and a failure. We must fight on. The stakes are too high to quit."

"Of course." I gripped her hand in my own and she looked me in the eye. "And we will rescue our friends. This I promise."

She nodded and went back to her meager meal. My words sounded hollow even to me.

EXCERPTS FROM UNIDENTIFIED DIARY
(translated from German)

. . . not believe that the Nazi Medical Association has yet again failed to find a test for blood that can reveal any Jewish taint. Seven years and still no Progress! Scientists? Idiots! Note—Maybe put Baron von F on this research. So far he has found nothing significant in the samples taken from the Brasov train victims and the skin samples collected at the castle Bran.

June 15

Had baked potato and linseed oil for lunch with a nice tomato salad. It is the beginning of the season and the tomatoes are exceedingly Savory.

Will order spaghetti for supper. Herr Wolf's Favorite Dish. It reminds him of the days and nights at the Osteria Bavaria. The little courtyard painted Pompeian red, the little temple in the back corner where Herr Wolf and his humble cohorts discussed Saving Germany. Transforming the World. And now we are in the process of doing just That. Some think that Herr Wolf is just after Revenge for his lowly origins and the manner in which he was treated in those early years. Oh, how those miscreants must shudder now, how they must tremble, but there is no such mundane feeling in the heart of the Man. He is just fulfilling a Destiny written by the Gods.

Herr Wolf had a bout of Meteorism. Sorry to say Dr. Koster's Anti-gas pills did little to alleviate the discomfort. And such Discomfort!

Blondi has accepted the attentions of Harras, the Shepherd! Herr Wolf has high Hopes for pups in the near future, if nothing else but to continue Blondi's Magnificent Lineage.

Herr Wolf has another reason to be exhilarated. Sitting in the dark of his private screening room with HH and watching the footage from Rumania, he was in such Thrall that his hot chocolate grew cold and the whipped cream became but a white slime and he, for a moment, forgot about his Stomach Colic. Physicians are Idiots, too!

The tests regarding garlic and the holy relics were informative, but not of interest to Herr Wolf, folktales and religious rubbish. But the healing properties displayed in response to the stabbings and gunshots—the implication is World-shattering.

IMMORTALITY!

At first Herr Wolf's thoughts were of forming an Immortal Army. Herr Wolf, like Wotan, God of War, riding before an Army of the Dead. Soldiers with the strength of ten men as proven by the first film, soldiers immune to bullets, bayonets, disease. (Ah, Pestilence! The most debilitating upon our forces) Even gas attacks! The latter Herr Wolf himself suffered under during his own military career. The Ordeal and its memory have never left him.

But after further consideration, this idea of an Army of Supermen soon lost its luster.

Immortality was not a dispensation to be handed out to the common man, the regular soldier, as if it were a canteen or haversack. Not even to the elite troops.

Immortality is Power. Power beyond the Realm and Compass of the middling man.

Who should receive such a Godlike gift?

The answer is clear.

But first—is the attribute transferable? That question must be answered.

Then the possibilities will be explored.

DATED: 16 JUNE 1941
TO: CSS REINHARD HEYDRICH, RSHA, REICHSFUHRER-SS
FROM: SS MAJOR WALTRAUD REIKEL
CC: HEINRICH HIMMLER, REICHSFUHRER-SS
(BY SPECIAL COURIER)

MOST SECRET

<u>THIRD INTERVIEW TRANSCRIPT</u>

INTERVIEW CONDUCTED BY MAJOR W. REIKEL, INTERVIEW
SPECIALIST CORPORAL SCHRECK. Also present is Company
Scribe. A military cinematographer with 35mm camera
records the proceedings.

The Subject appears more haggard than previously, is
barely able to raise his head as we enter.

Major R. speaks to Corporal S., who now wears a black
swath where his eye is missing. Major R. brandishes a
communiqué.

MAJOR R.: From the Fuhrer himself, Corporal! Your
Fuhrer!

Corporal S. snaps to attention.

MAJOR R.: Corporal, how would you like to perform a
personal service to your Fuhrer?

CORPORAL S.: I would die for him. For Germany.

MAJOR R.: You may have to do just that.

Corporal S.'s surprise is evident on his face.

CORPORAL S.: Die . . . Sir?

MAJOR R.: And return to life as an immortal. Think of it, Corporal. Immune to bullets! Stronger than you already are! You have witnessed such abilities yourself.

CORPORAL S.: How, Sir?

MAJOR R.: Make the vampire bite you.

CORPORAL S.: Bite me, Sir?

MAJOR R.: It is the way the transference works. Could you do this for your country? For your Fuhrer? Are you brave enough a man?

CORPORAL S.: I am, Sir.

MAJOR R.: To even ask is an affront to your courage. Of course you are. That is what I told Himmler.

CORPORAL S.: Himmler, Sir?

MAJOR R.: Yes, Schreck, your name is known in the very halls of the Reich Chancellery. Soon you will be honored there as a hero of the Fatherland, Corporal. Or should I say, Sergeant?

Corporal or Sergeant S. absorbs this information with a tremulous lip as Major R. approaches the Subject.

MAJOR R.: Hungry, my friend? How long has it been since you have fed? Maybe we can give you something to whet your appetite.

At the Major's direction, the Scribe and the Cinematographer leave the room. The Major joins us and locks the door behind us, leaving the Sergeant alone in the cell. We are told to observe through the bars of the door.

The Subject directs his attention toward Sergeant S., who lifts a steel crowbar he has brought with him. He raises it over the Subject, who braces for the expected blow.

But instead, the Sergeant uses the tool to pry at the spikes securing the subject. The chain across the Subject's chest is removed. Then the chains and spikes binding his hands to the wall.

The Subject falls to the floor. His ankles are still bound, but the Subject appears too weak to loose them.

Sergeant S. stands above the Subject, stands firm.

SERGEANT S.: Bite me. Make me what you are.

SUBJECT: Impossible. You have no merit.

Sergeant S. kicks the Subject.

SERGEANT S.: Bite me.

SUBJECT: I am most particular about what I put in my mouth, unlike a pederast like you.

SERGEANT S. rips off his shirt, baring his formidable torso. (It is worth noting at this point that the Sergeant is a former professional boxer of the heavyweight class, stands head and shoulders above most men, weighing at least 120 kilograms.) The Sergeant continues to kick the Subject.

SERGEANT S.: Bite me!

The Subject appears to feel the pain of each kick, but remains defiant.

MAJOR R.: Show it blood. Tempt it.

The Sergeant takes a moment to form an idea. He wears a necklace, a silver emblem of the SS runes, about his neck. Ripping the same free, Sergeant S. uses the edge of the symbol to slice his forearm. Blood seeps from the cut. Bending down to the Subject, Sergeant S. pushes the bloodied flesh toward the Subject's face.

The Subject's reaction is immediate. His fangs protrude, eyes redden. The Subject regards the Sergeant's arm with what could only be described as hunger--but restrains himself.

SERGEANT S.: Drink! DRINK, DAMN YOU!

The Sergeant grips the Subject by his hair, tries to force the Subject's face into the bloody arm.

Faster than can be seen, the Subject's hand snaps out and finds purchase in the Sergeant's neck, wrapping his fingers around the Sergeant's throat.

The Subject begins to stand. The Sergeant fights the Subject, pressing it down. Though the Sergeant outweighs the Subject at least two to one, maybe more, the Subject is able to slowly gain his feet.

Sergeant S. struggles, tries to free himself from the Subject's grip. He fails to do so, even though he uses both hands against just the one. The veins in the Sergeant's arms stand out in bold relief, the muscles bulge.

MAJOR R.: Fight it! Fight it, you dunderhead!

It is an impressive struggle, two beings of enormous strength in a physical battle of life and death.

Sergeant S. gives up that contest and wraps his large hands around the Subject's neck, attempting to strangle the Subject in turn.

NOTE: During this, the silver runes, still in the Sergeant's hand, make contact with the Subject's skin and appear to scorch the Subject's epidermis. The Subject reacts to the burning with a grunt of pain, rears away from the contact.

The Subject breaks free of the Sergeant's grasp, sinks his fangs into Sergeant S.'s neck near the jugular vein, which has gained prominence during the exertions.

MAJOR R.: You have done it, Sergeant! Success is ours! Now you must get away!

Sergeant S.'s battle to free himself becomes frantic. But his labours weaken as the Subject sucks his lifeblood.

MAJOR R.: Get away from him! That is an order! Escape, you fool!

The Subject finally pulls away. Blood drips from his fangs, drenches his chin. The Subject smiles at Major R.

SUBJECT: Thank you. I needed that.

The Subject has been transformed. No longer gaunt or haggard. Erect. Brimming with power.

MAJOR R.: Quickly now, Sergeant! Quickly!

Sergeant S., substantially weakened by the encounter, crawls toward the door. Major R. unlocks the door.

The Subject lunges for the exit. But he is held back by his ankle chains.

Major R. reaches for Sergeant S.'s hand.

The Subject pulls at his chains. They rip as if made of paper. The Subject leaps for the opened door.

Major R. drops the Sergeant's hand and slams the door shut. Just in time, as the Subject collides with the steel.

MAJOR R.: Sergeant! Come to the door!

The Subject stands between the door and the Sergeant, who is on his hands and knees.

SUBJECT: Do you think I do not know what you attempt?

With but one hand, the Subject lifts the Sergeant by the neck, completely off the floor.

SUBJECT: There is one issue you have not thought through.

The Subject throws the Sergeant against the wall. Sergeant S. falls to the floor, limp, moaning. The Subject plants a foot on Sergeant S.'s throat, applies pressure until a cracking is heard. It is apparent that the Sergeant is dead.

SUBJECT: One cannot go around leaving inferior copies of oneself behind.

Major R. dismisses the Scribe and the Cinematographer. As they exit the hallway, the Subject is heard pounding the steel door with his fists. The door has been reinforced specifically for this prisoner. The noise is most disturbing.

The Subject yells after them. "You can lead a horse to water! You can make it drink! But whether you survive the encounter is another matter entirely!"

EXCERPTED FROM THE UNPUBLISHED NOVEL
THE DRAGON PRINCE AND I
by Lenore Van Muller

After three days of trekking up and down the Carpathians, Lucille's father finally revealed the purpose of their wanderings. Their goal was to find the gypsies. The *tigani*, as some referred to the gypsies, had taken refuge in these mountains to escape the Rumanian Army's attempt to purge the entire country of their kind.

Historically they were among the original settlers of this land. The country of Rumania was named after them—the Roma, as they called themselves. But they were a minority, to be persecuted throughout the centuries. It was such hostility that had made them a secretive people—and a fierce fighting force.

Lucille found new hope in her father's announcement. If only these elusive people could be found, and found in time. But the expedition continued, up and down the narrow trails, enduring the cold winds, hot sun, and the thin air. Lucille's optimism began to fade, as they had yet to see another human outside their party, much less a gypsy.

The trio stopped at a small spring that splashed down the mountain's sheer side, a thin waterfall that trickled pleasantly over the rocks and down a cleft, then disappeared into the mountain once again. They filled their canteens and sat on the trunk of a stubborn, twisted pine that clung to the bluff, and they took the respite as a chance to sup on their diminishing rations.

"Our food won't last much longer," said Harker, the Patron Saint of the Obvious Observation.

"The area before us is vast, I know," Lucille's father remarked. "If we do not find them in the next day or so we will not find them at all. They might have fled so deep into these mountains they will not come out until the war is over."

He gazed at the peaks surrounding them. Lucille could not help but notice the dark circles under her father's eyes, his sunken cheeks, the slump of his shoulders. He was tired; his age and the strenuous march were straining what meager reserves he had left.

After their light meal, Harker excused himself for some privacy, tearing out a few blank pages from his journal. He scribbled in the damned thing at every opportunity.

Lucille turned to her father. "One more day for you, then we take you someplace safe," she told him. "Then Harker and I will continue the search."

"We will find them," her father stated. "Well, more likely they will find us."

"If we do connect with the gypsies, will they even help us?"

"We can only ask."

"They must help!" Lucille cried, desperation in her voice. "They must." She knew she sounded hysterical and muted the last phrase. She, too, was close to exhaustion.

"He is that important to you?"

"The Resistance is important to me," she said. "And he is important to the Resistance. The world is at stake, Father."

"I know what is at stake as well as you do," he chided her. "What I wonder is where your concerns lie. Freedom from oppression. Or something else? Something more personal?"

"Maybe all of those things," she said. "And more."

After a moment of silence he spoke again. "I fear for you."

"My safety?" she asked. "I think I have proved that I can take care of myself."

"You mistake the threat," he said. "The Prince appears to be cultured, civilised. But this is only a veneer. Underneath, he is like a wild beast, a lion that attacks at the first mistake of the one who arrogantly assumes to have tamed him. Even he admits to having slight control over his bestial tendencies. You are in danger every second you are with him. I know. I have seen the ruin he has left behind him, the depredation of innocent women. That you are named after one of his victims is only a cruel irony."

"The irony for me is that our search to free him only takes me farther from the Prince."

She felt sudden shame at her response. When she saw the fatherly concern in his eyes she was touched.

"I fear for your soul," he gravely concluded, then immediately apologised. "I am sorry, dear one. The old, like me, know so many sorrows and the cause of them."

They were quiet until Harker returned, and they once more set out on another goat path that wound around another mountain.

DATED: 17 JUNE 1941
TO: CSS REINHARD HEYDRICH, RSHA, REICHSFUHRER-SS
FROM: SS MAJOR WALTRAUD REIKEL
CC: HEINRICH HIMMLER, REICHSFUHRER-SS
(BY SPECIAL COURIER)

MOST SECRET

What follows is an update on our progress so far:

Our prisoner is an intransigent subject. For the last thirty-six hours he has been throwing himself against the bars and door to his cell. Repeatedly, with full strength, and without letup. His neighbours are complaining about the constant clamour--those who still have tongues in their mouths.

His fervour is such and the collision between the Creature and the steel is so forceful that it must cause the Creature great pain. Still, it persists despite any anguish it must feel. In fact, it has been reported to me that the impact is oft-times so vicious that it has dislocated a shoulder. The Creature then wrenches the dislocation back into place with its own hands. I have suffered such an injury and I can attest to the agony involved. And this has occurred more than once! Whether it was the same shoulder each time I cannot state as the eyewitnesses were so discombobulated as to be unreliable in that detail.

(For your consideration: The Creature's recuperative powers are a wonderment. It should also be noted that the spike punctures in his hands have healed completely and show not even scar tissue.)

The steel of the cell door and bars has already begun to show some distress, bending outwardly but not breaking--so far. An astonishing display of strength and resolve.

We have considered the possibility of an escape attempt, improbable as that may be (improbable becoming commonplace in this whole incident). I have set an MG34 heavy machine-gun emplacement at the end of the corridor near the Creature's cell. The machine-gun crew is supplemented by rotating squads of my personal SS. This is a twenty-four-hour detail.

There was a problem with further examination of the Creature, since it is for the moment unrestrained within the confines of its cell. So I devised an assault that would put the Creature back under my control.

In order for you to understand our problem: The window that allowed sunlight into the cell and served as our only control over the creature has been obscured. The vampire has stuffed the aperture with the late Corporal's blouse.

Two of my best men descended by rope down the outside of the castle. At the cell window they waited for my signal.

The timing was coordinated with the declination of the sun's rays. While I approached the cell door, the Creature watched me with a superior attitude, inquiring whether there was another German for his feasting on the menu today.

I ignored the jocosity and gave the order to proceed.

At that command, the two outside soldiers reached through the cell window for the obstruction that blocked the sunlight. The obstruction was subsequently removed and the light entered the cell to fill a major part of the room.

The Creature was forced to retreat to the one corner still in shadow.

We took the opportunity to fling open the cell door and two of my men dragged out Corporal Schreck's body. The door was immediately shut and secured.

Again the Creature quipped, thanking us for removing the corpse, commenting that leaving the body in his cell was unhygienic.

I was not interested in the Creature at the moment.

My attention was drawn toward the late Corporal, more specifically what he held in his clenched fist. The SS medallion he so cherished was still clasped in the dead man's hand. I pried it from his cold fingers and examined it. There was nothing out of the ordinary about the necklace, two centimetres by three, and a rather plain execution of the SS runes resembling two bolts of lightning. There was no indication of a manufacturer's stamp, just the notation stamped on the back that the material was 90 percent silver.

I turned my attention back to our prisoner, studying the burned impression of the SS runes still apparent upon his neck. This had obviously been made when the Corporal had tried to strangle him with the medallion still in Schreck's palm.

The resulting burn mark has not healed as have the other wounds he suffered in the struggle to free himself--cuts and abrasions as he tore his shackles from his wrists and ankles. There are no signs at all of these wounds, some deep, as demonstrated by healing of the spike-pierced hands.

Yet the burn mark remains.

Silver.

I have a theory--and with it a plan to subdue this Creature to our bidding.

FROM THE WAR JOURNAL OF
J. HARKER

(transcribed from shorthand)

JUNE 17, 1941

Lucy and I are both worried about her father. Another fruitless day of meandering about these mountain trails, some not suitable for a goat, much less an old man and a woman, no matter their innate hardiness. He is a man of iron nerve, indomitable resolution, self-command, and vigor, but his age has become a factor, and he is quite knackered.

Our rest stops have become more frequent, necessitated by Professor Van Helsing's shortness of breath, which, despite his denials, is not entirely caused by the thin air of our elevation. By my map, we have climbed to over fifteen hundred metres today.

Watching Lucy care for her father has shed a new light on her character; her tender ministrations reveal a solicitude and sensitivity I have not seen before, a feminine side to the fierce Amazon she usually presents. That this woman contains all these aspects in such a becoming form has only heightened my ardour. What occurred before I must admit might have been more of an infatuation, a momentary calf love, if you will, caused by such intimacy at a vulnerable moment for both of us. But now my affection has matured with my knowledge of the woman.

How to express this newfound emotional state, that is the question I must answer. And soon. Before Lucy and the Prince are reunited.

We stopped this afternoon inside a dense copse of gnarled, wind-tortured pines. Dr. Van Helsing needed assistance to even sit, and I could see that Lucy was also spent. I, too, was tired, sore of muscle, my ankle now swollen. But I was even more exhausted by how unproductive our search had been thus far.

Lucy agreed with me. She was pleading with the Professor.

"I'm sorry, Father, but this is a useless endeavour," she told him. "Tomorrow we leave the mountains, go someplace for you to rest. Then we can reassess our plans."

"We will never find the gypsies, ambling about like three blind mice, Professor," I added.

"You do not find gypsies," the Professor began his epigram again.

"They find you," a voice said from the shadows in the trees.

To our extreme surprise, the speaker stepped into view. It was Ouspenkaya, the gypsy leader I had met during the train rescue of his people.

He whistled and from behind trees and rocks there appeared a dozen armed gypsies. How we had been surrounded without being alerted in any fashion, I do not know. I had not seen or heard anything of their approach.

We were led back the way we had come, about a kilometre, on the same trail, the gypsies relieving us of our backpacks. That small courtesy gave me much relief, and my step became so much lighter that I forgot the misery I had been experiencing just minutes before.

At a cluster of oak scrub, a mass of bushes we had passed without a glance earlier that day, Ouspenkaya parted the foliage as if it were a curtain, and his men slipped through, into a hidden cleft in the rock.

He gave orders to a pair of his fellows to wipe away any tracks for a kilometre in both directions and then gestured for us to enter the revealed passage.

Stepping inside the mountain was like sitting in a West End theatre as the curtain rose to reveal a new world.

We walked into a huge cavern, a space to rival Winchester Cathedral, with a similar feeling of grandeur. A great bowl at least fifty metres high at its peak, with side vestibules much like a church, separated by massive stalagmites that rose off the floor like stately stone soldiers at eternal attention. From above, stalactites hung like a succession of Damoclean swords, creating the same insecurity in me that they could fall upon my head at any time. Some had joined their fellow accretions rising from below and had formed mighty columns, amplifying the basilica simile.

The whole chamber was lit by oil lamps and flickering candles, casting upon the walls eerie shadows that danced a macabre jitterbug.

"Stalagmite, stalactite, I could never remember which is which," Lucy remarked.

"Stalagmite from the ground up, stalactite from the ceiling down," I told her, proud of my erudition. "My geology teacher, Professor Milton Ford, taught me a handy little reminder: If it's tight, stalac*tite*, it sticks to the ceiling. If not, it might build up from the floor, stalag*mite*. Did you catch that?"

"Watch where you step, young Harker; that before you is bat guano," Van Helsing, in turn, edified me.

I performed a clumsy Highland fling to avoid the whitish pile, then craned my neck to search the cave ceiling for the vile animals, but saw none in the dark recesses.

Then, as my eyes adjusted to the dim light, I was able to survey more of my surroundings. The gypsies had converted the interior into a subterranean village.

There was a kitchen where a deer was being dressed, pots were boiling, and women were busy at makeshift tables and around open fires. In one of the side chambers I noticed a school was in session, the children squatting on logs, hunched over tablets by the light of hurricane lamps.

In another side vault, a young man was tumbling across the floor in a series of acrobatic somersaults before a cluster of older children who, in turn, imitated the youth's gymnastics with varying degrees of success.

We took a turn into a side tunnel and, to my amazement, a young woman appeared above me, seeming to hover in midair. As we came closer I was able to make out a wire suspended between two stalagmites that she walked upon as easily and as daintily as if she were crossing a ballroom floor. Our gaze met and I do not know if it was the firelight reflected in those dark eyes, but something made the hair on the back of my neck rise and the skin on my face burn. The latter I put to sun and windburn, but the former I could only explain as some gypsy spell.

Ouspenkaya was speaking and I tried to focus on his words.

". . . following you for the last two days to see if you had any soldiers on your trail."

"Were there any?" Van Helsing asked.

"None," the gypsy leader said.

"We were careful," I told him. "Careful and alert."

"So careful and alert that you knew we were stalking you?" Ouspenkaya asked.

I had no answer as we entered a narrowing of the cave tributary, a hallway of a sort that widened momentarily. Two gypsy men were smoking fish over a smouldering fire, the fillets laid out upon a grill of woven green saplings.

"What are you doing?!" Ouspenkaya shouted as he began kicking dirt over the embers. "No fires in this room."

The men apologised and scurried to move their operation to another location. I took their immediate and forthright obeisance as a tribute to Ouspenkaya's leadership and power among his clan.

"Why is fire forbidden here?" Van Helsing asked. "Is there some kind of cave gas?"

"No, the smoke would harm these." Ouspenkaya jerked a thumb upward. We looked. The roof was lower here, and, painted or daubed upon it were pictographs—what was obviously a horse, the image of two humans, one a woman with extreme feminine accoutrements and a male with exaggerated masculine qualities. At least, I hope they were exaggerated, for the man's balance and mobility, if no other reason.

"Cave paintings." Van Helsing gazed up in admiration. "Most likely Paleolithic."

"They're beautiful." Lucy's voice was hushed in awe. "They would put most of the art in the Louvre to shame."

And they were just that. We all paused to take in the wondrous sight. A small menagerie of animals had been painted with a delicate and charming hand. You could see the little form of a deer in full flight, a bear in fierce pursuit.

"There are over eleven thousand caves in Rumania and Transylvania," Van Helsing explained. "I was part of a mapping expedition in the twenties. There are probably more, hidden like this one. This *pestera*"—he used the Rumanian term for "cave"—"was formed by the leaching of limestone. Some are salt caves. Very ancient."

"We found the bones of more than one bear when we set up our home here," Ouspenkaya told us.

"*Ursus spelaeus.*" The old Professor nodded. "Cave bears. I'm afraid they have been hunted to the point where they are now a rare sight."

"To our benefit," the gypsy said. "Now have a rest, share our food, become settled among us. You have sanctuary."

Lucy turned to him. "Sanctuary is the last thing we seek."

EXCERPTS FROM UNIDENTIFIED DIARY
(translated from German)

June 18

Herr Wolf could not wait any longer. His curiosity has overwhelmed him and he ordered his private rail car and a train to proceed to Rumania. The war can be handled by cable and phone. Herr Wolf's doppelganger will make public appearances and speeches and show his face in the appropriate places to maintain the illusion that the Fuhrer is in Berlin. The double is but a superficial likeness, in Herr Wolf's opinion, but others aware of the deception say he has a remarkable resemblance. Herr Wolf has doubts but has found that any cursory similarity will suffice; people only look at the mustache. As for the speeches, the ersatz Wolf is hammy, demonstrating his former vocation (actor). The twin knows his lines, mimics the gestures, but speaks with no heart. He is sufficient. The audience responds, the public's expectation doing most of the work, more likely a response to the idea of the man than what they behold.

No one knows that Herr Wolf is absent, not even HJ, who would disapprove. HJ is always haranguing Herr Wolf about the safety of his person and attempts to control Herr Wolf's every movement. Much of this anxiety about Herr Wolf's welfare is just pretense, an attempt to wield more influence. Herr Wolf is aware of this ulterior motive and so is able to manipulate the man, and others who try the same tactic. This is how one fulfills his Destiny.

Of Herr Wolf's motivation—he could not help himself. He must view the mythical Creature for himself in person. The tests are not completed, but Herr Wolf could wait no more. Even if the capabilities of the Creature are not transferable, Herr Wolf must witness the phenomenon with his own eyes.

What is at stake is too great. This could be the key to Herr Wolf's own Legend, the Path to Valhalla. Herr Wolf has been Chosen by Supernatural means to save his Nation. This discovery could be part of the Greater Plan.

EXCERPTED FROM THE UNPUBLISHED NOVEL
THE DRAGON PRINCE AND I
by Lenore Van Muller

There was a certain comfort sitting around a fire of fragrant logs crackling and spitting sparks that wafted up into the darkness overhead. Listening to the gypsies with guitar and violin perform the *manele* songs lulled Lucille into a sense of safety she had not felt for . . . ages.

Since she had been a child, this oriental-tinted music would remind her of home and her mother's soft singing at her bedside. The memory was faint, her mother's face out of focus, as if a faded photograph, but it was there, and it gave her comfort in troubled times.

Later she heard these melodies from street singers along the Seine in Paris, a Spanish beach at twilight, once in New Orleans, Louisiana, and every time the music gave her solace.

She stood up and walked through the caverns, the music following her becoming more and more muted, the cave giving the songs a haunting echo, much like she heard in her dreams when she felt lonely or afraid. She came upon a small antechamber where a woman crouched over a mortar and pestle, grinding away as she muttered to herself in a cadent chant. Lucille squatted next to her, curious.

"What are you making?" Lucille asked. "A potion?"

The woman ignored her, continued her chanting until she was finished, then raised her head up to peer at Lucille. She was middle-aged, with a weathered, tanned face, and sported a nose that had been broken and angled to one cheek. But what stood out were the woman's eyes—one a piercing blue, the other deep brown. Lucille had seen this phenomenon only once before, in a Chinese dog.

At this moment those eyes were boring into her own, a deep look. Lucille felt like the woman was peering into her soul, her very being.

"You are a sister." The woman took Lucille's hands into her own. "In the diablerie. I am Vesta."

"I'm Lucille." She had been taken by surprise. "I, uh, only dabble."

"Dabble? What is this dabble?"

"I play at it." Lucille shrugged and smiled dismissively.

"There is no 'play,'" Vesta sneered, revealing a dead tooth. "The spirits can be harsh sovereigns."

She released Lucille's hands and instead laid her own palm over Lucille's heart.

"You have power," the witch said, for indeed that was what Lucille now recognised in the gypsy. "Power untapped. Oh!"

The woman gasped and stepped quickly away from Lucille as if pushed.

"What?" Lucille asked.

The woman grabbed her mortar and pestle and tried to walk away, muttering to herself. Lucille hurried after her, grabbed the woman by the shoulder, and turned her so that they were face-to-face again.

"What did you see?" she demanded.

"In my calling one learns very soon to never deliver anything but good tidings," she replied. "If what you see harkens bad tidings it is best to remain silent. Or lie. People like ourselves cannot lie to each other, so I say nothing. I will not reveal the shadow that looms before you."

"What shadow?" Lucille asked.

The gypsy woman didn't answer, rather set the mortar and pestle aside as she fumbled in the deep pockets of her patched coat, pulling out a handful of strange items. She picked through them, stuffing some back into the pocket until one item was left: a small leather pouch tied with a simple string long enough to be a necklace. The old woman had to strain onto her tiptoes to be able to drape the cord over Lucille's head.

"For when you lose your love," the woman whispered into Lucille's ear, the sound like crushing dried leaves.

And she walked away. Lucille did not pursue. She was left alone to ponder the dancing shadows cast by the flickering torchlight. There was light from four or five torches around her, and she had as many shadows surrounding her. Her shadows, like a gathering of Shakespearean witches, a coven of Lucille.

She fled the room, got lost in the myriad cavern corridors, and finally found her father and Harker sitting with the gypsy chief. She joined them.

"Oh, there you are," her father said. "We can now get down to business."

He turned to the gypsy and laid out the purpose of their mission—to form a band to rescue the prisoners of Castle Bran.

"No one else will come to our aid," Lucille added her own plea.

"We Roma understand this," he said. "In time, every country treats us like pariahs. We share this with the Jews."

He poured mulled wine, *vin fiert*, into her cup. She drank deeply, and heat coursed through her body.

"They hold our comrades hostage," Harker said. "Plus the Prince."

"Ah, the Prince." Ouspenkaya nodded. "In this land he has always been our protector. And he did save my precious daughter and many of my people. I am in his debt."

He glanced across the fire to where the gypsies surrounded the musicians. The women wore bright-coloured dresses, scarlet skirts with yellow prints, bright orange and green blouses, and scarves as iridescent as any butterfly. Lucille was envious of the display, but she knew if she wore such blazing colours she would only come off too garish. These women carried it with aplomb, giving an appearance of vivacity and joie de vivre.

She turned back to their leader. "You will help us, then?" she asked.

Her father interrupted.

"Do not let my daughter's resolve and precipitance pressure you," he said. "It will be a risky proposition. Lives could be, will be, lost."

Ouspenkaya grinned wolfishly.

"My people live hard, die harder."

DATED: 18 JUNE 1941
TO: CSS REINHARD HEYDRICH, RSHA, REICHSFUHRER-SS
FROM: SS MAJOR WALTRAUD REIKEL
CC: HEINRICH HIMMLER, REICHSFUHRER-SS
(BY SPECIAL COURIER)

MOST SECRET

The latest concerning our special guest:

   Last evening there was an incident. What follows I
have gathered from those present.

   Two guards were posted outside the Creature's cell
to monitor any further weakening of the steel bars and
much-besieged door. A Private Gustav von Wangenheim
and Corporal John Gottowt were assigned to the evening
sentry duty.

   Beginning their period of guard duty, von Wangenheim
approached the door, testing each bar, inspecting the
welds for damage and the door hinges (which were being
pulled from the wall and frame). This he did with
Corporal Gottowt standing a couple of metres away,
weapon at the ready. The inspection completed, von
Wangenheim looked up to find himself face-to-face with
the prisoner.

   Von Wangenheim froze as if entranced. His Corporal
inquired if something was wrong.

   Von Wangenheim replied that everything was fine.
Later, when clearheaded, he implied that the prisoner
told him what to say, forced him, as if he had hypnotised
him.

I think, in retrospect, that this may be a reasonable
assumption.

As von Wangenheim gazed into the cell after his
inspection, a mist floated from the prisoner's side
and hovered in front of his face. He watched this
remarkable apparition with only mild curiosity, telling
Gottowt that there was "nothing to be alarmed about."

(Again, later, von Wangenheim said that he was only
parroting what the prisoner ordered him to say.)

This mist then formed into the shape of a hand and
wrapped its foggy fingers around von Wangenheim's neck.
With this threatening ghost hand clutching his throat,
von Wangenheim heard the prisoner's next instructions
as if they were logic personified.

"Maybe you should open the door and make sure
everything inside is secured."

Von Wangenheim repeated the instruction as if it
were his own thought, and he was reaching for the key
to that door when Corporal Gottowt realised what was
occurring.

The Corporal grabbed the hypnotised man, tried to
pull him away from the door as he was attempting to
insert the key. But he discovered that the prisoner's
hand was in a vise-like grip around von Wangenheim's
neck.

Von Wangenheim, still in a trance-like state,
resisted Gottowt's efforts to free him. Gottowt's only
recourse was to first club von Wangenheim unconscious.
He did this with the butt of his rifle. Using the same
technique, he pounded the prisoner's hand where von
Wangenheim still hung in the creature's grip. By this
he was able to break the prisoner's fingers.

(It should also be noted that in the frenzy of
the attack and rescue, Gottowt also mutilated von
Wangenheim's ear and shattered the man's collarbone.)

The prisoner finally released von Wangenheim, who
fell to the floor.

A near disaster, I admit. But in retrospect, it also means that we have discovered another ability possessed by our guest. A means to enthrall others. Whether there has to be some proximity to the victim, and the range where the ability becomes effective, is to be learned later after more testing.

I will keep you informed as to any more developments.

Heil Hitler.

FROM THE WAR JOURNAL OF
J. HARKER

(transcribed from shorthand)

JUNE 20, 1941

We are off, like dirty socks, as my mum would say. The rescue party is scant; hardly what you think would be needful to assault a bloody castle. Ouspenkaya and eleven of his men, plus his daughter. I do not know how this girl will be anything but a hindrance, and I made the mistake of voicing this doubt within earshot of Lucy, who lit into me with a tirade about male condescension, which I bore with as much composure as I could muster.

To tell the truth, I am not that perturbed by the young lady's presence. The previous night, before we received word that the gypsy king would help us, I was watching a pair of young men play a dangerous version of mumblety-peg with daggers, an item which no gypsy man seems without (I am afraid to ask the women if they carry one). Facing each other, no more than a foot apart, they were throwing the knives at each other's foot, the launch point being some part of their anatomy above the waist, such as chin, elbow, forehead, and so on to acrobatic extremes, which the other had to imitate, the winner of each round choosing the throw position.

To return to my anecdote—I was spectating this sport when I felt a hand on my shoulder, and suddenly the young gypsy aerialist sat beside me. I remembered her name, Maleva, and greeted her in her native Romani tongue.

"You speak our language?" She smiled at me, her teeth a brilliant white against her tawny skin, contrasted even more by her raven hair and dark eyes.

"Only a few words," I told her honestly. "Languages are a hobby of mine. I have been picking up words here and there. You are the daughter of Ouspenkaya, right?"

She nodded. "He is at the *diwano*, where the elders discuss the *gajo* request."

"Gajo?"

"One who is not gypsy. You." She poked me in the chest with her finger, laughing. "I teach you gypsy words. What is your *nav*?"

"*Nav* . . . name?" I asked. She nodded. "Jonathan Harker."

She tried forming the syllables of my name then shook her head, wrinkling her nose.

"I do not like. I call you *rom baro*."

"Rom baro?"

"Means 'boss.' You are the Englisha boss, no?"

"Well, in a manner, yes. *Rom baro* . . ." I tested it. "I like it. Tell me another word. How do you say 'beautiful'?"

"*Pakvora.*"

"Then that is what I will call you. *Pakvora.*"

She bit her bottom lip and looked deep into my eyes. The effect was pixieish, most appealing. I was proud that I did not look away, in fact, gazed back and fell into the dark depths until I was lost.

"We have new names. Secret names. Tell no one. We are bound in this secret."

She reached out to me with a clasped hand, only the little finger protruding. I imitated the gesture and we joined those little fingers, like children making a solemn promise.

She then took my left hand into her own hands and gazed into my palm and traced the lines with her index finger. The fingernail tickled my palm in a most sexual manner. I have to admit that I was a bit aroused.

"You have been here before," she murmured. Her voice was low, just above a whisper, most seductive.

"Not really," I replied. "You mean Rumania? This is my first visit, actually."

"Your blood has been here."

"Well, my grandfather . . ." I realised with a shock that she had just divined my past. Was this some sort of gypsy magic?

She leaned into me, stared at my palm, her demeanor changed, registering surprise, then very serious.

"You are my savings," she said.

I was pondering this statement, ready to correct her or seek further elucidation, when she used her grasp on my hand to pull me toward her. She then kissed me on the lips, a mere peck, but a shock nevertheless. And I do mean shock, as I felt an electric charge that ran from my lips to the soles of my feet.

Before I could recover, she leapt up and dashed away. I felt that fever blush again, and it was a few moments before I could recover my composure. I decided to take a walk and unfluster myself.

I wandered the cave and marvelled at how the gypsies had made themselves a home here, how much resilience mankind demonstrates, over and over. No matter the depredations, the hardships, the calamity—man-made or the result of fierce nature—people find a way to survive, even find some remnant of happiness.

These musings were repeatedly interrupted by sweet, invasive thoughts of the dark gypsy beauty. Some of these exotic visions I was not proud of, as they verged on the side of licentiousness. In order to hold on to some respect for myself, I continued my survey of the quiet cave.

I found Lucy in the pictograph cavern, lying upon her back, playing the beam from her battery-powered torch across the painted ceiling. It seemed the moment to have a proper chin-wag with her.

I sat down next to her and took the opportunity to admire the beauty of her face as the ambient light spilled across her features, and I found myself comparing it to that singular allure of Maleva.

"Amazing," she remarked. "All that beauty and few people to appreciate it. Created by people who made their tools out of stone. This is what makes us different from the lower creatures."

"Do you include the Germans in your admiration?" I joked.

"Actually you should see some of the architecture the Germans are building. Some are quite beautiful in a brutish way. The best show in Berlin was when Hitler gathered together what he thought was 'degenerate art.' The show sold out repeatedly, defeating his purpose. And I have known some very artistic people who were complete sadists. No, art doesn't make us humane, just human."

"That brings up another subject," I said and laid back to join her in the admiration of the painted horse trapped in her ring of light.

"What would that be?" she asked.

"There is no future for you with him, you know," I told her.

"You're thinking of my future?" she asked

"I am concerned for your welfare," I said. "What can you look forward to? I doubt you can have children with him. And he is not going to die, age. And you will. Age. What then?"

"You've thought this out," she said, regarding me with those green eyes.

"I have," I said. "And only out of concern for you, not investing my own interests at all."

"Really?" She smiled softly.

"Honestly."

"Well, let us examine the logic of your argument," she began. "One, you assume that I care about my future. I am sorry, but this war has taught me that none of us can count on having a future. We are about to assault a castle where we will be outnumbered, outgunned, and have little chance of survival. If I have learned one thing in this conflict it is that you live by the moment—as it may be your last. And as for children . . . Who would bring a child into this world of death and destruction? Not I. Not I. As for making it to old age?" A short, derisive laugh escaped her lips. "Those are all peacetime indulgences."

She rose from the ground, dusted off her trousers, handed me the torch.

"Here. Be sure to lock up when you leave."

I lay there, absorbing what she had just said, playing my light across the ancient drawings overhead. I studied the delicate form and line. An artist, to be sure. I wondered how violent was the world he walked, where he not only had to battle his own kind but the very elements, had to fight just for a bit of meat. And still had the soul to create something so full of grace as this.

My view was suddenly eclipsed. A face hovered over my own. Maleva. The reflection of my torchlight filled her eyes with a sparkling fire.

She put a finger to her lips, which drew my attention to her ripe mouth. It was a voluptuous smile, swollen and sultry. She reached down and turned off my torch.

I was plunged into a darkness so black that I could not see my own hand, though I held it only inches from my eyes.

Then I heard a rustle of cloth.

"What . . . ?" I began to ask but a delicate hand was put over my mouth. Then her other hand took my own and moved it across naked flesh.

What followed was the most erotic moment of my life. Sight gone, I experienced everything by touch alone. It was flesh upon flesh, fingers and lips and tongues, exploration and discovery, until I succumbed to a sensual overload, unparalleled by any man, ever.

EXCERPTS FROM UNIDENTIFIED DIARY
(translated from the German)

Herr Wolf took a brief sleep (the only kind he can manage anymore). After waking and dressing (a new record), his valet HL provided a light breakfast—tea, biscuits, and an apple. Watching through the window of his private rail car, he saw vistas of Hungary then Rumania glide past. Grubby children stared at the train, some making vulgar gestures. The Rumanians are a vile, inbred race of dwarfs without any culture. There is a saying that there are three sorts of Rumanians—they are either pimps, pederasts, or violinists, and very few play the violin.

June 20

Herr Wolf arrived at the grimy Rumanian outpost in the midst of the day, purposely pausing at a sidetrack a kilometre from the Brasov station to wait for the sun to go down and the railroad station to be evacuated of prying eyes.

Through the windows Herr Wolf could see that the station was in the midst of repair: Scaffolding had been erected and stacks of lumber and building materials were scattered all about, and cement dust covered every surface. Examining the pieces of the structure that had not been reduced to ruin, Herr Wolf wondered why such a boring piece of junk architecture would even be reconstructed. They should raze it to the ground and start over. He would offer the locals some advice and maybe forward some examples of what he had erected in Germany. He passed these thoughts on to the secretary who travelled with him.

During the wait for night, Herr Wolf's thoughts drifted to his own Mortality. He had escaped Death repeatedly, the Miraculous Survival in the trenches at Ypres, the narrow escape from the podium bomb at the Sportpalast. He considers this a Divine protection; Fate has always had a Greater role for him.

This current opportunity is another gift from Destiny. Lately Herr Wolf has been haunted by the thought of what becomes of the Reich and Europe in a hundred years, a thousand years, without the proper Stewardship. Will it fall from neglect or corruption as before?

Herr Wolf has determined that he is irreplaceable; no military or civilian personage seems able enough to take his place. Even after his retirement to Linz, the Fate of the Reich may depend on him alone, and he must act to preserve what has been fought so hard to create. This is the next step in Herr Wolf's evolution to what Nietzsche called his "superman."

Herr Wolf has been given a Divine Historical Imperative to return Germany to a purer place, and it is only proper that Supernatural means be given to him to perpetuate that Reign.

With Immortality, he could become Master of the World; take his rightful place in history alongside Frederick the Great, Genghis Khan. No, do not think in those mortal terms. Take a seat alongside Thor, Odin!

There was a Brasov greeting party, a small contingent of SS as per the instructions cabled to the local German commandant telling him to expect the visit of a low-level dignitary.

There was a display of flags, Rumanian and German, a few threadbare and faded swastika banners, but the Commanding Officer was present to greet this visitor, and Herr Wolf commended him on that point of courtesy.

The compliment was lost on the poor soldier, a Major WR, as the soldier was quite discomfited when he recognised his guest. The Major fell all over himself apologising for the meager reception and the appearance of his troops, who looked fine considering they were field soldiers.

Herr Wolf attempted to put the Major at ease, informing the intimidated soldier that he was travelling incognito, that Herr Wolf's presence should not in any way be revealed—and that if this information was to leak, there would be dire consequences. Fatal consequences.

The Major had to be informed by Herr Wolf's valet, HL, that smoking was not allowed in Herr Wolf's presence.

Herr Wolf was transported quickly through the charming village of Brasov and further to the castle that housed the SS garrison. The area reminded Herr Wolf of the terrain around his own mountain retreat, the Berghof. The castle was quaint, a bit cold and damp as these places tend to be, smelling of mildew and wood smoke.

Supper was offered, mostly various meats, but Herr Wolf took no offence, the ruse of who was visiting the Major being so successful that the cooking staff had not been prepared for his vegetarian diet. He asked for some oatmeal soup, if there were any available. Herr Wolf told the Major that the elephant is the strongest animal in the world but eats no meat. The point was not taken. The Major is definitely a Leichenfresser. Herr Wolf could smell it on his breath.

The soup was brought to him by a toadying Lieutenant F. They had also set the table for twelve, and a message was sent to cancel the other invitees.

Herr Wolf filled a plate with what cheeses and breads he could find and sipped lime blossom tea while the Major related his various efforts against the local underground—mostly successful. Herr Wolf had already read all this in the dossier supplied to him, and he switched the conversation to the Major's background, again, which he already had discerned from the same file. But one can learn much about a man by the way he tells his own story.

The Major was modest without being servile, and when Herr Wolf brought up the soldier's fencing exploits and his performance at the Berlin Olympics, the officer declared how splendid the entire affair had been and how marvelous the experience was for him. The Major's distinctive Bavarian accent reminds Herr Wolf of his childhood days. The Major seems to be a stolid soldier, hard as Krupp steel. Herr Wolf wonders if a promotion and transfer to the Reich Chancellery might be prudent and useful. He will consider this. After all, this brave and obviously intelligent officer most likely could do better than Herr Wolf's Generals. The New Reich needs men of Imagination who confront the impossible and accomplish it—not the naysayers and defeatists who now compose his General Staff.

At this point, Herr Wolf's patience for the niceties was at an end, and he interrogated the Major about the purpose of this journey. The Vampire was still in custody, and Herr Wolf was eager to see the myth for himself. But the Major kept glancing at his watch, checking the window. Only when the first rays of dawn began to seep into the room did the Major finally deem it time. The sun was "at the proper inclination." They left the dinner table and descended into the bowels of the castle.

There was a curious aspect to the castle architecture: the dungeon had been fitted into the cleft of the mountain, so that it was possible to have windows even in the lower depths.

Along the way the Major spoke of his latest discovery, that the vampire was vulnerable to the touch of silver, that this metal could possibly be fatal to the creature. The Major had one of his men, a Private Venohr, who had previously worked in a Hamburg foundry, melt down as much silver as had been collected from the Jews and gypsies, plus some religious figures from a Zarnesti church that had harboured fugitive terrorists, and he'd had this smith create a silver sword for the officer.

Major R proudly showed Herr Wolf the results, a handsome blade in the sabre style with a Waffen-SS design embossed into the hilt. The Major remarked that the blade was a mite heavy and could not hold an edge very well, but would suffice for the purpose intended.

The Major's plan was to admit another human into the vampire's cell to be bitten, a person that the Creature might not feel so free to kill once the victim had been infected—a friend or possibly one of his terrorist compatriots.

Herr Wolf inquired as to whether the Creature would agree to feast on a friend. The Major's reply was that as an officer involved in the Warsaw Ghetto conflict and the Polish internment camps he bore witness to the fact that hunger triumphs over all social constraints. Herr Wolf's experience in the trenches of the Great War only confirmed the Major's hypothesis.

The plan then, after acquiring someone who had been bitten, was to use this infected person to bite one of our own and hence to control the dissemination of the gift.

Herr Wolf voiced doubts whether a new vampire would be any easier to handle than the one in their possession now.

The solution to that problem the Major had already pondered. He had found a victim who was already weak enough, morally and constitutionally, to do his bidding.

Meanwhile, they meandered down narrow stairs, curving and steep, always leading below, and then reached a level where a long corridor was lined with cells with large, barred steel doors. The passage was of grey stone with an arched ceiling, damp and oppressive as most cellars are. From the cells Herr Wolf could hear the moans and pitiful whimpers of the various guests, the voices echoing about, multiplying the misery within. The odours emanating from the cells were disgusting and foul.

The Major stopped at one of these. Inside a prisoner crouched in a corner, brooding with a dull, sullen, woe-begotten look on his face, huddled as if against the cold. The prisoner was unshaven, with sunken eyes, filthy clothes, and bloodied and grotesquely swollen hands that he held claw-like in front of him. He was suckling on one finger as an infant does. This motley semblance of a man proved to be British, and he was singing a vulgar song. The Major translated the lyrics. Something about a woman with overly large buttocks and a man with a tiny organ and their difficulties in coitus. The tune was familiar, but Herr Wolf could not place it and was haunted by his inability to name the song. This inane recitation at once belied the oft-repeated axiom that the ravings of the deranged are the secrets of God. Unless He is fond of mauvais ton.

When he finished his ditty, the Tommy became entranced by the progress of a very large insect as it traversed the cell wall. Snatching out a hand, this pitiful creature, obviously demented, shocked Herr Wolf by capturing the bug, a küchenschabe, and popping it into his mouth like a piece of zwieback. The crunch-crunch as teeth masticated carapace was loud enough to echo in the hall. Herr Wolf was particularly disgusted by this loathsome act, detesting all insects since that hated, bug-infested apartment in Vienna.

The Major told of a previous incident whereupon a guard saw a bird fly into the cell and seemingly disappear. Then a few minutes later the prisoner vomited a profusion of feathers.

Herr Wolf became slightly sick to his stomach, but maintained a stoic countenance as the cell door was opened and two guards entered to drag the prisoner out. He whined and keened like a rabbit in a trap. If weakness was a qualification for his selection, then the Major had chosen well.

Herr Wolf asked the prisoner's name. The response sounded Jewish, which explained the cowardly manner.

The guards dragged the prisoner—he was too frightened to walk—down the hall past a machine-gun position to another cell. This door was deformed, bent outward, but apparently maintaining some integrity.

This particular cell was flooded with sunlight from a window, the glare momentarily blinding Herr Wolf to the fact that, indeed, the room was occupied.

In the one corner not illuminated, lurking in the meager shade, was a presence. It took a moment for Herr Wolf's eyes to adjust. Slowly the figure was revealed. It was tall, pale, the skin luminescent as if lit from within by a lightbulb. The white streak in its dark hair, longish like a bohemian, gave it a theatrical look. Despite the sad state of its clothing, ripped and torn, the figure stood erect, with an inherent dignity.

After all, if the legends were true, this was a descendant of royal lineage. It did not flinch under Herr Wolf's inspection. Under a noble brow its ochre eyes bored into Herr Wolf.

Herr Wolf knew these eyes, saw them in the mirror every day. Herr Wolf met the striking gaze with his own, not to be intimidated, secure in the knowledge that he is able to stare down any man, from General to foreign dignitary. But then Herr Wolf remembered the Major's caution about the Creature's mesmeric abilities and broke the contact.

The Creature spoke a question, in Rumanian, and the Major translated. — Is it really you?

Herr Wolf commented that he could ask the same.

The Major drew his new sword and the cell door was cautiously opened. The Vampire did not move from the safety of his shadowy sanctuary.

The Tommy was tossed into the vampire's cell and the door hurriedly locked. The two prisoners regarded each other for a moment, the Englishman addressing the Creature as "Master." Nothing more was said for quite a few moments, during which the Tommy captured another insect, a spider this time, and ate it with some relish, but, thank the gods, none of that hideous, crunching noise.

After his disgusting repast, the Tommy approached the vampire with desperation in his eyes and made a request in English (the Major continued his translation): Would Master Dracula help him with the fly of his pants as his hands could not perform properly and he had to urinate. This appeal was made with such pitiful shame that Herr Wolf felt some momentary compassion for the man.

The Tommy had to move close to the Creature for this operation and we watched in anticipation, but the Vampire only did as asked. No teeth, no feasting, no blood. It was a humiliating task, but the Vampire's composure remained a sort of grandiose detachment.

In his days of poverty and pain, Herr Wolf would walk around the Hellabrunn Zoological Gardens in Munich, observing the beasts pacing their enclosures. Herr Wolf often did the same in his tiny lodging. One day at the zoo he heard a keeper announce that the feeding of the big cats was about to occur. Herr Wolf waited for the event, and when the raw meat was tossed to the lions, he watched in awe as the magnificent felines devoured their meal, fighting and snarling at each other.

He felt the same trepidation here, waiting for the Vampire to pounce.

Nothing else occurred over the next few hours, but Herr Wolf stayed at his post like a loyal sentry.

For quite a long time Herr Wolf paced, watched as the Vampire stayed in its corner, not moving anything but those cruel, mocking eyes.

The Major provided a chair for Herr Wolf in which he occasionally sat, but otherwise he continued to walk the corridor as was his habit. Upon a small side table a plate of savories was set for Herr Wolf's indulgence. Herr Wolf took his daily pills, regretting that he was missing his injections from Dr. M.

He attempted to engage the Vampire in conversation, asking about the incident that created his current state. The Vampire chose silence.

Herr Wolf inquired about the Prince's days of rule, hoping to bridge the gulf between them by sharing the burden of Leadership.

Again there was no response.

Herr Wolf knows the power of silence and proceeded in the same manner for a while. After a few hours, Major R brought in another chair and joined Herr Wolf for a light meal. The Vampire had been watching the column of sunlight that pierced its window as the beam crept across the cell. After a while the light disappeared completely. The sun set, and the bare lightbulb that hung in the corridor flicked to a dim glow. Yet the Vampire remained in its corner.

Fresh-baked black bread and cups of hot chocolate were brought down, and Herr Wolf allowed himself a brief respite. After Herr Wolf and the Major had supped, the Major relaxed his officious attitude and began to converse with Herr Wolf as with an equal, as if the bathetic ritual of breaking bread had erased the lines of authority. The Major was enthusiastic about Herr Wolf's conduct of the war, the speed of the new Nazi Empire's expansion. He praised Herr Wolf's military genius with not a note of sycophancy. He then rhapsodised about Herr Wolf's plan for the Vampire, the creation of a Vampire army. Herr Wolf did not correct the man for his assumption. The Major went on, imagining soldiers invulnerable to ordinary armaments, indefatigable, of superior strength, and so on.

This incited a sardonic laugh from the Vampire.

— A vampire empire! The Creature cried out and laughed more exuberantly.

The Major took umbrage at this outburst, but Herr Wolf knew what instigated the sarcasm.

The Vampire stepped into the artificial light and explained, derided the Major for his small thinking.

— A Vampire army is not in the offing, my friend. What leader would allow a lowly soldier more power than the leader possessed? No, the power of the Vampire would be passed on to one individual and one only.

With that, the Vampire stared directly at Herr Wolf.

Herr Wolf acknowledged the Vampire's conclusion. Wolf had been sickly as a child, still suffered from one ailment after another. The portent of an imminent death stalked him like a sinister predator: cancer, as his mother suffered, his most likely demise. The pain in his gut was a constant signal that he was not long for this world. His greatest worry has always been that he would not live long enough to complete his Destiny, his Struggle to restore the Fatherland to Glory.

The Major commented that this was only proper. — For this Reich to live forever it must be led by the man who created it.

Herr Wolf could not tell if this was just lip service, but he felt confident in the man's loyalty so the sentiment's truth did not matter.

Herr Wolf appealed to the Creature to join him.

— Between the two of us, we could rule the world, two great leaders, ruling an empire that would last longer than the Romans'.

The Creature became mute once more and sank back into the darkness, leaving Herr Wolf with a strange chill. Herr Wolf used all of his miraculous powers of persuasion, but the Vampire was not moved.

Finally, this one they call Dracula approached the bars and faced Herr Wolf, stating that during his many seasons he had learned that there were few solid truths.

— One truth is inviolate—too much power in one individual's hands always degenerates into misfortune, usually for others. I know this from my own singular experience.

There ensued quiet again as the Vampire retreated to the far wall. Another idle hour passed.

During this wait the Major presented Herr Wolf with a token of his appreciation in the form of Major R's pistol, a Mauser M712 he had inherited from his father, a hero of the German East Africa campaign in the Great War. It is a beautiful weapon, ivory grips and a custom holster of elephant hide. Herr Wolf accepted the gift with grace and laid it on the side table.

Nothing again occurred for hours. Dispatches were brought to Herr Wolf, relayed from his secretary at the station, updating him on events at the Chancellery and on various fronts, particularly on the Soviet line. Of particular distaste were the bulletins from Operation Eagle Attack. Despite the assurances and predictions of H and G, the Brits were still battling in the air without diminishment, much less defeat. At this rate, Operation Sea Lion will never be possible. We cannot invade that annoying Isle without total control of the air. Herr Wolf dealt with these missives, never taking his eyes off the cell.

There was an instant of activity in the cell when the Vampire approached the sniveling Tommy. Nothing more than whispers could be heard between the two, and the Creature returned to his previous position on the wall.

Herr Wolf was quite frustrated at not knowing what transpired between the two, and he suggested to the Major that he consider situating microphones in the cell to record any future clandestine conversations. The Major replied that this would be done at the next opportunity.

Herr Wolf inquired as to the last time the vampire had fed and how long it could go between feedings. The Major recounted that the late Corporal Schreck was the last victim, and, as to how often the Creature had to nourish itself, they had no idea.

Herr Wolf suddenly remembered the tune to the Tommy's coarse lyric—"Yes, We Have No Bananas!"

The Vampire remained erect in his corner, regarding us with the superior air of a Czar; the Tommy still huddled at the foot of the wall, rubbing his hand against the stone in a repetitive manner as one sees the mentally deficient do in an asylum. This manic activity scrubbed off the scabs on his palms and they began to bleed. This zoophagous creature was becoming excited in greater and greater degree, a shifty look in his eyes, which one always sees when a madman has seized an idea.

Senses dulled by the monotony, Herr Wolf was caught off guard when the Vampire finally acted. This occurred with such surprising speed that it was difficult to comprehend what exactly had transpired.

The Vampire had attacked the Englishman.

FROM THE WAR JOURNAL OF
J. HARKER

(transcribed from shorthand)

JUNE 21, 1941

After returning to Brasov, we rummaged in the ruins of the Van Helsing home for a change of clothes and to further arm ourselves from a hidden cache. We left the city just before sunset, passing through two small towns along the way. The buildings along the road had the dates of construction carved in their street-facing walls, deeming them a hundred, sometimes two hundred years old. Apparitions of blue smoke rose from their chimneys, thin souls abandoning their homes. Past the towns, the mountains on the left rose green and verdant. A sullen, black donkey watched our passing with bored disdain.

By the time we were at the base of the Bran Castle, night held full dominance. The castle was a yellow-limestone-and-brick edifice that commanded the crest of a small mountain, allowing a commanding view of the surrounding countryside as it had done throughout the centuries. A slender river cut through the narrow pass the castle commanded. Across the road and river stood the ruins of an imposing and ancient structure, constructed of smooth river rock, Roman in appearance, the ruins long abandoned and overgrown with vine and bush. The decrepit remains of a former ruler.

The clear line of the castle was a black silhouette against the deep blue night sky. There was something wild and rare about the place.

The castle had one rounded spire and a half-dozen peaked roofs on a variety of levels. Multiple chimneys spewed smoke that was instantly dispersed by the wind.

The sheer rock cliffs merged into the castle's vertical walls. The terrain below was a jumble of trees and thickets. Using that foliage, we darted from cover to cover, ascending the heights. Others of our party used the dense brush that grew alongside the curving access road to hide their approach from that direction.

The stronghold was built in 1212, then burned by the Mongols. The Saxons rebuilt when this was the border between Transylvania and Wallachia and used the fortress to keep out the Ottomans. Up until the recent conflict the castle had been the residence of the Rumanian Queen Maria. She had died three years previously and her heart had been ensconced inside the castle. I assumed that the dastardly Reikel feasted on it while he watched his torturer work.

I stood in a tangle of brush with Maleva, her proximity unnerving me a bit. She smelled of vanilla and some exotic scent I could not place. We reconnoitred the palace, and I realised how difficult the task before us seemed to be.

The entrance gate and the road that curved up to it were guarded by two machine-gun nests. An attempted breach there would cost us too many lives. And the walls were so steep as to defeat an alpine mountaineer. I remarked upon that.

Maleva turned to me. "Not for Maleva," she said and, giving me a quick kiss, she scurried to the base of the wall. I had difficulty recovering from this second demonstration of affection on her part, wondering if she did this with everyone, every man. Was she just a physically affectionate type of woman, or was she sending me signals that I was not receiving properly? Or maybe she was teasing me. What is my failing that the attentions of a female always vex and distress me so?

I was emotionally flummoxed and not paying attention to the job at hand. I tried to refocus and craned my neck to keep watch on the two sentries patrolling the parapets atop the castle. There were mercifully few guards on the wall, the inhabitants resting on the security of the precipitous revetments. And I have to admit that I was fearful about attacking such a formidable alcazar. Especially considering we were about to do so with a band of amateurs, not soldiers, not even experienced Resistance fighters but instead an untrained group of . . . there was no other word for them—entertainers. And one only a slip of a girl.

But then I, and the German occupants, had not considered the unique talents of Maleva. She clambered up the rocky slope like a child up a tree, finding handholds and footholds where I saw none. Upon reaching what appeared to be the smooth skin of the building proper, she jumped up to grab the sill of a lower window and from there leapt from staggered window to window with breathtaking agility until she was high enough to reach the out-thrust roof supports. Hanging from one of these massive beams, she hoisted herself up onto the roof itself. The feat happened so quickly and was so astonishing that I nearly forgot where we were and almost clapped my hands together in applause. Now who was the amateur?

From her precarious perch Maleva began to haul up the cord looped around her waist.

That slim twine was attached to a stouter rope she secured to the steel base of a lightning rod fixed atop the roof peak.

One by one, I and five of our gypsy legion climbed the rope, knotted every yard or so for the ease of our ascent. Once on the roof, we silently moved across the tiles, having shed our shoes and laced them about our necks. We made our way across the clay tile in our stocking feet or, in some cases, bare feet.

A good thing, too, for as soon as we achieved the rooftop we were able to spot the two guards on the parapets. They patrolled the square of the tallest tower, a Nazi flag flapping noisily from the pole over their heads. The Germans paraded around the rectangle of the tower, taking turns. The parapet was just above us, and one glance in our direction would give us away.

We crept cautiously toward the low wall, timing our movements for the brief moment the tower guard had his back to us. This occurred only during one short side of his box march. Our incursion took infinite patience as we waited silently for the man to complete the rest of his walk and give us his back once more. We were able to get only one of us across the distance each time.

When enough had crossed, Maleva and three gypsy men scurried over the parapet. One of the men ran up behind one Nazi sentry, leapt up onto the man's shoulders piggyback style, covered the guard's mouth with both hands, and hauled him over onto his back. Maleva rushed up with another of her fellows and, while he stripped the German of his weapon, she withdrew a knife out of her stocking and stabbed the guard in the heart, slipping the blade between his ribs with deadly accuracy. I noticed that she jerked the knife handle in a back-and-forth fashion, thereby slicing the heart. A much-practiced technique? Again, a swift and silent operation.

They moved on to the next sentry, this time Maleva simply slitting his throat from behind, and I was left with the question of why I keep getting entangled with women who are so ready, even eager, to kill. And so damned good at it.

EXCERPTS FROM UNIDENTIFIED DIARY
(translated from the German)

– It feeds! IT FEEDS! the Major cried out, whether from surprise or excitement Herr Wolf did not know.

The Tommy added his screams to the pandemonium as the machine-gun crews shouted queries as to what was happening.

The Tommy's blood-chilling howl resonated around the stone walls as the Vampire buried his face in the hollow of the man's throat. Then, just as abruptly, the Creature released his victim. There remained a smear of blood across the Tommy's neck and in turn across the face of the vampire, who hissed at us like a riled cat and, in so doing, displayed the elongated teeth of a predatory beast.

Herr Wolf admits to gasping.

Major R drew his new sword with a snick of metal against metal and ordered the cell to be opened.

FROM THE WAR JOURNAL OF
J. HARKER

(transcribed from shorthand)

Because the second parapet guard was dispatched as easily and quietly as the first, my doubts about the competence of the gypsies, and particularly the girl, were now forgotten. Hell, if I had a company of the blighters I could win the war.

Having eliminated the danger of being spied by the sentries, we were now able to walk from the outside wall to the inner and look down upon a small courtyard three storeys below. Throwing our rope over this side, we descended to the courtyard level. Maleva and two of the gypsies remained on the parapet to secure and keep watch from the high ground. I gave her a nod as I approached the rope and she smiled back at me, the white of her teeth like a beacon in the dark.

After descending into the courtyard one of the Romani, who knew the castle from when his mother read the Tarot cards for the late Queen Maria, led three of our party to cover the doors leading into the castle.

We gathered behind a generator that had recently been set in the courtyard. It smelled of diesel, the chugging and clattering only slightly muffled by the wall of sandbags stacked around it to the height of eight feet.

Our mission was to secure the main gate. Since the guards stationed there were expecting any possible trouble to originate outside, they had no suspicion that the danger lay within and behind them. Crossing the courtyard by staying within the shadows, I stopped my team within a few metres of the machine-gun nest. The gun and the men were facing the road that led up to the gate.

There were three men in the sandbagged position, lounging, smoking cigarettes. It appeared that one was sleeping in a sitting position. I assumed that they took turns napping, ready to wake their fellows when the Sergeant of the Guard approached. Beyond them were two more guards flanking the wrought-iron gate, both smoking, in that ease of one bored with monotonous duty.

Inside my gloves my hands were sweating. I took the gloves off and wiped my slick palms on my pants leg, switching my kukiri knife from hand to hand.

I could feel the cold stone through my socks and was eager to put my shoes back on, but I knew that the task ahead of me had to be completed before this luxury was afforded. It seems trivial that I was thinking about my feet and how the hasty killing of a man or two was all that stood between me and my comfort, but I suppose these are also the priorities of battle.

Remembering the lessons taught me at the spy finishing school, I crept forward and picked my target—the man sitting behind the machine gun, as I felt he was the most important. One pull of the trigger would alert the entire castle and we would have a massacre on our hands. Outnumbered and in close quarters, we would have no chance. I thought of Maleva and the brave attack she had committed just moments before and I leapt over the sandbags.

Reaching over my target's head, I stuck four fingers into his mouth, prying it open and pulling back on his upper jaw, stretching his neck to the fullest, then sliced the taut throat. Thank you, Training Sergeant Charlie Hall.

I turned in time to see my gypsies eliminating the other Germans. The gypsy next to me merely snatched the helmet off his guard and slammed the steel rim into the man's temple, thusly rendering the victim instantly unconscious, if not dead. The helmet rang like a bell and the gypsy issued the coup de grace with his dagger.

At the gates, the two guards suffered the same kind of fate. While the gypsies stripped the soldiers of their weapons and ammo, I strolled to the gate and waved a white handkerchief at the dark night beyond the castle road. Out of those shadows came Lucy, her father, Ouspenkaya, and the rest of our band.

We had breached the fortress.

EXCERPTS FROM UNIDENTIFIED DIARY
(translated from the German)

The Tommy lurched away from the Vampire, clutching at his throat, blood seeping between his fingers. He screamed at us who stood on the other side of the bars.

The Vampire crouched in the corner, fangs bloody.

The cell door was opened and two of the Major's men reached in to drag the Englishman out. It was imperative to remove him while he was infected and before the Creature could kill his victim.

The Major held his silver sabre at the ready as the Tommy collapsed to the floor. Clasping the Englishman's legs, the two soldiers tried to drag him out of the cell. But at the door, the bitten man resisted, grabbing at the frame to prevent his removal.

At this moment Herr Wolf should have realised that something untoward was afoot.

As the Tommy stretched under the pull of the guards, the man's neck was fully visible and it was evident that there was no wound upon the skin, that the blood there had originated from the bloody cut on his palm. Everyone had been duped.

Herr Wolf shouted an alarm. But it was too late to close the cell door. The Tommy had wedged himself in the doorway.

The Major shouted commands to his men. — In or out! But close the damned door!

The Vampire launched itself across the cell at blinding speed, forcing the steel door to fly open with such force that it slammed against the wall. It caught one of the soldiers betwixt wall and door and crushed him to death.

The Major was also knocked aside, propelled into Herr Wolf, and both fell to the floor in a tangle of arms and legs.

Dracula stood in the corridor, free, facing the machine-gun crew at the end of the hallway and six armed SS beyond.

The Major composed himself enough to shout an order to fire. Herr Wolf and the Major pressed themselves to the floor as the stupefied machine-gun crew gathered their wits about them and began to shoot.

The Vampire leapt straight into the air and clung to the ceiling. How it accomplished this feat Herr Wolf had no idea. Quickly skittering overhead like some insect, the Creature made fast for the gun crew. They elevated the gun barrel to track the vampire, but bullets ricocheted without hitting their target.

Dracula landed behind the gun crew and made quick work of the six SS soldiers stationed there for Herr Wolf's security. The vampire grasped one of them by his leg and swung the body like a cudgel to batter the other five. This demonstration of strength astonished Herr Wolf and thrilled him at the same time.

The Vampire attacked the gun crew next, feasting on one while choking another and kicking the third. The kicked man flew twenty feet down the corridor and hit the wall with a crunch of bone and splat of meat. Most amazing. And most unpleasant.

Dracula broke the neck of his meal then turned and fixed his gaze upon Herr Wolf, who felt the malign malice in that glare. For the first time since the trenches, Herr Wolf felt his demise was at hand.

EXCERPTED FROM THE UNPUBLISHED NOVEL
THE DRAGON PRINCE AND I
by Lenore Van Muller

As the gate to the castle opened, Lucille and her father entered to greet Harker. A splash of blood glistened on his sleeve. She embraced him and uttered a grateful sigh.

"You're safe," she said, not even pausing to look at the dead Germans being dragged away from the machine-gun nest.

"I'm flattered that you care enough to worry," Harker said, and she searched his face to see if he was joking or if that same old issue still perturbed him.

"We're not out of danger yet—rather, we have stepped into the lion's mouth," Van Helsing warned.

They left two of the gypsies behind to keep the gate secured and hurried across the courtyard to the castle's main entrance. They faced a massive wooden door set inside a projecting doorway of formidable stone, worn by time and weather.

Lucille looked above them, examining the frowning walls that lined the courtyard. Dark windows bespoke a sleeping enemy and promised little interference, but Lucille knew this quiet respite would soon change.

The door itself was old, scarred and studded with large iron nails. Easing it open, they found the entryway vacant. Two stairwells presented themselves, one curving up and one spiraling down. Harker turned to the gypsies accompanying them.

"Who knows where the Germans bed their troops?" Lucille was amazed that he asked this in their language. On the trip back to Brasov she had observed him conversing with the gypsy girl Maleva, supposedly learning her native tongue. Lucille had thought it a ploy, an excuse for the Englishman to spend time with the exotically beautiful girl. So he had actually learned something, as stilted as his elocution might be.

She was not surprised that he had been enchanted by Maleva. It seemed that the English male, so repressed, was quite vulnerable to the exotic women outside his inhibited little island. In India, the Far and Middle East, Africa, these pale, stifled men quickly succumbed to the unique charms of the foreign female. Lucille was just happy that his ardour was no longer aimed at her. She did detect within herself a twinge of jealous injury at how swiftly his attention had shifted—the fickleness of youth, she supposed—but mostly she was relieved that he had moved on.

One of the Romani raised his hand, a fifteen-year-old boy with eyelashes long enough for Vivien Leigh to envy. He explained that he had previously been a prisoner in this castle, forced to help collect and wash the bedding of his captors. Lucille recognised him as one of those rescued from the concentration camp train. A woman did not forget a boy as pretty as this one. He would break some hearts—if he lived through tonight.

"You come with me," Harker told the boy, then addressed Lucille and her father.

"Professor, I think it would be best if you remained in the courtyard to protect our rear. Lucy, if you could go below with the gypsy king and his men and release the prisoners, I will set a surprise for the Germans with one of Renfield's tricks."

With a sardonic grin, he hefted a satchel that they had recovered in the ruins of the Van Helsing basement. She knew it was filled with a few pounds of gelignite and another pound of screws and nails for shrapnel.

He clapped a hand on Ouspenkaya's shoulder. "And I will make sure Maleva is brought safely from the tower."

He saluted Lucille and the rest, then dashed up the stairs with a "Chocks away, and good luck all." The boy followed and quickly passed Harker to lead the way.

Lucille smiled at his commanding manner and again at the mention of Maleva. She was sure the two were sharing more than language lessons and if not yet it was definitely in their future. Again, if they had one after tonight. She was fully aware that they were but a dozen against a tenfold enemy.

Lucille followed Ouspenkaya down into the bowels of the castle. During Harker's instructions, the gypsy king had outfitted himself in an SS uniform pilfered from one of the dead gate guards.

Reaching the landing where the stairs ceased, they entered a short hallway that made a sharp right turn. The passage was lit by gas jets, this section of the castle not yet electrified. Their shadows were projected on the wall next to them, doubling their meager numbers as they sneaked up to the corner.

Peering around the turn, Lucille saw two German guards posted at a large door. Beyond the door, according to their guide, was a ballroom, and beyond that the passage to the subterranean prison where their comrades and the Prince were being held.

Ouspenkaya pulled a bottle of spirits from one pocket, jabbed a cigar into his mouth, and winked at us. He made a few adjustments to his German costume, smiled, and set off. Turning the corner, he staggered down the hall, bumping into the heavy furniture and bouncing off the wall. As he weaved his way to the guards at the door he spoke in slurred German.

"Good time in town tonight." He brandished his bottle. "Taste this stuff. What 'Old Shatterhand' called firewater. Got a light?"

He took a huge swig from the bottle, held out his cigar. One of the guards fumbled in his jacket pocket for a match and offered the flame to the gypsy.

Grasping the match hand with his own, Ouspenkaya puffed his cheeks and spewed alcohol into the air. The match ignited the spray and fire bloomed in the dark hallway. The human flamethrower sprayed the guard's face, engulfing the man. The German's hair and clothes caught fire. Another swallow and the gypsy set fire to the astonished second guard, frozen in place, staring at his comrade's sudden combustion. Both men began to howl.

As the torched men batted at their flaming clothes and skin, Lucille and her father sprinted down the hall and knifed them.

Stepping over the smouldering bodies, two gypsies pushed past them and opened the great doors.

The ballroom was empty, and they hurried across the parquet floor, leaving two gypsies behind to man the door and hide the bodies. The room was large, high-ceilinged. Overhead, crystal chandeliers wrapped in sheets hung like giant wasp nests. The walls were lined with mirrors, and Lucille saw herself and the gypsies in myriad multiples. She glanced at the reflections and the sight startled her. They looked like bandits, hard-boiled killers on a homicidal vendetta. Which was not that far from the truth.

Hurrying into the next room, only a small vestibule, they found another spiral stairwell, the steps leading one way—down.

At the edge of the stairs, Lucille peered over the railing to see the shoulders and grey cap of another guard. Ouspenkaya aimed his pistol at the man below. Lucille pushed the gun hand away and shook her head, whispering, "No, let us try to remain undetected as long as possible."

The guard was speaking to someone. "Bunkhouse rumours. Pah! Vampires and werewolves and monsters. Horse shit between two slices of rye bread."

Another voice answered. "I didn't hear about the werewolves. Where? Is that what killed Schreck?"

So there were two men at the bottom of the stairs. She circled the railing and could see the boot tips of the other soldier.

Ouspenkaya moved to descend the stairs. Lucille stopped him.

"My turn," she whispered as she handed him her Luger and stripped off her coat, then her shirt and trousers. One of the men began to protest, but she hushed him with a look. Under the clothing she wore a thin batiste camisole and panties, but no brassiere. Clothing she had rescued from the ruins of the Van Helsing home.

She found a few of the gypsy men staring at where her nipples were visible through the camisole and, rather than being indignant or embarrassed, she smiled with satisfaction. This would work.

Stepping over to one of the gas lamps on the wall, she removed the glass and dipped a finger into the accumulated soot. Applying the black around her eyes and a lighter usage onto the hollows of her cheeks, Lucille checked the results in the reflection of a glass-covered painting hanging on the wall. Satisfied that she was appropriately phantasmal, she started walking down the steps.

Ouspenkaya laid a hand on her shoulder, stopping her.

"What are you doing?" he demanded in a harsh whisper.

"What needs to be done," she whispered back, pointedly removing his hand from her clavicle.

"You don't have a gun," he said. "Not even a knife."

"I have these." She cupped her breasts defiantly, then began the walk down the stairs. She kept her eyes wide, raised her arms into her best *White Zombie* walk.

The two sentries first saw her feet, then her pale legs. One called "Halt!" but Lucille kept her slow, deliberate pace.

One of the guards aimed his Schmeisser at her, but his vigilance was modulated when her breasts came into view. The gun barrel dipped as his eyes riveted to the areolae easily visible through the thin fabric.

His partner's concentration fixed upon the same area.

Gas lamp flames danced shadows across the hollow-eyed specter appearing before the two men, an erotic vision from out of their dreams—or nightmares, depending on their Jungian bent.

"What the f—" one muttered.

Lucille, eyes wide and unblinking, maintained her sleepwalking enchantress act and walked toward the nearest guard, murmuring softly.

". . . help me, help me, help me . . ." She kept repeating the phrase. The Nazi in front of her was perplexed, aroused, allowing Lucille to come closer, closer.

"I'll help you," he leered. "With this." He released the machine gun and grabbed his crotch. Just what she was waiting for.

"Careful, Fritz," the other cautioned.

Too late. Lucille kneed good old Fritz in the groin. He genuflected in front of her. Snatching the Schmeisser from his hands, she clubbed him in the head with the butt.

The other guard roused himself and aimed his own weapon at her. Lucille moved to him, but her legs became entangled with the fallen Fritz and she fell.

The second guard stepped over her and put the barrel of his own weapon into Lucille's face. She scrambled to aim her commandeered Schmeisser at him. But the weapon had become trapped under Fritz's leg. She struggled to free it.

The man above her smiled and flicked off his gun safety. The metallic clack was like a thunderclap in the small room.

Lucille prepared to die.

Then a shadow fell over her and the guard. There was a muffled crash as the second guard hit the floor with a fierce Ouspenkaya upon him, stabbing the man repeatedly.

The gypsy had jumped straight down the stairwell, hurtling toward the guard, landing on him like a sack of grain, and driving the man to the ground.

With both sentries eliminated, the rest of their force rushed down the stairs and joined them. Lucy put her clothing back on and wiped her face with a proffered handkerchief. She received her Luger back from Ouspenkaya as another gypsy eased open the lone door on the landing.

"This is it. The prison," he announced.

And then they heard the familiar stutter of a machine gun.

EXCERPTS FROM UNIDENTIFIED DIARY
(translated from German)

Herr Wolf found himself unable to move as the Vampire strode toward him with vile intent in those red eyes. Herr Wolf knew his End was at hand. These last years he had been sure Death was impending—the assassination attempts, his ill health, one close call after another. He just had not expected his Demise to be at the hands of some mythical beast.

But then Major R stepped between him and Dracula.

— Step back, my Führer, the stalwart soldier cried and wielded his new sword.

With a flick of his wrist he quickly scored a cut upon the vampire's forearm. Dracula reacted as if scalded and stepped backward, clasping the wound.

— Silver! was his response.

The Major confirmed this statement and proceeded to attack the Vampire, who retreated.

Herr Wolf shouted an order to the Major not to kill the Creature. The Major replied that his intention was but to subdue. He drove Dracula back a few steps more and the Vampire was now cornered. The Major preened for a moment, relishing his victory, always a mistake.

With a shriek of fury, the Tommy leapt from behind Herr Wolf and crossed the hall to tackle Major R. The two tumbled to the floor, the Major losing his sabre in the tussle. Dracula instantly pounced upon the Major and sank his teeth into the man's neck.

Herr Wolf was transfixed, fascinated at bearing witness to this act. Then he remembered his mission, how crucial it was that Dracula not be allowed to kill the Major. Without even thinking, Herr Wolf found the gift pistol in his hand. He did not remember taking it from the stand next to his chair. He reflexively chambered a round and aimed, the movement bringing back a vivid recollection of his days in the Great War.

Herr Wolf fired at the Vampire, hitting it in the upper arm. Dracula cried out, lifted his face from his feeding, and released the Major, who fell to the floor, gasping, still alive.

– Silver bullets! the Major shouted in triumph.

This must have been true, as the Vampire writhed with some vigor, clasping the wounded arm.

Herr Wolf now had a clear shot at the vampire and fired again. But the Englishman threw himself into the line of fire and Herr Wolf's shots, five of them, hit the Tommy instead.

Dracula leapt to the fallen spy and lifted him clear of the floor and carried him away with his unwounded arm. They both disappeared around the corner of the corridor.

Herr Wolf rushed to Major R's side, hoping that the officer was still alive. He was and told Herr Wolf that they must vacate this area before the Vampire returned.

Staggering to his feet, the Major retrieved his silver sabre and directed Herr Wolf down the corridor and through a door that they secured behind them. Herr Wolf had to help the Major, who was bleeding profusely from his neck bite and demonstrated a profound weakness.

With the Major giving directions, they made their way through a maze of subterranean tunnels. All the while, Herr Wolf had one thought on his mind—if the legends were true, he now possessed his own Vampire, obedient to him! Here was Immortality! Idunn's apples were in his hands!

EXCERPTED FROM THE UNPUBLISHED NOVEL
THE DRAGON PRINCE AND I
by Lenore Van Muller

Lucille and the others waited until the gunfire ceased, then eased their way into the underground prison. The corridors were dark; the ceiling lights hung too far apart, leaving stretches of deep shadow. The bulbs were dim, as if the generator was overloaded. You could see the filaments glowing orange, and what light they produced barely reached the floor.

The partisans crept along, expecting to encounter armed Germans with every step. But strangely, the corridor was empty. A ring of keys had been found hanging from the wall next to an abandoned desk, a cigarette still smoking in the ashtray. Ouspenkaya directed his people to begin opening the cells.

They freed their compatriots, and Lucille found herself appalled at the state of her friends. Captivity and torture had rendered many of them unrecognisable. The filth of the cells, the damp, and the cold had drained them further.

They found Farkas and Mihaly, their bloody faces bruised, cut, and swollen almost beyond recognition by beatings. Only their joyful voices gave a clue to their identity. There were embraces, but both men were so physically broken that they had to be carried out.

Farkas called out to Lucille as he passed, his voice a husky wreck, "They slaughtered Pavel!" he cried angrily. "Find me some revenge."

As shocked and dispirited Lucille was at the condition of her comrades, her focus was entirely centred upon the whereabouts and fate of the Prince. The opening of every door became a tortured moment of tense revelation and subsequent disappointment as the Prince was not found. And a following wave of guilt swept over her as the poor wretch who was inside was led away.

Too many of the prisoners needed assistance and soon Lucy was accompanied only by Ouspenkaya, as the rest of her party had helped the weak toward safer ground.

They continued their search for more prisoners and the keep where Dracula might be imprisoned.

The corridor made a turn, and Lucille braced herself against the wall. She peered around the corner to see if any Germans lay in wait. But the fear was moot as the hall ahead was still, the fight there long over.

She turned the corner and walked past the bodies of dead Germans littering the floor. Incongruously, an empty chair and an end table sat in the midst of this carnage. On the table, laid out as if for a tea party, sat a cup of congealed chocolate and a plate with a single dried date and a bit of half-eaten cheese, this surrounded by a tableau of blood and death.

There was a smell of cordite in the air, the walls and ceiling pockmarked with fresh divots cut from the stone. A tripod-mounted machine gun lay on its side. Nine dead Germans lay in a growing pool of blood.

Another cautious step past the next bend in the tunnel and Lucille halted, stunned. The Prince was sitting against the wall holding a limp Renfield in his arms.

Lucy rushed over and went to her knees before them, examining both. Renfield had multiple wounds, one in his chest frothing blood in rhythm with the rise and fall of his chest.

His eyes were fixed upon the Prince, then they turned to Lucille.

"Sergeant Renfield, reporting for duty." He raised a mangled hand in salute, but the arm made it only halfway before his strength failed and the hand fell to the floor like a shot bird.

"Can you do anything?" Dracula asked.

Lucille shook her head. She had seen other men lung shot and knew that there was little to be done, especially with the other wounds and the loss of blood the Sergeant had suffered. His face was white and his lips blue as he tried to smile.

Not knowing what else to do, Lucille reached out and swept the dying man's hair from his eyes. How many times had she done this, tried to find some scrap of comfort for a man about to die.

"Let's everybody sing . . ." he began. But the song died on his lips. Lucille saw the life leave his eyes.

Dracula released the lifeless man and rose to his feet. He regarded Renfield for a solemn second.

"He died a gallant soldier," Dracula whispered. "Sacrificing his life for my own." He then turned to her and the gypsy. "I had hoped that you had fled to safety," he said to Lucille as he embraced her with one arm.

"You know me better than that," she whispered into his ear, her breath warm on his neck.

"Yes, I do." They kissed. It was as good as their first, and she felt herself melt into his arms. He pulled away and attempted a smile, but it did not last long on his lips.

"Hitler is here," he said.

Lucille cursed, first to herself, then out loud.

"Impossible." Ouspenkaya refused to believe it.

"Know that it is possible and fact," Dracula said and started back the way they had come. He clutched one arm with his hand.

"You are wounded," Lucille said. The Prince examined the flesh of his arm.

"Silver bullets," he remarked. "The Major is sagacious. Remove the offending bullet, please."

"I, I can't. I don't have any instruments, any sterilization," she protested.

"Here." Ouspenkaya handed her his thin-bladed dagger. Lucille was quick, not wanting to prolong the Prince's pain. She inserted the knife into the wound and pried out the spent round, which fell to the floor with a dull clink.

"We should suture that," she told the Prince, returning the dagger to the gypsy, who wiped the blade clean on a dead German's tunic.

When she turned back to him, Dracula was gone, running down the corridor so fast as to blur.

EXCERPTS FROM UNIDENTIFIED DIARY
(translated from the German)

The Major directed Herr Wolf to a room deep in the penetralia of the castle. Herr Wolf shut the thick door and barred it with a beam he found leaning against the wall.

The centre of the room was dominated by a large, circular opening in the floor. It was an old cistern, the source of water for this ancient fortress, most likely fed by underground springs. The water glistened under the wavering light from the gas jet, flickering in the draught of the castle's exhalations. Herr Wolf peered into the dark depths of the water and could see no bottom.

Herr Wolf turned from his examination of this architectural artefact to see the Major sprawled on the floor, writhing in the throes of great pain. His screams echoed across the chamber, the sound reverberating against the hoary stones. Herr Wolf's skin tightened at the sound and he searched for an exit, but realised that the barred door was the only way in or out.

He was trapped with a dying man. At least this was what he thought until, upon closer examination of the Major, he discovered that the man was instead undergoing some kind of transformation. His skin was turning pale, not the purple-lipped, yellow-skinned pallor of death that Herr Wolf had become so familiar with on the Western Front.

No, this was a profound change in the substance of the skin, metamorphosing into a glass-like translucence, the man's eyes reddening with burst capillaries. In the midst of an ear-punishing scream from the wretch, Herr Wolf was able to discern that the Major's eyeteeth had become fangs.

The transformation was happening before his eyes!

But then another thought occurred to Herr Wolf. He was trapped in this room with a Vampire. Would the transmutation affect the man's reasoning? Would he attack like some famished animal? Would his Ungodly thirst dominate his Common Sense, his allegiance to his Fuhrer?

As the Major ceased writhing in his physical anguish and grew still, Herr Wolf backed his way to the door. Clutching the pistol loaded with silver bullets he casually aimed it in the Major's direction. Then the Major rose unsteadily to his feet, slowly, carefully, as if an invalid finding his strength after a long recovery. He turned to face Herr Wolf, an expression on his face that could only be described as ecstatic, exultant.

It struck Herr Wolf that this moment was another event that would define his Destiny. This was the culmination of his Superiority over the rest of humanity. His victories over his enemies had repeatedly proved his Supremacy. Herr Wolf was no longer bound by the restrictions of ordinary human mores. He had Evolved into a super-human state and before him was the opportunity to take the next inevitable step, to rise to his rightful seat next to the Gods.

Immortality stood before him. Could he do this?

He thought of Dr. Schertel's declaration—He who does not have the demonic seed within himself will never give birth to a magical world.

Could he do this? He must.

HE MUST!

FROM THE WAR JOURNAL OF
J. HARKER

(transcribed from shorthand)

After parting with Lucy and her contingent, I followed the young gypsy boy, Sandu, up the stairs. The passageway was narrow, and my elbows constantly banged on the rough wall. The castle had been wired for electricity recently and rather crudely: Bare wire was stapled to the walls and ceilings; switches, outlets, and lighting had been installed with no regard for the chipping of marble, stone, or the mutilation of centuries-old hardwoods. Obviously these Nazi troglodytes bore no respect for history. To my embarrassment, I struck my head on the lintel of the first-floor exit with a resounding thud. The boy turned to me with concern, and I gestured for him to proceed.

On the third-floor landing, I committed the same foible. This time the collision of beam and my forehead caused a wound and blood to seep. The boy raised his eyebrows at me, then pointed to a door.

I eased it open and immediately the effluvium of men cohabiting together floated out like a miasmal fog with an accompanying musicale of grunts, snores, and coughs. Peering inside, I could see folding bunks crowded together in what must have once been a magnificent library. A small wood stove had been set against one wall, and the flue pipe ran up the wall to poke through a broken pane in the window. It was evident that the German savages were using the books for fuel; a pile of tomes, some torn into stove-sized bits, were strewn about the floor next to the stove.

This sacrilege roiled my gut and seemed reason enough to set the charge at the door. I attached a length of fishing line to the doorknob and tied the other end to a pull switch, which I then inserted into the charge. The whole package, a block of gelignite wrapped with nails, was set on the threshold. Then we crept up the stairs to another landing, to a door that accessed the roof.

Once outside, we stood adjacent to the parapet. I spied Maleva and her companions crouched behind the parapet walls, two of them aiming their weapons to the grounds outside the castle, one guarding the interior courtyard below.

Sandu gave a low whistle, and we were recognised. Maleva hopped over the wall and into my arms.

"We took the castle," she whispered enthusiastically. "Like the Errol Flynn."

I could not but help return the embrace with some enthusiasm of my own. The gypsy waif noticed the blood on my forehead and her instant show of concern touched my heart.

"We need to get you down from here before all hell breaks loose," I told her, whispering into her ear, which I noticed was within biting distance of my mouth. I wanted to do that and more. But the soldier in me overruled the man, and I led her and the rest of the gypsies toward the access door.

We started down the stairs and made it to the first landing, when we heard muffled gunshots below us. Then a klaxon blared its obnoxious cry all about. I halted my band of gypsies on the stairs, and I was just about to urge everyone to hurry down, when the charge at the library door went off.

The concussive force swept up the stairs and we all suddenly found ourselves thrown backward onto the steps. Clambering back to my feet, I began to descend the stairs. Turning the corner, I was able to see the library doorway. Smoke was curling up over the header, and an injured man, his clothes in tatters, bloody from a multitude of wounds, crawled out of the room on his hands and knees.

I urgently led the others down the stairs. We were almost abreast of the library when gunfire erupted from the smoking doorway. Bullets whipped past my face and impacted against the stone wall. I stopped and everyone backed up behind me. Sandu heedlessly pushed past me into the line of fire.

I grabbed the boy by his collar and yanked him out of danger.

"Back!" I shouted and fired a burst into the black interior of the library. I could barely hear because of the concussive effects of the blast, but I could feel the wood steps vibrate as the others ran back up the way we had come.

More gunfire poured through the library and I fired back until I was sure the gypsies were safe. Then I followed them up.

We reconvened our little party on the rooftop. Stationing myself at the door, I reloaded and fired a short burst from my Thompson every time a Jerry poked his head into the stairwell.

"Take the others down the rope," I called out to Maleva. She nodded and they climbed the wall again and made their way over the roof to where the rope still hung into the courtyard.

One by one, the gypsies slid down to safety. The Germans were now firing blindly at my position, poking their weapons around the corner to fire wild rounds in my direction. The roof door was being shredded by the constant fusillade and was no longer suitable for cover, so I stood on the other side of the jamb to return fire.

Maleva returned to my side. "They are all gone."

"Now it's your turn," I told her. She stared into my face and reached up to pluck a stone shard from my cheek. I reached my own hand to my face and found sticky blood pouring from the wound. I had not known that I was even hit.

"You must come with me," she said.

"I will," I said. "As soon as you're safe."

I knew this was a lie. It was a bad show all around. I was running short on ammo; I had but one magazine left after this one was spent. Maybe twenty-five rounds or so. Enough to hold them off until Maleva climbed down. But when I left the doorway I knew the Jerries would attack, and I would not have enough time to get to the rope, much less climb down, before they would be upon me. She did not need to know this.

She still hesitated.

"Blast it! Go!" I said but the rebellious fire I saw in her eyes made me try another tactic. "Please," I begged.

She nodded and sprinted to the wall and was over it and gone. I sighed in regret at what might have been and returned my attention to the stairwell.

Two Germans made a mad dash up the stairs. I emptied my magazine at them and they fell. While changing magazines I thought I heard Maleva yelling from the roof. I was thoroughly deaf from all the gunfire by now and was not able to make out the words.

Below, an arm stretched out to drag one of the wounded Germans out of my line of fire, and I let loose a couple of rounds at the reaching hand, missing and cursing myself for wasting ammo on such small targets. No more mucking about—I knew that larger ones were coming. I also knew that

I was in an untenable position. I could not withstand a prolonged firefight. This was one that I had little hope of escaping, and I fretted not. This was my job. Fair enough. I would fulfill this mission. Do or die, as they say. Do. Or die.

Then I felt a tap on my shoulder and turned to see Maleva and Sandu standing behind me, their shoulders sagging under the weight of a couple of satchels. They dropped them at my feet. Three Schmeissers, a proliferation of magazines, and a satchel full of grenades.

"The others, they attack from below," Maleva said.

"Well, we're not playing the game for candy." I grinned. "We will attack from above."

And this we did. Brandishing two Schmeissers, Maleva doing the same, with Sandu hurling grenades over our heads into the stairs before us, we charged the Germans.

It was madness, the gypsy girl at my side, both of us emptying two machine guns simultaneously, reloading during Sandu's grenade tosses, making our way step by step down the stairs. We had to step over, around, and sometimes upon the bodies, firing into any that stirred in the slightest, sometimes shooting the already dead just to make sure none of them were going to shoot us in the back after we passed.

At the library, we stopped to toss in six more grenades, if for no other reason than momentary paranoia. At this point we heard the gunfire below and proceeded to pin the last redoubt of Jerries between us and our compatriots. It was short work to eliminate this last obstacle, and we suddenly found ourselves in the brisk, fresh air of the courtyard.

I took a deep breath that was not redolent of cordite and blood. And found myself wrapping my arms around Maleva and giving her a proper kiss.

Of course this was the moment when her father and the Professor chose to exit the castle and join us.

I quickly pulled away from the girl and saw her father's face twist into a sardonic grin.

"So, did you save my daughter for me or for yourself, Englishman?" he asked.

"She saved me," I told him. "And I was just demonstrating my appreciation."

That received laughter from those gathered about. But the mirth was short-lived, as suddenly we were under fire again.

There was a gun battle at the gate as a lorry full of SS, returning from some off-post duty, was set upon by our gypsy machine-gun crew. I led my group across the courtyard to reinforce the gate defenders and join the fray, when we were suddenly under fire from above.

We all sought cover as bullets pinged off the cobblestones underfoot. I searched for our attackers and saw four rifles protruding from windows of the third floor. From that secure perch, the courtyard was a fish barrel for them.

Maleva and I crouched under an overhang of the building. The Professor and Ouspenkaya joined us.

"Where's Lucy?" I asked her father.

Ouspenkaya answered for him. "She went after the Prince," he said. "He went after Hitler."

"Hitler!" I could not contain my surprise.

"He probably came for the vampire," Van Helsing said.

"Hitler . . . ?" I was still trying to absorb this when I noticed a small group of people huddled against the wall across the courtyard. They were thin, wearing rags. The prisoners. Freed. That was good. Then I remembered.

"Renfield?" I asked.

"Dead," Ouspenkaya stated solemnly. "He died a hero."

"Of course." But I did not mourn. Instead I felt an anger bloom within me. "Then we shall repay his sacrifice." I began looking around, taking in our status, and searching for a way to join the fray.

"Our escape is completely blocked!" Van Helsing shouted over the gunfire. And we saw the gate machine-gun nest overtaken by the Germans as they drove the gypsies back and took positions behind the sandbagged position.

"We have to get everyone out before any Rumanian Army reinforcements arrive!" Ouspenkaya shouted. "I am sure the Germans called for them!"

They were all looking to me, and I realised that this was the reason I had been sent here.

I turned to Sandu, who had tagged along with me since our assault on the stairwell. "Any more grenades?" I asked.

"Five," he said, checking his satchel for confirmation.

"Enough," I said, looking up at the third-storey sniper positions. "Now if I could only find a way to deliver them."

I felt a tap on my shoulder. Maleva. The elfin face was smeared with gunpowder blowback and she looked like a Dickens street urchin. A street urchin with a peculiar sexual component, I must confess.

"I know how to get the apples through the window," she said cryptically and tugged on my sleeve to follow her. I allowed her to lead me back into the castle through a small door that led to a kitchen and then a door to a most claustrophobic stairwell. We hurried up the narrow stairway. I had to hunch over for the low ceiling; once again I found the walls so close that my shoulders brushed the sides. How small were the builders and occupants of these fortresses? Maleva held my hand the whole circular climb and I felt a strange dislocation, she and I holding hands like a boy and girl on a frolic in Hyde Park. There was a rush of emotion inside me reminiscent of those innocent days.

Once we made the fourth floor, Maleva directed me to a window. As the sound of gunfire increased in volume, my romantic reverie was shattered, and I was rudely reminded of our embattled situation.

Maleva used the butt of her Schmeisser to clear out the glass, and we both put our faces to the opening to survey the situation from on high. The machine-gun nest at the gate was now turned from facing the entrance road to aim inside the courtyard. An occasional burst from this emplacement kept the partisans trapped in the courtyard. The riflemen at the windows were one floor below us and fifteen to twenty yards to our right. These Nazi snipers were oblivious to our presence, firing down below at targets of opportunity. Two more were in reserve, taking over when their fellows emptied their clips and had to reload.

I thought of firing upon them, but all I could see were mere bits and pieces of them, not good targets, and my Schmeisser was not accurate enough for a sure hit in any case. Plus, we would be in another firefight and outnumbered at that.

I related this to Maleva and she gestured to the grenades.

"Much better, no?"

"Too far to throw with any accuracy," I told her.

"But I can get closer," she said and pointed to the telephone wires just below us, strung from building to building across the courtyard. A few of the wires ran from our window and just above the snipers' positions.

I remembered her tightrope act in the caves and smiled. While she took off her shoes, I told her that if she was discovered to come right back. I took the M24 stick grenades and prepared them, unscrewing the base cap to allow the ball and cord to fall out, then arranged them inside the satchel, stick end up so that the strings would not tangle. She nodded and slipped the satchel of grenades over her head to hang from one shoulder.

Then I helped her out onto the window ledge, where she stepped onto the wire as casually as I would step off an underground platform and onto a train.

Walking the wire, she soon crossed the distance between our window and the Germans. I rested my Schmeisser on the windowsill, keeping what I could see of the Nazi snipers in my sights in case they spotted her approach and I had to cover her retreat.

But they were oblivious as they took pot shots at any movement of the gypsies below.

Maleva reached into the satchel, withdrew a grenade, pulled the porcelain ball initiating the five-second fuse. Then I was witness to the most calmness and coolness under pressure I have ever seen. She counted off three seconds of the five before tossing the grenade through the open window. Obviously she had more confidence in the lowest bidder than the late Renfield and I did.

The Jerries had but a second to take notice of what had landed in their midst before it went off. And meanwhile she had taken a second grenade and repeated the amazing act.

The explosions blew out the glass from the surrounding windows, and a cloud of debris shot out into the courtyard.

Amazingly, Maleva never wavered on her precarious perch. I waved her back, but she turned her back to me and stepped over onto one of the other black cables and began making her way toward the machine-gun nest, reaching into her satchel on the remarkable walk.

There was no way for me to call her back. I tried shouting over the gun battle still happening below, but it was a futile exercise. And the last thing I wanted to do was draw attention to her. Besides, I doubt if she would have obeyed. Realising that she might need covering fire, I rushed away from the window and back down the stairs as fast as I could run, jumping the steps two, three, and four at a time.

I came out to find the situation still at a stalemate. I could see Maleva overhead, and I pointed this out to her father, who shouted for her to stop.

She ignored him and continued her dangerous trot across open air. But now every one of the gypsies was staring up at her—which, to my chagrin, alerted the Germans at the machine gun.

One of them lifted his rifle and took aim. I yelled a warning. The German fired. She was hit, in the arm or shoulder, it was hard to tell. I saw only a spray of blood and her twist, then teeter on the wire.

She fell, but caught herself with one leg, hung there by a bent knee as the satchel dropped to the ground.

The German fired again, mercifully missing this time. But his comrades took up the same action and instantly the air around her was alive with bullets like hornets flitting about the poor girl.

I do not know what came over me. I charged across the courtyard firing my Schmeisser. The Jerries momentarily ducked for safety, and I was able to cross the courtyard far enough to put myself under the dangling Maleva.

"Let loose!" I shouted at her.

She did, and I caught her in my arms. And for a moment, time stopped. She looked up at me, her eyes so wide, an incongruous smile on her lips. "See," she said, "you are my savings." I wanted to kiss her but I uttered only one word.

"Pakvora," I said. And she was just that: beautiful.

But this was no time to throw bouquets. The sound of gunfire interrupted this insane reverie. I saw the spark of bullets skipping across the cobblestones around us and I suddenly was aware of where I was and the danger we were in.

Then Ouspenkaya was beside us.

"Take her," I told him, and as he did so I snatched up the satchel. Reaching inside, I pulled the cords of every stick as I sprinted toward the machine-gun nest in a broken zigzag run that would have made my field hockey coach proud, heedless of the M34 belching flame and spitting bullets my way. I felt a tug at my jacket as a round tore through, but I did not stop.

When I was within throwing distance, I tossed the satchel over the sandbag wall and threw myself flat upon the cobbles.

The blast pounded through my body like a giant had slapped me into the ground with one great hand.

As I rose, the armed gypsies bounded past me to clean up the nest, and I became stunned at what I had just done. The feeling overwhelmed me to the point that my legs wobbled like my grandmother's tomato aspic.

I started back to where I had left Maleva, and I saw the weakened prisoners being carried and escorted out of the gates. Van Helsing was bent over a prostrate Maleva as Ouspenkaya hovered, and the Professor bound her shoulder in a hasty bandage.

I walked over, feeling suddenly very weak myself.

"Is it bad?" I asked, the guilt of allowing her to endanger herself weighing heavily on me. But the gypsy girl responded by leaping up from the ground and into my arms, kissing me. I felt the startling, incredibly sensual intrusion of the tip of her tongue.

"You saved me!" she cried, and I was immediately self-conscious. My eyes looked everywhere but at the girl.

My eyes lighted upon her father, who just shrugged in that European manner that says so many things at once.

I regained my senses and took a deep breath to calm myself.

"If Hitler is really in the castle, it is imperative that we capture him," I said as I gently pried my way out of Maleva's grasp and led them back into the castle.

"This is our chance to end this war. Now," Van Helsing declared as he and the gypsies followed me.

EXCERPTS FROM UNIDENTIFIED DIARY
(translated from the German)

Herr Wolf studied the bloodless face of Major R and felt himself take a few involuntary steps back, his fingers tensing on the Mauser pistol as the transformed man walked toward him. Being in the Major's presence gave Herr Wolf a feeling of malignant threat. Nothing that the soldier did or said communicated this sinister aura, but it still emanated from him like heat from a blazing fire. Herr Wolf could not help but back away.

The Major seemed to realise this trepidation and ceased his approach. The light from the gas lamps on the wall bounced off the cistern waters and rippled across the ghostly face.

— Mein Führer, you will have to order me to commit this deed, the Major said. — I cannot do this to you of my own accord.

The thought came to Herr Wolf that the consequences of this act could be very black. He could die. The Major might not be fully in control of his new state and be able to stop before draining Herr Wolf to the point of death.

Was Herr Wolf afraid? Possibly. Perhaps the act of submission needed to do this was what was holding him back. Herr Wolf had not subjugated himself to any person in quite some time.

But fear? He brushed aside any qualms. It certainly was not his Destiny to die at the hands of some mythological creature in the subterranean vault of an obscure Rumanian castle. No. "If you do not stake your life, life shall never be your prize."

Herr Wolf ripped open his collar, bared his neck to the cool, damp air.

— Do your duty, Colonel, Herr Wolf ordered, instantly promoting the man.

— And may God protect us, said the Colonel.

He stepped forward and laid one hand on Herr Wolf's head, another hand on the opposite shoulder, whether to steady himself or Herr Wolf was not exactly evident.

The Colonel opened his mouth to reveal two wet fangs, shiny white teeth, sharp and deadly looking. He lowered his head. At the first touch of these teeth Herr Wolf sprang back, maybe instinctively.

He ordered the Colonel to cease, that this action must be considered a bit more. Herr Wolf was too important to the Reich to risk his life precipitously. He decided that it would be better if the Colonel would accompany Herr Wolf back to Berlin. There they would decide the proper way to proceed.

This pause was difficult for the Colonel. Herr Wolf could see the sanguine craving in the man's countenance. But slowly, through sheer force of visible will, the soldier brought himself under control.

Herr Wolf proceeded to the door, lifted the bar, and ordered Colonel R to proceed ahead of him, as the Colonel knew the way.

They had not walked far when they encountered a breathless Lieutenant F, who, with great agitation, announced that the castle was under attack and reported to the Colonel that his troops were close to being overrun.

The Colonel instantly took command and declared that the Fuhrer must be evacuated immediately. Herr Wolf reminded the Colonel that he was under orders to accompany Herr Wolf to Berlin.

Herr Wolf followed the two loyal soldiers up and through a labyrinth of corridors and rooms, both large and small. The Lieutenant kept glancing back at his Colonel, eyeing his superior officer with puzzlement, then concern and apprehension. Herr Wolf, too, had noticed the change in the Colonel—a difference of appearance, of course, the bloodshot eyes and strange pallor—but also there was a certain carriage, an effortless motion that Herr Wolf had not noticed before.

Gunfire could be heard, becoming louder as they ascended the stairs. The castle was indeed under siege. Herr Wolf suddenly became aware that he was in jeopardy. He must not be captured!

At one recalcitrant door, the Colonel opened it with such prodigious force that he tore it off the hinges and tossed it aside like a discarded newspaper.

They entered a rather large vaulted room that was apparently being used to store ammunition and military supplies and ordnance, the familiarly marked crates and boxes stacked everywhere. Herr Wolf was pleased to see how neatly the provisions were arranged, a tribute to the professionalism of the Colonel and his command.

One wall was decorated with implements from the castle's medieval origins: shields and weaponry, halberds, maces, long and short swords. Lieutenant F walked directly to a massive, ornately carved mahogany bench, the back taller than a man. With a slight push it slid away from the wall; the ease with which he accomplished this was facilitated by a set of cleverly concealed wheels. A passageway was revealed, a dark, brick-lined tunnel of ancient construction.

The Lieutenant explained that this was an ancient secret escape tunnel to the road at the base of the mountain.

The Colonel led Herr Wolf across the room toward this subterranean passage, but this short journey was interrupted by the arrival of another.

The Vampire. Dracula!

The monster's focus was entirely fixed upon Herr Wolf, who felt a bleak dread clutch his heart in cold fingers.

— You. The Vampire pointed a long finger at Herr Wolf. — Your war is at an end.

His stride toward Herr Wolf was purposeful and laden with ill intent.

But then the brave Colonel R stepped between his Führer and the Vampire. He drew his silver sabre and faced Dracula, a Siegfried for a modern time.

— Take the Führer to safety, the Colonel commanded. — That is your priority!

Lieutenant G took Herr Wolf by the arm and drew him into the mouth of the tunnel.

Herr Wolf hesitated at the opening, not wanting to abandon the transformed Colonel, this chance at immortality. Still, there was the danger of Herr Wolf's imminent capture. That could not happen! He paused to watch the Vampire snatch a sword off the wall and step toward the Colonel's challenge. The Lieutenant rudely pulled Herr Wolf into the tunnel and pushed shut a thick concrete door, the hinges protesting with a screech of rusty steel.

Just before the door was closed, Herr Wolf saw a woman enter the room, a red-haired beauty, fierce of visage, a Valkyrian vision, brandishing a long-barrelled Luger. She rushed toward him, her fiery eyes fixed upon Herr Wolf's own, her determination much in evidence. And then she was gone as the closing door obliterated this amazing tableau.

EXCERPTED FROM THE UNPUBLISHED NOVEL
THE DRAGON PRINCE AND I
by Lenore Van Muller

Lucille searched every room, dashing about the castle like a rat in a pantry, ripping open doors, poking her head inside rooms, darting to the next, trying desperately to find the Prince. All to no avail. So many rooms. So many empty rooms.

Well, one room, a large linen room, was occupied, a German soldier with his pants around his ankles atop a girl, not much more than twelve or thirteen. She had her skirts bundled around her waist; he was plunging at her like he was driving a spike into a tree.

They both were startled. No more so than when Lucille shot the Kraut in the head and shut the door behind her. Lucille heard a small squeak from the girl. Then she moved on with her quest, which seemed to grow more futile by the moment. She heard the gunfire, the explosions of a major battle outside, but continued her hunt for the man she was now bound to, trying not to give up all hope.

She stopped for a second, to get her bearing in the labyrinth of the castle. The surety of her purpose was strong as ever, but she was completely lost in the castle's depths, having no idea where Prince Vlad had gone. The realisation stunned her, overwhelmed her, and she stopped dead in her tracks.

Then she felt a sudden heat on her chest, like a hot ember had fallen between her breasts. She quickly jammed a hand down her shirtfront, found her fingers clasping the leather pouch given to her by the mysterious gypsy woman in the caves.

She pulled it out, lifted the cord off her neck. The pouch was warm in her palm, like holding a little bird. She untied the neck and emptied the contents into her hand. A reddish powder, like rouge poured out, inert but warm. What was she to do with it? What were the gypsy's words?

"For when you lose your love"? At the time Lucille thought it was some spurious love potion that the gypsies foisted on the bourgeois. But what if . . . ?

The sound of explosions interrupted her musing, reminding her that other lives were in jeopardy. She had no time to dawdle, to muse over some useless powder.

Raising her palm to her face, she blew the dust off her hand. It formed a small, scarlet cloud and she was about to walk away when she noticed that the dust was not settling. The cloud hung in midair, the dust swirling inside the brume. She walked around this curious sight, then said, "Find him." Where the words came from she had no idea, neither the why of her actions. She just somehow knew what to do.

The cloud spewed a red finger that shot down the corridor in front of her. Lucille ran after it.

She began following a thread only she could see, a trickle of scarlet fog leading her onward to her love. She moved forward in a mad rush.

So fast was her progress that when she opened the door to what appeared to be a storeroom and saw the Prince at en garde with a Nazi officer, she at first closed the door, ready to move on, and even took a step away before the sight finally registered. The red cloud had evaporated, further affirmation that she had found him.

She quickly stepped back and re-opened the door. Yes, Dracula was here. Something else caught her attention, movement across the room, another doorway. A man stood there, short, dark hair hanging over his forehead, that little patch of mustache . . . Could it be?

My God, it *was* him! Dracula had told the truth.

Hitler!

"Get him!" Dracula shouted to her and she rushed across the room, but as she ran the door slid into place. It slammed shut inches from her face, almost trapping her outflung fingers. She clawed at the door but was unable to gain purchase, much less pry it open.

She cursed, turned back toward the Prince and his opponent. They were circling each other, sword tips making delicate arabesques in the air, eyes wary.

There was something about the German officer that forced Lucille to give him further scrutiny. His eyes, his skin, the manner in which he moved. A chill coursed through her body, her skin goose-pimpled.

He was a vampire.

Then she noticed the bloody smear on the German's neck, a black-red stain on the collar of his uniform. He had been bitten. And survived. Lucille now remembered his name: Reikel, the murderer of the Mayor, Janos, and so many of her friends.

"I don't fear you," the Nazi addressed Dracula and punctuated the statement with a dry laugh.

"You should," Dracula warned.

"I have your powers," the German said, grinning in triumph.

"You have some," Dracula answered. "But power is oft not enough, as many a tyrant has discovered."

Lucille observed that one of the Prince's arms hung limply at his side, the same arm from which she had removed the silver bullet.

The Nazi attacked. Swords slashed, clashed, Dracula parrying adroitly. The contact lasted but tiny bits of seconds, the thrust and parry of blades at a speed no human could match or even follow. To Lucille it was but a bright scintillation of metal against metal, then a withdrawal and more circling. They were testing each other.

"I was the captain of the Olympic Fencing Team representing Germany; I have won medals all over Europe."

"I do not know of what you speak," Dracula said.

"A contest. For medals. Have you ever seen a German officer with a scar on his cheek?" the German asked. "Dueling scars? They brag about them."

"I do recall a Hun with such a scar," Dracula answered.

Another thrust and counterthrust at blinding speed.

"We who know the sword call such men losers." The German smiled. Lucy could see his new fangs. "I have no scars. I make scars."

"I see. You have no scar." Dracula returned the grin. "Well, then we shall give you one."

And he did just that. With an almost invisible flick of his sabre, he cut the Nazi across one cheek. The SS officer was shocked, touched the cut. There was no blood, just a dark seepage.

Then Dracula attacked, driving the German back.

"You see, I fought no duels for medals. Or for vanity," the Prince declared. "I fought to defend myself, to evade death. A better teacher, do you not agree?"

And he slashed the German across the chest, slicing through uniform and skin.

"To maim," Dracula said as he managed another slash, this one across the German's forearm.

"To kill my enemy." This cut rent the Nazi's pants, exposing Reikel's thigh.

Lucille could see the sudden astonishment and growing panic in the German's eyes. He was forced to back his way across the room then retreat along the wall until he reached the door opposite.

Opening it with his free hand, still engaging the Prince with his sabre, he mounted a short attack and then ducked into the next room.

Dracula followed and Lucille was close behind.

This room was the ballroom Lucille had passed through earlier. It was a long rectangle, one wall completely mirrored like a ballet studio, the ancient glass corroded with brackish rivers and tributaries. In the near corner, a mirrored bar was set, a hint of modernity contemplated by the gilt-winged cherubs flitting about in the sky-blue ceiling.

The other wall was interrupted at regular intervals by ornate windows, starting waist high and extending to the ceiling.

Twenty German soldiers were now stationed at the opened windows, weapons aimed outside. As one, they all turned their attention from the castle grounds outside to the two men who were dancing across the parquet floor like a scene from a Douglas Fairbanks movie.

Lucille stepped back into the shadows of the doorway before the soldiers took their attention from the fencing pair toward her. She ducked behind the bar.

Dracula and the Nazi officer fought, blade clashing upon blade, the two combatants oblivious to their audience as Dracula drove the German down the length of the room. The SS men at the windows watched, mouths agape at the sight.

Reikel took another cut, a slice across his torso that made his tunic flap open to reveal his pallid chest. The officer was suffering from a dozen cuts, small and large, and he was tiring.

He turned to the troops at the windows.

"Kill him!" he screamed at them.

The soldiers turned their guns toward Dracula and began to fire.

Some of the bullets struck the Prince, knocking him back like invisible punches, hindering his attack on their commander.

Many of the shots hammered instead the mirrored wall, shattering glass that waterfalled to the floor in a crystalline deluge with an accompanying din that pained Lucille's ears.

The Germans stopped shooting for a second and stared in awe at a man who had just visibly been hit by a dozen bullets and showed no adverse effects except the impact.

Seeing the Prince battered by the gunfire, Lucille aimed her long-barrelled Luger and began picking off the Germans. Some of them turned their fire onto her, smashing the bar's mirrored cladding and tearing through the wood beneath.

One of the Germans emptied his weapon at her, causing Lucille to seek cover as the man sprinted past and out the door that led to the storeroom. She fired after him but missed.

Dracula turned from Reikel and charged the soldiers with his sword, slashing through swaths of grey uniforms as if they were cornstalks before a scythe. Men dropped to the floor, some not even realising that they had just lost an arm, just had a leg amputated, one not even aware that he was dead on his feet. Blood geysered from severed arteries.

Lucille killed three more, but then heard the dull click that meant her bolt was fixed back. She was out of ammunition and cursed herself.

But there was no need to worry. With a lightning slash, Dracula cleaved the last soldier into two pieces. He turned back to Reikel.

Lucille rose from her cover to watch them duel. She knew it was a fight to the death, but she had also seen the Prince's superiority over the German and was not concerned. She relaxed to watch the show.

Then something caught the periphery of her vision. She turned to see the soldier who had fled step back into the room. Perched upon his shoulder was a Panzerschreck, what the partisans called a stovepipe, a long tube that fired an 88mm rocket. He must have appropriated the weapon from the armoury they had just vacated.

Fear stole her breath away. The Prince might survive a few bullets, but she herself had destroyed a tank with one of these rockets. This would obliterate him.

Instinctively, she raised her Luger to shoot the soldier and remembered that the pistol was empty. She dashed across the room to one of the fallen dead.

The soldier with the rocket launcher struggled to aim his weapon at the Prince, who was in a dance of death that made him flit around the room.

Lucille ripped a pistol out of a dead man's hand, flicked off the safety, and aimed at the German in the doorway. His hand was on the trigger.

She shot him. Twice in the chest.

He staggered. In his death throes he somehow fired the rocket. The round went wild, struck the ceiling with a tremendous explosion. Plaster and slivers of wood rained down.

The white cloud of plaster dust was just beginning to settle when there was a creak of strained wood and one of the thick beams overhead plunged to the floor.

It struck Dracula, pinned him to the floor.

Reikel leapt out of the way, recovered, and climbed over the debris pile to stand over the helpless Prince.

Lucille shot Reikel. But besides his recoiling from the impact, the bullets had no more effect on him than they would on Dracula.

Reikel loomed over the Prince, raised his sabre high for the killing slash.

"Is it as the legend says, that a wooden stake through the heart kills the vampire?" Reikel mused sardonically. "Or does a silver blade suffice? Time for another experiment. I wish my scribe was here to record this moment."

Lucille suddenly found herself on her feet and hurtling across the room, throwing her body over the Prince's as the gleaming silver sabre descended.

She did not hear her scream as the blade penetrated her side, slicing through flesh and rib. She just felt all her strength drain from her body.

Dracula was struggling to free himself when Lucille's face suddenly appeared only inches from his own. Then he saw her eyes go wide in shock, the exhalation of her breath on his skin.

He felt her pain as if it were his own, as if they were twins joined in mind and body. Empathy unbound. Pain beyond endurance.

Whether Dracula's scream came from anguish, protest, or anger, he surged from under the beam that trapped him and charged after the German.

His attack was hampered, one leg injured, dragging behind him as he sliced at the Nazi, who was once again forced to back away from the onslaught.

Then Reikel attacked, wounding the Prince's dead leg, finally scoring on the vampire. The German smiled at his success.

"One cut?" Dracula asked. "Learn this much. I welcome the pain."

"Then I shall give it," Reikel sneered.

Dracula received another cut, hissed in agony.

"Pain reminds one of what it was to feel human." Dracula attacked toward the Nazi, receiving wound after wound while forcing the Nazi to retreat. "I embrace the pain."

He drove the German to an open window. The Major's legs were against the sill. He had nowhere to move; behind him were only open air and a deadly drop down the castle's sheer wall. Dracula smiled and, with a twirl of his sword, disarmed Reikel.

"Since you have such an inquisitive mind, one more bit of superstition you should know," Dracula told the German, blade point at the man's throat. "The stake through the heart does not kill the vampire. It only suspends life. To kill one such as we, you must behead the beast."

The German could only watch as Dracula's blade rose in an arc over his shoulder.

"But I am immor—"

His head tumbled to the pile of dust and debris. Dracula kicked the headless body over the sill, and it fell lazily to the grounds below.

Then the Prince collapsed. Crawling across the floor, over the bodies and debris, he called out in a mournful plea.

"Lucille . . ."

FROM THE WAR JOURNAL OF
J. HARKER

(transcribed from shorthand)

As we sought Lucy and the vampire, my thoughts swirled about my brain at the very idea that we might be able to capture Hitler himself. If not capture, then at least kill him. And end this brutal war. I could save Europe! I could save England!

In my haste I outran Professor Van Helsing and had to go back to help the old man up the stairs, as the whole engagement had exhausted his aged resources.

Room by room we searched. Then we heard a dull explosion that shook the foundation of the wing in which we were hunting. Dust drifted down from the ancient beams overhead, descending like a grey cloud.

Using this concussion as our focus, we hurried up yet another spiral stairway as fast as the Professor could manage, pausing occasionally so he could catch his breath.

The stairwell opened up onto a long room that was fogged with a haze of plaster dust.

We entered just in time to see Dracula swing a sword at a German officer, and we observed the same officer's head roll across the floor to settle at our feet. There was an expression of surprise and dismay on the disembodied face. I could see why. Scattered around the room was a score of his fellow soldiers, all dead, many in pieces.

Dracula dropped his sword and then slowly sank to his knees. He was in terrible shape, multiple gashes across his body. He began to crawl, not toward us but toward a large pile of rubble.

He cried out in a pitiful wail, one word, a name.

"Lucille!"

And then I saw her. She was sprawled on her back, bent over a broken beam. Blood stained the mound of plaster dust she lay upon, the dark pool spreading as we rushed over. Her clothing, too, was soaked in her lifeblood from a rent in her chest so deep you could see past the sliced white bone to a throbbing organ.

Her breathing was ragged and, as Dracula bent over her, she spoke in a thin whisper.

"Did you kill the bastard who killed me?" she asked him.

"I did," he answered. His voice, too, was but a rasp, filled with emotion.

I turned to her father, who immediately began examining his daughter, his fingers delicately probing. She gasped in pain at his touch and he muttered an apology.

"We must get her to a hospital," Dracula said.

Van Helsing looked at him, then me, and shook his head.

"She would not survive the journey."

"Then we must operate here," Dracula declared.

"This is beyond my abilities," Van Helsing said and his voice broke into a sob. "Beyond . . . any physician."

"Father, don't fret." Lucille lay a comforting hand on her father's. There were tears in his eyes.

"Do something!" I found myself shouting. "Surely you can do something!"

The Professor turned to me and gave a slight shake of his head, the saddest sight I have ever witnessed. I saw the man break down before my eyes. He raised his hands over his head in a sort of mute despair. Finally he put his hands before his face, began to wail, a cry that seemed to come from the very wracking of his heart. He raised his arms again as though appealing to the whole universe. "God! What have I done?"

But I refused to succumb to helplessness. I would not accept her death. Even if she had rejected my affections, I had fought beside her; we had shared danger and delight. I could not, would not allow her to die.

I knelt before Dracula, who had his arms around Lucy, supporting her head and shoulders.

"You can save her," I suggested. "Do so."

"No," the vampire stated flatly. "No. You do not know what you ask."

"Do it!" I screamed at him.

Dracula turned his eyes to Van Helsing. "You know."

"I do," Van Helsing replied with such sorrow as I have ever heard. "But—"

He left that one word hang in the air.

"DO IT!" I commanded with every particle of my being. "You can. And you will."

The vampire regarded the dying woman.

She managed a weak smile. Dracula slowly shook his head at her.

"You always get what you desire," he said to her. "Do you not?"

And he bent over her with all the solemnity of a priest before an altar.

EXCERPTS FROM UNIDENTIFIED DIARY
(translated from the German)

June 21

The good Lieutenant & I led Herr Wolf through the musty tunnel that meandered its way beneath the castle. There was only damp and darkness, following his shaky hand-torch, no sense of direction but down. This declination ultimately took them to another thick door that opened to a copse of trees and bushes at the base of the mountain.

There was the sound of gunfire and explosions emanating from the castle above them. The noise of a fierce battle. Herr Wolf knew that he was in Grave Danger and turned to his escort.

— We must leave immediately, he ordered. — The future of the Reich depends on my survival.

The Lieutenant scouted ahead, but found no threat. He did discover a vehicle, some Italian car with exquisite lines and a luxurious interior of fine leather, wood, and chrome.

Herr Wolf paused at the car door, stared up at the castle. Yellow flashes flared behind the windows, and the interior walls were briefly illuminated, each burst of light accompanied by the crack of gunfire and the blast of grenades.

Amid that skirmishing was the promise of Immortality, God-like powers. Could he risk going back? For personal reasons, yes. But without him Germany would Fall, the Promise crushed. He could gamble with his own life but not that of the Fatherland. He climbed into the car. Maybe the Colonel would manage to escape. For some reason Herr Wolf had doubts.

The drive back to Brasov and the terminal was without complication, and Herr Wolf's private train was waiting, engine rumbling and ready to depart as was standard procedure.

Herr Wolf had the Lieutenant stop the car some distance from the train. He thanked him for the successful rescue and then shot him in the temple with the Colonel's pistol. Herr Wolf was surprised that he still held the gun. He put two more rounds into the man's chest for insurance. There was a look of shock on the Lieutenant's face, death-frozen.

The Lieutenant was a witness to events that should never be spoken of and, thusly, a Danger to the Reich. The Fortunes of War.

This may have been the first man that Herr Wolf had ever killed with his own hand. Except for maybe the Tommy back at the castle whose fate, dead or not, was unknown. Herr Wolf contemplated this act and discovered that it did not bother him. In his opinion Conscience was a Jewish invention and not an aspect of a Great Leader.

The train ride back to Berlin was uneventful, and there was time to consider what had just transpired. Herr Wolf was disappointed in his actions, or lack of them. For a moment he had an opportunity to cross the Bifrost, the bridge to Valhalla, to sit with the Gods as an Equal, to live forever, to mentor his beloved Germany until the End of Time.

And he had balked. He had passed the cup. He was a coward.

It would not happen again. This was not over. If there is one such Creature, there is another. The search will be unending.

FROM THE DESK OF
ABRAHAM VAN HELSING

(Translated from the Dutch)

My worst nightmare has become corporeal. After the ordeal at the castle my tribulations have fallen upon me like the lamentations of Job.

I also have a confession. When the Rumanian relief sped to Castle Dracula they came upon an ungodly sight. From Brasov to Bran, all alongside the road, wooden pillars had been erected, stakes driven into the ground, and upon each a Nazi soldier had been impaled. Yes, an image from five hundred years past greeted the army.

And the perpetrators of this barbaric display? Not our ancient ally but two men of this so-called civilised era—Jonathan Harker and I, with some help from the gypsies. I suppose we perpetuated this act out of our profound anger and grief. I know this is no excuse, but the deed has been done. Have I lost all of my humanity? I remember chiding the Prince for just such savagery. Now who are the monsters?

And as for my dear Lucille . . . my emotion is in such excess that I cannot bear to contemplate her future.

What have I wrought?

God help us all.

FROM THE WAR JOURNAL OF
J. HARKER

(transcribed from shorthand)

June 22, 1941

We buried poor Renfield today. In the tiny graveyard next to a tiny church miles away from Brasov. He was a brave man, deranged or sane, and I will miss him. Hell's teeth, I wish I had known him before his impairment. From the personality he exhibited when he was sound, I think he would have been a more than decent bloke and a boon companion.

I read over his grave:

"They that fought so well—in death are warriors still;
Stubborn and steadfast to the end, they could not be dishonoured.
Their bodies perished in the fight; but the magic of their souls is strong—
Captains among the ghosts, heroes among the Dead!"

"Hymn to the Fallen." I do not remember the origin—Oriental, I think—but the translation was by Arthur Waley.

Van Helsing spoke:

"We who are pledged to set the world free salute this man. Our toil must be in silence and our efforts all in secret. We who are willing to imperil even our own souls for the safety of the ones we love—for the good of mankind, for the honor of our country and the glory of God, we treasure his sacrifice and someday will acknowledge it to the world."

But this seemed too solemn for a man who, even in his addled state, was a man too full of life, and so I resorted to another canto, singing softly to myself:

"Fuck 'em all, fuck 'em all,
The long and the short and the tall.
Fuck all the Sergeants and their bleedin' sons,
Fuck all the Corporals and W.O. ones,
'Cause we're sayin' good-bye to them all,
As back to the billet we crawl.
They'll get no promotion this side of the ocean,
So cheer up, my lads, fuck 'em all."

At first I sang alone, but then I found my voice joined by Maleva, a few of the gypsies doing their best with the language, and even Van Helsing for the finale. It brought tears to my eyes, I am not ashamed to say.

After the service I tried to console Van Helsing, who is as distraught over his daughter's survival as I think he would have been at her death. I fear that the strain of the past week has broken even his iron strength.

We walked through a dismal rain across the muddy cemetery and I asked him.

"So this is the end?"

"Not so. Not so." He shook his craggy head. "It is only the beginning."

I told him that I was not sure of his meaning. He told me that yesterday the Germans had invaded the Soviet Union and that many more brave men such as Sergeant Renfield (I swear that when this war is over I will find out his real name) will die before this nasty business is over.

But I knew that his burden came from the state of his daughter and what was to become of her.

This and the cloud that hung over these somber times, the overriding and frightening question—was Hitler bitten?

"Friend Jon," he said, wagging that monumental head, "there are strange and terrible days before us."

EXCERPTED FROM THE UNPUBLISHED NOVEL
THE DRAGON PRINCE AND I
by Lenore Van Muller

EPILOGUE

Standing on the balcony of a remote mountain cabin, Lucille watched the purple sky fade through the chroma of dawn, a soft magenta to a deep red and a quick blaze of vermilion. Dracula stood at her side, one comforting hand nestling her own. The once exotic coolness of his touch was gone, their temperatures now equal. She missed the difference.

Lucille knew this was the last sunrise she would ever witness.

The peaks of the Carpathians were a jagged black frame to the glorious display on the horizon. Then the sawtooth silhouette dissolved under the assault of pure fire as the sun slipped over the mountains.

Lucille felt a blast of heat upon her face. She threw a hand up to block the blaze, and her palm, too, burned as if she were standing under a midday desert sun. Then the scorching became too intense to bear anymore. She allowed the Prince to draw her back into the safety of the cabin's shade. He closed the door and the room was thrust into darkness.

It was curious; she found that she could see as well in the pitch-dark as she could in full light. Another lesson concerning this new state. Lately there were so many.

Dracula pulled her to his chest.

"I warned you," he said.

"I suppose I've always been the kind of person who had to learn the hard way," she replied.

"I have noticed this about you." He kissed her and she responded in kind. "Among your many remarkable qualities."

"I'm glad you're paying attention," she said and returned the kiss.

Then she pulled away, frowned at him.

"I'm . . . hungry."

THE END

ACKNOWLEDGMENTS

This book would not have been possible without the assistance of a great many researchers and specialists in authentication and other eccentric skills. Here are a few of those dedicated souls: Dr. Milt Ford, Edward Fejedelem, Marc Leepson, Ed Cray, Denise Pantoja, David Kanter, Adam Rodman, and always Lesa Meredith Duncan.

Thanks to everyone at Inkshares. The brilliant people at Girl Friday Productions who corrected my brain farts and plain old ignorance: Devon Fredericksen, Clete Smith, Dan Stiles, Mark Steven Long, and Phyllis DeBlanche. All of you made the book better than it was written.

And a special note of gratitude to Felicia Day for the little things, the big things, and everything in between.

ABOUT THE AUTHOR

Patrick Sheane Duncan began his film career as the manager of a small movie theater in Grand Rapids, Michigan. He later moved to Los Angeles, California, where he pursued screenwriting and film production. He has written screenplays such as *Mr. Holland's Opus, Courage Under Fire*, and *Nick of Time*. Duncan is also the writer/director of the critically acclaimed feature film *84 Charlie Mopic* and the writer of *A Painted House*. He is the producer of the HBO series *Vietnam War Story* and the cowriter/director of the documentary series *Medal of Honor*. He lives in Los Angeles.

LIST OF PATRONS

This book was made possible in part by the following grand patrons who preordered the book on inkshares.com. Thank you.

Alex Ackley
Andrew Fitz Simons
Charles Caraway
Charles R. Day
David Koble
Derek Victor Pounds
Doug Johnson
Elizabeth E. Krause
Felicia Day
Geoffrey Bernstein
Graham John Cann
Greg Zesinger
Hope T.
Ian Albert
James C. Crawford
Jeffrey N. Rapaglia
Jeremy Thomas
Jessica Talbot
Jonas Lee

Jonathan C. Oliver
Jonathan Nelson
Jon West
Joris Kemel
Karen Borsholm
Kevin Kane
Kyle Lockwood
Lexa and David Crooks
Matt Kaye
Michael Hsiao
Michael Welter
Reader Writer
Ryan A. Earles
Shanon Cole
Shelley R. Ward
Stephen Turczyn
Tom Atwood
Winston C. Weathers

INKSHARES

 Inkshares is a crowdfunded book publisher. We democratize publishing by having readers select the books we publish—we edit, design, print, distribute, and market any book that meets a preorder threshold.

Interested in making a book idea come to life? Visit inkshares.com to find new book projects or start your own.